"A realistic and touching image of . . . an operation as arcane and immense as rebuilding a nation. An insightful, impressively broad glimpse of a formidable mission."

Kirkus Reviews

"A politically-charged probe of overseas events and their links to American interests. Readers seeking a combination of political and psychological depth and struggle will relish this multi-faceted story of survival on different levels, with the powerful backdrop of Afghanistan pulling everything together."

Donovan's Bookshelf

"A tribute to human tenderness, resilience, and ambiguity in the face of war. A surprising account of love, redemption and understanding."

Robert Calderisi
author of *The Trouble with Africa: Why Foreign Aid Isn't Working*

WE'LL LIVE TOMORROW

WILL EVERETT

GALATEA

Galatea Press
www.galateapress.com

Publisher's Note:
This is a work of fiction. Names, characters, businesses, places, events and incidents are either the products of the author's imagination or used in a fictitious manner. Any resemblance to actual persons, living or dead, or actual events is purely coincidental.

Cover design by Pintado

Ordering Information:
Quantity sales. Special discounts are available on quantity purchases by corporations, associations, and others. For details, contact the "Special Sales Department" at:
sales@galateapress.com

We'll Live Tomorrow / Will Everett. -- 1st ed.
ISBN 978-0-9962871-0-4

In Memory of Barry Horn

AFGHAN WORDS AND PHRASES

afghani	Afghan unit of currency, abbreviated Afs
bacha bazi	The practice of using a boy for sexual play. The man who lays claim to such a boy is the *bacha baz*, usually a warlord of a person of power and influence. The boy is the *bacha*.
chowkidar	A night watchman
haram	An act forbidden under Islam
hijab	Head covering for Muslim women, ranging from a simple headscarf to a full burka
inshallah	As Allah wills it
muezzin	A man chosen by a mosque to offer the call to prayer
mullah	A Muslim scholar
qibla	The direction in which Muslims turn to offer prayers
shabnama	A Taliban "night letter" containing a threat of imminent peril
Shaitan	Satan
shalwar kamiz	Afghan traditional clothing consisting of loose-fitting trousers held by a drawstring and a knee-length shirt
shisha	A water pipe or hookah
shura	A convening of tribal elders for the purpose of making community decisions
tazkira	Identity card

MILITARY TERMINOLOGY

conex	A metal shipping container often adapted to provide accommodation on military bases.
DFAC	Dining facility
expat	An expatriate
FOB	Forward Operating Base
Hesco	Wire mesh container lined with heavy fabric and filled with rocks or sand for making walls or defense barriers.
MRAP	Mine Resistant Ambush Protected vehicle. Its V-shaped hull deflects the explosive force of IEDs and landmines, protecting troops on the move.
RPG	Rocket Propelled Grenade
VBIED	Vehicle-borne improvised explosive device

FOREWORD

HUMANITARIAN AID ATTEMPTS to alleviate suffering and improve lives for millions around the world. To succeed, these projects must have two things: the support of the people they seek to help, and a stable environment in which to work. One cannot build a dam during an earthquake.

After World War II, and during the Vietnam War in particular, aid was discovered to be a useful weapon against insurgent elements. When coupled with military objectives, aid can bring stability to war-torn areas plagued by insurgent violence. Give a farmer a steady source of income and he'll be less likely to hurl a grenade or bury a roadside bomb. Idle hands are the devil's workshop. People need money and they need something to do.

Such stabilization projects flourished in Afghanistan during the first decade of the Afghan war. They provided short-term assistance that helped restore order and productivity, particularly in agriculture, the primary source of income for Afghan people. Some of these projects were deployed by the military as part of its hearts and minds strategy, others by the United States Agency for International Development—USAID.

These projects—noble in intention, grand in design, military in execution—are unique in the history of international aid. They stand beside their conventional aid counterparts like a giant earthmover next to a wheelbarrow. They employed hundreds of thousands of Afghans to build bridges, canals, roads and reservoirs. They gave out tractors, innumerable metric tons of seed and fertilizer, planted millions of trees. If they improved lives, so much the better. Their real goal was to help win a war.

Those projects are mostly gone now, having made way for the kind of aid projects that strengthen education, governance and the economy. Whether they achieved their goals is a history still being written.

The practice of *bacha bazi* (or "playing with boys") dates back to Afghanistan's pre-Islamic past. Examples of wealthy or powerful men abducting boys into sexual slavery can be traced as far back as Alexander, who took possession of a Persian dancing boy when he passed through the area (though some accounts suggest the relationship may have been consensual). The 16th century Mughal emperor Babur is also known to have had a fondness for catamites.

Such quaint historical references are far removed from the horror faced by many unwilling initiates into *bacha bazi* today. Recruited from among the poorest of the poor, their suffering is often overlooked by the Afghan judiciary, which affords few legal protections to abused boys. Those who escape often have no resources to fall back on, and many end up returning to their former master. In rare cases where a victim brings charges against his abuser, it is often the boy—lacking money and influence—who is sent to prison on charges of immorality.

While the Afghan government pays lip service to ending the practice, *bacha bazi* is known to exist among the military, the police and the echelons of government. When the UN raised the issue before Hamid Karzai, the president's reply was laconic. "Let us win the war first, then we will deal with such matters."

The only Afghan government to succeed in defeating the practice was the Taliban.

PROLOGUE

SINCE I GOT BACK from Kandahar, everyone wants to know the story.
Which, in my recklessly simplistic way, goes something like this:

There was a boy who had known misfortune—not unusual in itself.
He was exploited, suffered in terrible ways, but his spirit was unbroken.
He fled a vicious master, wandered with nomads and found his place in
the world.

He met a man who had known misfortune—not unusual in itself. This
man was alone, having lost the love of his wife and the life of his beloved
son. He had suffered in terrible ways, but his spirit was weak. Suffering
had broken him. He wanted only a place of refuge, somewhere to hide.

War brought them together, an ugly war, a seemingly endless war.
Then war tore them apart.

Have I got it right? I want to remember, to preserve our last few
months before they fade away like a crazy dream. You inspired me to do

1

this, my dear Karimullah. Remember when I caught you scrawling one of our conversations in your diary?

Yes, Hunter, I sometimes write down what you say. Not because your words are especially wise or important, but because they will help me remember you when you are gone.

You had the right idea. Every so often a forgotten conversation will filter up from those last turbulent days. I want to strain out every word, preserve them like scripture. Your words are all I have.

You didn't change me. I'm still as cynical as ever—and just as fat. On the other hand, a big belly like mine makes a damn good writing surface. Just look at the way it supports this open notebook. I should patent the thing.

Outside, heavy Indiana snow is falling, gathering in big clumps on the window. Back where you are, the street vendors' carts are piled high with pomegranates. People are sleeping on their roofs in the cool of the evening.

There's no telling when you'll be here. Perhaps spring? I try to imagine you coming off the plane in your pale blue shalwar kamiz, *running up to me with your funny cockeyed grin.*

The Greeks understood about love. The knew that it had too many dimensions to be encompassed by one word. And so they gave us eros, agape, philia, ludus, pragma *and* philautia. *One of these must fit the way I feel for you, Karimullah.*

A name I never could pronounce quite right.

An emotion I still can't define.

Come quickly.

Find me.

BOOK ONE

1
Karimullah

What we speak becomes the house we live in.

Hafez

THE MULLAH'S VOICE was ugly, like a machine that stamped words out of sheets of tin. But the words he spoke were truth. *Sacrifice is the proof of faith.*

It was a holy feast day, and many had come to the Red Mosque to pray. Karimullah found himself wedged into a corner by strong-smelling, bearded men who thought he was a child. He sat with his knees together on the prayer rug. He raised his hands to his ears and said in a high, clear voice: *Allah-u-Akbar.*

When it was time to leave he stepped into his sandals and flowed with the crowd into the bright, dusty street lined with beggars. Behind him he heard voices. Were they speaking of him? He hurried his steps, realizing how stupid he had been to show his face in public.

* * *

At home his two friends were just waking up. So lazy, even during the holy festival of Eid, but he loved them. They were hungry, demanding: Where is the *biryani*? Where is the bread?

He changed into jeans and an Adidas T-shirt that Leandro Palafox, his supervisor, had brought him from America. He boiled water for the rice and chopped the meat. Chunks of lamb were soon sizzling in honey, olive oil and poppy seeds, such a beautiful smell.

Khan came up behind him to watch him work, yawning and scratching his balls.

— You know what that shirt means, don't you?

— It's a sports apparel company.

— It means All Day I Dream About Sex. Is that all you dream about, Karimullah?

He blushed. They always joked with him about sex. Khan and Sadiq had lost their virginity last year while they were working in Dubai, to the same whore. The sin of *zena*.

He was hardly the innocent they thought he was.

Soon the sleeping mats were folded away and the oilcloth was rolled out along the middle of the floor. The roommates leaned back on their elbows, sipping tea. Khan's normally coiffed hair was standing every which way, his face pinched and surly. They were handsome, jobless young men whom Karimullah still supported, though he had long ago moved out of the apartment.

He brought out the dishes of *biryani* and garlic yogurt so thick and creamy the spoon stood straight up. Khan and Sadiq were already tearing off hunks of bread and scooping food into their plates. Karimullah wanted today to be perfect. He had brothers and sisters in Kandahar whom he might have been cooking for, but they were dead to him now.

Sadiq said through a mouthful of rice:

— You should come back and live with us. We miss your cooking.

Khan snorted.

— Don't bother. He prefers the company of Americans.

For several months Karimullah had been living on the compound of an American aid project in the city. When the Taliban, learning that he worked for the foreign occupiers, had tried to kill him, his supervisor had let him stay there for safekeeping. Karimullah tried to visit his friends whenever he could, knowing that Khan and Sadiq would not lift a finger to do housework, feeling it was work fit for women.

— It's still not safe for me, Karimullah said, flashing back to the feel of a cold muzzle pressed to his temple.

— He's right, Khan. The Taliban memory is long.

After lunch the apartment smelled of deodorant and cologne. Khan and Sadiq came out of the bedroom wearing flashy jewelry, their hair gleaming with gel. They clapped Karimullah on the back and went out without saying where they were going.

Karimullah took out his rug and offered the afternoon prayer. Then he sat in the open window and watched the families walking past in their nice Eid clothes. It filled him with an indescribable loneliness. Khan and Sadiq had no doubt gone to see prostitutes, and on Eid, so shameful.

He saw Khan's cigarettes and took one out of the pack. He sniffed it down its length. Delicious. The danger of the prospect, commingled with a vision of what Khan and Sadiq must be doing at that moment, gave him a sudden erection. He broke the cigarette in half and tossed it out the window.

He began furiously cleaning the apartment. He swept the carpet with a thatch broom and cleaned the toilet with Dettol and rinsed out the slick algae-coated concrete basin where they showered.

Afterward he removed his clothes to bathe. He was always attentive to hygiene, knowing that cleanliness of body was *sunnah*, commendable to the Prophet.

Keeping his teeth clean was *sunnah*. Wearing a beard was also *sunnah*, but at twenty-two his was still patchy, so he kept his face shaved. He trimmed his armpit hair, clipped his nails and regularly tidied the hair around his genitals as it was commanded.

When he performed the latter he did so with only the tips of his fingers, avoiding contact with his penis, as it was *haram*, forbidden, to touch oneself. His former roommates liked to debate this matter endlessly. Sadiq said that it was only *makruh*—disliked—not *haram*. Better to succumb to masturbation than to the greater sin of *zena*, he said, though of course he and Khan frequently succumbed to both.

Karimullah, no stranger to defilement of the body, sought purity. He could not always control his thoughts, but he waged a daily war against the temptations of the flesh. And yet the body's urges were not always easy to resist.

And now, squatting in the basin and lathering his body with soap, he felt it happening. He tried to ignore it. But in moments like these his body seemed possessed by something wholly outside of him. He knew it was not the spirit of Shaitan, as some had said. It came from his dark past, a seed planted by men who had never asked his permission or sought his complicity, and which now and then arose from the cracks in his resolve like a prickly nettle. You could pull it out by the roots but it always seemed to come back.

And now he yielded to it. He tried to get through it as quickly and joylessly as he could, not as a fulfillment but as a purging of desire. And when the pollution shot out from his body he sprayed it down the drain, hating it, hating himself.

Napping on a cushion, waiting for Khan and Sadiq to return, he was awakened by a loud knock at the door. He lay for some moments as a terrifying range of possibilities flashed across his mind. The knock came again, more insistent. Was it Obaidullah, his former master? The Taliban?

A muffled voice said from the window:

— Open the door, *bacha*. I see you.

It was the mullah whom he had seen that morning at the mosque. He was a man of fifty who looked infinitely older, his face lined and darkly tanned. His turban at close range was filthy. Entering the living area as casually as if it were his own, he looked more like a day laborer than a holy man.

— I smell good food.

— It is all gone, Karimullah lied. We have only bread.

The mullah stared at him, one eye squinting shut.

— I saw you this morning, but I could not remember your name.

— And you remember now?

— Your eldest brother is Kaaseb. Your father is Abdul Bahram, but he is dead. You are Karimullah, the stain on your family's name.

Karimullah saw the small blue pouch tied to the mullah's waist, with its decorative gold tassels and the embroidered verse of scripture. He knew why the mullah was here: to collect the monthly offering.

Karimullah said:

— Only a fool would curse the man from whom he hopes to beg alms.

The mullah laughed.

— What man? Did a man enter the room?

— I know what you want.

— And I know what you want, *bacha*. I know all about you, working for the American invaders, betraying your country and your religion.

The mullah shoved the ornate pouch into Karimullah's chest. Karimullah held his gaze, his hand sliding into the pocket of his *kamiz*. He drew out a fifty *afghani* note and dropped it into the open maw of the pouch where he could see a swirl of dirty banknotes mostly of smaller denominations.

The mullah closed the pouch, his eyes seeming to drill into the young man.

— God sees you. He knows you. He knows what you do. Do not think those green eyes of yours can seduce Him.

— But are you God? Or are you just a man like any other?

The mullah looked as though he might strike Karimullah, or at the very least spit at him. But at that moment there were voices in the courtyard, laughter. He turned to go.

— Fear the judgment of God ... and of man.

Khan and Sadiq came inside sounding like ten people. Their breath was tangy with fruit and alcohol. They demanded food and tea.

Karimullah heated up the leftovers from their Eid feast. He reminded them that he must be back at the American compound before nightfall. *No!* they pleaded, dragging him from the kitchen.

Sadiq put on a CD by Farhad Darya. He closed his eyes and danced with himself in the middle of the room, sliding a hand suggestively down his torso. He pretended to lewdness because he thought he could win Khan's approval no other way. He was a sweet boy, Karimullah concluded, but weak of character.

Soon they were all dancing. Khan moved as if he was in a night-club, jutting out his arms and bouncing around. They were both watching Karimullah, who was turning and turning, like a coil tightly winding. He could feel heat and energy gathering in his muscles and loins. Without willing it, he found himself entering the dancer's trance.

— Go, dancing boy! Khan shouted, making room for him in the center of the floor.

They watched his slender body going through the familiar pantomime of seduction. And though Karimullah knew they felt no carnal desire for him, he could see them surrendering to his magic.

It was time to stop, time for him to go. If he was late he would not be admitted inside the compound. The guards at the gate would point their guns at him and motion him away like a stranger. And then what would he do?

There was silence now as a new song started, a slow one he recognized from his youth. It brought to mind a hotel in Kabul, a gathering of drunken Pakistani businessmen and the leering face of Obaidullah, his former master. But the dark memory soon vanished as he coiled his arms together like snakes, raking his fingernails over his arms, swaying to the sinuous rhythm of the song.

2

Our Souls are Weary

Death has a tendency to encourage a depressing view of war.
Donald Rumsfeld

I WATCHED THE PANORAMA of Afghan life passing outside the window of the armored vehicle. Old men in turbans squatted in the shade, heads turning as one to watch the passing of the shiny black Land Cruiser—chariot of the foreign-aid gods.

It was a morning in Kandahar like so many others, the fierce sun casting stark shadows. A city of darkness and light. Nothing much had changed while I'd been out on leave. Donkey carts trundled along with their top-heavy burdens. Ragged children were bent under burlap bags twice their size. The ancient exchange of goods and money went on as it had forever.

What did I know about this city that I had called home for the past two years? Not much. One of the oldest known human settlements. Birthplace of the Taliban. Despite a skyline bristling with minarets and cell-phone towers, it was a place where Genghis Khan or Alexander the Great might still feel at home.

It was the great feast day of Eid. Through the bulletproof windows I watched Afghan children skipping along in their holiday finest, the girls wearing colorful new shawls sparkling with sequins, the boys in the standard *shalwar kamiz*, an outfit somewhere between pajamas and a karate costume. They could all look forward to a day of feasting, and what a pleasure that would be after the dreary month of fasting they'd just endured.

Up front, my Afghan driver and the gunman next to him were staring rigidly ahead. Their faces were wrapped with kerchiefs to avoid detection from those watching from the sidewalk. They had dangerous jobs.

I called forward:

— *Eid Mubarak*, fellas.

I caught my reflection in the rearview and saw my father looking back at me: lined forehead, thinning hair, Deputy Dawg jowls.

The driver said:

— Thank you, Mr. Hunter.

It must suck being asked to work on the holiest day of the Muslim calendar, I thought. They should have been home with their families, watching their kids open presents, or whatever Afghans did on Eid.

— So how are things at the compound?

The driver moved his scarf away from his lips.

— Very big damage, sir.

— I saw it on the news. It's too bad.

— Yes, Mr. Hunter. Too bad.

I hadn't yet processed the true horror of what had happened while I had been away. Suicide bombers, a coordinated attack, a six-hour gun battle. A shoulder-fired mortar had struck the balcony just outside my very room. The blast had blown the door off its hinges and sent in a fireball that set lampshades ablaze. I would have been toast. Three members of our Afghan security detail had been killed.

Friends back home had urged me not to come back. Even my ex-wife declared a truce, begging me in a terse but emotional e-mail to come to my senses. But aid work was my life. I was fifty years old, not an age for new beginnings. Besides, lightning rarely strikes the same place twice.

As we neared the compound the vehicle began moving faster, like a horse expecting water and a nice bucket of oats. I felt my heartbeat quicken as we passed the familiar dome of the Red Mosque, and then the produce market, its stalls all shuttered for the holiday.

Soon we were at the gate marking the outermost entrance of the compound. We wove through a short obstacle course of concrete barriers, then turned down a narrow lane where two more steel gates rose to admit us like welcoming arms in a chorus line. A guard raised his arm in salute. I felt like visiting royalty.

The project office slid past on our left. Then we stopped before a tall steel door that rolled back with a clattering roar, admitting us to the residential heart of the compound. I was home.

Unfastening the Velcro belts of my body armor, I glanced around the garden, anticipating the worst. But everything looked as it had when I left three weeks earlier. The big eucalyptus trees were still standing, the roses still in bloom. I heard the hammers of workmen and the whine of power tools. The sweet smell of sawdust hung in the air. At the far end of the garden, laborers were carting away rubble while masons on ladders were repairing the perimeter wall. I could see the outline of a hole where the suicide bomber had blown himself up. I tried to imagine it, to feel it, but it was still an abstraction. And I knew it would remain so until I reached my room.

* * *

Lugging my suitcase up to the third floor, I found the door to my room propped against the opposite wall, its hinges weirdly twisted. The guesthouse manager, Ahmed, was supervising two workmen. Seeing me in the doorway he sprang to attention, a dazed smile forming on his fleshy face.

— Welcome back, sir.

My bed was out in the hall, the mattresses leaning one against the other like books. The room was nothing but a shell. The carpet had been taken up, exposing raw concrete. I couldn't find anything to connect it with my previous existence.

— When do you think you'll be finished?

The workmen were on ladders, watching me with trowels in their hands. The blast had left spidery cracks in the walls, which they were presently patching with cement.

— There is still much work. Many days.

I approached the large window that faced the garden. It was nothing but a gaping cavity now. Ten days ago someone had seen this window, *my* window, through the crosshairs of a shoulder-fired rocket.

I took another look at the mattresses in the hall. Lifting back the box spring I found a telling spray of dried blood. I showed this to Ahmed, whose expression became one of dawning pity as he realized I had not been told.

— A guest was staying in your room, sir.

— Guest?

— He was a visiting consultant from Pakistan. There were no vacant rooms at the time, so Leandro put him here.

— And he was injured in the blast?

Ahmed's eyes started away. He placed his fingertips together as he thought of the words he must utter.

— He was killed, sir.

It took a moment to process. A man came into this room, went to sleep in my bed, and never woke up. It might have been me, but it wasn't. It was a guy from Pakistan, come to make a little quick money. He had come in as a living man and gone out as charred bits and pieces in a body bag.

His things were probably still inside the wardrobe, which had been dragged out into the hall. Sure enough, I opened it and found unfamiliar underwear and socks, a cheap tie, a belt, some pants and shirts I didn't recognize. I took a shirt down from the hanger, turning it around as I tried to form an image of its vanished owner.

On an upper shelf I found a bottle of something called Rosepair Mustard Oil. I sniffed it. I had no idea what it was for.

— There are clothes in the laundry basket as well, Ahmed said.

I dug out a short-sleeved dress shirt still redolent of cologne and a smelly pair of black socks. I could read Ahmed's grave expression: *It could have been you.*

— Let's gather up all the clothes and personal items and get them out of here.

— Perhaps I could take a shirt or two. Changwani was the same size as my eldest son.

Changwani. I hadn't wanted to attach a name to this.

I went down to the garden for a smoke. Striking the match, I saw that my hand was shaking, not from what I had just seen so much as a crushing sense of fatigue.

The state of my room raised an obvious problem. I turned on my cell phone and rang up Leandro Palafox, the project's Director of Operations. A few minutes later the young Latino came springing into the garden, embracing me warmly.

— We didn't think you were coming back!

— I can see that. It seems I don't have a place to sleep.

He was still hugging me, and I gently pulled away. We moved to a nearby picnic table where he sat and lit a cigarette, crossing his legs at the knee. He was a thin, nervous guy in his thirties, famous in the compound for his fine clothes and his blatant effeminacy.

He cocked his head to one side, releasing a jet of smoke from the corner of his mouth.

— You don't look so good, honey.

— I just heard about . . . the guy.

— Changwani.

Again the name, as though everyone were conspiring to make sure I wouldn't forget it.

I'm no foreigner to death. I've worked in crazy places, seen bodies caught in trees, washed in from flooded rivers. The bodies of the slain. I don't worry about death. I'm not religious or even vaguely spiritual. I see death as just a powering-down, a flip of the big switch.

But this was odd. The company press release had said nothing about Changwani. Did the death of a man really mean so little when he was just a visiting consultant?

— Christ, Leandro, the guy's blood was still on the bed. I mean, why didn't anyone e-mail me while I was home?

Leandro patted my hand.

— I'll find you a room. In the meantime, you could always double-bunk with me, he suggested mischievously.

The trite remark left me speechless. I wanted to slap the designer sunglasses off his mousy little face. Of course, he and the rest of my colleagues had had ten days to get used to this. I was still on training wheels.

— I can sleep on the roof. Don't we still have that old army

17

sleeping bag?

— What about the mosquitoes?

— I'll deal with it.

— Tomorrow I'll put you in the training villa, just until things are back to normal.

The training villa was an old building out in a less secure part of the compound. It had classrooms downstairs and a few rooms upstairs where we put the sort of guests who didn't require much luxury or security (mostly Afghans). I didn't have much choice.

He added:

— Karimullah is staying there temporarily, so you won't be alone.

I sorted through my mental Rolodex of Afghan names, trying to attach a face. Then I remembered: the quiet kid who worked in contracts. There were vague rumors that he and Leandro were carrying on an affair.

— So how is everyone holding up generally?

Leandro turned his face away and shrugged. The attack had affected him more than he was letting on. I would never know what it was like to be awakened by a bomb blast powerful enough to blow a door off its hinges, or what it was like to sit in a safe room for six hours listening to guns and rockets and the screams of insurgents intent on killing you.

His lips were set tight.

— To be honest, Hunt, I'm not ready to talk about it.

— I understand.

— You really don't know what the worst thing in the world is until you see it first hand.

He rose abruptly, glancing at his backside and swatting at some dust.

— You sure you want to sleep on the roof?

— Just for tonight.

— I'll tell Ahmed to find you a cot.

He hugged me again, smiled bravely and walked toward the gate, his skinny drainpipe trousers making an urgent swishing sound. The tight pants, the challenging insouciance, only Leandro could get away with that here. In such a masculine environment he should have been the object of derision, and yet he had managed to become something of a beloved mascot. There was a kind of stubborn resiliency about him. No matter what you thought of his sexuality, you couldn't help respecting someone so unapologetically his own person.

Around sundown I fixed up the cot, choosing a place on the roof behind the big water cistern where I wouldn't be seen by the guards in the watchtowers. I zipped up the sleeping bag with only my face showing, like a fat pharaoh.

One of my colleagues was playing a radio in the room below; I could feel the bass thrumming through the cot's aluminum frame. I heard raised voices, laughter. I hadn't seen any of them except for Leandro. I knew I wasn't leading any popularity contests here, but their indifference surprised me.

I stared up at the starlight, so clear that I could see the wandering trail of the Milky Way. A blinking white light detached itself from the stars. Immediately behind it came another: drones returning from night missions on the Pakistani border.

My thoughts returned to the attack. The Taliban was still gloating over the event on its Voice of Jihad website, employing their usual poetic license in their version of events:

> The martyrdom-seeking Mujahedeen went from room to room, kill-ing the foreign invaders inside, then took up positions and killed the

enemy troops arriving for reinforcement. In all, eight of the foreign occupiers were killed and dozens more wounded.

As it happens, the visiting Pakistani was the only foreign casualty, a man known only to me by his smelly socks and the mysterious bottle of mustard oil.

It could have been me, but it wasn't. Some might say it was part of some divine plan. Even my ex-wife couldn't resist bringing in her new-age "guardian angels." I despised that kind of nonsense. What sort of god would exterminate one life in lieu of another? Was my life somehow more precious than Changwani's?

It took a long time to fall asleep. I dreamed that I was piloting a rocket bound for Mars. My son Maurice was in the cockpit next to me. We had just lifted off, a lot of smoke and flame showing in the small porthole window. I looked into Maurice's smooth, handsome face and saw that he was about to say something. But then the rocket abruptly went silent, the nose tilted and we began the awful death-ward plunge.

I started awake, hearing the call to morning prayer crackling from a loudspeaker at the Red Mosque. I didn't know what the words meant, but I detected a note of weary despair in the *muezzin*'s voice, as though he was saying: *Yes, we're at war, and our souls are weary. But we must make it through another day.*

The dream was still eerily vivid. I wondered what Maurice had been trying to tell me. It was a variation on a dream I'd had so many times.

Maybe it was the dream, or jet lag, or the plangent sadness in the *muezzin*'s voice, but right there, under a grey Afghan sky, I covered my face and wept like a baby.

3
Karimullah

Without the frown of clouds and lightning, the vines would be burned
by the smiling sun.
Rumi

IT WAS DARK WHEN Karimullah left the apartment, out of breath from all the dancing and laughter.

Smiling to himself, with his small backpack slung over one shoulder, he looked up and down the quiet street. Kandahar was his birthplace; he was a proud Pashtun. And yet the darkened windows seemed to watch his passage with pious judgment, as though they saw through to his dark secrets, his shameful past.

He exchanged a friendly nod with a man standing in the shadows in front of a tailor's shop. Rounding a corner, he glanced back and saw that the man was following him. He picked up his pace. Surely it was only a coincidence.

He was only five minutes away from the compound. He felt his cell phone vibrate and saw that it was a message from his boss,

Leandro Palafox. He didn't read it, for at that moment he realized that the footfalls behind him were coming faster.

Now he remembered the man. It was the slenderest of recollections, a flicker of memory as quick as a camera's shutter. But there are emotions that live on after memory fades, and this one made his heart quicken with terror. It was the mullah's eldest son.

He couldn't remember the man's name, but they had met at a party, the residence of one of Kandahar's district governors. Many warlords had been in attendance, each of varying power and prestige, many with a boy at his side. The boys were not dancers. They served only as shoulder ornaments, like epaulettes on a uniform, batting their eyelashes at each other, scowling at Karimullah.

Girls had been invited to the party, but when they saw the reaction Karimullah elicited among the men when he danced, they became enraged.

— Why did you invite us if you only have eyes for this boy?

The mullah's son had been watching from a darkened doorway while Karimullah danced. When the dance was finished, the man spoke quietly to Obaidullah. In a moment, slipping a banknote into his shirt pocket, Obaidullah snapped his fingers for Karimullah to come.

Karimullah followed the man down a hallway and into an unlit room. The man threw him onto a bed. Before Karimullah could protest the rough treatment, he felt a pillow come down over his face to stifle his cries. The man tried to unclasp the noisy embroidered blouse, which was ringing with the sound of a dozen bridles. Unable to breathe, Karimullah began striking out in panic.

He might have forgotten this incident as he had so many others were it not for the memory of his savior. One of the angry girls had been in the toilet down the hall when she heard the noise. She stood in the doorway berating the mullah's son, screaming at him to let Karimullah go. Her outrage brought others to the door. Now the man began to strike him, claiming that Karimullah had stolen from him. Seated in the back of Obaidullah's Volvo, Karimullah wept all the way back to Arghandab. From his master came not a word of sympathy or remorse, only the crackly blare of music from the radio. When they arrived at Obaidullah's orchard, Karimullah ran to his room, washed the smeared makeup from his face, unrolled his mat and offered a prayer of thanks for the girl whose cries had rescued him.

He had run into a street washed with bright halogen light. Not only could he see the man now clearly jogging toward him, a reflected gleam at the man's ear told Karimullah that he was phoning someone, perhaps the Taliban.

Tightening his grip on the strap of his backpack, Karimullah broke into a run. The backpack was slowing him down. He considered flinging it to the side of the road. But just then he saw the lights marking out the main gate of the compound.

He sprinted ahead for all he was worth, attracting the attention of the guards. They stepped into the street, bringing their AK-47s to their chests. One raised his arm, ordering Karimullah to stop.

Karimullah realized his error. The guards saw only a fast-moving person headed toward them with a parcel over one shoulder, perhaps a bomb. One guard had now lined Karimullah up in his sights. Karimullah threw the backpack into the gutter, confused by the dangers both behind and in front of him.

He screamed out his name, running with arms aloft like a marathon racer breasting the ribbon. They grabbed him to prevent him from colliding into a concrete wall. Breathless, he pointed back, trying to make them understand.

They aimed their lights into the street from which he had come. The lights danced every which way. But the street was empty, his pursuer was gone.

4

Do Not Spit Here

All paid jobs absorb and degrade the mind.
Aristotle

I DREADED GOING BACK to the office. My heart wasn't in it. But we all have to spend our days doing something.

Entering the building, I saluted the bearded Afghan farmer gazing down from the banner over the reception desk. His eyes were meant to invite pity, but to me they had always seemed threatening. With his hand planted on a scythe, it was as if he were daring you to drag him from the tenth-century agricultural practices in which he felt most at home.

Over his head was the logo of my employer, Global Relief Solutions, and at the bottom corner, the red, white and blue logo of our funder, the United States Agency for International Development—USAID—with its heartwarming tagline: *From the American People.*

Our project's name was emblazoned across another banner: Advancing Livelihoods and Agricultural Stability (ALAS). USAID had hit upon this sad acronym after the previous one, Advancing Livelihoods and Afghan Agriculture (ALAA), had been discarded because of its faint note of sacrilege. They always batted a thousand when it came to catchy project monikers.

On the second floor I opened the door onto a rambling expanse of cheap particleboard desks, more than sixty of them clustered according to our different departments. I breathed in the familiar office smells of instant coffee, roach spray and Afghan body odor.

The place was humming with activity. Copiers were thumping out copies, scanners were scanning and a pigeon-like coo of chatter filled the vast room. Arriving Afghans greeted each other with stiff hugs, unwrapping the kerchiefs that they wore to conceal their identities when entering the compound. Wearing the pajama-like *shalwar kamiz*, they looked like boys arriving for a giant slumber party or a martial arts competition.

My department was in back. Ramatullah, my chief deputy, rose when he saw me approach. He smiled, but warily. The boss was back.

— Ah, good morning, sir. Welcome!

Ramatullah came to my side, drawing out my chair, pretending to swat away some dust.

— How was your trip?

— Stressful.

I set my laptop bag on the desk.

— How is your family?

— Everyone's fine.

Ramatullah was in his late thirties. His tight *shalwar kamiz* called attention to his plump belly, a symbol of prosperity in this culture. He had a smallpox mark on one cheek that had left a hairless crater in his full beard. As he smiled he gingerly fingered the pockmark, a nervous habit.

26

— Well, I hope you had a restful and leisurely visit.

Was the insincerity in his voice real or just the result of an awkward grasp of the language? I had worked with him for two years and had never been able to penetrate the servile exterior. I liked Ramatullah well enough, but at a distance, the way you come to appreciate a good waiter.

I saw my field coordinators Nissar and Mohammed approaching at a distance. They were holding pinky fingers in that peculiar Afghan way. When they saw me their pace picked up. They shook my hand but seemed preoccupied, chattering in animated voices with Ramatullah. He turned away, calling back.

— I'll be just a moment, sir.

As I was plugging in my laptop I glanced around the office and became aware of a nervous hilarity sweeping through the room. Guys were gathering in the aisles, some doubled over with laughter. Was it something to do with me?

On my way to the coffee station I saw Behzad, our government liaison, waving to me from his desk. A wide grin showed that he was genuinely glad to see me, unless he too had caught the prevailing mood in the office.

I reached out to shake the young man's hand, but he came around and wrapped his arms around me in a backslapping American-style embrace that he'd perfected.

— So glad to see you back, Hunter. Sit for a moment. How is your . . . how was everything?

He nearly asked about my family. He was the only Afghan who knew something of my unhappy history.

— What is everybody so giggly about today?

He nodded toward the doorway where Faith Woodson, our human resources manager, was standing with arms planted on her narrow hips.

— You are about to find out.

Faith saw me, raised her hand and marched over, a little out of breath. A lock of dark hair fell over her eyes and she batted it impatiently away. She glanced uncertainly at Behzad and drew me aside.

— Hope you had a good trip, Hunt, but you picked a helluva day to come back. We had a ... situation this morning.

Gene Patmore, our training manager, strolled up behind her. The fasteners of his overalls gave a light jingle like the bells on a cat's collar. He gave me a sweeping pat on the shoulder, shaking his head sourly. He leaned toward Faith and said:

— I asked around.

— Nothing?

— There's no telling who he was or where he went.

She scanned the room.

— It could be any one of these guys.

I had noticed a perceptible drop in volume when Faith entered the room. Some Afghans pretended to work, while others buried their faces in their hands and shook with helpless laughter. Faith clapped her hands, silencing the room.

— All right, folks, you've all had a good laugh. Now everyone get back to work.

I looked at Gene, who seemed torn between official disdain and a desire to join the Afghans in their merriment. He hailed from somewhere in Nebraska, the only genuine farmer on our team. He laid a hand on my shoulder and whispered:

— Thought we'd welcome you back with a little drama.

— What happened?

— Just some monkey business in the ladies' cloakroom.

I turned back to Behzad and he gave me a sly wink. He was a

sophisticated, worldly young man, the only Afghan who wore a business suit to work. With his narrow, foxlike face he seemed younger than his thirty-four years. Seeing my confusion, he rose, took my arm, and led me outside to the smoking area. Two Afghans, seeing us, flicked their cigarettes into the foliage and went inside.

— A young lady walked in on him.

— Walked in on who?

Behzad lit two cigarettes and handed me one, squinting against the sun.

— That is what we are trying to figure out.

— I don't get it. What was he doing?

Behzad took a long draw on his cigarette, enjoying the suspense. But in a while I had the whole story. And it wasn't surprising. In a society where virginity was sometimes prolonged until a man's late twenties, the only surprise was that it didn't happen more often. I had to laugh.

— Did he ... finish?

— Thank God, no. Someone heard the girl's screams when she walked in on him. But when we got to the cloakroom he was gone.

— Can't she identify him?

— She did not get a good look at his face. Unfortunately, the rest she saw quite plainly.

— Poor girl.

— She was unlucky. They both were. I do not think he expected to get caught.

— He could have just done it in the bathroom like the rest of us do.

Behzad looked at me knowingly, a slow smile crinkling the corners of his eyes.

— Yes, perhaps he wanted to spice things up. Anyway, I am sure we will catch him.

I liked Behzad. He was irreligious, hopelessly immoral, incredibly intelligent. He served as our liaison with the Afghan government, navigating the maze of permissions required to get our projects off the ground. He attended the grinding government meetings that his American cohorts never bothered with. When something went wrong, it was Behzad who was called upon to iron things out. As such, he was seen as a person of power and stature. And this had made him a conspicuous target for assassination. He received threats on the phone so frequently that he joked about creating a special mailbox on his voicemail. *To leave a death threat, press one.*

It all came down to corruption, of course. Our partners in the Afghan government wanted only one thing: to cash in on the Americans before it was too late. After all, huge aid projects like ALAS wouldn't be around forever. But to get at the project's purse strings, they had to get past Behzad.

I followed him back inside. The mood in the office had relaxed somewhat, but clearly no one would be getting much work done today. Behzad leaned back in his chair and slapped the armrests.

— So how was your trip? You look a little ruffled.

I didn't have much to say about my three weeks off. I'd spent a little time in France where I put a hefty down payment on an old monastery, an impulse purchase that I was already starting to regret. Then I went back to the States to put my house on the market. I'd spent precious little time in Evansville since the divorce, but it was still the only place I thought of as home.

— So how did my guys behave while I was away?

Behzad peered in the direction of my work area. He shrugged.

— They come, they go. What they do while they are here, who knows?

I leaned over his desk.

— I like them. I just wonder how much I can trust them.

— They are Afghans, Hunter. If you set a trap, they will fall into it. Spare them such temptations and they will be fine.

— What do you think of my team leader?

We glanced in Ramatullah's direction. He was standing over one of the guys and pointing at his screen, ever the efficient supervisor.

— We have a saying, Hunter. The man who lives nearest the sugar-cane field always has a sticky handshake.

— So you think I should watch him?

I felt a twitch in my pocket. It was a text message summoning me to the Chief of Party's office. I sighed. Here came another wasted hour.

— Sorry, I've got to pay a call on the old man.

— By the way, Hunter, did you buy that strange monastery in France that you wrote me about?

— Did you check out the photo I sent you?

— It seems like a big place. Much too big for one man.

— Well, I'm a big guy. And I like being alone.

— That is an American peculiarity.

— It's more of a Hunter Ames peculiarity.

I made a cup of coffee in my beloved Indiana Hoosiers mug and took it downstairs. Someone had put up signs in the stairwell warning, in English and Pashto, *Do Not Spit Here*. Not surprisingly, one of the signs bore a telling streak of brown saliva.

I walked through Contracts and Tendering where Karimullah glanced up at me from his computer. In those days he was just another Afghan face. We had no idea where fate was about to lead us. If you had told me about the crazy events that lay in store for us I wouldn't have believed any of it.

Rising from a nearby desk, Leandro offered me a cheerful good-morning smile.

— Hunter, you look hunted!

— I'm off to see the chief.

— Uh-oh. Call if you need me. I've got your back, honey.

I called back:

— Stay out of the ladies' cloakroom.

He laughed and gave me the finger. Seeing this, Karimullah grew rigid.

Old Cleve Harbin had the only private office in the building. He motioned me into a seat opposite his desk while he finished up a call on his cell phone, turning away in his swivel chair so that all I could see was a puff of wispy white hair.

Everyone pretended to fear the Chief of Party, but to me he seemed harmless enough. Cleve Harbin was a career aid worker if there ever was one. He was in his seventies, a benign but neglectful leader who was too well liked and had climbed too high to ever lose his position. He made nearly three hundred thousand a year and would continue to do so for as long as he chose to work. Because he made so few demands, his American subordinates adored him. And to the Afghans who profited from his indifference, he was a godsend indeed.

I knew from his clipped tone that he was talking to someone at the USAID platform. For all of the chief's personal vagaries and outward laziness, he knew the project inside and out. Even now, eavesdropping at the end of this phone call, I heard him speak confidently on the previous quarter's infrastructure construction figures. This was my department. I'd never thought Harbin actually read my reports, but he seemed not only to have read them but to have committed them to memory.

The old man snapped his cell phone shut and whirled around in his chair.

— Welcome back, big guy. Good trip? Jet lag kicking your ass?

— It always does. I hear you guys got an ass-kicking of your own while I was away.

Harbin blinked at the impertinence.

— I wouldn't say anyone got an *ass-kicking*. Our security guys rose to the occasion. Besides, you know the GRS company motto. *For the world's most vulnerable people, in the world's most hostile environments.*

— It's too bad about Changwani.

He didn't seem to know who I was talking about. Then the corners of his mouth turned down in an expression that was more annoyance than regret.

— Yes, we were all devastated by that. Right there in your room, too. Of course, we didn't know him very well. Wait till you hear the stories, though. I tell you, our Guardian Angels were watching out for us that day. I know you believe otherwise, but let me tell you, God is real.

Guardian Angels, I thought. *Tell that to Changwani.*

I stared at the colored stickpins prickling in clumps across Harbin's map of Afghanistan, each one indicating a different project site. It was amazing how the program had grown.

Advancing Livelihoods and Agricultural Stability was unlike any aid program I'd ever worked on, with areas of operation dictated by military objectives more than humanitarian need. Originally funded for one year, the project was extended for another year, and then another. Its original budget of $45 million ballooned tenfold, and a modest food relief project metamorphosed into a half-billion-dollar stabilization behemoth that was hoped by many to be a key component in winning the war in the south.

I had a background in building irrigation systems in Gabon back in my Peace Corps days. As experience went, it wasn't much. I'd never built a road or a brick masonry reservoir. Harbin assured me that I'd catch on.

Suddenly all eyes—USAID, the State Department and the military—were on my infrastructure projects. My budget doubled, then tripled. The military said it was working; security was improving in some of the deadliest districts. IED blasts dropped in direct proportion to the number of projects initiated in those districts.

I couldn't keep up with the demand for new projects. I hired more field staff. I went to village *shuras* and told the elders: *give me more workers*. It wasn't hard. If I asked for a hundred men, I got them. If I asked for five hundred, more would be found. There seemed to be an inexhaustible supply of out-of-work young men ready to snap up those short-term jobs.

The only problem was money, not the lack of it but the suffocating over-abundance of it. *Burning money* was what we called it in the business. Global Relief Solutions received a nice commission from USAID on every dollar spent. Those profits depended on a steady burn rate, and that burn rate depended on my ability to design projects, get them approved and bring them to fruition.

My job wasn't to help people; I'd left those ideals on the shelf. I was there to facilitate the transfer of millions of dollars from the pockets of American taxpayers into the toughened hands of Afghan laborers and contractors. The jobs we created helped local citizens, and the projects they built supported local agriculture. And somehow or another this would help us win the war.

* * *

The chief startled me out of my reverie.

— We've got some new work coming your way. As you know, things are getting frisky again out in Zhari.

The old man swung around in his chair and aimed the green dot of his laser pointer at Zhari District.

— The military is taking fire on a weekly basis. They're finding IEDs all over the damn place. Colonel Waffa wants more of your famous construction projects.

I settled back in the cheaply made chair. Hearing a threatening creak, I sat up again, crossing my legs at the knee.

The Taliban had deep roots in Zhari. I had no staff there, no way to monitor the workers and make sure they were doing what they were paid to do. What Zhari needed was more hands-on agricultural training. The farmers loved it, and it made a difference. But training, for all the good it did, had a low burn rate. It cost nothing to implement but the wages of the trainers and whatnot. You had to run a lot of farmers through that kind of program to make a profit for Global Relief Solutions.

The Chief of Party had a mantra. He referred to it as something so absolute and unquestioned that it might have been chiseled into stone tablets: WHAT IS NOT SPENT CANNOT BE BILLED.

Now he was fiddling with his laser pointer, zipping the brilliant green dot across wall and ceiling.

— The military wants us to create jobs for *hundreds* of workers. We've got to help them. It's all in your lap, big guy.

— I'll need time before I can start things up in Zhari. I'll need to draft a work plan.

— I'll let Colonel Waffa know you're coming. Try to fly out there in a week or so.

Indignation was rising in my gorge. I thought of my colleagues on the project, with their light, predictable workloads. I felt like the child who'd been given twice as many chores as his lazy brothers.

I watched the chief playing with the laser pointer and thought: *It should have been you.*

5
Waiting for the End to Come

You are a little soul carrying around a corpse.
Epictetus

I KEPT MY TEAM LATE at the office that afternoon designing the new projects for Zhari. It was dark when they finally grabbed their scarves and flew out the door. Ramatullah stayed behind, going over the documents for a pair of brick masonry reservoirs that we had started in Maiwand not long before.

Reservoirs were easy to roll out, and they put lots of men to work. They enabled villages to store water that could be used for irrigation during the dry months. More importantly, as far as GRS was concerned, they burned through a lot of taxpayer money.

Ramatullah drew up an empty chair and watched me go through the various reservoir documents. I came to a roster of laborers with their photos and fingerprints in lieu of signatures, since most were illiterate. I studied the faces, all those proud young Afghan men with their unknown histories and hardships, their expressions as blank as precinct mug shots. Some were clearly too old to be doing this kind of work. I pointed at one of them.

— Why is this guy on the list? He's as old as Methuselah.

Ramatullah leaned closer and scowled, fingering his pockmark. The man in the photo had a weary face and a neatly trimmed grey beard that bespoke wisdom and intelligence. For all I knew he could have been an out-of-work professor.

— What the hell, if he wants a job, let him work. How many workers have we got?

— Nearly one hundred, sir.

He rose, collected the documents as gingerly as you'd take a vase from an errant child, and returned to his desk. He opened up his e-mail and began typing something, but it was just for show. The moment I left the office he'd be right on my heels. I appreciated whatever he was trying to prove. Few Afghans took the trouble.

I was late getting to dinner. By now the dining room was empty, with flies circling the dirty plates that my colleagues had left on the table. I opened the lid of one of the chafing dishes and found a bit of stew. Lifting the lid of the other dish I found only scattered crumbs and a dried fish head. Spying a plump bag of barbecue potato chips, my heart leapt.

Faith Woodson found me with my plate piled high with potato chips. She glanced at my bulging cheeks and smiled politely. Fatso was back.

With her back to me she opened a cabinet, stepped up on her tiptoes and grabbed up all the drinking glasses she could find. From another shelf she selected a variety of canned soft drinks and set them inside a plastic bag.

— We're having a little party on the roof. You should join us.

Did I have any choice? My cot and sleeping bag were up there. I was so wiped out from jet lag I could have slept on the wing of a moving plane. I glanced at my watch: only 8 p.m. It would be well after midnight before they'd had enough. I never understood how they did it. And on a work night.

My arrival had coincided with the punch line of a joke, and I assumed, as everyone does, that the eruption of laughter was aimed at me.

Jerry Janace called out:

— He made it!

They were all standing around the brick fire pit. An iPod was wired up to a pair of tinny, overstressed speakers grinding out heavy metal. I saw my cot and sleeping bag pushed to the side.

— Drinks on the table, someone called out.

Away from the glow of the fire everything was dark. Guy wires supported a collection of antennas mounted to the roof, and as I felt my way toward the table I tripped on one of them. Faith came up behind me, grabbing my arm.

— You drunk already?

— Just my usual grace.

She pointed the glow of her phone at the various bottles: gin, vodka and whiskey. She had always been polite to me, but in a calculated way, like the high school cheerleader condescending to the kid nobody else liked.

— Name your pleasure.

Sleep. And if it had been in a bottle I would have drunk the thing down in one go. There was nothing I needed on this table. Therein lay madness, and I knew it.

When Faith turned away I picked up the vodka bottle, let it clink against my glass, set it down again without taking a drop, then filled my empty glass with tonic water. Faith turned back, saw the full, bubbling glass and smiled appreciatively.

— Have all you want. We're not stingy here.

My colleagues made room for me around the fire. It wasn't cold, but the fire kept the mosquitoes at bay. The night was clear, the stars as pronounced as LEDs on black velvet. From the watchtowers on either end of the building our Afghan guards stared into the night, their AK-47s pointed skyward. The houses all around were dark, though no doubt our neighbors could hear the noise. They never complained. Maybe they were watching us right now like characters in some reality TV program, eager to see the latest craziness the drunk Americans could come up with. They would usually be rewarded with screaming, dancing and projectile vomiting by morning.

Faith was standing next to me, humming to a song she clearly didn't know. I nudged her in the side.

— Any updates on the day's mystery?

— You mean our Occupational Onanist? Mahmoud the Masturbator? Nope, nothing so far.

Miso, our Japanese-American communications director, was standing opposite us, her face up-lit by the fire, a sexy little Japanese dragon. She was smiling at Faith's joke, but because the chief was standing next to her she wasn't sure if she should laugh. That was her *modus operandi*: make no trouble, stay out of the way.

Old Harbin took a drink from his Coke and shook his head, as though the matter in question disgusted him (or we did for bringing it up).

Jerry Janace and Hank Diebold, muscular rednecks in their forties, were also reliving the morning's event. Morgan Hayes, our finance director and the only African-American on our team, was trying to edge in on the joke, smilingly ignoring his failure.

Jerry, Hank and Morgan—I thought of them as the Unholy Trinity. They had all dated Faith, though as Morgan had once quipped, "you don't date Faith, you just wait your turn." I recalled one alcohol-fueled skirmish between Jerry and Morgan when the latter realized he had been eclipsed by the former. Our poor chief had to tear them apart. Such was life in the Golden Cage, where relationships were really "locationships"—passionate and vital in the moment, dissolving like smoke when the project ended.

Not that I was immune. A few years ago, when the project was peopled by a very different cast of characters, I'd gotten involved with a gal from home office. Sherry Deal, brilliantly breasted, breathtakingly stout. *It is what it is*, she used to say, climbing on me as frankly as you'd mount a tractor. It wasn't bad. It wasn't all that great, either. But it was what it was.

— Hunter was a lucky sumbitch.

Hank Diebold said this from the iPod where he was queuing up a new playlist. Something started playing that he clearly didn't mean for us to hear—classical violins and a harpsichord.

Everyone was now talking about the attack. Faith reflected:

— I'd gotten up early that morning to take a shower. I never shower that early. But that's when it happened. *Boom.* If I'd stayed in bed five more minutes . . .

I admired the way the firelight picked out her angular profile. She was a good-looking woman, though a little skinny for my taste. Not that I'd ever been offered right of refusal.

She continued:

— I barely had my clothes on before Dusty herded us all into the safe room. We were trapped in there for six hours. You should have seen Daddy. It aged him ten years.

Daddy was her pet name for the chief. I glanced around, but he'd gone back inside. He never stayed beyond the time it took to polish off a single soft drink, wandering back to his room to deal with a never-ending torrent of e-mails.

— You missed all the fun. How were things back in Indiana?

Hank Diebold said this from across the fire, drinking from a big tumbler that I'd seen him fill almost entirely with vodka.

— Just the usual craziness.

He looked at me critically, perhaps trying to imagine the sort of craziness I might be capable of. Others were waiting for more. I didn't have their conversational ease. I didn't know how to relax and gab with people I worked with. They thought I was a snob, but the truth was, I couldn't think of much that would interest them.

— I bumped into an old colleague while I was back home. Had kind of a crazy night.

Hank had already started drifting off in search of more interesting fare. Now he paused, raising an eyebrow.

— Oh yeah? Tell me about it.

It wasn't much of a story. I used to teach history at the local high school, where my friend Ron White was on the English faculty. Now he was the assistant principal. We ran into each other one night outside of a convenience store. It was precisely the kind of encounter I could count on having when I wanted to be alone.

But it wasn't a bad night. We went to a strip club, had a few laughs. He remembered stories about my former teaching days that I'd so completely forgotten it was as though they had happened to someone else. Girls that looked like truck drivers kept coming up and offering us lap dances. Ron facetiously bought me one, picking out the tiniest girl of the bunch. She couldn't get her legs around me, so she rode sidesaddle for a while.

Ron and I went back to my place for a nightcap, whereupon Ron confessed he was gay, reached out to stroke my hand and asked if I'd like some help relaxing. All I could do was laugh, imagining the two of us in bed, like Laurel and Hardy.

Reaching the end of the tale I realized I'd made a tactical mistake. Hank was nodding studiously, his expression both thoughtful and alarmed. Little Jerry Janace had sidled up next to him, peering at me as through a misty window.

— Dude, you threw him out of your house, right?

— I hope you kicked his ass.

The two were staring at me, hoping for an ending that would spell the worst for the predatory homo, though neither of them would have said as much. With Leandro on the team they'd learned to keep their true disgust for the subject in check.

— Actually I put him up in my son's old room. He wasn't in any condition to drive.

Jerry frowned, spitting into the fire.

— Not me, man. I'm as open-minded as the next guy. But not in my house. It's against my beliefs.

Jerry Janace was a retired army sergeant. He was a stocky little guy, about five foot two, who compensated for his shortness with a tough, abrasive personality. He had none of the cultural sensitivity that sometimes stymied his fellow program directors. An aggressively religious man, he taped passages from the New Testament around his desk for the benefit of his Muslim staff.

Hank said:

— I'll bet we've got plenty of homos in the office. Kandahar is like the gay capital of Afghanistan. Dudes pay lots of money to watch boys dance. I saw it on TV.

Jerry was turning his glass so that the ice in the bottom clattered and spun. The conversation made him uneasy, which only made me feel deviously inclined to push it further along.

— They probably wouldn't call themselves gay. That's really a western concept. They might like other guys, but anal sex is taboo here.

Jerry winced as though he'd stepped on a nail. I added:

— Sometimes it's just an expedient. They can't have sex with women, and I guess goats can get kind of tiresome.

Leandro had joined the circle, fresh from a shower and wearing a yellow tank top, white sweat pants and apparently no underwear, to judge from the sharp outline of his diminutive endowment, upturned like a crooked pinky finger. He'd brought his laptop and was cradling it awkwardly as he clicked around in search of something he wanted to show me.

— Look at this, Hunter.

I covered my mouth, stifling a yawn that seemed too vast for my face. Over at the drink table I saw Faith hold up the bottle of vodka, but I shook my head.

— What's up?

— Pictures of the attack. I got them from Dusty.

Dusty was the leader of our private security detail, the eight Rambo-like warriors affectionately known as The Gunslingers. They lived a parallel existence on the compound, dined apart from us and generally kept to themselves. Seconds after the blast they had leapt out of bed, grabbed their AK-47s and were on the roof picking off insurgents in their T-shirts and underwear.

The photos on Leandro's screen showed ransacked bedrooms with curtains hanging in ribbons and glass all over the floor. Shattered mirrors. Black plumes of smoke over gentle, unperturbed trees.

— Here's a good one, Hunter.

One of the gunslingers was crouched beside a lump of something bloody, offering the photographer a victorious thumbs-up. Ammo was strapped on bandoliers crosswise over his chest. Leandro zoomed in on the thing at his feet, which turned out to be an eviscerated slab of human torso. He zoomed closer onto what was unmistakably a bundle of cock and balls.

For a sick instant, I thought these were the remains of the Pakistani consultant. I wanted to slam the laptop on Leandro's fingers. But no, this was what was left of the suicide bomber, projected hundreds of feet in the air onto the office roof.

— That's enough for me.

As I turned away, Leandro said:

— Oh, I almost forgot, I found you a room.

— Seriously?

He paused for dramatic effect, glancing right, then left.

— Well, sort of. I don't know if you'll like it.

I set down my empty glass. My hands were trembling with fatigue. I was trying not to smile with relief, setting an arm lightly over the shoulders of my savior, my mincing *deus ex machina*.

Hank Diebold whistled for silence. From his speakers came the opening piano notes of Queen's "We Are the Champions." His face was stern with emotion as he beckoned everyone around the fire, his glass held high. Leandro pulled me away.

— We'd better go.

Hank's booming voice followed us down the stairwell as he not so much as sang but shouted out the opening lyrics of hardship and triumph for the benefit of the surrounding homes. The music was turned up as loud as it would go.

Leandro took the stairs two at a time, calling up to me:

— You'll be hearing that a lot. Since the attack it's become a kind of theme song.

A guard rolled back the steel gate leading out of the residential part of the compound. I lugged the larger of my two suitcases while Leandro carried the other. Guards with machine guns stood in the shadows, alert to the unusual passage of two Americans into the less secure part of the compound.

The area comprising the guesthouse and the office was Zone One, the compound's nucleus. Here we lived and worked, a kind of *sanctum sanctorum*. Except when departing on road missions, I rarely had reason to venture into Zone Two. This area consisted of the small residential side street that we shared with a handful of Kandahar homeowners, a kind of poor suburb of Zone One. It extended to the front gate on the main road, beyond which lay Zone Three—Greater Kandahar with all its implicit dangers.

We walked in darkness past the mud-brick walls of a children's prison. Fifty or so kids were held there. It abutted the project's office, and from the roof you could look down into the courtyard and see the inmates at play. In the early days the kids would wave up at us in hopes of candy and cigarettes. Nowadays, after two years of disappointment, they just scowled and gave us the middle finger.

Before we arrived, this had been just an ordinary Kandahar neighborhood. As the project grew, so did our compound. Space was needed for storage and parking. The neighbors, wary of living so close to such a conspicuous target, were happy to rent out their homes to the Americans at many times the going price. One such structure was the training villa, a derelict two-story building near the main gate. It was to this building that Leandro now led me.

— The room is okay, Hunt. It's not the Taj Mahal or anything, but you'll be back in the guesthouse before long. Tomorrow we're running a cable over here so you'll have an Internet hookup.

He led me into a gravel courtyard where a lone tree stood in the center. I turned back in the direction of the guesthouse and could see the soft glow of firelight illuminating the night sky. The music had stopped but everyone was still shouting out the refrain. I wondered what all the shouting must have sounded like to the neighborhood at large, like spectators seated in the visitors section, vastly outnumbered but defiant that they were still and forever the champions of the world.

Leandro opened a creaky bedroom door and pulled the string on a bulb hanging from the ceiling: a narrow bed, a desk with a folding metal chair and an oval rug on bare concrete.

He sighed and shook his head.

— Like I said, hon, it's not the Taj Mahal.

— Really, it's fine, I said, setting down my suitcases with a feeling of icy desolation.

The room reeked of vanished humanity. The walls were painted a dark shade midway between orange and brown. I tested the bed, which sank with a dispiriting creak of ancient springs.

Leandro offered to show me the bathroom and kitchen down the hall, but for the moment I'd seen enough.

— Karimullah is next door. Otherwise the building is all yours.

He added with a roguish twinkle:

— Remember, he's mine. Hands off.

— No worries on that score.

— And don't let this place get you down. It's just temporary.

As we stood there, arms crossed, I became aware of the unusual silence in the building. No generators roaring in the background. No

47

drinking and shouting on the roof.

Leandro's expression left me in no doubt that this was an arrangement he himself would never have tolerated. No air conditioning, no satellite TV. It was the sort of accommodation one might foist on a visiting Afghan but never on an American. But this was me, after all. Agreeable, uncomplaining Hunter.

— I'll say goodbye then. Come on back to the party once you're settled in.

Leandro held his arms out to be hugged, his head flopping to one side. He snuggled up close with his face pressed to my breast, groaning a little. It was a little weird. I glanced down at his shiny hair and patted him reluctantly on the back.

Once he was gone, I leaned against the door, surveying my new home. Any of my colleagues would have marched right back to the guesthouse. But as I thought about it, I realized the room was okay. In fact, it might be damned fine. It reminded me of a long-ago posting I'd had in Sudan, a converted whorehouse. I had a feeling that I'd be here for some time, so I might as well make the most of it.

I needed to move my bowels. It was a strange time of day for that, but then my body was still on an American rhythm.

As I went out to find the bathroom I saw Leandro down the hall squatting next to a door. I realized it must be Karimullah's. He probably thought he was whispering, but you could have heard him out in the courtyard.

— *Just five minutes. I promise, I just want to talk.*

I moved toward the jostling smells of soap and mildew. Behind me Leandro was tapping louder, insisting on admittance. A mild disgust rose up within me but I pushed it down. My aversion was out of date, no longer socially acceptable. That's just the way some guys liked it.

I'd already been through this with my son. I couldn't understand

48

it then, and I couldn't understand it now. But it was no concern of mine.

6
Karimullah

What you seek is seeking you.
Rumi

IN THE EARLY DAYS Karimullah loved his job. He made eleven hundred dollars a month, and the work was satisfying. His boss, Leandro Palafox, was kind, if a little too affectionate, but this could be overlooked.

The security pat-downs he was subjected to each morning coming into the compound took some getting used to. Everyone had to be checked for weapons or for cameras on their cell phones, which were forbidden. But it gave Karimullah a proud feeling to walk through the gates and to show his ID card with the princely seal of GRS and the red, white and blue logo of USAID, *From the American People*.

One guard gave him trouble. Karimullah recognized the fierce, troubled yearning as the guard took him aside for a private inspection. *Hold your arms out*. The guard patted each sleeve of his *kamiz*, then the side of his torso. *Separate your legs*. The guard squatted and ran his hands slowly down Karimullah's buttocks, then from his ankles up the insides of his thighs.

Later, when Karimullah was leaving work, the guard took him aside for another pat-down. He said he must check for stolen office supplies and flash drives that might contain valuable information. Again the hands groped him through the thin cloth of his *shalwar kamiz*, touching him where no man's hands should go, breathing heavily with dark masculine desire.

Somehow the guard obtained Karimullah's cell phone number. He implored Karimullah to come out with him. Karimullah refused, but politely, as was his nature. When the guard followed him home and called up to his window, he complained to Leandro Palafox. The guard was fired. Karimullah heard rumors that he had joined the Taliban.

The first death threat came as no surprise:

— Leave your job or in the name of Prophet we will hunt you down.

He filed a security report, as per GRS company policy.

The second threat was more explicit:

— You were warned. Do not force us to kill you.

He filled out another security report, which was filed along with the first one.

Then came the phone calls. The man's voice was gentle, like that of a patient friend.

— Why would you work for them? Don't you know what they are doing to our country?

— They are trying to help us.

— What would your father think if he were alive?

How did they know about his father?

— And your poor mother, far away in Pakistan with her heart troubles.

He began to tremble.

— Your employers are infidel dogs. You should be ashamed.

He wasn't ashamed. He was prouder than ever.

In those days he was living alone in a room above a butcher's shop. In the evenings he lit a candle and studied his engineering texts. He didn't want to file papers and arrange contracts all his life; he wanted to build roads and bridges.

He awoke one morning to find a night letter, a *shabnama*, taped to his door. It warned him in unambiguous language to leave his job. He went to stay with his friends Khan and Sadiq for a few days. When he received no more calls or texts he returned to his room over the butcher's shop.

He never saw the faces of the two intruders. One held him down in a wrestler's hold while the other kicked him in the gut and groin. The first man produced a pistol, pressed it to Karimullah's temple and cocked the hammer.

— Let me be very clear. Unless you stop working for the Americans at once, you will die. Do you understand?

They took his cell phone and his laptop and his books on engineering, everything that they knew was precious to him.

He pissed blood.

For three days the butcher brought him food. When he returned to work, Faith Woodson, the human resources manager, wrote him up for absenteeism. He never told her about the attack or his bruised ribs or the blood in his urine.

He moved in with Khan and Sadiq. It was glorious. They stayed up late playing chess and watching movies on Khan's laptop. When he was well, Karimullah showed his gratitude by cooking lavish feasts for them and entertaining them with dances and tales from his days of wandering, omitting the parts he knew they would not want to hear.

One Friday after mosque he ran into his friend Noorullah from the office. They hailed a taxi and set off for a teahouse. A man on a motorbike pulled up beside them at an intersection, a black scarf concealing his face. He opened the back door of the taxi, aimed a pistol and fired twice. The first bullet shattered a window, the second shattered Noorullah's shoulder. The man sped away. Karimullah was unharmed.

The matter came to the attention of his supervisor, who was furious that Karimullah had not told him of the previous incidents. The anxiety of the preceding weeks rose up and poured out of Karimullah in tears. Leandro embraced him and said everything would be all right.

— You can live in the training villa. No one will hurt you there.

Karimullah thanked him through heaving sobs. As Leandro held him, patting him on the back, Karimullah felt his hand traveling down toward his buttocks.

As it had been, so it would always be.

He knew what men of this sort were like, the dangerous power of their lust. But he had nowhere else to go.

His supervisor treated him with surprising cordiality, like a house guest. Whatever Karimullah needed, Leandro was at pains to provide. Karimullah felt great shame. Perhaps he had misjudged his superior. His shame turned into pity for the lonely little man, though he remembered the words of the poet: *the lion is most handsome when looking for food.*

One night, when Leandro dropped by to check on him, Karimullah was profuse in his gratitude, remembering all the terrors he had so recently endured. And in that outpouring he blurted out that he loved Leandro.

It wasn't what he had meant to say, but he knew it was what Leandro had been in agony to hear. And because it was in Karimullah's nature to make others happy, he could not deprive this loveless man of something so easily given.

But those words, uttered in a moment of careless exuberance, would come to haunt him. At the office he could feel Leandro's eyes following him when he walked to the teakettle or went to the roof for prayers. When Leandro came to Karimullah's desk to instruct him in some task he would lean close so that his breath was hot in Karimullah's ear. He would send imploring e-mails with poems and sonnets that made Karimullah's heart twist in dread.

Karimullah's Afghan colleagues picked up on Leandro's strange ardor. While many had dabbled in mild forms of homosexuality in their youth, they had never seen anything so blatant, so *haram*. At lunch in the cafeteria for national staff, they sat away from Karimullah and wouldn't look him in the eye.

Leandro began talking about a future with Karimullah in the United States. He showed him photos of his house in Oakland, California. The house had a porch swing where, using Photoshop, he had superimposed photos of himself and Karimullah in a frame that said *Happy Together*.

Most odious were the surprise visits to Karimullah's room at the training villa. Leandro always brought some gift like fruit or toiletries. Once it was a set of expensive Calvin Klein underwear, which he then begged Karimullah to model for him.

It was an easy matter to allow Leandro to hold his hand while they talked. It was unpleasant but not unbearable when Leandro would reach under his *kamiz* to touch his smooth, hairless chest. His hand would move down to his navel, then to the bunched fabric at the waist of his trousers. Karimullah, remembering other hands and other men, would edge trembling away.

Karimullah didn't know how to make him understand that it was all a mistake. He would hide in darkened classrooms when Leandro was prowling around the building. He went more often to visit his former roommates, overjoyed to be among his own people, wanting above all to laugh again.

It was a relief when the infrastructure director, Hunter Ames, came to live down the hall from him. He was a quiet man whom Karimullah knew only through conversations about contracts. But it was puzzling. The training villa was no place for an American; it was filthy and unsafe. It must have been levied upon him as some sort of punishment. But for what?

Karimullah began saying prayers when it was not required to do so. He made special appeals for the health of his mother and her weak heart. He prayed for the redemption of his former master, Obaidullah, whom he hated. And he prayed for patience and wisdom in dealing with the unpredictable passions of his supervisor.

One night on the balcony, rising from prayer, he saw his new neighbor, Hunter Ames, standing nearby smoking a cigarette. He wore pajama bottoms and an enormous sweatshirt that swung with the weight of his belly. Had he been watching Karimullah's prostrations with the same wicked longing? Was he another one to fear?

Hunter said:

— Sorry, I didn't see you down there.

— It is okay.

— Cigarette?

— No, thank you. Goodnight.

That night Karimullah read several *suras* of the Qur'an. He didn't understand Arabic, but the sound of the words greatly soothed him.

In his journal he wrote: *I am lost in a wilderness, surrounded by wild beasts, and each day they draw nearer. There are times when death seems sweet. But God calls us to live in His mercy. We have no path other than that which is ordained.*

During the night he heard the footsteps of his new neighbor shuffling aimlessly up and down the hall. Fearing the man's intentions, he pushed a desk against the door. He lay for a long time without sleeping, staring wide-eyed into the darkness.

7

Last of the True Gentlemen

Wherever it lies, under earth or over earth, the body will always rot.
Plotinus

I PACED UP AND DOWN the hall, smoking. A single fluorescent bulb cast a pale bluish light. Stepping out onto the balcony, I nearly tripped over Karimullah, praying. I could see firelight on the roof of the guesthouse; I could hear the music and laughter. Faith had been texting me to come join them, but I had too much on my mind.

With a host of new tasks now piling up, I had begun to feel a growing sense of panic. We were rolling out infrastructure projects in five districts. They were eloquent in their simplicity—erosion walls, reservoirs and road projects that were scaled to burn the greatest amount of money.

I didn't know what to do about Zhari. I would have to fly out there and set up some *shura* meetings. Each tribal elder would demand priority for his village. One or two elders would walk out in a huff, then wait outside to be invited back in. The meetings followed a kind of dramatic arc, like opera, and before the final curtain went down the district governor and I would invariably sing an aria of triumph, joined by a chorus of eager old men. With so many laborers put to work, the military could count on a few months of relative stability. USAID could publish more success stories and the accountants back at GRS home office would have a flurry of new invoices to process. All that remained was putting my wide ass on a helicopter and getting out there.

But then, just to make things interesting, the chief asked me to oversee an inaugural ceremony in Kabul. The project was spending $20 million to distribute tractors and other farm machinery to agricultural cooperatives. This had been discussed at the most recent staff meeting, but as it had nothing to do with my program I didn't pay much attention—until I heard the chief announce that he had picked me to organize the event.

I followed him into his office.

— I've got a lot on my plate, Cleve. Miso is better at this sort of thing.

— She's too damn shy.

— But what the hell do I know about—

— You don't need to know anything. I just need you there to make sure the thing doesn't fall apart.

— Send Jerry, he's running the tractor program.

— The keynote speaker will be the U.S. ambassador. Would you send that redneck to handle a high-profile VIP event?

Old Harbin had a point. He continued:

— No one knows how to finesse these things the way you can, Hunter. You've got class. Hell, you're probably the only one among us who owns a tie.

I looked into Harbin's watery blue eyes. I knew he didn't think highly of me. I forgot to include attachments on e-mails, forgot to turn off my phone during important meetings. My shirts always came untucked. Twice I'd dropped my laptop and crashed the hard drive. But I cared about my job, something the chief, for all his growing complacency, could still appreciate.

As I continued pacing the hall of the training villa I heard the door downstairs swing closed with a resounding boom. It was a late hour for guests. I heard tennis shoes squeaking on the stairs. In a moment Faith Woodson turned the corner.

She started, seeing me at the other end of the hall.

— God, you scared me. I thought you might be lonely out here.

Puzzled, I held the door open to my room. We'd always been cordial but in a loose, disconnected way, like people who had never had reason to dislike each other nor cause to believe they'd ever actually become friends.

She surveyed the room, though there wasn't much to look at, just my open laptop, a shelf of books, and some clothes piled on the bed. I spirited away a pair of dirty boxers with my foot.

— Hope you don't mind me barging in like this. Just thought I'd come see how exile was treating you.

As she said this she picked up a framed photo of my son Maurice. It was one of the handful of personal knickknacks that followed me from one posting to another. Mementos from a lost world.

— Is that your kid? He's cute.

The photo had been taken on a beach in West Africa. The sun was behind him, leaving his face grainy and in shadow. He was seventeen. It was the last picture taken of him.

— That was almost ten years ago.

— He's a hottie.

Indeed, he was a handsome young man, with his mother's Greek eyebrows, olive skin and a smile so easy and natural it rarely left his face. Even as a boy he had one of those mature faces that suggested exactly what he would look like as an adult.

— Do you have a recent photo?

I took the frame from her, examining it. I'd be damned if I was going to sift through the ashes of the past for this woman's benefit.

In a moment she said:

— Divorce, huh?

— Something like that.

From her handbag she produced a bottle and two glasses. I could tell she was already a little drunk. She poured a disarming three inches of vodka into each of the glasses. From her handbag she opened a can of Orangina, glancing at me questioningly.

— It's not a real screwdriver, but close. Have one?

She was dressed in a red blouse and Capri pants that terminated just below her calves. A charm bracelet jingled as she poured soda into each glass, waiting for the orange foam to recede. She handed me one.

— Cheers.

She lay diagonally across my bed propped on one elbow, ankles crossed and one foot twitching. I sat nearby at my desk. Music played on my laptop, electro-ambient music with a soft, driving beat. I thought it might drive her away, but it seemed to be doing the opposite.

I announced in the cool, soothing voice of a DJ:

— *This* is a group called Carbon Based Lifeforms.

— Hmm, kind of sexy, babe.

She squinted up at me as at a bright light. *Babe.* She was drunker than I'd thought.

— Don't you like your drink?

I raised my eyebrows as though I'd forgotten it was there. I had a complicated relationship with alcohol. It attracted and repelled me. I'd seen it bring hilarity and I'd seen it wreck lives. When I was a kid I never feared my father less than when he had a few beers in him. It made him accessible, softened his edges. And it sent him driving off the Second Street overpass when I was fifteen.

Most of my colleagues drank. Our imprisoned circumstances almost dictated it. I liked a little bump in the evening to accompany a good book, but the crazy rooftop saturnalias were too much for me. So I mostly avoided them, earning the reputation of a snob and a recluse.

— You look like you've got the world on your shoulders, Hunt.

— Just a lot of work coming down at once.

— I heard about the Kabul ceremony. You'll do great.

— Apparently the old man thinks I've got the makings of a party planner.

— Daddy is always right. Anyways, you'll have fun in Kabul. Go to a restaurant, enjoy yourself. Sure beats this shithole.

— I won't have much time for that. I've got to get back and start work in Zhari.

— Well, make the most of it. How old are you, anyway?

— Forty-eight.

I had a habit of deducting a few years when I was with a good-looking woman. Not that Faith was my type. She was too thin, with black hair cut like a boy's. Odd that such a stick figure of a woman could arouse such frenzied interest from my conventional colleagues. Then again, she was the only woman around—apart from Miso, who was indifferent to the men's advances and therefore presumed to be a lesbian.

As we sat listening to the music I glanced at Faith in profile. She probably drank around a pint of alcohol a day. With her lean body she could count on her metabolism to carry her along for a few more years. Then one morning she'd sit down on the toilet and find her gut pooling in her lap like bread dough. Give it five years, maybe ten. I could tell her all about it.

Lighting a cigarette, she puckered one eye as if on the trail of a good mystery.

— You know, you're one of the only guys in the compound who hasn't hit on me.

— Really? What about the old man?

She widened her eyes as if to say: *Yep, even him.*

She blew smoke up at the ceiling, watching it dissolve into the shadows. I couldn't be falling for her, not Faith. It was just the weird alchemy of booze and isolation. Life in the Golden Cage. It did something to you.

She sat up and leaned closer to me, unknowingly directing a blast of stale, pungent breath.

— So tell me, why *have* you never hit on me?

I looked down at my glass. I could feel my ears burning.

— That's not really my style.

— So what's your style?

I pointed at my body.

— I didn't figure this was *your* style.

— Don't you like me?

— Sure. But you know, a man can appreciate a good-looking woman without—

— Without trying to screw her?

— Something like that.

She pointed at me, nodding.

— I like that about you. The last of the true gentlemen. Now pour me a wee bit more.

8

I Know About Your Son

Life is the flight of the alone to the alone.
Plotinus

WHEN I AWOKE I WAS still at my desk, my nose notched into the crook of my arm. My face felt wooden. As I raised my head I felt my pulse pounding with each miserable beat of my heart. My mouth tasted like I'd gargled with battery acid.

Faith was gone, the bed neatly made. Ambient music was still wafting hypnotically from my open laptop. I slammed it shut.

I squinted at my watch: nine o'clock. I let out a curse, stripped out of yesterday's clothes, slipped on a pair of chinos and a polo shirt, stuffed my laptop into my bag and was still getting into my shoes as I stumbled out the door.

My guys were all there, each staring attentively at his monitor. At least that. In my present grim mood it would have been too easy to strike out at those poor bastards.

Approaching my desk, Ramatullah, my deputy, seemed taken aback by my disheveled state, but said in the deferential tone of a flight attendant:

— Good morning, sir. Would you like coffee? Tea?

— Actually, yes. I'd like black coffee.

— Very good, sir.

The others were trying not to look at me. I should have taken a sick day, but there was too much to do. I had the inaugural event in Kabul coming up in a few days. There was a banner to be printed and a long list of arrangements screaming for my attention.

As the e-mails began scrolling into my inbox I recognized the name of my friend Bill Batson at the American Embassy.

> I hear you're organizing next week's inaugural ceremony for the tractor program. Running chain gangs not keeping you busy enough? Ha! Let's get together for dinner while you're in Kabul. We've got loads to catch up on.

I took a sip of coffee and realized I badly needed a piss.

I stood up and said to my deputy:

— How are those culvert plans?

— All done, sir. I e-mailed them to you. Did you not see them in your inbox?

— I'll have a look when I get back.

— I'm sure I e-mailed them.

My foot caught the leg of my chair, which in my blurred impatience I sent careening toward the wall. It bounced and rolled back, teetered for a moment on two wheels, then crashed helplessly on its side. People at other desks craned their heads around for a look. My team sat as if turned to stone.

On my way back from the restroom I stopped to chat with Behzad. I knew I could count on him to view my present distress with a minimum of judgment. Glad for the distraction, the well-dressed Afghan leaned back in his swivel chair and crossed his ankles, regarding my red eyes and greasy, sleep-swept hair.

— You don't look too good, my friend.

— I hardly know where I am.

— A question that has baffled mankind through the ages.

I took up Behzad's stapler and considered putting a staple through the webbing of my thumb. Behzad calmly took it from me.

— What is troubling you, my friend?

— Nothing that a sick day wouldn't cure.

— Then take one. Go back to your room. Afghanistan's problems will still be here when you get back.

— I've got too much to do. I'm flying to Kabul tomorrow.

Behzad was looking more than usually well dressed. A briefcase stood open on his desk. The air was stinging with cologne.

— Speaking of wasted time, I've got a meeting with the Provincial Governor today at his palace.

— That's . . . good. I guess.

Behzad sighed.

— Who knows? Two months ago he told the Chief of Party that he wanted me fired. Last week he offered me a job in his administration. Today perhaps he will want me killed.

It was an exaggeration, but not by much. Governor Wazir had long been Behzad's nemesis. USAID considered him a key partner in the rebuilding of Afghanistan, a man "committed to good government and ending the insurgency." According to Behzad and others, though, he was a criminal who ran the province like his own private fiefdom. It was hard to know who to believe, but the guy sounded like a real asshole.

— Well, good luck with the governor. You'll be fine.

— And you, have fun in Kabul.

Behzad smiled and added in a low voice:

— Try to combine business with pleasure.

I went back to my room for a rest. I really thought I was going to puke. The maid was sitting on my bed, paging through *National Geographic*. Startled, she drew her head-covering around the lower part of her face, her dark eyes glowing with resentment at the intrusion.

There were half a dozen of these women on the compound, drifting in every morning like a flock of warbling birds in blue burkas. This one was youngish, probably in her thirties. She was likely illiterate, enjoying the magazine for the bright, colorful pictures.

A minute later, fussing with the things on my desk, I saw her lean back on one arm, crossing her ankles and slapping a page of the magazine as though prepared to sit there all day. I cleared my throat meaningfully, and finally tapped her on the shoulder, pointing my thumb at the door. She gathered up her cleaning supplies and left, making as much noise as she could.

I locked the door behind her, took off my pants and threw myself on the bed. I mashed my face into the pillow and could pick out two different smells, like notes spaced an octave apart: the tangy fragrance of women's shampoo, the darker odor of my own sweaty scalp. Bits of last night's conversation were coming back to me, but it was like trying to reassemble pages that had gone through a shredder.

Something about wool underwear, and whether a woman's G-spot is biologically related to the prostate and . . . Robert Heinlein novels?

She had patted the space next to her on the bed, but I demurred with a shy chuckle.

— Afraid I might attack you? I promise I won't bite.

She complained that the room was hot, and next thing I knew she was out of her Capris and lying atop the bed in red blouse and black panties, one leg crossed over the other like the number 4. She had the cat-like look of a woman ready to pounce on an unwilling suitor.

I hadn't gotten laid in months, apart from one drunken night in France when I was on leave, an encounter I was still trying to forget. I knew that with Faith it would mean nothing, and for some men that might be an inducement. But I worked with three of her former swains and had heard enough gossip about their amorous defects to be wary.

And anyway, what was her game? Why go for an awkward roll with me when she could have gone the rounds with a gifted playboy like Dusty or Hank?

She besieged me with questions. The vodka had swept away all inhibitions and she was going to get to the bottom of Hunter Ames.

— Like buying that monastery. What's that all about? Don't you like people?

— I guess so.

Her voice had adopted a high, chainsaw-like edge that grew more abrasive with each drink.

— Then is it some kind of religious thing? But it couldn't be, because you said you have no religion.

— We've all got to live somewhere.

— But … a … friggin' … French monastery?

Now it was my turn to be curious.

— How did you even hear about that?

Eyes closed, she waved the question away as tedious and irrelevant. I could have told her it was none of her damn business. All I wanted was a quiet piece of land far from meddlesome neighbors where I could retire in sweet anonymity. And where could you live more anonymously than among the French?

— And what about your kid? Is he coming out to live with you?

She must have seen the change in my expression. Or did she know more than she was letting on?

— No . . . he won't be coming.

I turned up the music and went out for a piss. When I got back, Faith was dead to the world. Her face in sleep had the innocence of a saint. I knelt as close as I dared, listening to her breathe. Moving downrange I found the mound of her pubis partially concealed by her up-drawn thigh. I touched the tiny rose on the waistband of her panties. It would have been so easy.

Now, a day later, I felt both nauseous and weirdly amorous. I needed to throw up. I needed to masturbate too, but I resisted, not wanting to confuse cause and effect. I had no feelings for Faith Woodson. The pleasure she had to offer was carnal, to use that stuffy biblical term. Of the flesh, not of the spirit.

No, what I wanted wasn't sex but something else. I couldn't have said what it was, but the longing was enough. It was a reminder that one or two filaments still carried signals from my black, stifled heart.

A light still burned, however feebly. The light of hope. The desire to live again.

In the afternoon I felt a little better. I worked with Nissar on graphics for a large banner that would hang behind the ambassador and appear on TV stations all over the country. Nissar was the laziest and vainest member of my team, a handsome boy who wore a thin gold bracelet on his hairy wrist. He watched my stress with slouching indifference, as though posing for the cover of Afghan *GQ*.

We had gone through four drafts of banner designs, but Nissar resisted my ideas, insisting on an elaborate wedding font for the project acronym. I'd had enough. I scrawled with a black marker BIG AND BOLD, MAKE IT POP! and slapped it on his desk.

In a while he came to me with a final proof. He had incorporated a photo of rolling farmland and hayricks and grain silos, a scene unlike any farm that had ever existed in Afghanistan, but it got the point across. Beneath the English, the text was translated into Dari, which might have been Sanskrit as far as I was concerned.

— Did you check the translation carefully?

— It is perfect in every detail, exact to your specifications.

I e-mailed it to the printer.

I worried all afternoon about the damned banner, calling the printer every half hour to check its progress. I was flying out in the morning and had agreed to pay twice the going rate for same-day turnaround.

My hangover had returned with a sinister, eye-popping vengeance. Vodka was sweating from my armpits and probably from my crotch, if anyone had dared check.

At four-thirty the office began thinning out. My team glanced at me and at each other, wanting to leave but unsure whether to abandon their boss in his grim fury.

My phone rang: it was security, informing me that the printer was waiting at the front gate. I nearly cried with relief. My team rose and grabbed their scarves. Nissar shook my hand firmly.

— I hope you are happy with it. I did it exactly to your

specifications.

A guy on an idling motorbike was at the gate with the banner rolled up under his arm. He spoke no English. I indicated for him to unroll the banner on the ground for inspection. At ten feet wide it spanned the road.

Everything looked good. It had metal grommets on each corner as ordered. The ink was nice and bright, Afghan flag in one corner, American flag in the other. At the bottom, the logos for USAID, Global Relief Solutions and the Ministry of Agriculture, Irrigation and Livestock.

ADVANCING LIVELIHOODS AND AGRICULTURAL STABILITY

ALAS

FARM MACHINERY GRANTS

A PROJECT OF USAID

Below that was the translation in Dari.

I heard the scrape of approaching feet. It was Karimullah, coming from the direction of the office. He was tapping a text message on his phone. He had nearly passed when curiosity led him to the thing unrolled on the ground. Later we would remember this as our first real conversation.

— Pretty nice, huh?

He moved his lips silently as he scanned the text. At close range I realized he was not the young boy I'd thought he was. Faint lines fanned out from the corner of his eyes, hinting at a hard youth. He had a clean, appealing smell.

— Who made this banner, sir?

— One of my guys, Nissar. Why, what's wrong?

He squatted and ran his finger over the English text, then down to the Dari.

— These words are confusing.

71

— What do you mean?

— It says: big, bold and ... make it pop?

He glanced up at me, shielding the sinking sun to gauge my reaction.

— That son of a bitch.

— I don't see any corresponding text in English.

I thought of the mock-up I'd slapped on his desk. The whole team was probably laughing about it right now. From Karimullah's ashen expression you would have thought it was he who had been responsible.

I shouted:

— Why the hell didn't the printer catch this?

I looked around, but the motorbike was gone. By now several Afghans were gathered around the banner and speaking to each other in their language. Someone laughed and said:

— Hey, mister, make it pop?

Jaw set, I rolled up the banner, threw it over my shoulder like a rug and stormed off to my room in the training villa.

I should have had someone else check it. Maybe Nissar had expected me to, and we would all have had a good laugh. I'd have to check with Faith about disciplinary action.

Well, there would just be no damn banner for the event. I'd group together some posters behind the podium and hope that no one missed it. What else could I do?

I lay on my bed in the gathering darkness. Why did situations like this still surprise me? The printer didn't give a damn. He would still get his money; ALAS could always be counted on to pay its bills without kicking up a fuss. Invoice us for the moon and we'd pay it. What is not spent cannot be billed.

My hangover had modulated into something hellish and

unforgiving. I wanted to blame Faith, but she hadn't exactly shoved the bottle down my throat, had she?

I began packing for Kabul. I grabbed two paperbacks, the usual complement of socks, underwear, T-shirts, dress shirts, slacks and khakis. I grabbed my journal, though I hadn't written a word in it in months; the last entry was from back in April.

I skimmed through it, wondering when I'd lost the capacity for self-examination; the entries read like notes from an appointment diary—this happened, then that, then that. Notes of a man on autopilot.

I heard a light tap at my door. I opened it and saw my neighbor, Karimullah, standing in the dark hallway. In the dim hall light his clothes appeared ghostly, diaphanous.

— I am sorry to disturb you.

— What's up?

— I feel bad about your banner, sir.

He said this to his folded hands, head bent, if not in deference to my station than certainly to my dark mood of before.

— It wasn't your fault.

— Perhaps I can help you fix it.

We carried the rolled banner to the balcony where Karimullah flipped on an outside light. The floor had been swept, open cans of paint standing at the ready.

He poured some white paint into the sawed-off bottom of a water bottle and began whitewashing over the Dari text. He was wearing his baggy Afghan trousers and an undershirt that had crept up his back, revealing a prominent tailbone and smooth caramel skin. When he finished, ink was still showing through, so he blew it dry and applied a second coat.

I tried to engage him in small talk, but my attempt at familiarity

73

seemed to embarrass him. He was still too attuned to my earlier rage to accept the friendly overture. Did the kid think I was going to beat him?

I struggled between a desire to admire his initiative and a conditioned mistrust. These Afghans always wanted something, a letter of reference, a promotion. I'd probably find out soon enough.

I went back to my room. I had resumed packing when I heard a quiet knock. Faith Woodson poked her head in.

— Just thought I'd check on you. I didn't see you all day. Were you at the office?

— Physically, I suppose.

— You were pretty hammered last night.

It amazed me how well she'd bounced back. There was life and loveliness in her pink cheeks. I wondered what time she had left that morning, and who might have seen her.

She leaned against the wall, staring at me with a wry expression.

— We caught him.

— Who?

— The Cloakroom Chicken-Choker.

— Seriously?

— He came back to the scene of the crime. Caught him red-handed, as it were. It was one of our drivers.

I laughed.

— He should learn to take his hand off the gearshift.

Faith drew a bottle from her handbag and sat on the bed beside my open suitcase. She brought out two glasses and began pouring when I said:

— None for me, thanks.

The lip of the bottle settled with a clink against the second glass. She glanced at me through one eye.

— Seriously?

I smiled casually, feeling a guilty tug. There was nothing I needed in that bottle. I wouldn't have been surprised if there was still alcohol in my system from the night before.

— I've got an early flight. And I'm still a little out of it from last night.

— Are you sure I can't tempt you? How about just one?

Clear liquid splashed in the glass.

— No, I don't want any. I'm not feeling well.

The silence in the room seemed magnified by the call to prayer outside my window. I thought about turning on some music but that felt too much like a concession. This was my room and if I wanted to pack my suitcase in silence, then by God why shouldn't I?

She held her glass and stared straight ahead, making no attempt to conceal her boredom. I could try to find the thread of the night before, bring her back. But I wouldn't be able to resist the vodka for long. Not because of any physical need for it but out of a misguided sense of politeness. I knew myself.

Tomorrow morning I'd be in a twin-engine plane not terribly unlike the one that periodically figured into my worst nightmares. I shuddered to think of another hangover transposed onto that bumpy flight.

I signaled my resolve with a yawn. Message received, Faith knocked back the contents of her glass and gathered her things. I had been remiss as a host. She had reached out to me, finding not the pleasant, garrulous colleague of the night before but a temperance mother fussing over an open suitcase.

— Well, maybe another time, she said, the hardness in her voice giving me a strange flutter of anxiety.

— I'll walk you out.

75

— Don't worry, I don't want to be a bother.

At the door she stopped and turned around. Her expression was a strange mix of hostility and pity.

— I googled you at the office today.

We stared at each other. She shook her head, smiling thinly.

— I know all about you.

— What's that supposed to mean?

— I know about your son.

The single outdoor bulb was inadequate for Karimullah's task, so he had dragged out a lamp on a long extension cord. He had marked out lines for the Dari text with a straight edge and a pencil and was now dipping a calligraphy brush into glossy black paint. He then began composing the swirling, sickle-shaped letters of his language.

I walked out to the rail and listened to the rumble of big trucks on the main road, groaning under God knew what mysterious loads. Behind me I heard Karimullah call out:

— Be careful. The house is old and the railing is not secure.

I drew up a chair. It was satisfying to watch Karimullah work, so engrossed in the minutiae of each sweeping arc. He made no mistakes. Now and then he sat up, shaking life into his wrist or popping his back.

— Looking good, I said, suddenly an expert in Dari.

— It will be finished soon. You will fly to Kabul tomorrow?

— Yes, have you been there?

He resumed working, his voice soft and hesitant:

— I lived and worked there.

— I'm staying at the Excelsior.

— It is a lovely hotel. I worked there briefly, carrying suitcases for guests.

For people like me, I thought.

I tried more small talk, but Karimullah was absorbed in his task, or pretended to be. It was nice just sitting in silence, listening to the sounds of Kandahar at night. I needed something to focus on besides what Faith had just said.

In a while Karimullah rose and invited me to inspect his work. The damp black letters gleamed in the lamplight. I decided I'd have to revise my feelings about the lazy, shiftless nature of Afghans.

It had turned out to be a pretty good day after all. I was kind of glad now for the mistake with the banner. I knew this hour on the balcony was something I would remember for a long time, a souvenir of my Kandahar sojourn that I would keep with me always.

Of course, the kid was probably up to no good. They usually had something up their sleeve.

Those were my thoughts at the time. Oh the slander, my poor Karimullah.

9
Kabul

Beware lest in your anxiety to avoid war you obtain a master.
Demosthenes

A TAXI DROVE ME to the restaurant where I was to meet up with my old friend Bill Batson. The sky was fading to red and the streets were turgid with rush-hour traffic. I felt a delightful flutter of anticipation.

My friends loved to complain about the difficulties of life in the Afghan capital. They complained of the snarled traffic that made it so difficult to get out to the restaurants that catered to foreigners throughout the city. They complained of the expensive supermarkets and how difficult it was to find certain brands of cereal. Life was so isolating. It wasn't at all like back in Boston or New York.

Come to Kandahar City, I told them. Come live in a guarded compound that you might not leave for weeks or months on end. Where the eyes of the Taliban are always upon you. Can't find your brand of cereal? Come to Kandahar City, where visiting a market would mean death. Yes, come to Kandahar.

This was going to be fun. After Kandahar City, with its grim piety and bland uniformity of belief, with its hatred of pleasure and its stern and dreary wholesomeness, Kabul seemed inexpressibly alive, irrepressibly energetic, fascinating and free.

I was running late, but it didn't matter. On the sidewalks I counted more jeans than traditional Afghan clothes. I saw cool guys with crazy coifs stiff with gel. They had attitude, they had personality. And what a shock, turning a corner to see three Afghan women wearing not burkas but headscarves, walking arm-in-arm and laughing.

Laughter. In Afghanistan.

Bill was waiting for me in the foyer of the Artemis Restaurant.

— Great to see you, big boy.

We embraced, Bill rocking me back and forth in a dance of welcome.

— You too, buddy, I grunted through his embrace.

He was wearing a white business shirt with a bright red tie sitting a little crooked in his collar. He had gained weight in the face since I had last seen him, his wolfish good looks replaced by puffiness around the eyes and the first signs of jowls.

The restaurant was teeming with life. The cacophony of laughter and raised voices made me feel like I was in a Brooklyn sports bar and not an expat watering hole in Kabul. The lights, the colors, the gorgeously dressed women—everything seemed in conspiracy to heighten my senses, as though the Universe had judged me worthy of the only reward this ruined country could provide.

While we waited to be seated I studied some framed photos of Old Kabul lining the wood-paneled walls. Afghan teens in a 1960s record store. The staid and elegant Darul Aman Palace. Men in suits boarding a streetcar. Afghan girls in skirts (!) picnicking in the gardens of the Paghman Palace.

All gone, of course. The management should have included the "after" photos: the Darul Aman Palace now a bombed-out ruins, the Paghman Palace gardens stripped of every bush and tree. For all its vitality, Kabul was unmistakably a casualty of war. Of too many wars.

A fat Russian waitress wearing too much makeup ushered us to an outdoor table near the swimming pool. She drew out a chair for Bill and slapped two bound menus on the table. Reggae music was playing and the cool breeze made fake palm fronds dance and clatter overhead. I hadn't brought a sweater, forgetting how nippy the nights could be at this altitude.

Our *matryoshka* stood waiting while we tried to come up with a drink order. I ran my eyes down the wine list: a bottle of Beaujolais, a hundred and twenty dollars. Jesus.

— Just a gin and tonic for me, I said.

— Martini, straight up, splash of bitters, Bill said with the insouciance of a regular.

She turned away, writing this down. Bill looked at me and smirked.

— It's great to see you, fatso. I'll bet you're glad to be outside of the wire.

— I've only been back for a couple of weeks and already I'm getting that cagey feeling.

— I remember the days.

I glanced around.

— Don't take this for granted, Bill. You don't know how good you've got it.

Bill shrugged, acknowledging his superior posting but not wanting to rub it in.

— Well, you get used to it. Kabul has its own challenges.

— You know that moment in The *Wizard of Oz* where everything suddenly shifts from black and white into brilliant color? That's what this is like to me.

— You're such a kid, Hunter. But I know what you mean. Kandahar sucks. You need to get out of there.

— Kandahar isn't the problem. It's the captivity.

— Well, the State Department would welcome you with open arms.

Bill Batson was in his late thirties. He worked in the visa division of the U.S. Embassy processing applications from Afghans hoping to immigrate to the United States. Dealing with people of all walks of life had given him an elastic personality that at some times seemed charming and at others hopelessly insincere.

When the drinks arrived we clinked glasses and sat back, studying the glowing tips of our cigarettes.

Bill said:

— So, Hunt, how's the aid business?

— Changing. It's different since the military drawdowns started. Harder to get around. We do everything by remote control these days. We rely on our Afghan staff for everything.

— You've got the Afghan Army backing you up, don't you?

I knew he was being facetious.

— They're not going to help us. And it's too dangerous to go out without military support. That's the great paradox.

— What is?

— Afghan society is supposed to be improving. It's time to start rolling out longer-term development programs. But we can't, it's too hostile out there. So we're stuck.

Bill's attention had drifted to the fake flower lolling in a vase on our table.

— I thought you guys were creating a more stable society. You build bridges. You put picks and shovels in the hands of would-be insurgents. You pay them to dig canals instead of burying roadside bombs. You mean it's not working?

As a former USAID staffer, Bill knew all about the extravagant waste that took place on projects like ALAS. With enough martinis he could go on all night about the well-meaning but doomed aid projects he'd seen in this country. As a State Department employee he brought home about two hundred a year tax-free, as did so many others like him. He was currently saving up for a Manhattan apartment. If cleaning canals and building roads was extravagantly wasteful, what about this war *wasn't*?

— So I want to tell you about a girl, Bill began, fiddling with his napkin ring and feigning boyish reticence.

— Another one?

Bill laughed.

— No, listen, this one is for real.

— Someone you work with?

— Sort of.

The waitress arrived with our appetizer, an onion blossom. We each tore off a piece and dipped it into the orange sauce in the center of the onion.

Our friendship was built around Bill's dubious romantic intrigues. I wouldn't hear from him for months, and then an e-mail would arrive full of impassioned details about some new girl, usually a colleague. And as I had little to offer in trade, I compensated by being an enthusiastic and non-judgmental audience.

— So what about this girl? I nudged.

— Well, you know we're not supposed to get involved with the clients. She came in to be interviewed for a Special Immigrant Visa.

— Hold on. She's Afghan?

— Yep. Her name is Zariah. Isn't that a gorgeous name? *Zariah.* Bill twiddled two fingers in the air, as though conducting those three musical syllables.

— Shit, Bill. That's kind of dangerous, isn't it?

It was just the reaction he had been hoping for. He leaned back in his chair with a mischievous twinkle in his eye, surveying the nearby swimming pool where floating red and green lights clustered at one end, whipped there by the driving breeze.

— She wants to come back to the States with me.

— You can't sponsor her. You'll be fired.

— She doesn't need a sponsor. These special visas are given to Afghans whose lives are put in danger because of their work for the U.S. government. She'll get a nice plump stipend, free airfare and healthcare benefits. It's a great deal. She could go anywhere in the States, but she wants to be with me.

— No kidding, in your million-dollar Manhattan apartment.

— You don't get it. She's in *love* with me. She used to be one of our translators. Then the Taliban tried to kill her and she went into hiding. *Zariah.* Don't you love it? And let me tell you, these Afghan women mate for life.

I looked down at my greasy fingertips and, resisting the urge to suck them clean, reached for my napkin.

— So what happens next?

— She has her final interview next month. If all goes well—and I'll make sure it will—she'll be heading stateside in January.

He took out his smartphone, came around to my side of the table and clicked through a series of photos. He zoomed in on a girl whose hair was hidden in a tight *hijab* that pulled her lusterless eyes into slits. Her expression was as resigned and impassive as in a coroner's photo.

How would it end, I wondered. Did it matter? Lovers came and went. Let him enjoy it while it's new. As I saw it, the real question was: what did she need from Bill and for how long could he meet those needs? Love, like everything else, was predicated on self-interest. Maybe she loved him, but would she love him just as much when she became the holder of an American visa?

Bill went back to his side of the table. The conversation about Zariah went through a few more turns until I discovered that Bill didn't really know much about her. He'd raked out every sparkle from the sand, and from what I could tell he hadn't come up with much. What seemed to matter for him was the romantic potential more than the thing itself. He was in love with a love story.

It was getting chilly, so after dinner we moved inside. At the gleaming brass-topped bar we ran into three of Bill's embassy friends who were well into a bottle of Jack Daniels. Bill called out for two more glasses. I knew the longer I stayed the harder it would be to leave. I had no interest in revisiting yesterday's hangover, and I'd already had two gin-and-tonics with dinner.

Bill said:

— Have a seat, Hunt. Stay awhile.

— Too noisy for me. I think I'll head back to the hotel.

Bill's friends protested, feigning wounded disappointment. Dragging out a barstool, I agreed to have just one.

I didn't get the names of Bill's friends, two men in business shirts and a black woman with a big, seventies Afro. The woman came over to my side with her drink.

— So, Hunter, Bill says you work down in Kandahar. What do you do?

84

— I build infrastructure projects. Irrigation canals, roads.

— USAID?

— Global Relief Solutions. We're funded by USAID.

— Sounds exciting.

Music was blaring through overhead speakers and we had to shout to be heard.

— It can get pretty lively down there. Our compound got hit recently.

Her eyes widened.

— No kidding?

— Suicide bomber. Coordinated attack.

— Anyone get killed?

I thought about mentioning Changwani, then thought better of it.

— A few guards.

— Oh, Hunter.

She placed a hand lightly on my arm. Her face was lean and angular, widening a little at the top like Nefertiti. In her eyes I was startled to see real compassion. I gave her a point-by-point description of the attack, tacitly omitting the fact that I had been out on leave at the time. By now Bill and the others were moving around so they could hear better.

— Shit, why didn't you tell me any of this? Bill said reproachfully.

The woman frowned at him.

— You moron, he's probably still in shock.

— Damn, Hunt. I had no idea. Were you hurt?

— No, but it really tore up the compound. You should have seen my room.

The woman leaned closer.

— So how much longer do you think you'll be in Kandahar? Might be time to get out, don't you think?

— We've got another six months, unless USAID gives us an extension.

— Making any headway?

— You mean are we improving lives? I suppose. We're doing what we're paid to do. We build things, we train farmers, we put people to work.

— But is it working?

If it weren't so loud in the room I would have given her the usual bullet points about how projects like ours took time to create measurable results. I was trying not to stare at her full, gorgeous lips.

I didn't want to talk about my job. I was still in the thrall of these new surroundings and the pounding music. But from the quaint tilt of her head I sensed that she genuinely cared. I began to wonder if this might be leading somewhere. I discreetly sucked in my stomach.

— Billions were spent keeping our military in Afghanistan. Now we have to build on our former successes to keep momentum.

The woman broke in (and by now I really wished I knew her name):

— Right. We spent billions fighting the war, and we'll spend billions more on projects like yours trying to undo the damage.

— We don't . . . it's not like that, really. Most Afghans are farmers, so that's where the aid money needs to be spent. Once that happens, you'll see a real impact, not only in agriculture but also in reduced Taliban recruitment.

— But isn't every year a little worse than the year before?

I drew confidentially closer, bringing my fingertips together. I really wanted her to understand this.

— But just think how bad it would be if these projects didn't exist. Bad as it is, can you imagine how it would be if these farmers couldn't bring in a crop? They'd have to find an alternative source of income. The insurgency preys on that.

Her voice was hardening by degrees.

— You think an irrigation canal is going to stop a guy from joining the Taliban?

— The point is to built better livelihoods, create a stronger society. Help me here, Bill.

But Bill raised his hands in surrender, wanting no part in it.

The woman was staring at the rings of one hand lying flat on the table, smiling as at some peculiar irony there.

— And you think that's going to happen when? One year? Five? Ten?

I was becoming confused. I looked at my empty glass and wondered if another drink would loosen up my tongue or just befuddle me even more.

— Look, the Afghans are at war—

— I thought the war was basically over. Isn't that why we're downsizing our troops?

— It's their war now. We've got to help them.

— Millions died in the Congo. *Millions.* Why didn't we help them?

I ignored this and plunged ahead.

— Tens of thousands of Afghan troops occupy those remote bases. They're just sitting ducks. Do you know what one bad guy with an RPG can do? But if that guy is back home helping out on his family farm, because thank God they've got real irrigation at last, he's not going to answer the Taliban's call. You see?

— Then why is security deteriorating? Why are more and more troops still dying? Why is Karzai so scared of the Taliban that he wants to bring them to the bargaining table?

— I don't know about that. But I think we're making a real

difference.

— How?

I felt impotent under her piercing gaze.

— Let me tell you about our sapling project—

— Ha, no need. I can read the so-called success story on the USAID webpage.

— A million saplings! Do you know how many jobs we created just for the laborers we hired to plant the trees and clear out the—

— You can hire all the guys you want. And by the way, five dollars a day? That's disgraceful. But go ahead and hire every working-age male in southern Afghanistan. It's not going to change the fact that every day new insurgents are pouring over the Pakistani border. It's like The Three Stooges. You know how they're in the basement trying to fix a leaky pipe, but while they're working on a leak over here, another leak breaks out over there. And soon the basement is flooded.

Bill Batson picked up on this, leaning over and slapping the bar.

— That's right, Hunt, the Three Fucking Stooges. You're Curly, man!

The woman was staring, waiting for a reply. I picked up my empty glass, set it down again and found a truant cuff thread that needed my attention. I thought, why can't we just have a nice conversation?

— If you're so down on American aid, why are you here? Why don't you just go home and find something that you believe in?

When she didn't respond I glanced up and saw her staring vacantly at the opposite wall.

— I used to believe. I really did. I guess when I look at you I see myself a few years ago, eager to help these people and make a difference. But it can't be done. There's nothing you can do.

— Nothing at all? What about the small changes? If the big ones don't work, maybe—

— The only changes that matter are the ones that come from the Afghans themselves.

I felt her hand sympathetically graze my back as she drifted off in search of a bathroom. Bill and the others were off and away on a discussion of American politics. I was preparing a return volley, but it suddenly seemed more important to get the hell out of there before she returned. Things were starting to get muddled.

I set a wad of money on the counter and left without saying anything.

10

Karimullah

Why do you prefer to crawl through life,
when you were born with wings?
Rumi

WHEN KARIMULLAH WAS A BOY his father drove a truck between Kandahar City and Mazar-i Sharif in the north. He told his young son that he hauled flowers, which was not far from the truth. It would be years before Karimullah learned that the flowers he delivered were opium poppies bound for processing centers in Tajikistan.

Karimullah was ten years old when his father's truck plunged off a snowy mountain highway near the Salang Tunnel. On the afternoon of the funeral his older brother, Kaaseb, told Karimullah he would need to find a job.

— There is no more money. If you will not work, you will not eat.

Kaaseb, whose name meant "earner," understood about money.

He found work for Karimullah in the bazaar carrying tea. The child had balance and a natural aptitude for service. He could run through the stalls with a heavy tray balanced on his fingertips and nothing would spill. He had a prodigious memory and knew exactly how much money to collect at the end of the day. But most in his favor were his striking green eyes.

The merchants asked for him by name. *Not you*, they would say, waving off another boy. *Send Karimullah, the one with the eyes.*

Everyone was captivated by those eyes, so different from the mud-brown eyes of the other boys. They were as deep and brilliant as emerald or tourmaline. They were like the flash of a mirror over a still, green pond. They seemed to hold the sun.

One day Kaaseb took him to a restaurant to meet a man from the nearby district of Arghandab. They sat together on ornate rugs and ate the finest food Karimullah had ever tasted. Obaidullah, a wealthy pomegranate farmer and businessman, watched the boy without speaking. At the end of the meal, Kaaseb asked Karimullah:

— How would you like to learn how to dance?

Obaidullah told Karimullah to stand. He removed the boy's blouse, or *kamiz*, and turned him this way and that. He examined the curve of Karimullah's back. He asked him to stand on one foot, then the other, holding his arms out at his side.

He told Kaaseb that the boy might have the makings of a dancer, a body neither too tall nor too short, feet that had not been prematurely damaged by hard work.

Karimullah was sent away while the men spoke about money.

By then Karimullah and Kaaseb and their many siblings were living alone. Their father was dead and their mother had gone to Lahore to seek treatment for her weak heart. And so, as the eldest brother, the decision about Karimullah's future fell upon Kaaseb.

— I don't want to go, Karimullah said. I am happy carrying tea.

— You will receive an education from Obaidullah. You will receive training. Besides, there is no room for you here.

— But I don't want to go.

— You will go! Kaaseb roared, raising his hand as if to strike him.

And so he went.

He lived in an outbuilding behind Obaidullah's main house, one that had once housed goats and still smelled of wet fur when it rained.

He received no education. He received no training.

He awoke when the pomegranate pickers arrived each morning. It was the time of the fall harvest and it was his job to shimmy up and pick the fruit that clung to the highest branches. It was an old orchard, and the trees had been pruned to grow straight and tall. He would climb the trunk as high as he dared, hold himself out by one arm and reach out for the fruit with the other, dropping the fat pomegranates into the hands of the waiting pickers.

The orchard was the largest in the district, occupying some eighty *jeribs* of land. Karimullah and the men worked sixteen-hour days in the rush to bring in the fruit before the first rains. By nightfall his arms were numb. He was sure they must have grown several centimeters in those first few weeks.

Soon the harvest was in. The ground lay strewn with dry, broken pomegranates that would be turned into compost for next year's crop. At last Karimullah could rest his body, his arms, his legs.

Obaidullah came to his room.

— You have passed the first step of your training. Your arms and legs are strong. You will now learn to dance.

A young man named Babur was his dancing instructor. His name meant "happiness," and yet Babur seemed one of the gloomiest people Karimullah had ever known. He was about twenty-five, with a face pitted with acne scars and dark, embittered eyes.

But Babur was kind to Karimullah. He showed the boy how to comport himself. He made Karimullah balance books on his head and taught him how to walk a tightrope suspended between two trees. He also showed him how to care for his skin, especially around his feet and ankles, the parts of the body at eye level with the viewer.

Babur taught Karimullah how to think in rhythms. Most dances were in a 7/8 meter. They would clap: *ONE-two-THREE-four-FIVE-six-seven*. But to truly feel the music it was important that Karimullah learn an instrument. Babur showed him the fundamentals of the *dombura*, a two-stringed instrument with a long, slender neck attached to a rounded bowl. Soon Karimullah had excelled beyond his teacher, and in the room that smelled of goats he stayed up late inventing his own songs.

It was always on his mind to ask Babur why he seemed so unhappy. Was it because of some tragedy in his past? But Babur's manner didn't allow for that level of familiarity. They must be teacher and pupil, no more.

When Karimullah was twelve, Babur began teaching him the dances. Karimullah had the poise, the agility and the strength. He lacked only the rudiments.

— You will dance only for men. And to those men you must become an illusion. You must make them forget you are a boy.

— If they want to see a woman dance, then why not train women to perform for them?

— Only a woman of ill repute would dance in the company of men who are not her relatives. You know that.

— Then I must pretend to be a girl?

— No, you must be yourself—your most beautiful self.

Just as a painter must understand the construction of the human anatomy before he can paint a portrait, so Karimullah had to understand how the body moved beneath the obscuring *shalwar kamiz*. And so they trained in thin loincloths, Babur drawing Karimullah's attention to the movements of his hips and pelvis and rear.

They studied dances of joy, Babur setting the tempo on tuned drums called *tabla*. They studied the Herati dance of *ghamzagi*, with its mood of seduction. By now Karimullah knew that dance was more than just movement of the body. It was expressed through the eyes and lips as well: coyness, flirtation, remorse and joy.

They danced in a shaded clearing. As Karimullah followed Babur's slow, patient instruction, he would pretend that he was looking into a mirror, spinning when Babur spun, raising a hand and snapping his fingers when Babur did the same. Babur watched and nodded. Now and then he even braved a smile.

— You are ready to take the next step. You must learn how to sing.

Karimullah knew many of the traditional songs from his mother, but his voice was puny. A voice teacher was brought from Kandahar City to teach Karimullah how to supplement his dances with beguiling *ghazals*. The teacher was pleased with Karimullah's high voice and helped him strengthen it against the day when his voice would drop in pitch.

Babur, who was a poor singer, laid hand to heart and swore that Karimullah would one day please many with his songs. And then his countenance darkened and he wandered away.

At the end of his second year in Arghandab, when Karimullah was thirteen, Obaidullah halted his studies so that he and Babur could help with the harvest. By now Karimullah could climb the trees with ease. The pickers were amazed by his agility. Babur had added

94

gymnastics to his studies, and Karimullah now swung through the trees as though the branches were parallel bars.

One evening in a clearing, lit by lamps high in the trees, the pickers gathered to watch Karimullah in what would be his first public performance. One played the *tabla* while Babur strummed the *dombura*. Karimullah went into a slow dance of his own invention. The pace accelerated and the men began clapping as he pushed back his sleeves, spinning in circles. Then he froze and moved slowly among them, eyes wide so the men would not fail to be dazzled by their green brilliance.

He was an illusionist. Because it was impossible for a woman to dance among them, these rough men would have to fall in love with him. And they did. The circle grew closer and their hands reached beseechingly towards him. They muttered intimate endearments, fell at his feet, wept with joy.

Obaidullah, standing outside the circle, nodded to Babur and said:

— I think he is ready.

Babur's face paled.

— He is still very young, master.

The older man turned away.

— You must now prepare him in matters of the flesh.

11
Taliban Country

If a man knows not to which port he sails, no wind is favorable.
Seneca

I PRESSED MY FOREHEAD against the helicopter's porthole as the shrieking machine rose vertically into the sky. A blinding cloud of dust blotted out the window, but in seconds we shot high above it.

These helicopter journeys always felt a little like time travel. From three thousand feet the war became just another memory in Afghanistan's complicated past. Here was the gentle simplicity of mountains and desert, nomads with their camels walking along trails dating back to the Mongols. With a pocket camera I tried to capture something of the landscape's harsh beauty through the dirty window, but I knew I couldn't. It could no sooner be captured in pixels than it could be understood with words.

The helicopter was flown by two florid-faced Russians up behind a plywood door sealing off the cockpit. I could smell strong cigarettes defying the red warnings stenciled all over the walls. Even with earplugs I could hear them erupt in bawdy laughter, the craft lurching a little with each outburst. I wouldn't have been surprised if they were passing a bottle.

We were bound for FOB Pasab, Zhari District, deep in the heart of Taliban country. Most of the villages there had only limited access to irrigation, hence the abundance of opium in the district, poppies being a dry crop. I was thinking that we might rebuild the old canal intakes so that more water could get to area farmers, maybe put up some water storage reservoirs.

The projects would burn enough money to keep the chief off my back, make GRS happy, keep hundreds of workers off the Taliban payrolls and improve vital infrastructure. I could see everything connecting like an intricate circuit board needing only the infusion of American dollars to make it light up.

The USAID inaugural ceremony in Kabul hadn't been a complete disaster, though it was close. I could cross out party planning as a possible career move.

Dozens of gleaming new tractors had been put on display by the project's vendors, but on the eve of the event no one could find the keys. Then the embassy sent word that the ambassador wanted to be photographed chatting with real Afghan farmers. But ALAS was a southern project—how would I find farmers in Kabul? I called Bill Batson, who managed to send over twenty Afghans from God knows where. Perceiving my distress, they demanded a hundred dollars apiece for the one-hour event. And they didn't look anything like farmers.

But the media came out in force, and my anxiety was forgotten in the excitement of reporters and flashing cameras. The ambassador gave a fine speech, flanked by the flags of Afghanistan and the United

States. Behind him hung the banner that had caused me so much grief. You could tell it had been altered; under harsh TV lights the painted-over section was duller than its glossy surroundings. But that hardly mattered. Each time I looked at it I recalled the disaster that Karimullah had so willingly helped me avert. If he was trying to win points, he had succeeded.

I nodded off, jolting awake as the helicopter pitched in a mountain thermal. Soon FOB Pasab came into view, the tents and Quonset huts and aircraft hangars arranged with geometric precision around pencil-thin gravel streets. We began a shuddering descent.

Once the helicopter had touched down, the pilot came out, dropped the stepladder and indicated for me to get out. With my backpack and duffle bag over either shoulder I hunkered low under the spinning blades. Then the engine rose in pitch and I was left in a cyclone of spinning sand as the helicopter rose into the sky. I set out across the quiet helipad in search of the command center.

I hadn't been around FOB Pasab much since it had been handed over to the Afghans. Back in my day it was FOB Wilson. As I walked toward the command center I passed a few Afghan Army soldiers lounging around in the shade with their shirts unbuttoned. I got the feeling that discipline had come down a notch or two since the handover from the Americans.

I found the command center in the same place it used to be, a plywood building bristling with antennas. The door opened onto a wide amphitheater where young Afghan soldiers sat behind flat-screen monitors and laptops. Huge screens dominated the front of the room with radar images and aerial photographs of the battlespace. It was like walking into NASA mission control before a launch.

I was relieved when an American soldier approached me, a young man with close-cropped black hair and a Mediterranean complexion. His tab said D'ANGELO.

— Can I help you, sir?

— American? I thought you guys had all left.

His guarded smile suggested that we were part of a rapidly shrinking minority, with shared memories of the good old days at FOB Wilson.

— There are still a few of us left. We're just advisors now.

He gazed at me a moment too long. I knew the look: no uniform, out of shape. It wasn't a judgment as much as a moment of naïve surprise, as though he'd forgotten about that world left behind and the overweight creatures who inhabited it.

— Follow me. Major Frost will sign you in.

I followed d'Angelo up the risers where we approached a youngish American whose red hair was cut so close to the scalp it must have felt like coarse sandpaper. He was eating what I recognized longingly as a Little Debbie Oatmeal Creme Pie.

I introduced myself and described my mission. The major looked at me as though he didn't have a clue what I was talking about.

— I'm a civilian with GRS.

— I don't know that acronym.

— Global Relief Solutions. We're trying to start up an irrigation project here. It's a USAID thing.

— Does the colonel know you're here?

— Not yet, but I'm hoping he'll help me schedule a field visit.

— He's tied up in meetings right up till dinner.

D'Angelo had moved away and now the major turned back to his screen. It was time for me to move along. Just then he turned back to me.

— Wait, are you the guy who came in on that helicopter a little while ago?

— Right.

He pulled a cell phone from the pocket below his nametag, eyeing me strangely.

— One moment. I think I can get Colonel Waffa to see you.

I followed him down a narrow fluorescent-lit hallway to a small office. He left me alone there.

A few minutes later I looked up to see the colonel framed in the doorway. His dark Afghan face gleamed with sweat. He seemed out of breath and rather pissed off.

— Are you the aid guy?

Major Frost came in behind him. Before I could say anything, the major mumbled something into his ear. The colonel took a step toward me and extended his hand. The hand was calloused and strong.

Col. Waffa had the air of someone who'd just come in from a field mission, his gestures a little too expansive for indoors. He was around fifty, deeply tanned, with a perfectly bald head—like Eisenhower on the old six-cent stamps. Like most middle-aged Afghan men he had a plump belly that hung like a feed sack over his belt. This alone made me think we'd be on friendly terms.

The colonel sat on the edge of a desk as I described my proposed meetings in the district. As he didn't venture to interrupt, I kept talking until I could think of nothing more to say. Then the colonel, staring down at his boots, said coolly and evenly:

— Help me to understand what the *hell* your helo pilot was doing flying into *my* battlespace without giving his call sign or asking for clearance.

Major Frost leaned against the wall, folding his arms in a gesture of solidarity. I coughed into my fist, feeling stomach acid bubbling up into my throat.

— I really have no idea, sir.

— No idea.

— I don't know anything about—it's really not—

— It is not *my* responsibility to teach your pilot how to avoid getting blown out of the sky.

— It's a lease. I'll let the Chief of Party know—

— I do not want to hear about any Chief of Party or whatever the hell you people call your CO. You're in *my* battlespace. You play by *my* rules.

I was a little awestruck by his self-assurance. Watching the veins of his forehead inflate into a throbbing V, I knew better than to defend myself. I suddenly felt like the child who had been unjustly spanked.

— Gentlemen, I don't know what happened out there, but I'll get to the bottom of it.

— You are damn lucky you did not get blown out of the sky, friend. You may not know it, but you had a howitzer pointed right up your ass.

Major Frost nodded slowly and meaningfully. Then, abruptly, Colonel Waffa smiled, the throbbing vein on his forehead deflated, and he clapped me on the shoulder. All was well. He turned on his heel and said:

— Major, we have a guest. Do not just stand there. Make him feel at home.

Home was a musty transient tent where a dozen soldiers were billeted, mostly specialists on loan from other bases. Bunk beds were arranged on either side of a narrow pathway littered with dirty socks and trampled copies of *Stars and Stripes*. The main light was off for the benefit of the night-duty soldiers who were sleeping.

I could just make out the dark masses of sleeping bags on the bunks, many of them occupied. I took an upper bunk, which creaked precariously as I made my way up the wooden ladder. I glanced down and saw the eyes of the soldier below snap open with alarm.

A few visiting American soldiers were visiting FOB Pasab to help with the handover. I caught snatches of conversation as they came in from patrols. Things didn't sound good. FOB Pasab, I learned, was being shelled every week. The soldiers were itching for a real fight, but opportunities to engage the enemy were few. And their Afghan Army cohorts had little interest in shooting at guys who might turn out to be cousins. They longed for the old FOB Wilson days when they could go out and kick ass when the situation demanded.

— We don't even know who the enemy is anymore.

Another answered from a nearby bunk:

— No shit. One minute some guy is launching a mortar, the next minute he's just a dude minding his goats.

They agreed it was a fucked-up way to fight, but none of them raised the obvious question: *why are we still here?* They were in Asscrackistan (as they called it) because that's where their country had sent them. They weren't philosophers debating moral imperatives. They were soldiers who knew their duty. One day they'd all return home, and whatever happened to Afghanistan after that—a coup, a civil war—was not their problem.

Major Frost dropped by to let me know that a *shura* would be convened for my benefit the next day in Senjeray, a village about an hour's drive away. I'd be traveling in an Afghan personnel carrier, leaving at the obnoxious hour of 5 a.m.

— But why Senjeray? Couldn't the elders meet here at the district center?

— There's been quite a bit of kinetic action lately, and they don't feel comfortable coming here. Don't worry, you'll be in good hands.

There was something in his tone I didn't quite like, a weird enthusiasm I didn't trust. He added:

— You'll have them eating out of your hand. You're bringing jobs and money, aren't you?

I got down from my bunk and started setting out my clothes. Frost watched me take from my backpack the white *shalwar kamiz* that I always wore when attending meetings with Afghans, so wrinkled now that it looked like crepe paper.

— You like to go native, huh?

— It's usually a good idea. We're their guests, so it's good to dress the part.

The major considered this skeptically.

— Let me give you some advice. If you want to win sympathy out here, you should try to look military.

— But I'm not with the military. I don't have a uniform.

— Khaki pants and that camo T-shirt you're wearing will get you a lot farther than some Afghan man-dress. I'm just saying, if those elders think you're one of us, you've won half the battle.

— Really?

He winked.

— Trust me.

12
Shura

Do not act as if you were going to live ten thousand years.
Death hangs over you.
Marcus Aurelius

THE ALARM ON MY cell phone went off at 4 a.m., a screaming torrent of notes that left me more stunned than awake. The men stirred in their bunks around me, groaning.

I was still awaking by degrees as I stumbled toward the embarkation point an hour later. I would be transported by the Highway One minesweeper convoy. I had my helmet and backpack in one hand, body armor in the other and a satisfactory breakfast of oatmeal and bacon warming my stomach.

I arrived just as the patrol sergeant was briefing the soldiers on the convoy. I approached the circle and leaned on my knees, completely winded. The sergeant looked up from his clipboard and said in English:

— Are you the civilian on this run?

— Yes sir. Hunter Ames.

— You almost missed the show.

I wheezed:

— Sorry.

He barked something in Pashto and the soldiers moved toward a row of battered personnel carriers. I was directed toward the payload area of what was really just a glorified Humvee, nothing like the mighty MRAPs I'd traveled in when the Americans were here in force. I piled into the backseat with my legs drawn up under my chin. Soon, with a great roar, the vehicle lumbered out of the base onto Highway One.

The rocky ride lulled me to sleep. I awoke an hour later as we bounced over a cattle guard leading into the Senjeray combat outpost. Like FOB Pasab, it looked a bit worse for wear. Garbage was standing in charred piles. Two mongrel dogs were playing an angry game of tug-of-war with some soldier's shirt.

We exited the vehicles and the patrol leader did a head count. In a moment someone gestured to me with two wiggling downturned fingers that we were going on a foot patrol.

The sun was peeking out between the cleft of two distant hills, the sky a perfect gradient running from white to blue. It was turning out to be a gorgeous Afghan morning. We marched along a gravel road lined on one side by a fetid green ditch. Our destination lay about a kilometer ahead of us. At Frost's suggestion I was wearing my camo shirt and khaki pants. I was rather glad I hadn't worn what he called my Afghan man-dress. I felt like one of the guys.

Going on these foot patrols always brought home the symbiotic nature of our relationship. Most of these Afghan soldiers were illiterate, some couldn't count and few could have told me their birthdays. But for the time being they held my life in their hands.

Two small children stood in the brambles on the opposite side of the ditch, watching our passage with shy wonder. It was a good sign. They were the proverbial canary in the mineshaft, as I knew from previous foot patrols. When there are no kids around, you can be sure some bad shit is about to go down.

Soon more kids flushed out of nowhere. Older boys came up and gave the patrol the thumbs-up. Apparently they hadn't yet learned about the middle finger in this village.

It was good to be out of the wire, to be marching with armed men whose only purpose at that moment was to see to my safety. The risk of assault was certainly present; Senjeray had always been kinetic. I didn't believe I would die, not here. But somehow the intrusion of death and its unlikelihood gave me a startling sense of joy. Bill Batson could keep his fancy restaurants. I had the best job in the world.

In a while we approached a low cinderblock building with a fancy roof that rose in tiers, like a pagoda. The meeting would take place here, a young man told me, introducing himself as Assad. He said he would be my interpreter. He had a lean, handsome face and a close-cropped haircut that seemed in imitation of his vanished American colleagues.

I followed Assad down an unlit hallway. The building had a dank mildewy smell, not unlike the training villa. As we approached a room at the end I became aware of a low rumble of voices. An Afghan standing in the doorway spotted us and called out something into the din.

Assad looked back at me and muttered:

— I do not like the sound of that.

— What's going on?

He didn't reply, but motioned for me to pass in front of him.

Some forty bearded old men rose from where they had been sitting on the carpeted floor. They all wore the *shalwar kamiz* with colorful turbans and ceremonial vests. Some had their beards and fingernails hennaed a bright orange. It was like a casting call for the Arabian Nights.

I smiled, shaking a few of their hands. Some were cordial, while others avoided my eyes. Right away I sensed that something was wrong, like an orchestra whose musicians were all slightly out of tune. Still smiling, I mumbled to Assad through the side of my mouth:

— What's going on here?

He raised his hands for silence and addressed the men in a strong, commanding voice. I sensed that some breech of hospitality had taken place, for which the men were now being reproved. Sure enough, a pot of tea was sent for and I was shown to a folding aluminum chair, the only seating in the bare room. A platter of nuts and raisins was set on the rug before me and soon a scorching hot glass of tea was placed in my hands.

I surveyed the unsympathetic faces, trying to cajole them into smiles. The *shura* was one of the earliest forms of democratic representation. Each of these old men hailed from a village whose rights he had come to protect. Though they might have seemed like just a bunch of illiterate old men, each was a personage of great renown in his home village.

A sudden change of energy swept through the room as the district governor strolled into the doorway. He was a short, balding man whose entrance brought the first smiles I had yet seen on the elders. He wore a bright green robe over his shoulders with arms that were far too long to be anything but ornamental. The elders welcomed him like a saint or a savior, crowding around him and seizing his hands.

Assad brought me over to him. The governor appraised me critically, head tilted, as though he thought he might want to sketch me later. His smile was eager, while his eyes betrayed a grimness he seemed at pains to conceal.

When the elders were all seated, one rose and opened the *shura* with a prayer. The old men all turned their palms up toward heaven. Assad gave me a light nudge to indicate that I should do likewise. This was followed by a speech by the district governor, none of which Assad seemed to feel warranted a translation. It was one of those slow diatribes whose sole purpose was to reinforce the speaker's authority upon his audience. If that was the case, he needn't have bothered. The old elders were as rapt as schoolgirls.

His speech over, the governor took his place in a big wooden chair that had just been brought for him. The disparity between the governor's throne and my rickety aluminum chair seemed to have some larger symbolic meaning. Assad whispered:

— It's your turn. Just introduce yourself. Tell them what you came here to do.

I stepped forward.

— Thank you, governor. Thank you all for coming. I'm here on behalf of the American people, who want the people of Zhari to have peace and prosperity. But that can only come through a stronger agricultural base. We can help you. You have a water crisis here. We can provide . . .

Assad translated, and I found it amusing the way he tried to impersonate my slow baritone. As I was listening, one part of my mind was thinking: *this is fun.* I was doing the kind of diplomatic spadework I enjoyed most. It was the most rewarding part of my job, the part I would remember long after the rest had faded.

Assad caught up and waited for more. I took a breath and launched into a coda that repeated my earlier points about the need for cooperation and the role of American aid. As I dispatched my final words, raising my arms in a vaguely evangelical way, I rather wished someone could have snapped my picture.

A low murmur began to spread through the room, like the approach of a train. With my closing remarks now repeated in translation, the murmur grew menacing. I scanned the wrinkled, angry faces and realized that the bounds of hospitality had been stretched to the utmost.

The elders were shaking their heads. They had heard enough. They took to their feet and descended upon me en masse . . .

13
Death is One Possibility

All alone! Whether you like it or not,
alone is something you'll be quite a lot!
Dr. Seuss

BACK IN THE TRANSIENT TENT I sat on a bunk and pulled off my boots one by one, dumping sand through the slats of the wood-pallet floor. Two American trainers were sitting on a bunk across from me as I wearily recounted the fiasco.

I hadn't actually been hurt, though as I described the talon-like hands tugging at my shirt and arms, and the enraged voices all clamoring for my attention, it did begin to feel like an assault. They may not have drawn blood, but they'd certainly done a number on my nerves.

One of the privates laughed and said:

— So you actually picked up your chair?

— I sort of freaked out.

— Damn, sir.

— I needed something between me and those crazy old men. The district governor obviously wasn't going to do anything. He seemed to be enjoying the show.

The soldiers looked down at their boots, smiling and shaking their heads. They were dipping snuff, spitting discreetly into plastic bottles. They were close enough that I could smell the combined odors of sweat and body spray wafting from their uniforms.

One said in a heavy southern accent, probably Mississippi:

— So where was your Afghan patrol?

— They were outside guarding the building.

— So all you had was your terp? Damn, bud.

The young men shook their heads and exchanged a look that I translated as: *typical fucking Afghans.*

I recalled the surge of adrenaline when it sank in that I might be in physical danger, that I'd made some very broad assumptions about Muslim rules of hospitality.

— Picking up the chair was foolish, I admitted.

The two guys—identified by their tabs as LOPEZ and FRANKLIN—erupted in laughter.

— Shit, I would have done more than that. Excuse the language.

— I would have bitch-slapped those motherfuckers. Pardon my French.

While grateful for their solidarity, I knew it had been a rash and immature thing to do. I was surprised at how quickly some of the elders darted away, alarmed by the impetuous act, while others seemed to welcome the challenge. *Bring it on.*

— I got scared. And it was wrong. You can't talk about peace and then try to hold off a bunch of old men like some kind of lion tamer.

Lopez sputtered, imagining the overweight civilian trying to fend off a roomful of Afghan elders with an aluminum chair. Franklin said in a low voice:

— It sounds like a setup. That DG knew what was going to happen to you when you went in there.

I knew I had been missing some vital piece of information. At the end of the uproar, the district governor, clearly on the side of the old elders, raised his arms like Moses, speaking of dead bodies and retribution. They wanted reparations, not reservoirs.

Assad ran outside to alert the patrol. In a moment the Afghan soldiers burst into the room, sidearms unholstered. They saw me brandishing my chair in a corner and assumed I was the cause of the commotion. On the march back, I gestured for them to stop so I could be sick in a ditch.

Lopez said:

— Buddy, you picked a pretty bad time to try the hearts and minds thing with these people.

Franklin nodded in agreement.

— These people hate us right now.

— More than usual?

Lopez broke in:

— Buddy, it's off the radar.

Soon I had the whole story. A few days before my arrival, two insurgents had been caught on video planting IEDs around the district center. An American helicopter piloted by Afghan trainees went in for an air strike. On its first pass it blanketed the ground with fire, killing one of the insurgents. They saw what they thought was the other insurgent stepping out onto the roof of a nearby house with an AK-47. They flew in, guns blazing, and the house went up in a cloud of dust.

Upon later review of the video, however, it was found that the person on the roof was in fact a woman, and she was clutching not a machine gun but a rolled-up burka that she was hanging up to dry. It was possible that the insurgent had entered a different house altogether. Two women and four children were killed in the incident, and according to Franklin the local populace was going apeshit.

— They haven't been this pissed off since that soldier went on a killing spree in Panjwayi.

Now it made sense, the opaque references to damages and retribution. The elders hadn't expected to meet with me—they wanted a meeting with the army. They were grieving, and probably offended that the best the army could come up with was some fat guy in a camo T-shirt offering them erosion walls and sluice gates. Was this why Frost was so adamant about my looking as military as possible?

The dead women and children would be added to the war's roster of collateral damage. Such a strange term, I thought. Collateral— something off to the side, incidental.

New soldiers entered the tent bringing rumors of an American civilian who'd chased the Zhari district governor around the room with a chair. One by one they were introduced to the chief protagonist himself, surrounding my bunk like uniformed acolytes.

The newcomers all wanted to hear the story firsthand. Shouts of laughter went up as I recounted for the fourth or fifth time how I'd fended off the disgruntled old men. I tried to play down my fear, though without it the story came off with an uncomfortable note of bravado.

It made me feel a little drunk. I wasn't used to this much attention.

That night I lay on my bunk contemplating the future. I was finished with Zhari, the capricious Col. Waffa and the scheming elders. Cleve Harbin had earmarked a million dollars for Zhari. He'd have to find some other way to burn through all that money.

Wanting something to cheer me up, I thought about the two reservoirs that were underway in Maiwand. The most recent report from my deputy, Ramatullah, was glowing. I fired up my laptop and went back through his photos, looking for the affirmation that Zhari clearly wasn't going to give me.

And then I sat up, detecting something curious. The photos didn't look much like the Maiwand I remembered. Maiwand is a mountainous district, but the photos showed a flat, desert landscape more like my present situation. My bullshit alarm started ringing.

I hopped off my bunk, stepped into some flip-flops that were too small for me, probably the property of the snoring soldier in the bunk below, and walked outside. The spring-loaded plywood door closed with a sound like gunfire.

It was late, but Behzad picked up on the first ring.

— Dearest Hunter. How are the natives of Zhari treating you?

— I've got a hell of a story for you when I get back.

— Tell me now. Afghanistan just lost a very important cricket match and my heart is in the cemetery.

— Another time. I need a small favor.

I explained my errand without trying to sound too anxious. If something fishy was going on, stealth was important. I didn't want to give Ramatullah time to tidy up. On the other hand, maybe there was a logical explanation. It wasn't fair to punish Ramatullah for the mortification I'd suffered in Senjeray.

— Bring the monitoring team, but don't give them any advance notice. Just count the workers, take some photos.

— I know how the game is played, dear friend. Afghanistan may not produce the best cricketers, but we excel in sneakiness.

The next morning in the DFAC I stared out over the sea of

Afghan uniforms and saw an arm waving in my direction. I carried my tray to the table where Assad, my translator, sat alone. I squeezed into a chair opposite him. He seemed unable to meet my eyes.

— I was embarrassed about the meeting yesterday. It was not right.

— I suppose I've been through worse.

— Really?

I thought about it.

— Well, probably not. But the damage was minimal. Don't worry about it.

I looked at the food on my paper plate: scrambled eggs, sausage and French toast sticks. Assad was eating a spartan meal of an apple and a bowl of Cheerios.

— The district governor wanted a target, and there you were, a foreigner. His power is based on how people judge his actions. He needed them to see him act decisively.

I took a sip of scalding, bitter coffee.

— Well, I'm glad I could be of service.

— Please do not judge all Afghans by the belligerent actions of a few.

— I could be wrong, but I think people want the same things everywhere. A little money in their pockets, a secure future for their children.

— But no one can bring these things to Afghanistan, not you, not the military. They must come from within. Afghanistan will never succeed until it becomes the master of its own destiny.

It was almost exactly what that woman had told me in Kabul.

— And when do you think that will happen?

He took a breath and thought about it.

— When we find a real leader. It must be someone who rises up from the people, like Atatürk.

— What do you think of Karzai?

He snorted.

— Karzai was never the people's choice. He rules by fiat.

I had formed a positive opinion of Karzai after seeing him once on a BBC interview, amazed at his impeccable English, his polished accent. He always seemed to be photographed with children. But then, wasn't Stalin?

Assad's voice sank in volume.

— I am flying to Kabul next week.

— Vacation?

— I am trying to get an American visa. My contract ends soon, and it's not safe for me here.

— I've heard.

— Once you work for the foreigners, you are a marked man. Two of my friends were interpreters. They were both killed when they returned to their home villages.

— Seems like Afghanistan's best and brightest are all trying to get out.

— Would *you* stay in this country?

— It isn't my homeland.

I fished out a business card from my wallet.

— Look me up when you get to America.

He studied it and nodded, glancing up at me.

— Do not stay here, sir. Go back to Kandahar City.

— Why?

— This place is a powder keg.

The sincerity in the young man's voice moved me.

— Bad things happen all the time, Assad. Bombs fall and people die. But these things usually happen to other people. The odds are always in your favor, remember that.

I added to myself: *And if something terrible happened to me, so what? We live, we die. It's the circle of life. What difference does it really make one way or the other?*

Assad said:

— Death is one possibility, but not the only one. Some things are worse than dying. Just take care of yourself.

I held his gaze for a moment, then picked up a fork and went to work on my scrambled eggs.

I wasn't mystical about the future. I certainly didn't believe you could invite trouble simply by talking about it. But the kid's dark ruminations made me uneasy. It threatened the indifference that I had so carefully cultivated in regards to my own fate, and upon which my mental balance depended.

14

Karimullah

The wound is the place where the Light enters you.
Rumi

i.

AND SO KARIMULLAH DANCED.

He danced at weddings, he danced after harvests, he danced for businessmen who had negotiated favorable deals.

He danced for mullahs, he danced for farmers, he danced for bankers and warlords.

Obaidullah would drive him to these events in his black Volvo with tinted windows. The boy's sequined dancing outfit would tinkle softly as they moved through the dusty streets of Kandahar City. On the back of the headrest in front of him was a mirror where Karimullah would check his makeup. He thought: Paris, Rome, New York! For his master had promised him this and more. At night he dreamed of castles in the sky.

Babur, who knew a little English, had incorporated language

study into Karimullah's daily regimen.

— The country is full of foreigners. You never know, you may one day dance for diplomats and presidents.

Karimullah was allowed to keep the coins that the men tossed at his feet and the banknotes they tucked into his waistband. He understood that their hosts paid Obaidullah large sums to see him dance, but this was never spoken of. He never saw any of it, though now and then Obaidullah would meet with Karimullah's brother Kaaseb and slide an envelope across the table. This was never spoken of either.

Babur, watching him count his tips, was astonished at his success.

— You are only fifteen, and already you make more money than I did in my prime.

They stacked the coins and bills by denomination and entered the amount in a ledger. Later they took the money to the bank.

— This money does not seem real, Karimullah said. It is too easy.

— It will not always be so easy.

— Why? What do you mean?

But Babur turned away and gave no answer.

There was no pomegranate harvesting for Karimullah that year. His body must remain soft, his skin could not be bruised.

Obaidullah brought him to parties so that he could see other boys dance. Though they might be beautiful, their movements seemed forced and clumsy. And there was often an underlying sadness about them. This mystified Karimullah, but he paid it no mind.

By then he was known throughout the province. His body had grown that summer so that his arms and legs seemed oversized and gangly. But even the small constellation of pimples on his forehead did not deter his admirers. If anything, it only whetted their desire.

Babur was put in charge of his increasingly busy schedule. He rode along in the black Volvo and was ready to intervene if Karimullah's audience became too enthusiastic in their ardor. Certain things were permitted—a hand that caressed his ankle, a kiss that did not linger too long on the cheek. Anything beyond that would bring Babur to his feet, wielding his *dombura* like a club.

It was thanks to Karimullah that his mother was receiving the best medical treatment in Lahore for her ailing heart. One of his sisters would soon be married, and it was Karimullah's money that would help furnish her dowry. The old family house had been renovated, the living room now dominated by a flat-screen TV.

Kaaseb said:

— So what do you think of your new life?

It was clear that Kaaseb felt he was to be credited for Karimullah's good fortune.

— It is good, but I think I shall not do this much longer.

Kaaseb's expression hardened.

— What do you mean? You will do it as long as Obaidullah needs you.

— I want to go to school. I don't want to be a dancer all my life. I want an education.

— If you quit, you will get no support from me.

Karimullah knew he'd never need Kaaseb's support, as he had secretly saved many thousands of *afghanis* already.

— You have everything any boy could dream of, Kaaseb continued. You would be a fool to throw it all away.

His expression said something more: *I won't allow it. We depend on you.*

By then, word of Karimullah's grace and beauty had reached the Afghan capital. Obaidullah appeared in his room with a suitcase.

— Pack your best outfit and all your makeup. Bring your *dom-bura*. It is time for you to experience Kabul.

It was his first trip on an airplane. All the traffic and commotion of Kabul made him feel as though he were already in Paris. He saw young men wearing jeans and flashy shirts in the latest styles. He even saw women without the burka, wearing only a simple headscarf. They stayed at a fancy hotel where Karimullah had his own bedroom and bath. He was sad that Babur was not there to share the adventure with him.

Something was different about Obaidullah. He had always seemed remote and preoccupied, but there was a new furtiveness in his manner. He spent his days in meetings, during which time Karimullah was not permitted to leave the hotel. Through the wall separating their rooms he overheard Obaidullah shouting at Babur on his cell phone, but couldn't understand what their argument was about.

That night Obaidullah came into Karimullah's room and sat on the edge of his bed. He had been out with business associates and stank of cigarettes and alcohol.

— You have matured as a dancer. You have great talent. But more will be required of you. Do you understand what I am speaking of?

Karimullah sat up, shielding his eyes from the light.

— What do you mean?

— Until now you have teased men with your gifts. Now you must learn how to give them the pleasure they crave.

Karimullah felt a coldness creep up his body. He instinctively drew the bedding up to his chin.

Obaidullah continued:

— You should have learned these mysteries from Babur, but I find that he has been remiss in your education. So you shall learn them from me.

121

Obaidullah matter-of-factly stripped off his blouse, revealing the hairy prominence of his belly. He stepped out of his trousers and then his undershorts. Karimullah stared in alarm at Obaidullah's swelling penis. Obaidullah spat into his hand.

— Turn over on your stomach.

And so the horror began. It was not exactly a surprise. It had always hovered like a shadow on the periphery of his consciousness—a foreboding, a sense that it had all been too easy, that something more would be asked of him.

But it was not asked, it was simply taken. And this, he sensed, would not be the end of it, nor the worst.

The next evening Obaidullah took him to a party for some Pakistani businessmen. It was held in a suite of rooms at the Intercontinental Hotel, on the promontory of a high, forested hill.

The businessmen appraised Karimullah through the smoke of their cigarettes. One had a razor and was dividing a powdery substance into rows along the surface of a mirror. They did not want Karimullah to dance to Afghan music but to a harsh electronic music that he had never heard before. Karimullah was still in pain from the night before. He felt frightened and clumsy. It was as if he had forgotten everything he had learned about his art. But the businessmen, bending over the mirror with the white powder, didn't want art.

He was sent to the bedroom while they played cards and drank vodka. He didn't hear what they were saying, but he began to understand that he was the prize they were playing for.

Such was his induction into the hidden world of *bacha bazi*. Now he understood Babur's secret sadness. Now he knew what lay behind the disturbed faces of the boys he had seen dance at those parties in Kandahar City.

Obaidullah, reading his thoughts, said to him on the flight back:

— Don't even think about leaving. Whatever your intentions, I will know them. Wherever you go, I will find you. And don't think your friend Babur can help you. By now he is far away.

It was true: Babur was gone. Everywhere that Karimullah looked for him—on the streets, in the bazaar—he met with only puzzled shakes of the head. It was as if Babur had never existed.

From the gardener he learned that Babur had returned to his family in Badakhshan Province. He had left in haste, taking everything he could carry in a single rucksack. The old man added in a hoarse whisper:

— He left a note for you. Look inside your pillowcase.

Karimullah ran back to his room and read:

I could not prevent what happened to you. I was supposed to prepare you in all things, but in this I could not. I should have warned you. But you will endure this as you have endured much worse. Fear not, young prince. I will come back to you when I can. We will live tomorrow.

Karimullah crumpled the note when he heard footsteps outside his small room. Obaidullah opened the door without knocking.

— Get dressed. Tonight we have guests, and you will perform.

Babur was wrong. Karimullah had never endured anything worse than this. It was exactly as if he had lived for years in the presence of a caged beast, protected from its violence by iron bars, and now the door of the cage stood wide open.

That beast was Obaidullah. Throughout the years of his training, Karimullah had learned to fear and respect his master. But whatever benevolent force had once kept Obaidullah at bay—was it God? or perhaps Babur?—was gone now, leaving Karimullah as vulnerable as a snail that had lost the protection of its shell.

When his brother next met with Obaidullah, the envelope of money he received was thicker. Kaaseb knew what was happening; Karimullah could feel his brother's shame and disgust. He knew that Kaaseb would never let him return home now. He was a prostitute and had brought shame to the family. He would forever be shunned, an outcast.

It was at this time that Karimullah was befriended by the unlikeliest of people—Obaidullah's taciturn wife, Afsana. One evening he returned from a party where three wealthy farmers had had their way with him. Arriving at his room, weary and disconsolate, he found a small package at his door. A note said (with many misspellings): *There is grace in suffering. Everything happens by God's will.*

Opening the parcel he found a stuffed green bear with a silly smile that made Karimullah laugh through his tears.

The next day he found Afsana hanging laundry out to dry behind the house. Her blue burka was drawn back over her head, but seeing his approach she cautiously lowered it.

— I wanted to thank you.

The muffled voice replied:

— You have no reason to thank me.

— You showed kindness to me when I needed it.

— I know nothing of what you're speaking about.

He understood.

There were more gifts, always small but comforting—a bar of American candy, a collection of religious writings, a pair of camel's hair mittens. When he tried to thank her she would refuse to acknowledge the gifts.

— I know not what you mean.

— Thank you, Afsana. Thank you, blessed one.

He would have embraced her, but as he was not a member of the family this would have only shamed her. So in return for her kindness he looked for opportunities to help out. He would come to her aid when he saw her carrying firewood. When it was time for the castration of the young male goats, another of her duties, he took the burdizzo out of her hands and performed the odious task himself.

They did not speak or touch, and yet he felt her sympathy and compassion as warmly as an embrace.

Obaidullah had correctly anticipated his desire to escape. When he went to the bank one day to draw upon his savings, he found that his account had been emptied. All his money was gone, leaving him as poor as the day he had arrived five years before.

The urge to flee came over him as it never had before. With it came a sense of panic, a terrifying presentiment of doom. But where would he go, and how?

A year passed before he summoned up the courage. It was an evening when Obaidullah was entertaining his business partners for tea. Karimullah knew it must be now. He went around to the back of the house and climbed in quietly through Obaidullah's bedroom window. He could find nothing of value but a cheap watch of Obaidullah's. Then, with great misgivings, he opened Afsana's jewelry box. He greedily pocketed all of her necklaces and rings.

He ran to the market and found a man who bought the items without questioning their origin. The amount he received was pitiful, but Karimullah's only thought was to find a bus bound for Herat, near the Iranian border. Surely his Persian brothers and sisters would welcome him.

But Obaidullah's network extended far and wide. The next morning, when the bus stopped at a Taliban checkpoint, everyone had to present their *tazkiras* to the armed men who moved down the aisle. Karimullah was taken off the bus, handcuffed and driven back to Arghandab.

Obaidullah was frighteningly calm. Not wanting to damage his source of revenue, he did not beat Karimullah. Instead he made the boy drink a tall glass of water. When he had drunk it, Obaidullah calmly poured him another. When he had drunk that, Obaidullah poured him another, until Karimullah thought his stomach would burst.

Obaidullah ordered him to undress, tied him to the four corners of his bed and flattened his penis against his abdomen with strapping tape so that he could not urinate. He bound Karimullah's mouth so that he could not scream, then left him there.

When Obaidullah returned two days later, Karimullah's belly was distended like a melon, his head burning with fever.

Freeing him, Obaidullah said:

— You will never do this again. If you do, I will catch you. And next time, you will die.

Karimullah learned to endure his lot as best he could. In time he was able to shut off his emotions, throwing himself into a kind of trance when the deed took place, becoming as limp and unresponsive as a corpse. He could only believe that his suffering was part of some larger plan that it was his destiny to fulfill.

One afternoon he overheard Obaidullah talking on his cell phone. He was assembling his largest and most profitable evening yet, an orgy of dancing, drugs and sex.

Karimullah waited until Obaidullah was out of the house, climbed into his open bedroom window and again found Afsana's jewelry box. New jewels had replaced the ones he had stolen before. He grabbed them indiscriminately, stuffed them in his pockets and ran to the market where the same man offered him the same pittance.

He considered the options at his disposal, knowing that whatever bus or taxi he took, Obaidullah would find him. He ran far outside of Arghandab, wondering what to do.

In the far distance he heard the lowing of livestock. It was late spring and tribes of Kuchi nomads were passing through Arghandab on their seasonal migration to Ghazni Province. They were a rough people, in appearance close to beggars, and slept in tents made from feed sacks and blankets. But they were his only hope.

He approached the Kuchis as they were taking down their tents and gathering up their sheep and goats, preparing for the long northward journey.

— Let me come with you. I will tend your animals. I will gather your firewood.

The men looked dubiously at the delicate youth.

— We have our own boys who can tend to those things.

— Then I will wash your clothes and cook for you.

They shook their heads.

— Our women can do that.

Karimullah studied the weathered faces of these illiterate men, their expressions dulled from staring all day at the hind quarters of sheep and goats. Beyond them he could see the scattered lights of the Arghandab Valley where by now Obaidullah must be alert to his absence.

In desperation he rolled back his sleeves and extended his arms, imagining silver bells in either hand.

— Then . . . I will dance for you.

ii.

So began his life with the Kuchis. He danced by the fire and slept beneath the stars. He taught their children how to dance, and pleased the men with his entertainment. At first the wives mistrusted him, cursing him under their breath for the hypnotic effect he had upon their husbands. But they too fell under the spell of his vivid green eyes.

The journey was hard, taking them through the rugged heart of the Hindu Kush. But the Kuchis knew the ancient passes and corridors, and to Karimullah, for whom the landscape was strange and new, it was nothing short of a grand adventure.

He settled into their quiet domestic routine. He tended flocks in lush river bottoms where the winter snowmelt flowed fast from snowcapped peaks. He would bathe in the shockingly cold water and lie out to dry on smooth black stones. The sun had never seemed so golden, the water had never tasted as sweet.

It had been a long time since Karimullah had been so happy. Obaidullah was far away, and with each passing day those terrible memories began to fade. The Kuchis accepted the story of his sad origins without question, how his parents had been killed, leaving him to fend for himself. Many fathers eyed him as a prospective husband for their daughters.

Karimullah was no longer asked to dance for the Kuchis. But there were some who cast a longing eye on him. They were primitive mountain men who knew little of the outside world. He had awakened in them a desire that they both cherished and feared.

He rewarded their attention with kindness, trying to ignore the warnings of his intuition. But just as a shadow edges nearer with the rotation of the sun, or as a rumble of thunder precedes a storm, so did Karimullah feel the approach of his familiar enemy, the dreaded lust that transformed men into monsters.

These were powerful men awaiting only the right opportunity. He knew that he needed an ally.

Karimullah was not the only outsider dwelling among the Kuchis. Sardar was a boy of about his age. He had fair hair and pale skin inherited from his mother who hailed from the ancient Kalash people in the Chitral Valley. Sardar's father had been a great man among the Kuchis. Now, father and mother dead, Sardar tended his herd alone, living in a small tent away from the tribe.

From the start, everyone said that Karimullah and Sardar should be friends. But for months they had avoided each other. One morning, after they had reached Ghazni Province, making camp on a high plateau, the two shared pasturage. Nothing was said, but from then on the two young men worked their herds together, lunching in the tall mountain grass and engaging in mock battles where their laughter could be heard echoing against the steep canyon walls. They prepared evening meals together. The nights at Sardar's fire soon stretched into morning, and little by little Karimullah and Sardar began sharing a tent.

No one questioned the arrangement. It seemed perfectly natural that the two outsiders should gravitate toward each other. Those men who had once cast a predatory gaze upon Karimullah now turned away in resignation.

That summer on the Ghazni plateau the two were scarcely apart. As the lush valley grass became scarce they led their flocks farther from the tribe, following the narrow river bottoms between steep hills. Often they would stay away for many days, indulging in a world of their own making, one populated by the animal gods and fairies of the Kalash, which Sardar recalled from childhood myths told by his mother. With his face bathed in firelight, he spoke of Peri, the pagan mountain deity who helped find food and vanquish enemies. He knew, or pretended to know, the chants that would invoke the god's presence, singing them out in a voice that echoed off the silent hills. Sacrilegious though these stories were, Karimullah could not help but be enthralled.

Sardar told Karimullah of the Festival of the Budulak, a rite of passage for Kalash boys. At a certain age the boy is sent to the mountains with his flock where for a summer he lives on nothing but goat's milk. His return is celebrated with a festival during which he can have intercourse with any woman he chooses. Among the Kuchis, of course, such practices were completely unheard of.

This was Sardar's greatest longing, his desire to know the body of a woman. It was a recurring theme in their fireside talks, where Sardar raised a paean to the ample breasts, the tender lips and that rarely glimpsed portal of all earthly pleasure. But what Kuchi girl would ever have him?

To Karimullah, sexuality was an alien land. He knew what it was to feel love, as he felt for Sardar or for his mother. He understood fear and the other emotions. But where the body's desires were concerned, he felt a peculiar remoteness. Occasionally he felt the need to pleasure himself, but it was a purely physical exigency, like moving his bowels, with no connection to his emotions. And it was for this that he hated Obaidullah most of all.

One night, drunk on a beverage made from fermented goat's milk, Sardar became strangely amorous. It started out as a game. Perhaps he only meant to test Karimullah's ambivalence, or perhaps his needs had undone him at last. When Karimullah rebuffed his approach, Sardar became angry.

— You are just drunk, Karimullah pleaded. You will regret this.

Sardar persisted, and when Karimullah refused, struck him. For a moment they only stared at each other. And then Sardar threw him to the floor of the tent and began tearing at his clothes.

Overcome by the older boy's strength, and paralyzed by his own confusion, Karimullah yielded as he had done so often in the past.

This happened one moonlit evening at a camp overlooking Ghazni City. It happened on a day when their combined flocks were down at the river in a deep niche in the hills that created a natural enclosure for the dogs that guarded them. While Sardar lay drunkenly asleep, Karimullah was hugging the dogs in farewell. And then he was but a shadow slipping over the mountain's rim, a hide bag slung over one shoulder.

It wasn't just the attack, for which he knew Sardar would beg his forgiveness. A summer of dizzy, satisfying experiences was coming to an end. A summer of great change, of joy, of freedom, had given way to autumn. Any day now the tribe would be readying for the southward march, tearing down sheep pens and bundling their tents. Back to Kandahar Province.

Karimullah had anguished over this decision for many sleepless nights. He knew he could not go back to Kandahar and risk being found by Obaidullah.

He had heard there were good jobs in Kabul. Many foreign organizations were now in the Afghan capital working to rebuild the shattered country. They paid good money to bright young men and women who could speak English. Perhaps he could save money and go back to school and one day pursue his dream of becoming an engineer. Sardar had only provided Karimullah with the impetus he needed, awaking him to the vivid terrors of that world left behind.

And so he began the long walk. A dozen times he wept, already nostalgic for those Kuchi faces and voices he would never see or hear again. But his pace quickened, as though Obaidullah himself were at his heels.

Tears streaking his face, he followed the stars toward Kabul.

15

Phantom Workers

To avoid criticism say nothing, do nothing, be nothing.
Aristotle

THE NIGHT BEFORE my return to Kandahar City a dust storm rose up from the desert like something out of the Book of Revelation. A scorching wind whistled through the transient tent, making it balloon and contract like a paper sack. I jumped awake, hearing high-voltage capacitors shorting out across the base. In the morning the air was thick as brown fog and I knew, even before a text message from Leandro confirmed it, that my helicopter flight had been canceled.

With time to kill, I went for long walks around the base. I met a guy named Jim Bland who worked for the U.S. Department of Agriculture. He introduced me to some of his colleagues who had an office inside a nearby tent. I couldn't imagine what USDA was doing in Afghanistan. Not much, from the looks of it: one of the guys was playing Tetris and the other was updating his Facebook page.

— So what are you guys doing here?

— Starting up new ag projects, or trying to. An air strike killed six civilians and the Afghans are pretty pissed off.

— Yeah, I heard about that.

— We've been getting hit every damn week. Rocket attacks. IEDs on the highway. They captured a twelve-year-old suicide bomber last week, a little girl.

— Shit.

— Yeah. Seems like the more money we pump into this place the more they hate us for it.

— Ain't that the fucking truth, a voice said.

It was dark as I tried to find my way back to the transient tent. I passed Afghan soldiers sitting in canvas chairs in front of their tents, the red embers of cigarettes rising and falling. Now and then I caught a whiff of marijuana.

I stopped to visit a portable toilet. While I was pissing into the blue murk I held my cell phone up to read the graffiti on the plastic wall, a mix of Pashto and English. My throat constricted when I read, scrawled beneath the usual drawings and obscenities:

Rest in Peace

PFC Brandon Mullins

WE MISS AND LOVE YOU, BUD

You were never far from such reminders. I hadn't seen much of the war when it was in full swing, but it was moments like this that reminded me of those who had. Now they were gone, their buddies were gone, and what had it been for? It was easy to forget the body count, to think of the war in terms of seed and fertilizer vouchers or canal projects. All these soldiers had gone home with the memory of someone who'd been killed or wounded. They understood the cost of this war in a way I never would.

* * *

The next morning I lay atop my sleeping bag in my boxers, still damp from a shower. There was no one else in the tent. I pondered my hairy belly, watching it move up and down with my breathing. It had the precise shape and curve of a tortoise's shell. I flicked it and heard it resonate like a drum.

I'd never quite gotten used to being fat. Every morning came the parallax between the self-image I carried in my mind—the lean, energetic Peace Corps worker—and the version that confronted me in the mirror: the jiggling belly with its shaggy crucifix of chest hair. It bothered me, at least for the time it took to put on a shirt and get on with my day. Then it became just another part of me, like my brown eyes and thinning hair.

It was 10 a.m. I knew I should get some work done. I was incorrigibly lazy when away from the office. Seemed like I was always fighting off the urge for either sleep or masturbation.

I opened up my laptop, logged into the camp's Wi-Fi and saw an e-mail from Behzad. The subject line was ominous: DO NOT SHOOT THE MESSAGER.

He had just gotten back from inspecting the reservoirs in Maiwand. I went right to the photos attached to his e-mail and was a little confused. They presented quite a different work site from the one in Ramatullah's e-mail. The first reservoir seemed to be moving along on schedule. They had started framing and laying rebar for the cement floor. Maybe Ramatullah had sent the wrong photos earlier.

But where was the district center? The reservoir was supposed to be built under the eye of the district governor to prevent squabbling and water hoarding. But all I saw was a house, and a rather sumptuous one at that.

Behzad's message confirmed my worst suspicions:

Three problems, Hunt. They are building this thing a good 10 km away from the district center. The villa you see in the background belongs to Haji Ahmad Resha, a powerful warlord in the area. From what I can tell, this reservoir is going in as his private swimming pool.

I closed my eyes, clinched my sphincter and read on:

Then there is the matter of the second reservoir. We went to the site and found a reservoir there, but it was an old one from my grandfather's time. It had been drained and painted to look new. See attached.

I didn't want to see attached, but reluctantly opened a file labeled "Alleged 2nd Reservoir." The whole thing was so terrible I looked down and saw my belly quivering with irrepressible laughter.

Third problem, you are paying for 100 workers, but we counted only 40. And none of them match up with the men on your roster. Some of them are children. You must come back and shut this thing down, dear friend. Sorry to wreck your day.

Phantom workers. You gather up a bunch of men in a village, pay them for their picture and thumbprint, then do the actual work with a fraction of that number. At the end of the week, a hundred guys get paid, and except for the payroll officer and the guy who arranged the thing, no one is the wiser. But who was behind it?

I took a walk around the base, slammed my fist into sandbags, did some cursing. When I got back to the tent I felt myself slipping into a state of gloomy resignation. I knew Ramatullah was to blame, but how could I prove it? And how much corruption was still out there, begging us to find it? It was like the game of Tetris I'd seen the guy playing in the USDA tent, puzzle pieces demanding quick reaction as they dropped from the sky. Eventually, of course, you couldn't keep up with them all.

Haji Ahmad Resha's swimming pool would have cost the American taxpayer just over a hundred grand. Maybe that wasn't much in the big scheme of things, but the thought that my deputy was happily pocketing a bribe on top of a generous salary made my toes twist in anger.

Ramatullah would deny everything, of course. He would blame the construction company, which would blame the village elders, who would blame the district governor. Round and round the accusations would fly.

I would have to shut down the project and order an audit of all the infrastructure projects in Maiwand. No, I would audit *every* project on my tracker. Everyone would be pissed off—Quality Assurance, the USAID platform and especially the Chief of Party.

The old man had never actually said it, but the words were always on the tip of his tongue. *For God's sakes, Hunter, who cares if the work gets done? We've got to spend the damned money. What isn't spent cannot be billed.*

I slid my laptop under my pillow and climbed down from the bunk, needing a piss. I was stepping into my warm-up pants when—

... I spent a few seconds reestablishing my place in the universe, like a computer clunkily rebooting. I pulled myself up from the floor, as though thrown there by some malignant hand.

It's late afternoon in southern Afghanistan.

I'm in Zhari, Kandahar Province.

I've got a hell of a headache.

I heard a ringing in my ears like cicadas on a country night. I was aware of a siren rising in volume outside and the hurried tramp of boots going past the tent, one side of which was now open to bright, incongruous daylight.

I quickly pulled on my warm-ups. My hands were shaking. I threw on a shirt, getting the buttons wrong in my haste to get the hell out.

I stepped out into a brown haze. There was no wind, only a stillness underscored by the ghostly apparition of soldiers running past with stretchers. They shouted for me to get out of the way.

Clearly there had been an explosion, and it must have been damn close. Others like me were standing in various stages of undress, looking around. I recognized the backside of barrel-shaped Jim Bland hurrying past. He turned when I queried him, shouting:

— Incoming mortar, I think.

Following the direction of the smoke, I saw that the thing had struck one of the conexes directly behind the transient tent. I went around for a look.

The conexes were arranged like an orderly row of white steel shoeboxes. On one of them the steel door was hanging by a twisted hinge and smoke was billowing through a hole in the roof. A number of us stood at a respectful distance, waiting for the extent of the carnage to be revealed. We stepped aside as a medic backed out of the doorway carrying one end of a stretcher. It held an American soldier. One of his arms was limply scraping the ground. I focused on that arm, not wanting to see the rest. The two stretcher-bearers moved away at a light trot toward the infirmary.

I heard the words *recoilless rifle* and *eight-two millimeter round*. Whatever it was had turned the conex into a cauldron of spinning shrapnel. The wounded soldier was a night-duty security specialist sleeping between shifts. *And what an almighty wake-up that must have been*, I thought, my throat suddenly tightening with remorse when I noticed a second stretcher leaning beside the door. Two Afghan medics emerged from the conex wearing surgical facemasks and gloves. They snapped off their masks, leaving a pale square in the grime. They spoke in low voices to an arriving officer, then carried the stretcher inside for the recovery.

I got out of there. I didn't need to see what was carried out of that conex to know that it would haunt me forever.

The small contingent of American soldiers on the base was deeply affected by the death of Lt. Scott Warren. Within hours his photo had been enlarged, framed and placed on a stand in front of the command center. He was a boy of nineteen from Macon, Georgia. A memorial service was announced for the following day.

Dinner that evening was a somber affair. The Afghan soldiers were silent, listening to the Americans rage. They'd been through this before.

It seemed surreal to put food in my overfed, living body after what I had seen that day. For a moment I just stared into space. I was tired, but it was more a kind of existential lassitude, a sense that my work (and by extension the meaning of my life) had been devalued. I knew I was reaching a tipping point. Making a living wasn't always enough. It had to mean something.

Of course, a war zone isn't exactly the place to go searching for the meaning of life.

I thought about that night in Kabul when the woman from the embassy put me in the pillory. She had a point. The war was supposed to be over, and yet things continued to get worse. And what were my infrastructure projects really accomplishing? You could hire every worker in southern Afghanistan and it wouldn't stem the flow of insurgents pouring through the undefended Pakistani border.

What was it all for? I thought of the soldier carried out of the bombed-out conex, and Lt. Scott Warren, the one who hadn't made it. Then I thought of the other soldiers, more than a million of them, who had rotated through Afghanistan, and the billions spent to keep them there. And things were just as bad as ever.

Yeah, that bitch had a point, I thought. Maybe we should just pull up stakes, cut our losses and get the fuck out.

Forget humanitarian aid. Fuck their roads and canals. Fuck their future.

16
Karimullah

Stay close to anything that makes you glad you are alive.
Hafez

THE FIVE YEARS THAT Karimullah spent in Kabul marked his transition from boyhood to manhood. He would be his own man from now on. He sent no news to his family back in Kandahar. He was determined that somehow, in this crazy city, he would succeed.

He would not dance. No, he would reinvent himself. He would study engineering and be respected as a man among men.

But he had a long way to go. His arrival in the capital found him homeless and hungry, his Kuchi clothes in tatters. Babur had instilled in him one precious piece of advice: nothing was more important to one's success than clean clothes and a good pair of shoes. With the tiny bit of money he had managed to save he bought a white *shalwar kamiz* and some sturdy shoes.

He went for a shower and a haircut at the local *hammam*. Then, clean and respectable in his fine new clothes, he went to all the best hotels in the city, places where he knew he was likely to meet foreigners. For this was another important piece of advice he had received from Babur:

— Your own people have little to offer. To succeed, you must make yourself useful to the foreign invaders.

The manager of the Excelsior Hotel was impressed with his poise and confidence. He agreed to try the young man as a night porter, carrying luggage. Because he spoke some English, he was given the foreign guests, who tipped him well. He was soon able to rent a tiny room.

He began taking classes from an organization that helped Afghans earn their high school diplomas. He took courses in English, building on the lessons learned at Babur's feet. With this and his job he was lucky to find four hours' sleep in a night, but it didn't matter. In weary moments, nothing roused his fighting spirit more than his memories of Obaidullah and the terror he had left behind.

He began applying to aid organizations in the city. But everywhere he went the answer was the same. It didn't matter that he was willing to do anything, from proofreading documents to cleaning toilets, or that he spoke fair English with an almost posh British accent. He had no experience.

One night at the Excelsior he carried the luggage of an American woman journalist who took an interest in him. She was doing a story on the problems facing Afghan nomads. When she learned that Karimullah knew of the Kuchis first hand she persuaded him to submit to an interview. And because he could not discuss the Kuchis without talking about how he came to be with them, he told her of his life as a dancer, omitting the obscene parts.

Penny Jones was the sort of woman one saw only in American

movies. She had dazzling blonde hair and wore denim jeans and over-sized T-shirts bearing strange proverbs like: *I don't suffer from insanity—I enjoy every minute of it.* And: *I put the FUN back in dysfunction.* She was from Texas. She called him "sugar" and "honey." When she interviewed him in her hotel room she would sprawl out on the bed while he sat rigidly in a chair. It was a little unsettling. Didn't she know what this might do to her reputation, being alone with a man who was not her husband?

She told him he had the most beautiful eyes she had ever seen. But he had heard this so many times. He sometimes wished he could pluck them out; they had brought him nothing but trouble.

She wanted to find some Kuchis and do a photo essay on their lives. It was summer, nearly a year since he had left them. He reckoned they were back in Ghazni, but the highways were too dangerous for foreigners. If she were discovered at a Taliban checkpoint she would certainly be kidnapped or killed.

— Then I will stay off the highways and travel in disguise.

— But how will you find them? The Kuchis are a secretive people.

— Well, honey, I think you oughta come as my paid guide. How do you like that idea?

He liked the idea quite nicely. They set off in an old battered Corolla that would attract little attention, following a course that Karimullah hoped would not bring them in contact with the tribe he had traveled with before. Much as he wanted to see Sardar and the others, he was too ashamed of the manner of his disappearance, which had been an insult to their hospitality.

When it was impossible to go any further by car, they continued on horseback. It was just like something out of James Michener, she told him. They bathed in chilly rivers, cooked over an open fire, slept in two small tents. Penny Jones shocked him with her immodesty, strutting about the fire in nothing but a towel. He wondered if she had once been a prostitute.

After a week they encountered a band of Kuchis. Reticent at first, the nomads warmly welcomed them when they heard Karimullah speaking their dialect and using their own peculiar slang. Penny Jones and Karimullah made camp among them for two weeks.

The American woman was certainly unlike any woman he had ever encountered, indecorously crawling on the ground in her effort to get the perfect photograph. The Kuchis didn't know what to make of her. They smilingly indulged her as if she were *dewana*, a crazy person.

She was euphoric over her photos, showing them to Karimullah on her laptop that she recharged each day with a solar panel. She spoke of the many awards and honors that would be bestowed upon her thanks to him. She said she owed him everything, surprising Karimullah with a long, slow kiss on the lips.

One night, on the journey back to Kabul, she appeared inside his tent. She put her finger to his lips and was frank about what she wanted. He wondered if he was mistaken. Could a woman really ask such a thing? But as she began taking off his clothes she left him in no doubt.

There was much he had to learn, of course, but Penny Jones delighted in being a patient teacher. He did whatever she wanted, even devising a few techniques of his own. All along he was terrified that she would discover the hollowness of his affection, the empty chamber in his heart.

If he could have told her about his past it might have been different. But this was unthinkable. He would have sooner lifted back the lid on a septic tank and asked her to peer inside. And so he simply tried to be the man she wanted him to be, to say the things that would please her, to touch her in ways that would make her sigh.

At last they reached Kabul, their time on the road over. Fearing that he had ruined her for marriage, Karimullah did what he felt must be done. But Penny Jones only laughed at his grave proposal of marriage.

As payment for working as her translator and guide, Karimullah received as much money as he would have made carrying bags at the Excelsior Hotel for a whole year. As Penny Jones prepared to go back to America she gave Karimullah the number of a friend who ran a small aid project that worked with slum children.

— They won't pay you much, honey, but you'll get plenty of experience.

He was confused. One minute they were lovers, the next she was leaving him forever. Had he done something to offend her? Had she discovered his secret?

They were supposed to have a final dinner together at the Excelsior Hotel. But she didn't show up, and when he inquired at the front desk he was handed a note:

Can't do it, sugar. I'm just not good with goodbyes. Ring me up if you ever get to Texas. Here's to some good memories, Kari. You're one in a million.

That was her pet name for him: Kari. He knew he would probably never hear that name uttered again in his lifetime. He went back to his tiny room and wept. Not because she had left without saying goodbye. Not because he loved her. But because he felt so bitterly, awfully alone.

* * *

But he had a new job, one that would finally put his talents to good use. The Kabul Children's Trust was a small organization administered by a group of elderly American schoolteachers. The pay he received was scarcely more than he'd made as a porter at the Excelsior Hotel, but the job was many times more rewarding.

Each morning he smiled at the stern women in business suits who ran the organization, their hair sprayed stiff as grey helmets. They were nothing like Afghan women, with their frank, outgoing manner. Karimullah thought Americans were the most intriguing human beings he had ever met. And of course the women doted on him like a beloved grandson.

His supervisor, Marsha Kohn, was president of the organization, a dignified older woman as eccentric and mysterious in her way as Penny Jones. She drove around in her own Jeep and lived in a house with just a single guard, or *chowkidar*. She wore trousers like Penny Jones and couldn't be bothered to cover her hair. It was a wonder to watch this elderly American woman weaving through Kabul traffic, honking and gesturing aggressively at the other drivers.

The organization ran schools and clinics in the poorest districts of Kabul. Karimullah worked in procurement, locating cheap sources of food and clothing and school supplies. And as this meant dealing directly with Afghan vendors, it gave him his first taste of the corruption that gnawed at the edges of such projects like a predatory disease.

The vendors asked him to process forged invoices for goods that were never delivered, assuming that he would want a cut in the action. To them it was like a game, concocting one scheme after another by which the well-meaning American women could be swindled out of their money.

But it could not work without Karimullah's complicity. And so

146

the vendors put him under siege. At first they were friendly and ca-joling. *Everyone does it, my friend. No one will ever know.* Seeing that he was obdurate, they resorted to the brute tactics of their kind.

When Karimullah came to work with a cut on his forehead and one eye swollen shut, he lied to Marsha Kohn and said that he had fallen down the stairs. He moved like an old man, wincing from the pain of bruised ribs.

When it happened again, this time leaving him with a broken nose and a cut lip, Marsha Kohn told him to pack his things.

— But I am fine, I was just boxing with a friend.

— No more of your bullshit, kid. You're coming to live with me.

And so he left his tiny room and moved into Marsha Kohn's house in Shar-e Naw, close to Haji Yaqub Square. It was enclosed by a high brick wall, with a rabbit hutch, some chickens and a beautiful flower garden. Again he found himself living in an alien but exciting world. It was the sort of life Karimullah had seen only in American films, an unending round of dinner parties and funny croquet games and drinks—oh, how those American women could drink. Karimullah enjoyed taking them on outings to the National Museum and bowling at Strikers. Marsha Kohn called him her right-hand man. She made no decision without consulting him, for who at the Trust knew the plight of the poor better than Karimullah?

As his English improved she taught him how to write business letters. He helped her with grant applications and reports. He sat in on staff and board meetings. Whenever Marsha Kohn was pressed to make a difficult decision, she never failed to consult Karimullah for guidance. She would hug him roughly and say:

— Together we will change this unhappy country, Karimullah, you and me.

Each morning Farzam, their *chowkidar*, would slide back the big steel gate as they left for the office together in the Jeep. He was an unsmiling man with a beard as full as that of any mullah. Toward Marsha Kohn he was polite and deferential as became his station. He watched in taciturn silence as she laughed and embraced men who were not her husband. And in the morning he carried off the garbage bags full of clanking liquor bottles. As Farzam was of Tajik descent and Karimullah was Pashtun, they were ill disposed toward each other from the start.

One night at dinner, the party prevailed upon Karimullah to drink a glass of red wine. Normally he was shy at these gatherings, speaking only when he was addressed. But the wine opened some wellspring inside of him. He found that he was clever and funny. And when the ladies offered him another glass, how could he refuse?

Since he had left the Kuchis he had not danced for anyone. It was a part of his life for which he felt a mixture of nostalgia and disgust. But in his elevated state he found himself bragging about his skills as a dancer. And naturally, pretending to be dubious, Marsha Kohn and her friends demanded a demonstration.

There was no Afghan music in the house, but Marsha Kohn put on a CD of Dvořák's *Slavonic Dances*. With no costume and no finger cymbals he nevertheless pushed aside the furniture, rolled back his sleeves, closed his eyes and imagined he was back in Obaidullah's orchard in the days before his passion had been defiled.

The ladies gathered around, clapping in time with the spirited music. They reached into their big purses and jokingly threw coins at him. On the final crash of cymbals he threw out his arms and dropped his head, winded. The women broke into wild applause.

Karimullah looked up and saw Farzam watching through the front window. The meaning in his cruel, level gaze was unmistakable.

You might fool these American women, but I know what you are, bacha.

In the two years that Karimullah worked for them, the Kabul Children's Trust prospered. It was featured in a story by CNN and made the Forbes list of America's top charities. The office expanded and Karimullah was promoted to operations manager. He continued to ride to work with Marsha Kohn in her Jeep, but now he wore a suit and carried his own a laptop computer in a fine leather satchel.

What happened next took him by surprise, but in the end it was to be expected. A balloon can only rise so high before it must finally come back down.

A change came over Marsha Kohn. Lines of worry creased her formerly carefree brow. Gone was her jaunty, carefree spirit. Each evening she stayed late at the office on emergency videoconferences or going over spreadsheets and ledgers. The terrible words were on everyone's lips: *bookkeeping error.* And later: *accounting fraud.*

Marsha Kohn instituted a fifty percent pay cut across the board and moved the office into a smaller building. But this wasn't enough to offset the precipitous drop in revenue. Her dinner parties were now grave gatherings. It was amazing to Karimullah how a chain of events originating on computer screens in New York could move with such terrible speed to their house in Kabul.

The Christmas holidays came. Marsha Kohn put up a tree in her living room and Karimullah helped her decorate it with strings of colored lights. But it was not a merry Christmas. The Fund had put out an urgent appeal on its website, but by the end of the year the windfall of contributions that Marsha Kohn said they needed, and for which Karimullah prayed seven times a day, had not transpired. Americans seemed to have lost interest in the plight of starving

Kabul street children.

The Fund had reduced its operations like a spotlight shrinking down to a single dot. Marsha Kohn laid off everyone at the office and closed out the books. Karimullah assisted with the disposal of assets, handing over the computers and office furniture to various charities. Marsha Kohn called everyone she knew trying to find work for Karimullah. She said she would not leave Afghanistan until she knew he was provided for.

Then she remembered a friend working on a USAID-funded agricultural project in southern Afghanistan. They were hiring for a number of positions, and the pay was excellent. There was only one problem: the job was in Kandahar.

— You know I cannot go back there.

— You'll just have to suck it up. I'm sure things have changed.

Easy for her to say. Things hadn't changed in Kandahar in a thousand years. When she saw his face drain of color she took his hands and said:

— Good things happen to good people. I have confidence in you, kid. Once you've established yourself, others will see your gifts and you'll soar to new heights. And anyway, times are tough all over. Beggars can't be choosers.

He awoke one morning with the sense that something was not quite right. It was too quiet. At the front gate he discovered that Farzam, the shady *chowkidar*, had vanished without collecting his wages, leaving them unguarded.

Karimullah and Marsha Kohn drove to the office to gather the last of their things. It was a mournful visit, Marsha surprising Karimullah by breaking into heart-rending sobs. Karimullah wept too, holding the elderly woman as tenderly as a flower of thinnest porcelain.

She shooed him away, tearfully reminding him that they had a farewell dinner to prepare; several of their Kabul friends would be joining them that evening. As she departed in the Jeep she asked Karimullah to pick up her laundry from the dry cleaners while she went home to start cooking. She waved goodbye as she sped off through the Kabul streets.

The sun had set when he returned in a taxi to their neighborhood. Marsha Kohn's dry cleaning lay across his lap in rustling plastic. The taxi slowed at a police checkpoint. A great traffic jam had formed and an ambulance shrieked to be let through. A terrible odor of smoke and cordite hung in the air. The driver rolled down his window to find out what had happened from the other motorists.

— Another rocket attack, the driver said.

— In this neighborhood?

— They hit a house just up ahead. You know that old American woman who is always racing around in that funny truck? I knew they'd get her one of these days.

Karimullah felt his heart turn over. As the taxi began to move forward he jumped out and began running the other way. The driver called after him for his fare, but Karimullah was soon dashing blindly down a side street, not knowing where he was going but that he must get far away. He knew what the Afghan National Police were like. If they found that he had been living with the American woman, no force on earth would be able to save him from prosecution.

Fortunately he had his wallet and his *tazkira* with him. He took a room at the Mustafa Hotel, turned on the TV and waited for the morning news. By now his fear was melting into grief as the reality of what had happened began to sink in.

Surely she hadn't been killed. It wasn't possible.

When he heard the strident theme music for Tolo TV News the next morning his heart was beating so fast he thought it might explode. Then came the images. A terrible fire. Police cars. Neighbors peering through open gates. And then a photo of Marsha Kohn taken from the website of the Kabul Children's Trust.

He spent the next three days at the Mustafa Hotel wondering what to do. Kabul would forever be linked in his mind to the sweet, eccentric Marsha Kohn. A woman who had only wanted to help others. A brave, dear, wonderful woman.

He stared at the card she had given him. It bore the name of a program called Advancing Livelihoods and Agricultural Stability, and the logo of USAID—*From the American People.*

Kandahar has not changed, he thought. It will never change.

— But yes. Yes, Marsha Kohn, I am a beggar and I cannot be a chooser. It is time for me to return home.

BOOK TWO

17

The Monastery of Meuze

Sometimes even to live is an act of courage.
Seneca

FRANCE IS PUTTING ITS sacred buildings up for sale. Not all of them, of course. But enough that agencies are springing up to market these *anciens édifices religieux* to foreigners.

You can buy monasteries and convents, some attached to farms, some with chapels, some with crypts. Some come with the ruins of dead villages, tracts of forest, lakes and hills and streams.

These buildings come in a wide range of prices and conditions. Two million dollars will get you a vast 50-room complex on a Narbonne hill looking out on a topiary garden. It boasts three salons, two chapels and a 25-acre park—"B&B ready!"

A million will get you a restored fifteenth-century priory in the Languedoc. Recently updated, it features archways and terraced courtyards and lava tile roofs supported by enormous rafters milled from forests that haven't been seen in anyone's memory.

The cheaper options have potential, but they require more creativity. Monks and nuns didn't always inhabit stone castles adjacent to major freeways and other conveniences. Three hundred thousand will buy a promising little presbytery in a peaceful Provençal village. But the ceilings sag with mold and rot, and the cracked foundation will need hydraulics to set aright.

A little cheaper and you'll find yourself in something with four walls and no roof, with small bushes growing out of the *meurtrières* where medieval bowmen once sighted the enemy. It's never seen electricity or modern plumbing. That's part of its charm—and why it's been on the market for years. There is nowhere else to go, nothing more affordable or more derelict.

It was to this end of the spectrum that I one day stumbled.

I was in France on leave. I had flown into Bordeaux and rented a car, thinking it would be fun to drive around and see the countryside. It didn't matter where, it didn't matter that I was alone. I wanted green meadows and hills and the feeling of motion.

It was charming, of course, driving the forested back roads of lower Aquitaine. I stopped where I wanted, for as long as I wanted, sometimes for days. I gazed upon ancient fields of battle as recommended by my Michelin guide. I never stayed long, leaving straightaway for the next village, the next church, the next castle. In no time the little Fiat was littered with baguette crumbs and smelled of *cabecou* cheese and Hunter Ames.

It rained, but I didn't care. The landscape turned hilly, the blue Pyrénées grew larger, the roads more vertical. I felt that I had discovered this place, that it was mine. I sat in restaurants and cafés where no one spoke to me. I didn't care. I stayed in hotels and pensions. I went to the movies. I did exactly what I wanted to do. Or I did nothing at all, and that was fine too. With each day I could feel the straightjacket of Afghanistan loosening its grip.

One day I stopped for a piss on the roadside somewhere in the Hautes-Pyrénées. The road was narrow and through the trees below I could see a small village flanking a stream. Red roofs and grey stone, wildflowers in the meadows. I drove down for a look.

It was a charming village, as clean and orderly as a Disneyland attraction. I had lunch at a café with a stone terrace. There was no one around, just the waiter and me. He was a friendly old man, nicely dressed in a waistcoat and bow tie. He said he hadn't had a customer in two days.

The village of Meuze, he told me with regret, was dying. The farmers could no longer compete with the huge monoculture farms that were popping up everywhere. There were no jobs, and so people were flocking to the cities. Everyone was giving up, leaving, abandoning this picturesque place to the whims of natural selection. Just look around you, he said, pointing out the many windows with signs that said À VENDRE.

I decided to stick around for a few days.

He drew a map on a napkin. It directed me to a boutique hotel operated by a certain Madame Roche and her husband, who (the waiter warned me) suffered from an aggressive form of dementia. I reached l'Auberge des Charmes and, sure enough, a bewildered man sat watching me from a rocking chair in the garden. I waved, he scowled.

I bought snacks and soft drinks and hid away in my room. I watched movies on my laptop. I napped copiously and guiltlessly, jacked off like a teenager. I found a fat Stephen King paperback in the lobby and devoured it in three days. Each evening I walked into town and had dinner at the restaurant with the friendly old waiter and the stone terrace.

The proprietor, Yvette Roche, worried that I might be bored. But then, she said, this *was* the most boring place in all of France, what had I been thinking?

She didn't get very many guests anymore. She gave me the same refrain as Philippe, my waiter friend. Families were moving out in droves, old families that had been here for hundreds of years. But what were you going to do, with all the new European Union farm tariffs and regulations?

She was a lovely woman, thin and elegant with that geriatric sexiness that only the French can pull off, like Catherine Deneuve. She tended a full, lovely garden, and of course her husband, who passed his days in his rocker. Occasionally he wandered off in a daze and someone from the village would drive him back. No one minded. He was practically the only diversion left.

The Roches kept a few dozen sheep that they raised on rocky land adjoining their hotel. The sheep didn't bring in much income, Yvette explained, but it was something to do. They had a stable boy who came each morning to feed the animals and move them from barn to pasture. Once in a while Yvette would run the sheep higher up the mountain so they could roam the way their ancestors did.

One morning, dressed in a bright blue windbreaker, she invited me to join her. It was pelting rain so she loaned me one of her husband's jackets. Her border collie, Badou, knew what was up, and leapt around us as we trudged toward the barn. Yvette opened a door in back and the sheep shuffled out and moved dutifully uphill. She brought them to a level place where the grass was mixed with clover and the view was breathtaking.

The land had been in her husband's family since the Revolution. Its story was complicated, involving Cardinal Richelieu and Marat and one of the Louies. She was telling me this in French and I got all twisted around in it until I heard the word *monastère*. Picking up on my curiosity, she stood and asked me to follow.

A stone path led down through a canopy of trees. We picked our way along a small stream until the trail opened onto a wide green meadow. At the far end of this meadow stood the monastery, or what was left of it.

It was actually a complex of buildings consisting of a dormitory, a chapel, a dining area, a barn and outbuildings, some of which were no more than piles of wood and stone. The only structure more or less intact was the dormitory. We stepped through tangles of briars and weeds and looked inside gaping holes that had once been windows. Rodents scurried in the darkness. It smelled like a grave.

The thing was more than two centuries old. Years of dampness and rot had caused many of the mighty roof timbers to collapse. The rooms were now exposed to the elements, speeding up the general disintegration. I was amazed that it was still standing.

We examined the remains of what had been the church, positioned at the focal center of the other buildings. There had been a fire at some point in the past, and the thing was nothing but a shell with blackened niches and tall columns supporting blue sky. Saplings sprouted from cracks in the floor. We kicked up plastic water bottles and other garbage left by hikers.

The monks had put up a brave fight, she mused, taking my arm for support. The Dominican brothers had built their monastery at the furthermost limits of the country, far from the revolutionary upheavals in the capital. They lived quiet lives, farmed grapes and made raisin wine (she'd unearthed a bottle years ago, the cork still tight).

During the Second World War the monastery was still fit for habitation, but only barely. A group of Ursuline sisters hid Jewish children there, surviving until the last days of the Occupation when a Vichy collaborator tipped off the local *kommandantur*. The children were herded off to the camps and the Ursuline ladies all went to prison.

Yvette and I sat up drinking in the garden that night. She found my interest in her old monastery both charming and peculiar. In the French way, she wasn't content simply to acknowledge my enthusiasm, she wanted to dissect and analyze it. Was I perhaps experiencing some religious calling? Or was it an archaeological interest? When we had finished the bottle of wine I let her open another one, knowing I'd be wrecked the next day, but it didn't matter. Somehow I sensed that my life was about to change.

There may have been a third bottle. It was well after midnight before we went our separate ways, embracing a moment too long, Yvette's nails suggestively raking my back. I was having trouble standing upright. She walked me to my room and asked if I wanted company. For answer I ran to the bathroom, knelt before the toilet and puked up a purple waterfall.

18

The Children's Prison

To perceive is to suffer.
Aristotle

THE CHIEF OF PARTY leaned back in his plush leather chair until the skin accordioned under his chin.

— So, Hunter, I heard things got kind of frisky out in Indian country.

I was still reeling from the explosion at FOB Pasab, still choking up when I remembered the service for Lt. Warren. The chief didn't understand, but how could he?

I cleared my throat, passing a document across his desk.

— I'll get right to the point, Cleve. This is a list of infrastructure projects that I'm shutting down. Some are closed for good. The projects in Maiwand, for instance. We're finished there. Haji Ahmad Resha can finish that swimming pool on his own dime. The others are on hold pending an audit.

Harbin reached for his reading glasses, frowning. He flipped through the stapled pages and shook his head at what he read.

— What about Zhari?

— I don't think we should work there.

— But this was specifically requested by the military.

— It's too dangerous. We won't be able to monitor anything out there. We might as well just pour taxpayer money into the sand.

— Do you have a contingency plan? Or do you just plan on sitting on your budget and seeing if it will hatch on its own?

— On page three you'll see a list of proposed sites and projects. I'll have to run these by USAID, but I think they'll fly.

As Harbin squinted at the page I thought about the meager list it contained. I had gone through my files and chosen seven projects that I could vouch for with any certainty. Mostly these were variations on small construction projects that had been done before, in villages where I would have no trouble monitoring the laborers myself. It wasn't much, but it was the best I was willing to commit to.

In a while Cleve set the document down, removed his reading glasses and pinched the bridge of his nose.

— There's an old Afghan saying, Hunter. The snake-bitten man is often afraid of striped ropes. Would you say that accurately describes your situation?

— Sir, my department is riddled with corruption. Before I fired Ramatullah—

— You *fired* him?

— He was a liar and a thief.

— I hope you're sure.

— I got a written statement from two foremen.

— Just be damned sure. I don't want the Afghan labor courts blowing smoke up my ass.

— There's no doubt. The only question now is how many other

projects he screwed us on.

I had a sudden image of deferential Ramatullah, the good waiter preparing my morning coffee. So eager to please, nervously stroking the pockmark on his beard. I hadn't had the pleasure of sacking him personally. When word of the discovery reached him, he stopped coming to the office. Faith had fired him by e-mail.

Harbin exhaled and once again leaned back in his creaky chair.

— Look. We've got five months left on the project and thirty million dollars to burn. Then we're out of here. The very last thing I need right now, the *very* last, is for word to get out that we can't monitor our own programs.

My heart was beating so fast that I was beginning to feel a little lightheaded.

— Sir, I won't be complicit in fraud.

The chief put his hands together in a placating gesture, as though attending to an unruly child.

— No one is asking you to do anything dishonest. We all want the same thing: to improve the lives of these people and get back home to our families.

I rose.

— I'm glad we understand each other. And by the way, how long do you plan on keeping me out in the training villa? My room in the guesthouse was fixed up ages ago.

His eyes shifted away.

— Jerry was having some kind of plumbing issue, so we moved him into your old room.

Seeing my expression, he added.

— Oh, you know I couldn't very well put him out in Zone Two.

— Why not? It's good enough for *me*.

Harbin laughed.

— You and I are cut from the same cloth. We slept on mud floors back in our Peace Corps days. These guys are soft. I need you to be tough for me. Can you do that, Hunter?

Waheed was running the department now, not because he was the best or sharpest of the lot but because he would be easiest to control. Never before would I have made a hiring decision on such grounds, but things were going to be different from here on out. Ramatullah was brilliant, and look where that had gotten us. No, better this slow, nearsighted fellow with bad breath.

As soon as I was back at my desk I became aware of Waheed's looming presence beside me, hands folded over the front of his *kamiz*.

— What is it?

— Sir, I was just telephoned by the office of the governor of Panjwayi District. He would like to submit a formal petition for a road rehabilitation project.

— That's fine, but don't promise him anything. We're not moving forward on any roads until the results of the audit come back.

— Sir, he wants that I should visit him at his palace.

Engrossed in my e-mails, I didn't look at him.

— No. Any discussions can happen here, in my presence. Or pass it on to Behzad, it's his job. The last thing I need is for you to get cozy with the Panjwayi district governor.

— Sir, please do not suggest—

— I'm not suggesting anything. I'm giving you an order. No meetings with government officials outside this office. Understood?

Waheed padded soundlessly back to his workstation. I rubbed my eyes and leaned back. Poor homely Waheed, with his buckteeth and his lisp. But I'd be damned if I'd apologize now.

I went up to the roof for a smoke. The sky was as lead-grey as my mood. A cool, damp wind swept through the trees down in the courtyard of the children's prison. It would be a rainy night, a rare thing in this part of the world.

The door to the roof opened behind me and Faith Woodson came out. She was busy unwrapping a pack of cigarettes and didn't notice me until it was too late. She hesitated, then strolled indifferently toward the parapet, standing a comfortable distance away from me.

I hadn't spoken to her since that night before my trip to Kabul. I still wasn't sure how things had become so damned awkward between us. Rejection? Did it really come down to such a childish emotion?

The wind carried her smoke in my direction along with the aroma of perfumed shampoo. Bitchy as she might be, she did turn me on, I couldn't deny it.

Maybe it was the scent, but a childhood memory suddenly projected in the cinema of my mind. One New Year's Eve when I was a boy, my parents went out with my aunt and uncle to a party, leaving me alone with my four cousins. I was thirteen and my cousins were all a few years older. An older girl was staying with them at the time, I never found out why.

No sooner had the grown-ups departed than the girl went back to the master bedroom. My cousins, all boys, got their wallets out. They took turns going in to see her while I watched *Love, American Style.* Then they told me it was my turn.

She must have been twenty or twenty-five. She had a thin face and long, straight hair, like Cher. She was probably high on something. I found her waiting for me in my aunt and uncle's king-size bed. She raised the blanket to admit me, though without much enthusiasm. My cousins had pre-paid.

She kissed me, sticking her tongue deep into my small mouth. She guided my hand over her breasts, to her flat stomach and on down. By then, having gone the rounds with my cousins, she was pretty lathered up down there. She took my fingers and slid them right in. She seemed to like that. While I kissed her, my lips pecking over her face like I'd seen on TV, she deftly unzipped me and shimmied my Toughskins down my thighs. She took my erection in hand, guiding it toward the center of the universe. And at that very moment I heard a door slam, followed by the voices of my aunt and uncle.

— Looks like rain, I said.

Faith grunted.

— Mm.

With her elbows on the parapet and the cigarette close to her chin, the wind tousling her hair over one eye, she might have been standing on a bridge in Paris rather than a dusty roof in Kandahar.

What was the connection I felt between Faith and that long-ago babysitter? Just a case of boyhood *coitus interruptus*? How I'd cherished that stickiness on my fingers, with its acrid, coppery taste. Wanting to see her again, I took the bus over to my aunt and uncle's house a few days later, only to learn from my cousins that she had left town. I never saw her again. She had come and gone like a wraith, leaving only the faintest physical manifestation—the taste of cherry lip-gloss and cigarettes. And like any ghost, she was still just as mysterious and real as she'd been four decades ago.

Faith was glancing over at me. The directness of her stare unnerved me. I began scratching at a loose piece of plaster, not realizing that I was bouncing against the edge as though my belly were an exercise ball.

— Why are we fighting? I muttered.

— You tell me. Are we fighting?

— If I say no, does that mean we can be friends again?

She snorted.

— What are we in, seventh grade?

I heard shouting and laughter and looked down into the courtyard of the children's prison. A dozen kids were kicking around a big
wad of butcher paper wrapped with string. Kids always know how
to make do, I thought. They don't worry about the nuances of their
relationships. They just get on with it.

I blurted out:

— We're all so damned sophisticated and careful. But just look
at those kids. Give them a ball made of garbage and they're happy.

She stabbed out her cigarette and turned back toward the door.

— Whatever. Oh, don't forget you have a meeting with Hank.

— Shit, I almost forgot.

— My pleasure.

Hank Diebold was going out on leave and I would be watching his
department in his absence. Hank ran the grants program, which gave
out tractors to agricultural cooperatives. The chief knew how well
Hank and I got along. No doubt this was payback.

I thought Faith had left, and was startled when she called out
from the doorway:

— I could have been a good friend to you. What happened to your
son was a tragedy.

I was leaning over the edge, watching the kids. I had nothing to
say to this. She added:

— Just so you know, I didn't tell anyone. And I never would.

19

I Will Find My Tribe Right Here

Whosoever delights in solitude is either a wild beast or a god.
Aristotle

I SPENT TWO WEEKS in Meuze, that drowsy, timeless village in the foothills of the Pyrenees.

I dined at the restaurant with the stone terrace. I got to know the local shops and shopkeepers. I took walks with the venerable Yvette Roche on the lonely hills behind her hotel.

One evening after old Monsieur Roche was put to bed, Yvette and I sat in the garden with a candle, a transistor radio and a bottle of wine. A distant AM station was playing French crooners from the last century—Maurice Chevalier and Charles Trenet and Jean Sablon. A church bell tolled the quarter-hour. The breeze carried a note of lavender. I was about to explode with the Frenchness of it all.

Yvette asked me how I'd enjoyed my *vacance*, and I told her I'd never been so happy. And I meant it so truly, so sincerely, I felt tears come to my eyes.

What made me feel like I belonged here? Its people were not my people, its traditions were not my own. I could barely stumble through the simplest of French sentences. And yet I felt an eerie affinity for this gloomy place and these sad people.

Yvette put her hand over mine.

— You have spent your life in exile, moving from one project to another.

Her voice was low, like that of a sultry Delphic priestess. She continued:

— You have no home, no people. You had a wife and a son, but they are gone now. Our distant ancestors sought the security of their tribe. You are a man searching for his lost tribe.

— But why here, why now?

— Old people should not be alone. You are only fifty, but the clock is ticking.

She held her watch to her ear in an unnecessary bit of theatrics. I nodded to show that I got the point.

— The strength you had in youth to confront the world alone is fading. Your spirit knows it must start preparing for the end.

Yvette was right, bless her French heart. You didn't have to search the world for the place you needed to be. You just needed to accept the place where life had brought you.

I went back to my room and scribbled down all I could remember of our conversation. It was already fading, like fragments of a dream. She poked her head in to say goodnight.

— Stop running, monsieur. A rose can't bloom in a stiff breeze.

The next morning I joined her in the garden for coffee and croissants. I thanked her for our talk the night before.

— So have you decided what you want to do, Monsieur?

— I want to make you an offer on that old monastery.

Had she anticipated this? She walked inside and came out with an ancient property survey rolled inside a tube. She cleared the table. The brittle document was a museum piece in itself, all brown and crinkled like a treasure map.

I followed her hovering fingertip. Surveyor's markings indicated the hills and streams, a snaking path leading to what an ancient quill pen had captioned LE VIEUX MONASTÈRE. Nearby was a *bois* that no longer existed, a stream that did and a section dotted with small crosses, probably a cemetery.

As we hiked out to the monastery that afternoon I had a chance to revisit my feelings from the night before. I found they had not changed. But as I scrutinized the crumbling walls and collapsed roof beams through the lens of my limited financial resources, I wondered how it could be done. One half of the old dormitory was serviceable. Windows, some plaster work, a new roof, I could live there. But what about plumbing? What about electricity?

I pictured a vegetable garden in one weed-choked corner. I could see a piano under a vaulted ceiling, myself seated beside some clucking village schoolteacher beating time with a pencil. I could smell a pot of *ratatouille* simmering in the kitchen, see cordwood piled high for winter. Solar power. I'd live off the grid. Fresh spring water. An aproned cleaning woman named Isabelle. We'd have an affair.

People in the village would hear about the odd undertaking, of course. I'd invite my waiter friend, Philippe, over for dinner, and the postman and Yvette and my growing collection of friends and acquaintances from Meuze. I'd show them my garden and my fledgling grapevines. We'd hold glasses of wine in the moonlight. We'd sing songs around the piano.

My new friends. My people. My lost tribe.

And if that didn't happen, if I remained alone, I was prepared to live with it. My happiness didn't depend on other people. I would soon have reason to reconsider that premise. But as far as I was concerned, strolling the hills that afternoon, human companionship was optional. I could take it or leave it.

In a while we wandered silently back to the house, absorbed in our own thoughts. Yvette took my hand and didn't let it go until we were within hailing distance of the hotel. Her husband watched us from his chair in the bay window, scowling as always.

They'd had no offspring. No doubt the old man would die first, leaving Yvette stuck with an unprofitable hotel and lots of worthless land. When she died, the property would pass into the hands of the state. (And with an estate tax of forty percent, who would have wanted to inherit it?)

The subject of money made us both shy and evasive. Yvette tore a slip of paper in two. She wrote down a price and folded the paper in half. Then I did the same. When we saw what the other had written, we burst out laughing. We'd written down nearly the same figure.

My thoughts swung from one extreme to another. I was a lucky man. No, I was doomed. It was a chance of a lifetime. No, I was a fool! But by any definition, the deal was a bargain. She had set aside forty acres that would convey with the monastery. It included a fine portion of pasturage and stream, and of course the crumbling pile of stone that I might one day call home.

Things were moving a little too quickly. I didn't trust my impulses. How would this seem months down the road? *What the hell were you thinking, Ames?*

I called my ex-wife, Jane, for advice. There was no one else I could turn to. Her husband was listening in on the extension, but I didn't care. I told her about my trip, how I'd stumbled upon Meuze, and so on. I described the monastery at length, the rocks and hills, the view. She was oddly silent. I barreled forward, describing Yvette and her husband and the people I'd met.

Finally she spoke. She said it was the loneliest, saddest prospect she could imagine. I'd never learn French. I'd never find friends. To the villagers I would always be an eccentric outsider. And what the hell did I know about renovating old buildings? It was insane. Not just insane, it was pathetic. Not just pathetic, it was . . . she couldn't find the words. In the pause I realized she was choking back tears.

She hung up, and it took me a full hour to make the connection. How could I have forgotten?

I told Yvette the story that evening at dinner.

— When our son was still a toddler, Jane and I worked with the Peace Corps in Gabon.

— That's an unusual place to raise a child.

She offered me a quick, insincere smile, as though hoping this wouldn't be a long story.

— We left when he was four years old. One day we heard him screaming. He'd been bitten by a snake; his arm was swollen twice its normal size. Two weeks later we were back in Indiana. We got our teaching certificates and became schoolteachers.

We were dining at the restaurant with the stone terrace. Yvette and I were the only customers. She turned over the leaves of her salad, wondering how any of this concerned her.

— We stayed in touch with an evangelical minister named Pastor Kibula.

Yvette made a little grunt of assent, as though she had expected a pastor to enter the tale at this point.

— All the time we were back in Evansville he wrote, begging us to come back. Each time one of those blue onionskin envelopes came in the mail we'd have to brace ourselves for tears.

— You should have told him where to go.

— No, we sort of needed it. Helped keep things in perspective. And by the time Maurice was seventeen, we started thinking maybe it was time to go back.

I paused for a sip of wine, adding:

— It turned out to be the worst mistake of our lives. But anyway, Kibula sent photos of this home he had found for us, a ruined nineteenth-century farmhouse badly in need of repair. I think that's why Jane was so sad on the phone today.

You didn't have to be Sigmund Freud to see that I was trying to accomplish in Meuze what Jane and I had failed to accomplish in Gabon. That in some obscure way I was trying to atone for the tragic course of events that followed.

Yvette saw it right away.

— Perhaps you think your family would still be together if you'd stayed home.

— I know this monastery won't bring my son back.

— But it would be a nice place to hide, wouldn't it?

Philippe came out and lit the torches usually reserved for large parties, casting the table in a warm orange glow. The soft lighting took a decade or two off of Yvette's age, giving me a glimpse of the young woman she had once been. I seized her hands across the table.

— What difference does it make whether I bide my time in an old French monastery or in Kandahar or anywhere else? Aren't we all just looking for interesting things to do while we wait around to die?

— That's a uniquely depressing way of looking at things. But realistic, I'll grant you.

She raised her glass, adding:

— I'm not a spiritual person. Life has made me what I am. But you must create some reason for going on, even if it's just the joy of living in the next moment. The writer who said 'no man is an island' was probably right. We're tribal creatures.

— I will find my tribe right here.

— You already have me.

We drank and drank and drank. We laughed and smoked and drank and smoked and wandered back in arms to L'Auberge des Charmes. When it was time for us to go to our respective ends of the hotel she turned toward my room. This time I didn't throw up.

It happened without words, without apology, without promise or pretext. She was three years younger than my mother. I didn't care.

The next day we found an attorney and I arranged a wire transfer for the down payment. I left the following day, flew home to Indiana and put my house on the market.

I meant to call Jane and tell her the news. I meant to visit Maurice's grave as well. But I never got around to it. Maybe I didn't want to admit to either of them what I knew deep in my heart: that the whole idea was hopelessly ridiculous.

20
Rain

Life has the name of life, but in reality it is death.
Heraclitus

I WALKED UP TO the second floor of the guesthouse and found Hank's door ajar. A suitcase was open on his bed.

Hank came out of the bathroom in only a pair of sweatpants. Given that he sometimes went to the gym twice a day, usually during office hours, it was no surprise to see the chiseled, well-proportioned dimensions of his bare chest. What took me aback was the presence of a bright silver hoop piercing his navel.

Reading my thoughts, he glanced down and flicked at it fondly.

— Like it? Chicks friggin' dig it.

— I can imagine.

Finding myself standing at parade rest, I took my hands out from behind my back, but then didn't know what to do with them. I drew the seat out from behind Hank's desk and leaned far back, nearly tumbling.

— You okay, bro?

— I'm fine, just preoccupied.

Bro. The fake fraternity. Did he know—and only pretend to ignore—just how much I disliked him?

It occurred to me that there wasn't a soul left on the project whom I could call a friend. I got on with everyone well enough, but it was more like the relationship of shipwreck survivors in a life raft, bound not by shared values but by common hardship and adversity.

Hank sat on the bed across from me, leaning back on one elbow. He was forty, deeply tanned with close-cropped military hair. He had already e-mailed me the spreadsheets with the status of his machinery grants. I just needed to be on hand to sign documents and attend the occasional meeting while he was on leave.

— Oh, and tomorrow you've got a meeting with the contractor— I forget his name—the guy who's selling us some wheat threshers.

— I'll look at the procurement docs.

— Just be at the meeting. You know how it is when Afghans meet with Afghans. All kinds of deal-making will start going on if you're not there. Bring the contracts guy with you, Karimullah. I trust him.

— Don't you trust your deputy?

— Shit, no.

— I trusted mine.

Hank raised one eyebrow: *And look where that got you.*

— So I hear you've been really shaking things up in Infrastructure.

— I found some phony projects in Maiwand. Phantom workers.

— You've gotta stop thinking you can control things, Hunt. Go with the flow.

— But we're stewards of American treasure. You're a taxpayer. You want to just throw money at these people without accountability?

— As long as the money gets into the economy, our job is done.

— Really? So when we set out to build a reservoir and discover that a warlord instead bribed the contractor to build him a swimming pool, that's okay?

— You're paying the contractor, and he's paying his laborers, and that's the name of the game. You're still keeping those would-be insurgents gainfully employed.

— But these projects are supposed to help the *people*, not just one or two corrupt Afghans who escape detection.

Hank sighed.

— You're missing the point, bro. Either way, the money stays in the Afghan economy. And that's our mission.

— That's *not* our mission.

Hank's last gig had been in contract farming. The organization he'd worked for had been hired by USAID to jump-start the chili pepper industry in Helmand Province. The idea was that if you hired a certain number of dust-bowl farmers to produce nothing but chili peppers, export trade would transform the economy of the region. But no one had asked the local traders if they wanted chili peppers. And as it happened, they didn't. And so the local farmers found themselves with many metric tons of chili peppers and no buyers. USAID finally unloaded the peppers on a local orphanage. The project was quietly disbanded, and what the orphanage did with the peppers was anyone's guess.

Hank leaned back and widened his legs. The knobby curl of his penis strained against the stretched fabric of his sweatpants. The intrusion of this personal detail annoyed me, as though it gave his argument the backing of superior manhood.

— I don't know what kind of vendetta you're on these days, Hunt, but don't poke your nose into my projects. Don't start any friggin' audits.

I laughed falsely.

— You don't have anything to *hide*, do you?

— I mean it, dude. If you start looking for skeletons in the closet, I'll come back and kick your ass.

I blinked at the physical threat. It had never occurred to me that Hank might be concealing a mystery. And now he had practically handed it to me tied in ribbons.

I rose.

— Well, I've got my own troubles to think about.

Hank raised his arms to put on a T-shirt, showing off his ripped torso. As I was walking out, he called back in a relaxed, joking voice:

— Remember, bro. Curiosity killed the cat.

Leaving the guesthouse, I was surprised to see rain streaming from the roof straight as tinsel. The temperature had fallen. It would be damned good sleeping weather tonight.

The downpour seemed to double in intensity as I sprinted through the garden. It was pitch black out. The guards watched from their dry huts, carbines slung over their shoulders, as I picked my way miserably around the puddles, my shirt clinging to my chest.

When I finally reached the training villa I opened the door to my room, switched on the light and stared in amazement. The floor was gleaming with water. The rug had filled like a sponge, giving a loud squish as I took a step inside. I looked up and saw water dimpling the ceiling. The papers on my desk had flattened into a kind of decoupage.

I stripped the bed and found the mattress completely soaked. I let out a loud, irrepressible curse.

In the kitchen I found a few battered pots and pans. I arranged them along the desk and floor and bed, which soon brought a symphony of metallic pops and pings in varying registers. It was like a game of Twister trying to get around them all.

As I was coming back from the kitchen with more pots I encountered Karimullah unlocking his door. Aware that something was amiss, he followed me into my room.

— This is terrible, he said softly, surveying the many containers set out to catch the drips.

— Have you got the same problem in your room?

— No, my room is fine.

— Lucky you, I groaned, positioning a wooden salad bowl under a drip beside my bed.

Karimullah's *shalwar kamiz* was so drenched it had become almost see-through. Ringlets of dark hair were flattened against his forehead as though painted there in glossy black.

As I began to deal with the mess on my desk I felt a hand on my shoulder.

— I am going to change out of these wet clothes. I will have tea ready in fifteen minutes. Come. Forget about all this.

21
The Unhappy Elephant

*The unlike is joined together, and from differences results
the most beautiful harmony.*
Heraclitus

IT WAS LIKE stepping into Ali Baba's cave. Or the court of the
Kandahar Prince.

Thin, ballooning scarves of many colors were draped from a single point in the ceiling, giving the room a soft roseate glow. The bed
was larger than mine and shrouded in mosquito netting so that it
resembled a white grotto. A richly colored rug of deep blues and reds
covered the floor, at the center of which stood the tea things and a tall
hookah. The room smelled of sandalwood incense and body spray.

Karimullah, now in dry clothes, was seated cross-legged on the
rug like a grinning sultan. From a speaker on his desk came the clank
of recorded wind chimes.

— Do you prefer black or green tea?

I sat across from him, crossing my legs with difficulty.

— Whatever you're having.

— Let us have green, he said to himself, lowering two teabags into the steaming pot.

— This is a beautiful rug.

— It is a Kuchi design. Or did you know that?

— I don't know anything about rugs.

— The design is actually a map. See this? It depicts the Kuchis' seasonal migration route between Kandahar and Ghazni. They make that journey twice a year.

I studied the rug.

— Are you a Kuchi?

He shook his head, wearing a benign, tranquil expression. It was amazing the sort of peace the young man imparted without really trying. I remembered the time with the banner. I could almost feel my anxiety subsiding with each passing moment.

— I traveled with a Kuchi tribe long ago. I had an American girlfriend who was doing a story on them. You would like the Kuchis.

— You think so?

Karimullah leaned over the pot and danced the teabags around.

— You feel deeply about people, Mr. Hunter. It is something I noticed about you. The Kuchis are much like that.

He said this so earnestly that I wondered if he was having fun with me. But I hadn't yet gotten past the last thing he'd said.

— You had an American . . . girlfriend?

The pause was unintentional, and I regretted it.

— I had hoped to marry her.

— What happened?

He pondered his words.

— It did not work out. She felt she was too old for me. I could not convince her that she was being absurd. Let me show you a

181

photograph.

Without rising he stumped over to the desk and took down a framed photo. It showed a slightly younger Karimullah standing with a blonde woman in a Panama hat. Their faces were pressed close together and it was impossible not to notice how radiantly happy they were.

I handed it back, nodding appreciatively.

— Did you keep in touch with her?

— No, we lost contact. Would you like sugar in your tea?

— I'm sorry to hear that.

He looked away. The rain on the roof became louder, sounding like pebbles rolling endlessly from a tin pail.

— Such things happen. Sugar?

We had finished the tea and now Karimullah was lighting the coals of the tall water pipe, or as he called it, the *shisha*. I had gone back to my room and changed into my own *shalwar kamiz*, happy for an excuse to wear it. Now I leaned back comfortably with a cushion plumped under one arm. Unconsciously adopting the young man's syntax, I said:

— The rain is beautiful, is it not?

He sighed.

— It is one of the most beautiful sounds.

Wind chimes were still tinkling from his open laptop. We glanced at each other for a moment, long enough that I at last realized what it was that made the boy so attractive: it was his serenity, his repose. With most people a direct stare was enough to bring a flush to my face and cause me to look away. When Karimullah looked at me it was like taking nourishment, the way a leaf must feel under the rays of the sun.

— You've created a unique atmosphere here, I said, hating the avuncular tone that had crept into my voice.

I drew too hard on the hose, causing a minor explosion inside the water pipe. I gagged and spat out the wooden mouthpiece. Karimullah sat up with concern.

— No, it's okay. I haven't used one of these things since college.

— The tobacco is strong. Do not smoke it if you do not enjoy it.

— No, I like it.

I tried again. This time my lungs accepted the heavy smoke with its strange woody taste.

For the first time I felt like I was truly in Afghanistan. The misfortunes that had brought me to this moment—exile to the training villa, the deluge in my room—now seemed almost providential.

Karimullah sipped his tea and said:

— I told you about the American woman. Is there someone special in your life? Or is that an intrusive question?

— There's no one special. Not in a romantic sense. I'm divorced.

Karimullah nodded gravely.

— I am sorry.

— It's okay. We stayed friends. Her name is Jane.

Karimullah seemed to blink away the awkward intimacy. Then I remembered there was an Afghan taboo about men speaking frankly of their wives, or perhaps even ex-wives.

— Did you have children?

I should have anticipated the question, but it caught me off guard.

— Yes, we had a boy.

He accepted this at face value. I didn't elaborate and he didn't ask for more, as though he felt he had delved far enough. I was relieved. The subject of Maurice's death had a tendency to monopolize a conversation and shift everything to a minor chord.

Karimullah took the hose of the *shisha* and stared at it, absorbed in a thought of his own.

— You seemed surprised when I told you about my American girlfriend.

I felt myself reddening. He went on, not looking at me:

— Did Leandro suggest that he and I were perhaps more than just friends?

— Well . . . I know he cares for you very much.

His voice hardened.

— We are not lovers. We have never been lovers. This exists only in his imagination.

I cleared my throat, feeling as uncomfortable with the topic as he did.

— It's none of my business.

— But I want to tell you. I want to tell the world.

For a moment I saw a crack in the young man's calm exterior. His lips were compressed and he stared intently over my head, as if expecting the party in question to materialize behind me.

— Like I said, it's none of my business. Do you have family here?

Karimullah sank back, wrapping his arms around his bent knees.

— Not anymore. I have brothers, but they are nothing to me now. My mother lives in Pakistan, but I rarely speak to her. I am basically alone.

I took a slow draw from the water pipe, enjoying the resiny taste and the sound of the bubbles.

— I'm pretty much alone too. I have some friends in Kabul, but that's about it.

Karimullah's eyes became glassy, as if musing on things far away.

— I had a friend in Kabul. Her name was Marsha Kohn. I wish you could have met her.

— American?

— Yes, a very sweet and . . . unusual woman. She ran an organization that helped Kabul street children. I have never met a woman like
her before or since. It was she who helped me obtain this job.

— Are you still in touch with her?

He lowered his forehead against his knees. When he raised his
head his cheeks were flushed and mottled, his eyes shiny.

— Forgive me, Karimullah said wetly.

I felt a little embarrassed in the face of such undisguised feeling.
Karimullah smiled, his chin quivering.

— She was such a devil. It was from her that I discovered my
great weakness.

— What is that?

— Red wine!

I returned cradling a bottle of Chilean merlot and two glasses.
It wasn't a great wine, though I'd paid dearly for it back in Kabul.
Greedy with anticipation, Karimullah shoved the tea things aside,
then settled on his knees close beside me. His green eyes startled
me with their sudden brightness. I stared a moment too long, then
uncorked the wine.

Karimullah settled back with his elbow on a pillow and I did the
same, our heads close together like conspirators. We clinked glasses.

— Mm, this looks very, very good, Karimullah said, holding out
the glass to admire the wine's crimson gleam.

I looked down at his fingers on the glass. Karimullah wasn't frail,
I realized now. He might be lean, but he had good shoulders, and his
legs and arms were well developed, like those of an athlete.

He held out his glass and said:

— A good friendship is like this wine. It must be respected. Do not take too much from that person, or you will regret it the next day.

— But don't be afraid to partake deeply either.

— My religion says wine is wrong. I am not a scholar, but I find it hard to believe that God would create something so beautiful and then forbid us to touch it. That would be so . . . mean. Perhaps those ideas were put there by man.

Perhaps it was all invented by man, I wanted to say. But now, topping off our glasses, Karimullah abruptly changed the subject.

— I want to say something personal. But please do not be offended.

— You could not offend me if you tried.

— The Afghans call you *khapaa fil.*

— What does that mean?

— The Unhappy Elephant.

I snorted out the wine mid-sip. I sat up, wine dribbling down the front of my shirt. Karimullah rose in alarm.

— I am sorry. I knew you would be offended.

— They call me *what?*

— The elephant is a wise, noble creature. As are you. But you seem to carry a heavy burden.

Karimullah was dabbing at my front with a napkin, but I waved him away, wiping away tears of laughter.

— You are weeping?

— No, no. It's just funny. The Unhappy Elephant. I always wanted to be a character in a children's story.

Karimullah was scanning my face intently.

— I should not have said it.

— I suppose I'm unhappy sometimes. This project, sometimes I feel like I'm in the wrong place.

His eyes slid downward. I could tell there was something more he wanted to say.

— There is . . . a sadness. It clings to you. It follows you like a cloud.

I couldn't tell what he was getting at, but his intuitiveness impressed me. It was as though he could see right through to my dark and miserable core: to the horror itself. But he played along, realizing perhaps that he'd trespassed.

— What is it that saddens you?

I sighed.

— I don't feel like I'm helping anyone. It's ironic. Back in the Peace Corps we didn't get paid jack, but—

— You made a difference.

— In small ways, yes.

— Then make a small difference here.

— I was on the roof today watching the kids in the children's prison. And I was thinking, here we are spending half a billion dollars on seed and fertilizer and building roads and canals, but what the hell are we doing for those forgotten kids?

— The child prisoners, you care about them?

Did I? They were thugs, murderers, thieves. I felt no missionary zeal when it came to those shitheads. But there they were, under the literal shadow of the project, and none of us had given them a second thought.

— I just think it's an example of how we fail on such a huge scale, while on the small scale we don't even try. Have you seen the motto of Global Relief Solutions? *For the world's most vulnerable people, in the world's most hostile environments.* Who could be more vulnerable than a bunch of child convicts? Prime Taliban pickings.

Karimullah stared into his glass, pensive.

— Do something for those prison kids.

— It's not my department.

— It is no one's department, and that is why nothing is done for them. Your problem is you think like an American. You want to do everything on the grand scale or not at all. Just do one small meaningful thing. And when you have accomplished that, do another.

Just then we heard a terrific *whump* coming from next door. We sat up, looking at each other.

— I think it came from your room, Karimullah said, leaping up.

I cautiously opened the door. The pots that I'd set out to collect the dripping rain were full. But what caught my eye was what looked like a pile of snow lying across my bed and desk. I looked up at the ceiling and saw damp concrete where the plaster had given way.

Karimullah approached the bed and ruefully examined a handful of the stuff. Picking his way among the saucepans and bowls, he came to my side and took my elbow.

— Forget about this. Put on your sleeping clothes and come back to my room. You cannot sleep here tonight.

22
Wild Irish Rose

To get everything you want is not a good thing. Disease makes health seem sweet. Hunger leads to the appreciation of being fully fed.
Heraclitus

KARIMULLAH MADE A PALLET for me on the floor, but it was hell on my back. At some point, hearing me twisting and moaning, he insisted that we swap places. It was awkward enough sleeping in the same room with him, much less taking his bed. I had to remind myself that everything Leandro had told me was horseshit. I don't know what I was so worried about. I'm sure I was as much an object of lust to him as a St. Bernard.

I fell asleep to the gentle clatter of wind chimes pouring out of his laptop. When I awoke I glanced over and saw Karimullah on the pallet. The open, unguarded face was beautiful in its simplicity, the closed eyes like twin smiles.

I hurried out to avoid being seen by the maid. As I was dressing I was nagged by a sense of déjà vu. I kept seeing his garishly decorated ceiling with the colorful fabrics. I had the feeling that I'd been there before. And then I realized what it was.

When my son was fourteen, he and his mother used to go to the thrift store. That was their thing. They'd come back with old board games from the seventies, fussy kitchen appliances (a device that would *only* make French toast, another that would *only* make fondue), and clothes by the truckload, whether they fit or not, the main criteria being their comedic value.

One day my son walked in clutching an armload of fancy women's dresses—organdy and taffeta and tulle, the kind that rustle—and carried them out to the garden shed. Jane and I exchanged a look—so now we have *this* to deal with— but we didn't talk about it. That's the kind of family we were: sweep it under the rug.

He had always been a mysterious boy. Sensitive beyond his years. An old soul. A bunch of old-lady dresses wasn't exactly surprising.

The garden shed had recently become his personal hideaway. It was an old clapboard structure with big windows and lead sash weights that danced inside the wall when you opened the window. It leaned about ten degrees to one side and was nearly entirely wrapped in vines.

I'd planned on tearing the thing down, but Maurice loved that damn shed. He swept it out, patched the holes with cardboard and ran a long extension cord from the house. He'd take his portable record player out there and belt out tunes like Barry Manilow's "I Write the Songs." I can still hear his sweet soprano voice, clearly audible from the back patio where Jane and I would drink our sundowners and watch dusk descend upon the garden. He loved being alone. He didn't seem to need anyone, just a place of his own. I didn't dare tear it down.

I couldn't get those ball gowns out of my head. Was my son in there playing dress-up? I was fairly liberal about that sort of thing, but this was my kid. Didn't I have a right to know?

He must have anticipated his old man's curiosity. One weekend a lock appeared on the door, the kind with a three-digit combination, a thousand possibilities. You could run through them all, digit by digit, in about ten minutes. But it didn't take nearly that long. I knew my son too well—666, the little devil. The lock fell open.

I wanted to respect his privacy. I knew what I was doing was wrong. But with a glance back at the house I furtively opened the door.

What I found made me ashamed of myself. He'd cut those old dresses into strips of color and draped them from one corner of the ceiling to the other. At night, with the light on, the room must have been bathed in dazzling color.

He'd contrived a bed out of a stack of old blankets. The old gardening shelves were piled with paperbacks. Covering the walls were photos clipped from magazines. There was nothing unusual in that, until I realized they were all photos of men, the hunks of the day: Backstreet Boys, Hanson, Jason Priestley, River Phoenix. I just took it all in. All over the walls, floor to ceiling: men.

Leonardo DiCaprio, John Stamos, Keanu Reeves.

It was his business, I reminded myself, not mine.

I lay staring at the ceiling, trying to see it through a fourteen-year-old's eyes. I caught a whiff of something pungent, and saw beside my elbow an overfull ashtray. Kools. My son's a menthol man. Better to focus on the cigarettes than the other. His business, not mine.

I was about to go out when I spied on a high shelf the neck of a bottle peeking out from behind a slanting book. Wild Irish Rose.

I screwed off the cap, took a sniff, hoping it was just full of grape juice. I was ready to believe anything.

My son is fourteen, I thought. So he likes a little nip of fortified wine. It could be worse.

I didn't talk to him about it; Jane said we should watch and wait. But I couldn't shake the memory. It was always there, like a subtitle that never changed.

— Dad, can you help me with my algebra?

Wild Irish Rose.

— I'll be out in the shed. Call me when it's time to eat.

Wild Irish Rose.

Parents want to be proud of their children's strengths, but I think I loved Maurice even more for his weakness. I didn't know how he obtained the stuff, and I didn't ask. Kids always find a way. At least he was doing it in a safe place.

As I said, he was a loner. But that's not to say he was unsociable. He was in the Boy Scouts, where he accrued merit badges and ascended to the rank of Life Scout by age fifteen. And then, just shy of Eagle, he dropped out. He was in the school band, where he played the clarinet. He went to marching competitions and whatnot. Again, he rose in the ranks, achieving certificates and medals. His picture was in the local paper. And again, age fifteen, he dropped out. It seemed to be the year of letting go.

The shed marked the beginning of his withdrawal. Soon it was all we could do to coax him out of there, for by now he had pretty much taken up permanent residence. A therapist suggested agoraphobia.

When he was sixteen the clouds parted and we had a glimpse of the old Maurice, the one before the change. A new friend, a kid named Corby, started coming around. Corby was a country boy. He wore ratty jeans, T-shirts that had lost the elastic around the neck, tennis shoes bound in duct tape. He was from somewhere in the South and spoke with an accent. His dad would drop him off in a beat-up station wagon with an NRA sticker on the back window.

I liked Corby. He was polite, had good table manners, always insisted on helping with the dishes. We weren't able to drag much out of him about his family, except that it was just Corby and his father and they lived in a trailer. The father worked in an auto repair shop.

By now Maurice had a TV and VCR in the shed, so there wasn't much reason for them to hang around with us. But Corby always found some pretext to watch movies or eat with us. It was Corby who introduced us all to Yahtzee, explaining the rules in his slow drawl and never failing to congratulate Jane when she made a good roll. He could hardly take his eyes off her.

You got the feeling that this kid had found something he needed in our little family. There was a kind of winsomeness about him, around Jane especially. One night while she was in the kitchen getting dinner ready he came up from behind, put his arms around her and snuggled up close. It wasn't anything crude, more like something a five-year-old might do, or a terminal patient who'd lost all sense of boundaries. Jane just stood there with a wooden spoon suspended over the spaghetti sauce. She wanted to turn and hug him back, but he was sixteen, a tall boy with a preternaturally low voice, "a haunted house of psychosexual conflicts," as she put it.

He spent every weekend with us. It was Yahtzee Fridays, Movie Night on Saturdays and Monopoly on Sunday afternoons. Maurice endured it for his friend, but you know how kids are. The last place they want to be is sitting around a table playing board games with their parents. Corby raved about my potato pancakes. I had to admit, I rather liked the attention. He brought new warmth into our home, galvanized us as a family in a way sometimes only an outsider can do.

One night Jane called me out to the porch, wearing a sly smile. In the evening stillness we could hear them singing. Corby didn't share Maurice's love for Barry Manilow. He was all about The Beatles, and this at a time before The Beatles were cool. Out came my scratchy vinyl records and young voices singing two-part harmony. Corby wasn't much into the benign early Beatles, he was all White Album and *Abbey Road*.

I'm sure they got up to some drinking out there. One night I looked down from my bedroom window and saw Corby leaning against a tree having a piss. Music was blaring from the open door of the shed. He seemed to have a hard time standing upright.

One Sunday morning there was a knock at the door. The man standing there was a little on the scruffy side, holding a battered cap in his hand as though he were the hired help. He was a true prefiguration of what Corby might one day be, same face, same blue eyes framed in a ray of fine wrinkles, his tow-colored hair touched with grey. A calm man, restrained but dangerous.

I invited him inside, but he hemmed and hawed, scraped his stubble—didn't have time, needed to speak to his son. Same slow, patient drawl, but what was picturesque on the boy seemed on the man to hint of darker things.

I went to the shed to wake him. I should have knocked, but the door was ajar so I peeked inside. Empty wine bottles. Spilling ashtrays. And two teen boys spooning in their underwear in an attitude that suggested more than casual friendship. I wasn't exactly surprised.

I quietly closed the door, knowing the shame of boys, then knocked loudly and insouciantly, telling Corby he had a visitor.

A while later the bleary-eyed, just-awakened kid got in the station wagon and his father drove him away. I watched from the front stoop.

A dazed Maurice came running up from behind, pulling on his jeans. The station wagon was packed to the roof with clothes and other junk. Corby stared at us through the passenger window. I raised one hand, but he just looked at me.

We never learned what prompted the father's sudden visit or what the trouble was. But that was the end of Corby. Maurice asked at school and found out that he had been checked out, destination unknown. Their trailer was empty. We thought we might get a call or a postcard, but we never heard from him again.

Maurice's only reaction was a terrible calm. For days a candle burned in the windowsill of the shed, like a beacon for the lost. And then the light in Maurice went out.

23
Lessons Best Learned Young

We can easily forgive a child who is afraid of the dark; the real tragedy of life is when men are afraid of the light.
Plato

JANE AND I HAD never been model parents. We were products of the selfish seventies; we didn't want to lose ourselves in parenting the way our parents had. We gave Maurice freedom to make his own decisions and learn from his own mistakes. Too much rope, you might say.

Keep in mind, we were Peace Corps hippies at heart, even during the years when our careers turned toward teaching—what we referred to as the Decade of Clipped Wings. We had always planned to go back to Africa. Bringing up a kid in Africa is not impossible, just awkward. A moody teen even more so.

We felt a sad nostalgia for our former selves, the ones who'd slept on mud floors and suffered dengue fever and dysentery and malaria. We were heroic. We were saviors of the poor, the malnourished, the underprivileged. It's what we were cut out for. It's what gave our lives meaning.

Maurice didn't remember anything about Gabon. What then did he really know about *us*? He grew up among the bric-a-brac of our former life, a houseful of batiks and African trade beads and gloomy masks. It was part of our shared mythology. Ours, not his.

What do we ever really know about our parents? They exist to meet our needs, adjuncts to pleasure and pain. We may love them or hate them or ignore them, but in the drama of childhood they are supporting actors. They push the plot along and their decisions shape our destiny, for good or ill. But for the most part they are simply part of the surrounding environment, vital but invisible, like oxygen.

That changed for a while during the Corby period. But with the boy's mysterious departure we were treated to a darker reprise of the earlier Maurice. He drew back inside that ramshackle shed. He came indoors for food and provisions, a few clean clothes now and then. We watched him trudge off to school in the morning and come home in the afternoon, crouching under a burden of unhappiness as heavy as his oversized backpack.

Jane tried to talk to him, but I knew this was a wound not to be probed, especially by parents. Just leave him the hell alone, I told her.

— We can't bring Corby back. He misses his friend. Let him grieve.

I sat on the screened back porch with a vodka and cranberry juice, staring at those two oblong windows in the back of the garden. You could almost feel the pain radiating from that corner like heat. It's not that I didn't care. It's not that I lacked the words. I just didn't feel it was my business to meddle.

Looking back, I should have intervened. The alcohol, the smoking. What had happened to our son the clarinet player? The Boy

Scout? Jane thought it was the gay thing. I only hoped that was all it was.

I pitied him in his misery but I didn't try to draw him out. Sometimes friends stick around, sometimes they leave you. But life goes on. These are lessons best learned young.

This was his own private battle. Let him grieve, I told her. Let the boy grieve.

That summer he got a job with a maintenance crew repairing swimming pools. He worked with two guys in their thirties, tough rednecks but decent enough. Bill and Phil would come pick him up early each morning, honking in the driveway. He'd run out there in shorts and a sleeveless work shirt, tanned and fit and as handsome as I'd ever seen him.

Clearly hard work was what the doctor ordered. His thin arms were soon toned, his chest rippling with muscles. His two coworkers gave him the jobs they didn't want, but he didn't care. He filled his days acid-washing pools and digging trenches for electrical conduit while Bill and Phil lounged under a patio umbrella drinking beer.

They'd tease Maurice good-naturedly. He told me how one day at the YWCA they emptied a hamper of girls' gym shorts over his head. They seemed to delight in his innocence, instructing him in the ways of the world, reliving their youthful follies. He ate it up.

It never occurred to me to suspect anything. Why should I? My son had a summer job. He worked on pools with a couple of hard-core good ole boys who wore bandanas and drove a beat-up pickup. He was only sixteen, a bit naïve, but what was the harm in it?

It wasn't long before all the Bill and Phil stories started to make me a little anxious. Was it jealousy? They had captured his interest in a way I no longer could. A boy of four or five will idolize his father.

To a sixteen year old you're just a speed bump on the highway of life.

One night they took him out to shoot pool. He came home stumbling drunk. Bill, he confessed, had pretended to be his father and the bartender had let him drink all he wanted.

I protested, sure. I grounded him for a weekend. But what else are you going to do? You've already taught them all the lessons they're going to learn from you; at that age all the new ones come from experience. My real concern wasn't the drinking, it was keeping him out from under the shadow of darkness. He was happy, and that went a long way.

— I'm just glad to see you getting out and having some fun.

It was after midnight and I'd come out to the shed intending to wax nostalgic about my own checkered adolescence, such as it was. If these guys could be his comrades, why couldn't I?

When I flipped on the lamp he recoiled, drawing up a sheet to hide his nudity, but not before I'd seen the bruises on his chest and legs. When I asked him about them he was noncommittal.

— It's nothing. We were just horsing around.

And then I saw something else. I drew back the sheet and saw a small blue tattoo on his shoulder: two triangles, one wrapped inside the other, formed out of a single bending line.

— What the hell is this?

— Don't worry about it.

— Tell me.

— It's just something I got in town. I thought it looked cool.

— Why didn't I see it before?

— Dunno, Dad. Maybe you weren't paying attention.

This said into the corner of his pillow, eyes closing, a drowsy cherub with beer on his breath. A moment later he was snoring.

I had no idea what the tattoo symbolized, but from its vividness it seemed a recent acquisition. The larger triangle seemed to be coiled protectively around the smaller one. It looked like the emblem for some sort of club.

But it was the bruises that concerned me. I tilted the lamp and turned the sheet down a little. Horsing around? Impact bruises would be randomly spaced, but these were clustered on either side of his torso as though he'd been restrained.

Every parent has a sixth sense for the thing he or she most fears. I couldn't prove it, but I couldn't help thinking that something was going on with those pool guys.

Jane said I was crazy. I laid out the evidence for her, the bruises, the disappearances, the drinking. But I never could win an argument with Jane. I argued from the heart, from the certainty of intuition, while she fired back with cool rationality, as neat and elegant as a thrown dart.

— He drinks with them. They goof around. So what?

And then she turned the tables on me. What was I so worried about? Maybe I was afraid of losing my son to people he found more interesting.

— More interesting? Please. Bart's got a Playboy bunny on his mud flap.

She shrugged, turning back to her crossword.

— Well, I think you're imagining things.

Perhaps, but maybe Maurice was right, maybe I hadn't been paying attention.

24
Welcome to Our World

The object of life is not to be on the side of the majority,
but to avoid finding oneself in the ranks of the insane.
Marcus Aurelius

I ARRIVED AT THE OFFICE early, opened my daily planner and began thinking about the day ahead. I felt refreshed and energetic. My coffee tasted great, and for some reason I didn't feel the usual need to augment it with a morning cigarette.

I glanced at my schedule and saw that I had a meeting that afternoon with the contractor, Nazeem Farah, who would be supplying ALAS with two hundred wheat threshers. With only a vague idea of what a wheat thresher was, I flipped through the badly photocopied pages and was surprised to find it a substantial piece of equipment indeed, standing taller than the smiling Afghan farmer shown shoving a sheaf of wheat down the hopper.

I was glad Karimullah would be attending the meeting. Last night had been fun. We had talked about God and morality and why evil exists in the world—a lot of bullshit, really. But it was interesting. The kid was no dummy.

And yet there was something detached and alien about him. His kindness was too formalized, really a caricature of hospitality. It didn't seem entirely real.

Waheed and the rest of my staff were now taking seats at their workstations. They had all become model employees since Ramatullah's termination. I figured I could count on maybe another week of good behavior before the laziness and lollygagging resumed.

I opened an e-mail from Leandro. *Don't forget our 2 p.m. meeting, hon! P.S. Just got the note about your ceiling. I'll put in a work order.*

I was about to send him a reply when a pop-up balloon told me that another e-mail had come just behind it. It was from Karimullah. We communicated now and then on contract matters, but I sensed this note would be different.

> I did not hear you leave this morning. I had to ask myself, was it a dream? Lovely wine and an enchanting new friend. Would you like to have lunch with me in the Afghan cafeteria? If so, meet me downstairs at 12:15. Otherwise I will see you at the meeting with Nazeem Farah at 14:00.

Rising to stretch, I wiped my hands on my legs, as though they were oily. I felt odd, I wasn't sure why. Not since my college days had I reached such depths with another person so suddenly. This must be what scuba divers feel, rising to the surface after a very deep dive.

How long had it been since I'd found a new friend? Friendship began in darkness and uncertainty, a pulse transmitted into the depths, like sonar. And how beautiful and satisfying when that signal was returned.

* * *

I'd never eaten in the Afghan cafeteria before. Like wearing a *shalwar kamiz*, it was the sort of thing I would have done were it not for the derisive scrutiny of my American colleagues, who viewed interactions with Afghans as more of an occupational hazard than something that might be enjoyed.

I took up a tray and joined the queue, my presence telegraphed down the line of Afghans in nudges and glances. An old man in a dirty apron dumped a mountain of basmati rice on my plate, followed by a ladle full of beans and big hunks of fatty lamb. It smelled glorious. Another guy handed me a bottle of water and I turned to confront the long commissary-style tables where it seemed every Afghan eye was upon me. In the far corner, away from everyone else, I saw Karimullah waving in my direction.

— You made it!

— I wouldn't have missed it.

He smiled broadly, rising to shake my hand. I noted rings under his eyes from our late night and felt weirdly proud to have been the cause of it.

— Welcome to our world. I think you are the first American to eat down here. You do us a great honor. It's like the arrival of the Queen of Sheba.

— Or the Unhappy Elephant.

— Not today. You do not seem unhappy.

— I'm not. It was kind of you to let me sleep in your room.

Even as the words left my mouth I felt like a dork. Karimullah eyed me suspiciously.

— Why would I not have helped you? Do Americans just leave their friends to sleep in the rain? There is no kindness between friends, only respect, love and duty.

— Never mind. Ignore me.

— Kindness is what you show to a dog in the street.

We said nothing for some time. Then I heard him mutter under his breath: *Shit!*

I followed his eyes to Leandro, standing primly in the doorway. He was staring right at us, taking in the situation. He was on the verge of turning back, but then marched toward us, ignoring the whispers of the Afghans to whom this must have seemed like an expat invasion.

He handed me a folded piece of GRS stationery. His voice was all business.

— We didn't see you at lunch. The chief asked me to give you this.

He was standing with his hands in his back pockets, a pose intended to suggest casual indifference. His head was turned completely away from Karimullah, as though the latter were beneath his notice. The space between the three of us was crackling with tension.

Just a reminder about today's meeting with the machinery contractor. I won't be able to join you, but please be on time.
— Cleve.

I slid it under my plate.

— That's fine. Thanks.

— Nothing important, I hope.

Initially reluctant to approach us, Leandro now seemed unwilling to leave, as though asserting his right to stand wherever he goddamn well wanted.

— It's about that meeting this afternoon. Are you coming?

He smiled thinly.

— Of course I'm coming. Karimullah will be there as well to translate.

This said as though of an absent third party. I glanced at Karimullah, whose face was bent toward his plate like a scolded child.

— Well, see you there, he said and marched off.

The Afghans at the other tables watched him go, then the chatter in the room rose perceptibly in volume.

— What's going on with you guys?

Karimullah glanced at me, shook his head minutely but said nothing.

I went down to the conference room a few minutes before the meeting with Nazeem Farah was to begin. I went through the blue contract folder, not quite knowing what I was looking for or what this meeting was supposed to achieve. All I knew was that there was some concern about the contractor's ability to fulfill the order, though his track record seemed favorable.

Leandro was setting out bottles of water and toffee around the long table. He was impeccably dressed in a white Oxford shirt and a blue tie, his shiny black hair so neatly combed that the part seemed to have been made with a ruler. As always, he carried a rich medley of fragrances in his wake—body spray, deodorant and cologne.

I said lightly, trying to loosen things up:

— You okay, Leandro?

— Of course I'm okay, Hunter. Don't you know, I'm a busy, important person.

It was said in jest, but I suspected it revealed more about his convictions than he'd intended to let on. He looked like he needed a friend just then, but what could I say? What did I know about the thwarted desires of homosexuals?

The door creaked open and Karimullah entered with a binder clutched to his chest like a shield. As he began to move toward the place at the table next to me, Leandro said in a schoolmarm's voice:

— No, you'll need to sit on this side, by me, so you can translate. Nazeem Farah will be across from us.

Karimullah meekly obliged, drifting around the table and drawing out the chair beside Leandro's. He offered me only a flicker of a smile.

Side by side, forced to endure each other's company at uncomfortably close range, they looked like boys who'd been called into the principal's office after some playground skirmish. Leandro opened his notebook, lips pursed, scooting his chair microscopically away from the other as though he might be contagious. His neat, professional attire seemed to belittle Karimullah's simple *shalwar kamiz*. I fought an urge to drag the whole thing out into the open and be done with it.

But just then the Afghan receptionist poked his head in.

— Mr. Nazeem Farah, he said, then stood back to admit a stern, bearish Afghan, very dark, with a commanding presence and a plump round belly.

This latter detail automatically gave me a companionable feeling about him. I rose and introduced myself, realizing too late (despite his emphatic nods) that the man spoke not a word of English. I introduced Leandro, who stood imperially at attention, and then Karimullah.

As the man glanced at the seated Karimullah, his face underwent a transformation. Maybe it was Karimullah's piercing, electric eyes. I'd seen others do the same double take.

Karimullah glanced at the man and then down at his empty writing pad. Leandro had to give him a little kick before he stood and offered mumbled greetings, all the while avoiding the man's eyes.

25
Karimullah

Sell your cleverness and buy bewilderment.
Rumi

AFTER THE MEETING WITH Nazeem Farah, Karimullah ran back to the training villa, staring with the fixity that only pure terror can produce. He bolted to the bathroom, wracked with painful diarrhea, as though his insides had turned to hot jelly.

There was no mistaking the fierce eyes, the calloused hands, the proud bearing, the eyebrows that met in the middle. For years Karimullah had tried to forget that face. And there it was again, not softened by age but hardened, like old leather. Who was Nazeem Farah? *This was Obaidullah.*

For forty-five minutes he had tried not to look at that face, translating the proceedings with his head buried in the contract folder until Leandro barked at him to speak up. When he did look into Obaidullah's eyes, the communication he received was as clear as spoken words: *For five years I have hunted for you. You think you're*

safe here, sheltered by the Americans. But your days are numbered, danc-
ing boy.

He ignored Leandro's angry text messages recalling him to the
office. When Hunter Ames came by to check on him, Karimullah
pretended to be more ill than he was. It broke his heart to lie to the
kind American, but there was nothing Hunter could do to help him.
There was nothing anyone could do.

His dreams that night were violent reruns of all the forgotten as-
saults that had taken place under Obaidullah's dark gaze, the farmers,
husbands, businessmen and politicians who'd forced his legs apart,
mashing his cheek against dirty rugs.

At some point in the night he sat up, recalling the plight of his
neighbor. He went next door and found Hunter rolled up in a blanket on the hard box spring of his ruined bed. It was as sad a sight as
he had ever seen. He urged Hunter to come back with him and was
thankful for the warm, snoring presence in the room. Even the whis-
tling farts that surprised him out of sleep were oddly comforting. He
realized how much he cared for this silly, blundering man.

Wanting to take his mind off Obaidullah, Karimullah revisited
the subject of the children's prison. If Hunter showed no interest, he
would help the children himself. Even if nothing was accomplished,
he would be blessed for his good motives, for it is written: *Actions are*
recorded according to intention, and man will be rewarded or punished
accordingly.

Hunter, he was happy to discover, had already been mulling the
idea.

— But what can we do for them? I can't think of anything.

— Let the prison tell you what these children need. They will know better than you.

He had seen this happen so many times on ALAS, canals constructed for farmers who didn't want them, reservoirs built where no reservoir was needed. He couldn't decided if the Americans were arrogant or just so impatient to do good that they forgot to ask.

The prison director was a suspicious man who thought they had come bringing complaints about the boys' bad behavior. They met him in his dank, low-ceilinged office. From the other side of the wall came the sounds of adolescent voices, frenzied from too much time indoors.

Karimullah translated each exchange with great care and only the mildest (and most necessary) of embellishments.

The director said:

— For three years you Americans have lived among us with your loud parties and your noisy generators. When the Taliban attacked, did you worry about us? Did you think of us when body parts were raining down from the sky? Our windows are still shattered from the blast, and winter is coming. Why this sudden interest in our welfare?

Karimullah mulled this carefully, then translated:

— He is grateful for your interest in their welfare and sympathizes with your sufferings from the Taliban attack of several months ago. Because of the advance of winter, he asks that you assist with the replacement of some broken windows so that the training can be conducted in a dry, warm environment.

Hunter nodded eagerly, writing everything down in his sprawling, unreadable hand.

— But what kind of training does he want? How can we help these kids?

Karimullah translated the question, and the director rolled his eyes up to the ceiling.

— These children are hopeless! Half of them are political prisoners who will run to the Taliban the moment they leave this place. The rest are homosexual or retarded. If you point at the sky and say it is blue, they will say no, it is black. They don't even have the initiative to mend their own clothes. Do what you want, but you are wasting your time.

Karimullah translated:

— He says that the children lack hope in their lives and future. Many are in danger of joining the Taliban because of their illiteracy and lack of family support. He says they have no skill in mending their clothes.

He added quietly:

— You know, Hunter, the city is full of tailors in need of assistants. Tailoring would be an ideal skill for these boys.

Hunter was hunched over his notebook now, a groove denting the middle of his forehead.

— Right, we could bring in sewing machines and teach them how to make clothes. Perfect!

Seeing the American's attitude of deep concentration, the prison director now said to Karimullah:

— What is he writing down with such industry?

— I explained to him your desire to bring changes to this prison. He will come back to you with a plan.

— But what about me? I cannot undertake extra work without compensation. It is only fair.

Hunter looked up, pen aloft.

— What's he saying?

— He is amazed by the speed with which you write.

Hunter looked at the pen in his hand. Karimullah continued hesitantly:

— And he suggests that perhaps funds could be set aside for any extra expenses that the prison might incur for this training to take place—unforeseen charges and so forth.

Hunter said under his breath, as though there were any chance of the director understanding him:

— How much extra do you think is fair? Five hundred dollars a month? A thousand?

Karimullah brought his fingertips together, weighing the matter. Like most low government officials, the prison director made very little money and so could best be approached by appealing to his greed. This was that magic moment where any of Karimullah's colleagues would have turned to the director and brokered a deal. *I can get this guy to give you a thousand a month, but you must give me half.*

— I think a hundred dollars would be sufficient.

Hunter tipped his head to one side.

— Really? That's not much.

— In a place like this, it is a great deal.

The director was eyeing Karimullah anxiously, wanting to know the American's decision.

— He will give you fifty dollars a month to spend at your discretion.

The director calculated what this came to in his own currency.

— That's not enough. It should be at least . . . one hundred dollars!

It was precisely what Karimullah knew he would say.

— I will see if he is amenable to that.

Karimullah had listened in on enough of Obaidullah's business deals to know how such matters were conducted. Even if the director had been offered a thousand dollars he would have demanded twice that.

With this thought came the memory of yesterday's meeting with the so-called Nazeem Farah, and Karimullah once again began to feel nauseous with dread.

Back in the office, Karimullah sat quietly at his computer working on a procurement request for a bridge to be constructed in Spin Boldak. Even with his limited knowledge of engineering he knew that the price was inflated, that the contractor had more than doubled the estimate. But none of the Americans cared, so what could he do?

Seated nearby, Leandro was toiling over a document with his chin propped in his hand. Every few minutes his eyes slid languidly in Karimullah's direction. Karimullah's only thought was for Leandro to finish whatever he was doing and get out so that he could inspect the files of the so-called Nazeem Farah.

At last, in the early afternoon, Leandro rose from his desk and closed up his laptop.

— I have a Skype conference I'm going to take in my room. I probably won't be back. I expect you to keep working until five p.m. Is that understood?

Karimullah nodded without looking at him. "Skype conference" was code for a long afternoon nap.

Once he was gone, Karimullah went to the file room, locked the door behind him, took a deep breath to slow the wild beating of his heart, then took down the contract folders for Nazeem Farah, Inc. He had been waiting all day for this.

His first order of business was to find out whether Nazeem Farah, Inc. was a real business. In order for a company to provide services to a USAID project it had to be authenticated with an official business license. Karimullah found a photocopy of the license in the binder. It said that Nazeem Farah Inc. had been in business for nine years "providing a range of agricultural goods such as seed, fertilizer and machinery." All the necessary stamps and signatures were there. Karimullah turned the sheet in his hand. It looked valid enough, though everyone knew how easily such things could be procured on the black market.

Next he looked for a copy of Nazeem Farah's identity card, or *tazkira*. He found it. There was Obaidullah's photo on a document that was pure fiction. Name, address, date of birth, all lies.

It was not such an easy matter to obtain a counterfeit *tazkira*, as the main database was located in the Afghan capital. Of course, anyone could make one using Photoshop, but an attached memo affirmed that Leandro himself had seen the original *tazkira* and vouched for its authenticity.

Karimullah looked up. *Leandro?* When had he met Obaidullah? And why would he have concerned himself with such a trivial matter that was usually left for local staff?

He went through the documents again, and discovered an anomaly. All contract documents at the office were printed on American-size 8½" x 11" paper. The paper was air-freighted from abroad expressly to prevent the sort of tampering that Karimullah was now looking for. As he expected, the *tazkira* for Nazeem Farah had been submitted on standard A4 paper, such as would be found in any Kandahar shop, which meant the copy had not been made in the office. He had simply submitted this forged photocopy to ALAS, which Leandro then accepted as authentic.

Karimullah was surprised to see that the so-called Nazeem Farah, Inc. had done business with the project twice before. Three months earlier, his company had provided five hundred picks and shovels for canal-cleaning projects in Dand District. This was curious. Why would Obaidullah have concerned himself with such a trivial contract? But turning to the next, thicker binder Karimullah saw that the distribution of hand tools was just a good-faith exercise, one meant to demonstrate the ability of Nazeem Farah Inc. to render service. Having proven itself in this small contract, the company had been chosen for a far more lucrative one a few months later.

Karimullah sat down on the floor, carefully going through this larger second contract. In it, Nazeem Farah, Inc. had been contracted to provide 22,000 bags of urea fertilizer for $1.5 million. There was nothing unusual about the contract itself, which Karimullah recognized as a standard-form template. He glanced over the spreadsheets showing deliveries and payments. He saw that Nazeem Farah Inc. had delivered the fertilizer in two parts. First a third of the fertilizer was delivered, the bags had been counted and approved by the warehouse manager and a payment of $544,000 had then been processed, with the remainder to be paid upon fulfillment of the rest of the contract.

Only a few days after delivering 8,000 bags, Nazeem Farah Inc. had submitted an invoice showing that the remaining 14,000 bags of fertilizer had been delivered, valued at $950,000. It was an incredible amount to have been delivered in such a short time. But, sure enough, there was the warehouse clerk's affidavit showing that indeed 21,984 bags of fertilizer had been checked in.

Karimullah had carried many a bag of fertilizer while working on Obaidullah's orchard. He could recall their exact dimensions and how they looked piled in the back of a delivery truck. It had taken two days to unload this second delivery of 14,000 bags of fertilizer. During an eight-hour workday, a bag of fertilizer would have to have been taken off the truck every four seconds, with no breaks. It was theoretically possible, but on purely human terms it was completely unlikely. No matter how many workers were involved, it would take a minimum of fifteen seconds for each worker to be handed a bag, take it to the stack, then return for another. And what about prayer breaks and tea breaks and the general laziness of Afghan workers? No, it was impossible to imagine so much fertilizer being delivered in two days.

Maybe, he thought, the staff had stayed late to complete the deliveries. It wasn't unreasonable that Nazeem Farah, Inc., wanting to fulfill its quota on time, had bribed the ALAS workers to stay on, or had brought additional workers. Karimullah could have looked up the warehouse time sheet records, but he knew this was pointless, as the workers were logged in exactly at eight a.m. and logged out at five p.m. every day, regardless of what hours they really worked, which were usually far less.

That night he lay awake on the pallet listening to Hunter's booming, sonorous snores. He was happy for the company. He had grown used to the American and would have been sad to see him go. Not since Babur had he felt so comfortable with another man.

He wanted to warn Hunter about Obaidullah, but how? Despite the dubious business license and Obaidullah's counterfeit identity card, what proof did he have that Nazeem Farah was involved in corrupt activities? And what business was it of his anyway?

As his eyes began to grow heavy, he saw spreadsheets scrolling down from the dark ceiling. Row after row of urea fertilizer, column after column . . .

He sat up, suddenly wide awake.

— The database.

Hunter's snores terminated on a grunt.

— *Hrnh?*

Karimullah rose from the pallet, changed out of his sleeping clothes and into the *shalwar kamiz* he had worn that day. The dark bulk of Hunter sat up in bed and said in a sleepy voice:

— Where are you going?

Quickly pulling the *kamiz* over his head, Karimullah slipped on his sandals and grabbed his key.

— It is nothing, just a task I forgot to do at the office. Go back to sleep, dear friend.

There must have been drinking and carousing the night before, to judge from Leandro's sallow appearance the following morning. He arrived an hour late, his clothes looking wrinkled and slept in. No doubt he would find some way to make Karimullah suffer for it.

Karimullah made a pot of strong coffee for Leandro, as he did every morning. From his desk he watched as his supervisor downed a cup, black, then poured another one. Karimullah knew better than to approach him in his present mood.

After lunch the color seemed to come back to Leandro's cheeks. At around 2 p.m. he prepared to leave, another "Skype conference."

Karimullah cleared his throat. It was now or never.

— Sir, there is something I must bring to your attention.

Packing up his laptop, Leandro glanced at him sourly.

— What is it?

Karimullah rose, assembling the words in his mind, striving for an approach that would convey firmness without blame.

— I may have found something wrong with the procurement database.

He slid a page across Leandro's desk. The latter glanced down at it with misgivings.

— What is this?

— It is the spreadsheet for the fertilizer contract we concluded with Nazeem Farah, Inc.

— Since when did you start auditing our contracts?

— I was putting together the documents for the two hundred wheat threshers when I noticed a problem with the last procurement. The database seems to have been changed.

Karimullah was standing at attention beside Leandro's desk, hands behind his back. He knew he must present the matter as neutrally as possible so as not to imply Leandro's complicity, though by now he was certain of it.

Leandro sighed indifferently, but Karimullah saw his eyes dart frantically across the page.

— There's nothing wrong with the database. It's the same database we've always used.

— I am sorry, but one of the columns has been removed. Don't you see?

The document lying between them had many columns, one for project code, item description, the number of bags of fertilizer ordered, and so on. The final column showed the actual number of bags that the warehouse clerk had counted off the truck. But one telling column had been removed: nowhere did the spreadsheet record the *value* of the goods received.

In pointing this out to Leandro, Karimullah was careful not to impugn the honesty of either his boss or the warehouse manager. He simply wanted to demonstrate that he was doing his job.

Leandro stared sullenly at the paper, the morning's grimness returning.

— I guess you decided you hadn't hurt me enough, so now you want to wreck my career.

Karimullah was confused.

— This has nothing to do with my relationship with you, sir.

— The hell it doesn't.

— I am simply trying to determine—

Leandro was now staring at him with absurd pathos.

— *Que je souffre*, Leandro whispered.

Leandro always encoded his most ardent feelings in the French language. Karimullah didn't need to ask what he meant. The protruding lower lip and the limpid heaviness of his eyes said enough.

He knew this was the time to be strong, to resist his habit of trying to make others happy. Of course, only one thing would have made Leandro happy, and how easy it would have been to give it to him; he had certainly done it enough times against his will. But it would only feed Leandro's delusion and turn a mild nuisance into a millstone.

— You sicken me, Karimullah whispered, surprising himself as he heard the words he had never dared utter.

Leandro must have read the thoughts behind Karimullah's flaming eyes. He took a quaking breath, stared at him and said quietly:

— I don't understand why you hate me so.

A last, feeble appeal to Karimullah's pity. But the new emotion was speaking for him now as he bent down and whispered close to Leandro's ear:

— Hatred is an emotion of which you are not worthy.

Leandro leapt up, glanced around to see who was in earshot—only Cleve Harbin's secretary, Belourine, who passed through to the chief's office as though she had seen and heard nothing. In a sudden gesture he grasped Karimullah's face in both hands, as though he might kiss him. His fingers pressed down into Karimullah's flesh and he uttered through clenched teeth:

— Why don't you go complain to your new boyfriend!

Karimullah grabbed Leandro by the wrists and after a momentary struggle, freed himself from the vice-like grip. Leandro's expression was deranged, there was no other word for it.

Karimullah knew that anything he said at present would be like a match dropped into a pool of gasoline. Leandro wasn't concerned in the slightest about the manipulated database. He could not see beyond his wounded pride, his unappeased desires.

Karimullah remembered the evening when he'd made the terrible mistake of telling Leandro his story. He could still recall the manic change that came over his supervisor, fueled on one hand by jealousy and on the other by a frantic desire to experience the mystery that so many others had known. He even began undressing, as though the lurid tale had simply been a prelude to sex. It was the only time Karimullah had ever come so close to striking another human in anger.

Thankfully at that moment an outer door closed, footsteps could be heard in the hallway, and the two turned away from each other.

The ALAS warehouse was in District One, some distance from the compound. Karimullah hailed a taxi near the main gate, knowing that it was dangerous to be outside of the compound, but this had to be done.

He found the night watchman crouching beside a small open fire. Karimullah presented his ALAS badge and the guard rolled back the metal door. He began to follow, but Karimullah assured him that he knew the way.

Larger items like seed and fertilizer were usually stored in the back where the corrugated aluminum roof rose several stories in the air. As he strode ahead he became aware of the heavy odor of ammonia and urine, the residual of many thousands of bags of diammonium phosphate and urea fertilizer that had come through the place. But when he reached the pallets where the bags were usually stacked, he saw only powdery dust.

He returned to the watchman.

— Where is all the fertilizer? There should be more than twenty thousand bags back there.

— Yes, some fertilizer came through here not long ago.

— But where did it go?

The old man stroked his stringy beard, weighing the matter. Karimullah figured the man made about six or seven dollars a day. He probably had a wife and nine or ten kids and far more weighty matters to consider than the existence of $1.5 million dollars' worth of fertilizer.

— I believe it was taken to that metal container in back.

Before Karimullah could ask, the watchman began going through a ring of dark, oily keys.

— Shall I take you there?

— Yes, at once.

Karimullah sensed that the mystery was about to deepen. As they walked toward the shadowy bulk of a storage conex, Karimullah knew it was impossible to cram so much fertilizer into such a small space. His curiosity was growing by the moment.

The old guard was enjoying the distraction. He spoke to Karimullah of the things he had seen pass before his gate that day. Karimullah was only half listening to him.

— I counted three carrot trucks coming in from Pakistan. One of the trucks had to stop because children were running alongside it and pulling carrots through the slats.

He went on to recall the days when produce trucks were all going the other way, a glorious processional of Afghan melons and pomegranates, cereals and vegetables, all bound for merchants in Lahore. But no more.

— Ah, what would we do without our Muslim brothers, the Pakistanis.

— The Americans are helping us too.

— *Pfff*, the guard said.

— Without the Americans you would not have a job.

— Without the Americans we would not be at war.

— Would you prefer to see the Taliban in power?

— Ach, those days were not so bad. We had safety and security. You could leave your door unlocked at night.

— You did not mind that your girls had to be kept indoors and were forbidden an education?

He shrugged.

— I have no daughters.

In the end it all came down to self-interest, Karimullah thought, watching the guard sort through his keys and insert one into the lock. The door opened with a rusty cry, and a pungent blast of ammonia greeted them.

— Is this what you wanted to see?

The guard shook life into his flashlight and panned the beam across the neatly packed bags. Karimullah wondered if his eyes were deceiving him. As in some peculiar dream, the bags of fertilizer were just ahead of him, and yet they also seemed small and far away.

He stood on his toes and drew out one of the topmost bags. It was light; he could hold it in just one hand. He read the label. Suddenly all energy drained from his body and he leaned against the doorway for support.

Yes, Obaidullah had delivered the requisite number of bags, only they weren't 50 kg bags at all. They were the 2 kg bags used by housewives and gardeners.

It wasn't the warehouse manager's fault. He had approved them because he had no idea he was supposed to be receiving 50 kg bags. That column had been conveniently removed from the spreadsheet.

Such a simple deception.

Karimullah had come to the end of the riddle. He had found the key that turned the lock on a door he didn't want to open, but now must. Obaidullah would soon receive a wire transfer of nearly a million dollars for fertilizer that was not worth one-tenth of that. And there was only one person who could have helped him get away with it.

26
Crimes of the Offenders

All cruelty springs from weakness.
Seneca

I SPENT MOST OF THE next few days in meetings with USAID explaining my project cancellations. Voices were raised. There were threats. How had I allowed things to come to such a pass? Didn't I know what was going on in my districts?

They didn't want to hear about rogue employees, and they certainly didn't want to hear any criticism of our partners in the Afghan government. I scrawled diagrams on the squeaky whiteboard to show where money was leaking from the project.

— If a man is bleeding to death, you don't treat him by pumping him full of more blood, do you?

— Then stop the leaks, Ames.

— Am I empowered to fire Governor Wazir? Shall I start arresting village elders?

Returning to my room that afternoon I was greeted by the cheerful smell of fresh paint. The ceiling repairs had been completed, and the peeling walls had been scraped and repainted—pink from the waist up, grey down to the floor. And a new bed had appeared, the mattresses still wrapped in plastic.

I lay down, sweaty and tired, going through all the things I wish I'd said that morning. I was nearly asleep when my cell phone rang. I saw Karimullah's name—misspelled as KARMULLIAH.

— Were you napping?

I sat up.

— Almost. How are you, buddy?

— You asked me to tell you when the sewing equipment arrived at the prison. Well, it is there. The sewing machines have all been unloaded.

— That's great.

— The child inmates are very excited.

— I'll be right over. Will you meet me there?

Karimullah laughed.

— Do you think I would let you go into that den of lions by yourself?

Karimullah was waiting for me outside the prison, squatting with some old men who were sharing a pot of tea. When he arose, smooth-faced and smiling, the comparison he made to those wrinkled greybeards struck me as a kind of foreshadowing of the old man Karimullah would be in fifty or sixty years—one that I myself would not be around to witness.

He knocked at the blue metal gate of the prison. In a moment a small rusted-out hole was suddenly filled with a human eye. The bolt was withdrawn and the gate creaked open.

The prison director was waiting for us in his office fingering a set of red prayer beads. He shook my hand absently and muttered something to Karimullah, who leaned toward me and said:

— It has been a busy morning. One boy tried to escape while the sewing machines were being brought in.

— Did he make it?

— No, he was apprehended before he crossed the Zone Three gate. He has been confined.

— I'm sorry to hear it.

One of the child prisoners entered the room with a platter of steamy cups, like a bedraggled waiter. Taking one, I glanced up at a chalkboard over the director's desk. It contained a long column of Pashto words, with a tally beside each, as on a baseball scoreboard. I asked Karimullah what it said.

— These are the crimes of the child offenders.

— Read them to me.

Karimullah found some of the words hard to translate: homicide, theft, kidnapping, arson, sodomy . . .

As I started to laugh, he asked:

— Did I mistranslate?

— I'll bet those kids learn more about some things *in* prison than out of it.

— Sorry, I do not understand.

The prison director was nudging Karimullah for a translation. Changing the subject, I asked to inspect the sewing machines.

We followed the director down a cave-like passage. I had to bend to pass through a low doorway, feeling Karimullah's hand on my crown like a cop hustling a suspect into a squad car.

We entered the muddy courtyard that I had seen so many times from the office roof. There was the brick wall that the prison shared with our building. A concrete patio led into the dormitory where the prisoners slept. And there they were, squatting on a dusty red rug, a couple dozen boys watching my every move. They looked more like orphans than prisoners, with none of the swagger I'd seen before. At close range they seemed forlorn, hopeless, ready to grab the first lifeline thrown their way.

Nearby stood the sewing machines on their lacquered wooden stands. As I drew closer, the boys edged away to let me examine the machines. They were black and shiny and quaintly old-fashioned, powered by a hand crank like something from my grandmother's time. On the base was a metallic sticker with the imperative branding of USAID—*From the American People.*

I read those words that I had seen so many times before and felt a lump in my throat. I imagined these machines loudly alive, each manned by a little fellow intently pushing a strip of collar or sleeve under the needle.

I thought of the sweat and toil of the American people who'd made this small gift possible. It was easy to imagine their approval. The other projects, maybe not—all those expensive tractors that would be stolen by government agents, all those tons of seed and fertilizer that might never make it into the soil, the corrupt work projects that benefited village power brokers and scumbags like Ramatullah. But this was different. No warlords would stand to profit. It was simple, tangible training, and its impact could be monitored and tracked as these kids went back into the world.

What could be expected from an investment of six thousand dollars? Not a lot, even here. But if it changed the life of just one kid, who could call it a failure?

I asked:

— Where is all the fabric?

226

Karimullah spoke to the director who now approached us.

— It is locked up. It seems some miscreant already stole some.

— Tell him we can get more, not to worry.

And then I extended my hand and looked into the worn, bearded face, holding contact with the man's eyes.

— Thank you for the interest you have taken in the welfare of your prisoners. A great change will come to the lives of these boys because of your efforts, and you will be remembered by them for years to come.

Karimullah offered a translation that seemed much longer than the original, no doubt padded with platitudes and honorifics. The director, still clutching my hand, looked at me wryly. Then a gleam came into his eyes and he began to nod.

Karimullah said:

— Is there anything else you would like to see?

The boys were staring up at me with their mouths open. I reached down to tousle one's hair but he jumped as though I were going to strike him.

— We'll come back once the training has started, see how they like it.

We were walking back toward the low wooden door when I saw what looked like a large pet carrier. Fingers were clutching the metal slats, and inside I glimpsed a face bent awkwardly up toward the light.

— There's a child in that cage, I said to myself, moving in that direction. Karimullah drew me back.

— This is the boy who stole the fabric. He is being punished.

The director was gesturing impatiently for a translation. Karimullah said in a low, confidential voice.

— Do not pass judgment on the things you see here.

— There is a *human being* inside that cage!

It was too small for the boy to sit up, so he was lying on his side, his body bent double. I caught a smell of excrement. There was no telling how long he'd been in there.

Karimullah pulled me away before I could see more.

— They practice the old ways here. There is nothing you can do.

I hissed:

— It's an outrage! Let me talk to—

— We should go, Karimullah said, turning me toward the exit.

— Please give the director my *best* wishes, I spat.

— Just walk, Hunter. Walk away.

27

The Coward's Form of Suicide

Courage is knowing what not to fear.
Plato

THAT EVENING THE COMPOUND was on high alert. Afghan National Police had discovered a cache of AK-47s and shoulder-fired rockets at the Red Mosque, along with several dozen fake army uniforms. In reviewing the security tapes for the past twenty-four hours a vehicle was seen repeatedly driving past the compound, clearly with mischievous intent.

Dusty, our security manager, a square-jawed ex-military officer, informed us at dinner that rooftop gatherings were to be suspended for the next forty-eight hours. My colleagues looked down at their plates and groaned. I didn't care one way or the other.

Cleve Harbin cleared his throat dryly.

— Any idea what the bad guys were up to, Dusty?

— All indications suggest they were planning a raid.

— On us?

— That's the most likely scenario, sir. With the fake uniforms they would have been able to bully their way through the front gate. After that, anything is possible.

Miso, our communications director, was sitting next to me, daintily picking at a salad. Her hair was tied in back with a rubber band, a swath of which fell in front of her face. I had always thought we should be friends, though we could never seem to move beyond the professional. She kept to herself, and judging from the time stamp on her e-mails she put in an incredibly long workday.

— Should we be worried? she now said in a tiny voice.

— It seems to be under control, but we need to take precautions.

He added that only essential movements would be conducted outside of Zone One.

There was a murmur along the table. Then Faith Woodson said:

— Where does that leave *him*?

She indicated me. The expression on Dusty's face left me in no doubt that my exile in Zone Two had been completely forgotten by project security.

— Right. I'll need to look into that. Hunter, we may need to move you into the guesthouse for a while.

Everyone turned in my direction. Faith, who had seen this coming, was clearly delighting in the awkwardness of the situation.

— All the spare rooms are taken. But I guess he could always pitch a cot on the roof. He seems to like that.

I'd seen her turn openly hostile toward her former swains, so this didn't surprise me. It was the flip side of her unpredictable personality; she was so pretty and charming when you indulged her, but what a bitch she could be when scorned. How long would it be before she leaked what she had found out about me online?

I said through a mouthful of salad:

— I'm staying in the training villa. I'm not sleeping on any damn cot.

Dusty wasn't sure whether this was a joke or a challenge.

— Well, I'll get back to you about that. Keep your cell phone on.

— And what about Karimullah? Did anyone think about him? If I'm in some kind of danger, he is too.

Dusty clearly had no idea who I was talking about. And then, farther down the table, Leandro muttered:

— He's an Afghan, he'll be fine.

I leaned over the table.

— He's a human being, just like we are. What's wrong with you people anyway? These folks risk their lives working for us. They're in *much* greater danger than we are. And you don't even give them a second thought!

Leandro touched his napkin to the corner of his mouth, leaning over the table so he could see me.

— Your devotion to the Afghans is touching, Hunter. I didn't know you and Karimullah were so … close.

Dusty said:

— Afghan nationals fall under a different set of rules.

This was too much. I dropped my fork onto my plate with an angry clatter.

— So are their lives less important? Is their blood less red? Is their pain less real?

Dusty was a good guy. We'd always gotten along. But he didn't like being painted into a corner. And like most of the security guys, abstract ethics wasn't his strong suit.

I turned to Cleve Harbin:

— Don't you have an opinion, *Daddy*?

The old man shot me a look. Only Faith had ever been brave

enough to call him that to his face.

— None whatsoever. As far as I'm concerned this is Dusty's business, and we need to submit to his instruction.

I was no one to pontificate on the treatment of our local nationals, having never been very fond of them as a group. But Karimullah wasn't a group, he was an individual, and I cared about him. How long had it been since I'd had cause to feel protective toward anyone? It was weirdly intoxicating.

Outside, lighting a cigarette, staring out at the garden in the fading light, I heard the door open behind me. I knew from the sigh and the slow shuffle that it was Leandro. I didn't turn around.

— So, are you getting some of that? I hear it's pretty good.

I looked at my cigarette. And then it dawned on me what he meant.

— You'd better walk away, son. Right now.

— You know he's a professional, don't you? He has *years* of experience. That ass has seen more action than the toilet of a Greyhound bus terminal.

It was an odd confrontation. I knew I should turn around, but I was afraid of what I might do to him if I looked into his eyes. And yet the accusation intrigued me, I couldn't deny it.

— I don't know what's going on with you boys, and I really don't care. But *you* need to start acting like a professional.

I could feel him drawing closer. When he spoke, his voice was right behind me.

— Enjoy him while you can, hon. He's not going to be around here for much longer.

No sooner had I returned to my room in the training villa than Dusty's warning was reinforced by an explosion out on the main road. The traditional fighting season would soon be drawing to a close as cold weather drove the insurgents to cover, and the Taliban could always be counted on for a dazzling season finale.

Karimullah knocked and stuck his head in.

— Wow, did you hear that?

— That one was too close for comfort.

— Do you want some company? I do not feel like being alone.

He went back for the *shisha* while I poured the wine. I debated whether to tell him about the incident with Leandro, and realized it would just poison the evening.

We set the contraption on a chair at the head of the bed and lay facing each other with our heads propped on our elbows. Karimullah was washing his clothes that evening and wore gym shorts and a bright white tank top that brought out the caramel richness of his skin.

I had been going through photos of the monastery, and now Karimullah drew my laptop toward him and began clicking through them. I watched his face transit through a variety of emotions: surprise, pleasure, amusement . . .

The thought of the old monastery suddenly gave me a leaden feeling. It was a commitment, for one thing (Jane used to say it was hard for me to commit to green bananas). And it was a commitment that would consume a huge chunk of my savings.

I thought of my last conversation with Yvette Roche. It didn't re-awaken the spell, what I thought of as the Magic of Meuze. The place felt weirdly alien to me now, as though I'd only seen it in a movie. What had I been thinking? Such total isolation—it was the coward's form of suicide.

I thought back on the sexual episode with Yvette, which neither of us had mentioned since. A cynical thought crossed my mind: the old cougar probably thought she'd scored a steady boyfriend.

— I don't understand what is in these photos. Was it a suicide attack?

I laughed heartily and closed the laptop.

— No, it's just an old property I found it in France. I thought I was going to buy it, but now I'm not so sure.

Karimullah nodded, but his mind was clearly elsewhere. For days I had sensed that something was wrong with my friend. He seemed cagey and evasive, his smiles forced. I missed the old spontaneity that would send him running into my room on any pretext, sometimes just for a hug. No doubt it had something to do with Leandro.

I took a hit on the water pipe, the cherry smoke filling my lungs. I released it over my shoulder through puckered lips to avoid blowing smoke at him. He laughed and said:

— That is a funny face.

— What is?

— When you let out the smoke. It is cute. *You're* cute, Hunter.

Sitting up, and not letting myself cross-examine what I was about to do, I took Karimullah's hand in my own, holding it as if I was about to give the nails a good manicure.

— Tell me what's been going on with you. Is something wrong?

Karimullah stared at our hands, his smile vanishing.

— Things are not good in my department.

I was filled with a sudden, smoldering rage.

— You don't have to put up with him, Karimullah. There are rules. You should go to HR.

— I would never try to get Leandro in trouble. And besides, do you think Faith Woodson is going to take my side?

— Leandro is taking advantage of his authority and putting you in an uncomfortable situation.

Karimullah frowned.

— There is more to it than that.

He took a breath, adding:

— I really cannot talk about it.

I gave the hand a squeeze and let it go, taking up the hose of the *shisha*. I wasn't going to push him.

In a moment he said:

— What do you do when you know something that could cost the job of people you work with? Do you report it, even though it would be of no particular benefit to yourself?

I let the smoke fill my lungs, listening to the water popping and gurgling in the bowl of the pipe. I held my breath a moment, feeling my face redden, then let the smoke out over my shoulder in the manner that Karimullah had found so endearing. This time he didn't smile.

— That depends on the scale of the offence. Have you uncovered some corruption?

— I think so.

— Can you say who it is? One of your associates, like Zahir? Or Ahmed?

— I really cannot say.

— How bad is it?

— Very bad. A million and a half dollars.

I sat up.

— *What?*

— I found a … discrepancy.

— And you think Leandro was involved?

— It could not have happened without his complicity.

— Jesus, a million and a half dollars? Has the payment gone through?

— It will go out tomorrow.

— Which department? Was it mine?

— No, not yours. Oh, I want to tell you, Hunter. Truly. But the matter is … complicated.

I felt a stab of resentment, as though I had been denied some presumed benefit of our friendship. Didn't he know he could trust me? My egotism subsided when I saw that Karimullah's face had darkened, blood rising to his cheeks in patches.

— There is a contractor providing goods to the project. He is someone I know to be a very dishonorable person.

— How do you know him?

— It is too long a story. But he saw me in the office, and I know that he means to do me harm if I impede the transaction.

— I can't help you if you don't tell me.

— Everyone has one truly shameful secret, and this is mine.

— If this person did something to you without your consent, you have nothing to be ashamed of.

Karimullah took a sip of wine, paused to reflect, then downed the glass without tasting it.

— In part it was my fault. I was vain in my youth.

— I doubt that.

— It is true. I should have stopped it right away, but something within me believed that if I endured the cruel treatment it might one day lead to fame and fortune. Castles in the sky.

— I don't know that much about you, but I believe you're a good person with the best of intentions for yourself and for others. I believe you have love in your heart and a kind soul.

Seeing Karimullah's lips begin to tremble, I went on more fervently:

— I care about you, kid. Knowing you has been like opening the curtains in a cold, dusty room. I want you to trust me, to accept me as a true friend.

Karimullah recovered his composure, his face becoming almost statuesque. He nodded slightly, his eyes lusterless and dead.

— I do trust you, Hunter. I would trust you with my life. Perhaps it is only fitting that I trust you with my story.

— Only if you feel comfortable.

— Let us put away the *shisha* and get ready for bed. May I sleep on the floor beside you?

I patted the bed.

— That's silly. There's room enough for you here.

— I will return in a moment with my pallet. Turn the light out, please. I would prefer that you heard this in darkness. It is shameful. There are parts that may shock you.

Had it not been for the dawn call to prayer, floating in on bands of morning sunlight that bled through a part in the drapes, we might have gone on talking right up to breakfast. Karimullah lay on the pallet with his hands clasped under his head. I was hugging the edge of the bed and staring down at him, seeing him but not seeing him, the way as a kid I used to stare at a radio during the *CBS Radio Mystery Theatre*.

He drew up the sheet and turned on his side, intending, as he had so many times already, to go to sleep. The bottle of wine, still half full, stood nearby. We hadn't needed it. Sometimes alcohol can put wheels under a conversation, but the past night had called for cool sobriety.

He whispered:

— Are you awake?

We exchanged a sleepy smile.

— You're amazing, kid. My father drank, my mother was a

237

depressive, I thought that qualified me for a shitty childhood.

— Children should not have to suffer.

I yawned.

— I don't know, maybe they should, just a little. You have to eat a peck of dirt before you die.

— But it should not be forced down your throat.

In light of the incidents we had been discussing, the sexual connotation brought an awkward turning and shuffling of feet.

— You're right. I don't mean to belittle your suffering. If I could go back in time I would burn Obaidullah's orchard to the ground, grab that sad little dancer and bring him someplace safe. All a person can do is try to make the best of it. Either that or let it destroy you.

The call to prayer had stopped and I could hear Karimullah breathing through his nose. I heard the light pop of his stuck lips as he said:

— I suppose these things do not make any sense to an American.

They made more sense than I could have possibly explained. Throughout Karimullah's long tale I began drawing the obvious parallels to Maurice. There was a crucial difference, of course: one boy had suffered against his will, the other seemed to have invited it. But what did I know? I'd never had a conversation with my son like the one I'd had this night. He'd offered me only the tiniest, blurriest insight into his sad past, as stubbornly puzzling and grainy as an image taken with a pinhole camera. Karimullah, on the other hand, had simply thrown back the drapes.

There was nothing more I would ever know about Maurice. The files were closed, the case notes written, the boxes in dusty storage. But Karimullah had given me a lot to think about concerning my own complicity. Why had I stood idly by when I knew something was wrong, especially at the end?

The light in the room seemed brighter. Down the hall I heard the clunk and wobble of the maid dropping a pail. Karimullah's words were so soft I scarcely heard him.

— I think I really am falling asleep now.

I've been asleep for too long, I wanted to say, still hugging the side of the bed, watching the rise and fall of his thin blanket.

Far too long, I thought. *But I'm waking up.*

28
The Beauty of the World

What is a friend? A single soul dwelling in two bodies.
Aristotle

THE TAILORING CLASS WAS held outdoors to take advantage of the cooler weather. Twenty boys sat in a circle on the frayed red rug where they took their meals. Each held an embroidery hoop in one hand while carefully drawing a needle in and out of stretched fabric to learn basic stitches.

The instructor, Tulai, walked among them surveying their work. He was a young man with a full Amish-like beard running along the underside of his jaw. Of the six tailoring teachers I had interviewed, Tulai's quiet intelligence had singled him out. Spotting us, he raised one arm in greeting and came over.

— They are very receptive boys. And because this keeps them out of trouble, the director is most grateful.

I got out my camera.

— I'd like to take some photos if it wouldn't disturb your class.

— Go right ahead. We are learning the fundamentals of hand stitching. Next we will practice making hems.

— Can't you do the hems on the machines?

Tulai nodded like a wise man enduring a well-worn riddle.

— The skill must be learned before it can be imitated. This is Kandahar. Machines break down.

I stood at the front of the group, trying to frame the boys in the jumpy display of my camera. I decided to come down to their level, but as I squatted I fell forward on my knees, snapping a picture of the rug.

The boy closest to me erupted in laughter. He looked to be about thirteen. He had short dark hair with jagged bangs and pale skin that looked almost Caucasian. I took some shots at close range showing his young hands at work. I knew that some of these photos were going to come out damned good, and it inspired me to take even more. I couldn't help but wonder what he was in for, and where he would go when he was eventually released back into Afghan society.

In a moment Karimullah came up behind me and touched my shoulder.

— You sit with them and I will take your picture.

I surrendered the camera and saw the boy with the jagged bangs looking at me hopefully. Still on my knees, I moved to his side and felt him sink back as into a plump easy chair. I put my chin on the boy's shoulder just as the camera beeped. I had the sensation of my heart filling and breaking in the same instant.

Karimullah looked up from the viewfinder, tilting his head to one side.

— How nice. You look like father and son.

It was odd, but the kid *did* look a bit like Maurice. And as this realization sank in I suddenly wanted to get away from him.

Another boy got to his feet and came around behind me, peering around my thick neck as though a second head had sprouted there. Others put down their work, surrounding me like petals on a flower.

As Karimullah framed the photo, I felt a hand pinch my ear. I turned, staring into a grinning face. It was the kid who looked like Maurice. He laughed, emitting breath so foul I had to turn away.

When the boys were back at work, I leaned toward Karimullah.

— What do you think that one is in here for?

— I will ask.

He turned and spoke with the instructor.

— His name is Hamid. He is a thief.

— What did he do?

— He broke into a bakery and stole bread, he and his three brothers.

Karimullah spoke again to the instructor and added:

— He was stealing bread for his family. The brothers were not found. And because he would not inform on them, he must now serve their punishment as well.

I stared at him in disbelief.

— You can't make someone serve someone else's sentence.

Karimullah sighed, weary of these endless intrusions into things I would never comprehend.

— These are the old ways, Hunter. Do not think you can change them.

I excused myself for a piss, more to see the condition of the outhouse than anything else. It was every bit as ghastly as I'd expected, the walls black with dampness and mold. The smell was so bad I had to hold my breath, willing myself not to look down into the shit-caked hole.

When I came out again I was remembering the cage where the kid had been kept in solitary confinement a few days ago. It was gone, but as I neared the group on the patio I saw a sulking figure standing off by himself, his wrists tied with rope. He was older than the others, probably around seventeen.

I took Tulai aside.

— That's the kid, isn't it? The one who tried to escape?

The sun was now perched above the far wall and Tulai raised his hand to shield his eyes.

— Yes, he was released from solitary confinement yesterday.

— Find a place for him.

— In the class?

— If he's interested, make room for him.

— I do not recommend that, sir. He is a political prisoner. His only desire is to escape so that he can rejoin the Taliban.

— What's his name?

We approached the boy, who became suddenly cagey and fearful, his eyes darting back and forth between us as though we meant him harm. Tulai questioned him in a stern voice, then said to me:

— His name is Alaamzeb.

I extended my hand. The boy only stared at it. His eyes were luminously white against all the dirt and bruises. There was intelligence in his eyes, this much I was sure of, though whether for goodness or mischief, who could say.

In a moment his hand came tentatively forward and grasped mine with surprising firmness.

— This is the sort of kid we need to be reaching out to, Tulai. Put him in the class.

Karimullah leaned toward me and said:

— Alaamzeb is an unusual name.

— What does it mean?

— It is difficult to translate. *Alaam* is world, *zeb* means beauty.

— Alaamzeb. The beauty of the world?

— Yes. But I am afraid he will not find much beauty in this world.

— You had a hard life, but you found beauty, didn't you? Life is what we make of it.

Karimullah was quiet for a moment, then turned his face up to mine.

— You are right, my friend. There is a beautiful world out there, for Alaamzeb and for all of us.

I thought of our long conversation of the night before and felt myself blush with shame. *Life is what we make of it.* Such an easy, trivial thing to say.

Karimullah thought we should go back to the office and watch from the roof, maybe take some more photos.

It was one of those oddly clear late afternoons in which Kandahar's rooftops, domes and minarets had an almost ethereal clarity. The sky was radiating bands of pink and gold behind the Arghandab hills. A few sad little paper kites were whirling and tumbling in the breeze.

— Hunter, how do you do it?

— Do what?

— I was thinking about this while we were at the prison. You are a prisoner too. Do you not get a little crazy, stuck in this compound all the time?

— I never really think about it.

— There are places in Kandahar I could show you if you were free. Such lovely places.

— I would like nothing more. But it's just not possible.

— No, I suppose it is not.

I sighed.

— It's fun to imagine the places we might go.

Karimullah turned to me, smiling wickedly.

— We can do more than imagine. Come with me.

Leaving the office, we began walking in the direction of the training villa, past the handful of residences that shared this part of the street. Karimullah slowed, eyeing the guards ahead at the main gate. He stepped into the recess of a doorway and pulled me in with him, tapping on a steel door. In a while a slat shot open and I looked up to see a pair of eyes watching us.

— We must wait a moment so that the women can be sent to the private part of the house.

I felt a pleasant surge of adrenaline, wondering what in the hell he was up to.

In a moment the gate opened with a cat-like squeal and Karimullah led me inside. It was the garden courtyard of a simple two-story house. A sidewalk led up between two rectangular plots of grass lined with rosebushes exploding with color. A blanket was laid out on the grass and it was apparent that the family had been enjoying the cool of the afternoon before our arrival had sent them scattering.

A plump man with a flaming red beard came down the steps of the house, smiling warmly at Karimullah. I shook the man's hand and Karimullah said:

— Meet my friend, Muhammad Ali.

I looked into the man's eyes, trying not to laugh, thinking: *he floats like a butterfly, stings like a bee.*

— It's nice to meet you, Mr. Ali. I'm sorry if we've disturbed you and your family.

As Karimullah translated this, the man frowned, flinging his hands in the air as though disavowing his family's existence.

A boy came out of the house with tea things on a tray. We followed him onto the grass. Karimullah and Ali spoke for some time and I heard my name repeated, which Karimullah pronounced in Pashto as *Ontah*.

Muhammad Ali was probably around my age. To judge from the gleaming Land Cruiser parked nearby he was probably of the professional class, perhaps a doctor. As he spoke to Karimullah his hand could not stop reaching out to stroke the young man's arm.

— He says that in all these years he has wanted to meet one of his American neighbors. He thanks you for rewarding his patience.

— It's my pleasure. How do you two know each other?

I found it difficult to take my eyes off the hand stroking Karimullah's arm.

— It is a funny story. I was coming out of the main gate one night on my motorbike when he was coming in. We nearly had an accident. I fell off my bike and he brought me inside.

— I didn't know you had a motorbike.

I wondered what other secrets Karimullah was keeping.

— Over there.

It was parked under the shade of a tree. It was blue and rather small, not more than 150cc, and covered in dust.

— Mr. Ali lets me park it here for safekeeping. He still feels guilty for almost hitting me at the gate.

I sipped my tea while the two friends spoke at length. I was starting to feel querulous and edgy. Karimullah's hand on my arm startled me.

— Come, I want to show you something. This is the real reason I brought you here.

Karimullah sat up, righting his trousers, and gave me a hand up.

I followed him behind the house where the Ali family laundry was hanging from long drooping lines. Karimullah brushed back a damp sheet as though it were a curtain, giving the moment significance. But there was nothing on the other side but a blue metal door set into the wall.

— Are you ready?

Karimullah unbolted the door. It was stuck and he had to pull with both hands. It opened onto a bustling side street. Produce merchants were shouting their prices from ancient carts and from dark stalls. Women in blue burkas appraised produce, haggling with the vendors. It was the beating heart of the city, and I needed but step across the threshold to become one with it.

I stepped forward, arousing the curiosity of a group of men in turbans who were reclining under the shade of a wall. I raised my hand in greeting. The men looked at each other. One started to rise.

Karimullah saw this and drew me back inside. He closed the door and slammed the bolt home.

— I just wanted you to see it. I wanted you to know that it was there.

For two years I had lived in a bubble, insulated from the day-to-day reality of a city I knew only from the windows of armored Land Cruisers. I hadn't known until then how badly I'd wanted to remove those barriers, pierce the membrane and step into this gritty, dangerous city. Yes, it was here all along, and yet it might as well have been a movie set.

Karimullah led me back into the garden.

— I know you must abide by the project rules, but one day perhaps we can take a walk together in the city. Of course, we would have to be careful. I would not want anything to happen to you.

I said quietly, almost to myself:

— That doesn't matter.

He glanced back at me.

— What do you mean? Of course it matters.

— I don't know. Sometimes I think we put too great a price on preserving our existence. You live, you die. It's the circle of life. What's so important about me?

My words trailed off, and he gave me only a quizzical backward glance. I hoped he would change the subject. It was a mistake dragging this sweet kid into my existential darkness.

As we reached the picnic blanket he poured some tea and said:

— Of course, you could go in disguise.

I laughed, pointing at my face.

— How are you going to disguise this American mug?

Karimullah pretended to consider the question, though I had the feeling he'd gone through the scenario already.

— The most obvious way is to cover you with a burka.

— Ha, you know where we can find one big enough?

He smiled.

— I know some young tailoring students who might be persuaded to make one for you.

I watched him sip his tea, holding the bottom of the hot glass with the tips of his fingers. I drank mine straight down, wanting the caffeine more than the flavor. I was still reeling a little, not just from lack of sleep but from the sudden depth our rapport had taken the night before.

He had entrusted me with his life story, opened a window onto a world I never could have imagined, awakened feelings that I didn't know what to do with. Obaidullah's crimes were not mine to avenge, and yet I badly wanted another meeting with that bastard.

Parts of his story had returned to me throughout the day, like scenes from a long movie. The fatherless boy hustling tea in the bazaar, sold by his brother into indentured servitude. I recalled his season with the Kuchis, his struggles in Kabul. Those two iconic ladies, Marsha and Penny. And all those nameless, faceless abusers. There was no telling what sort of horrors he'd endured. I wondered if he had ever been tested for HIV.

I would help him. Somehow, some way.

I knew the risk I was taking, emotionally and otherwise.

I'd lost one son already. There was nothing I could do about that. But *this* one wouldn't get away.

29
The Adirondack Principle

There is truth in wine and children.
Plato

MAURICE QUIT HIS JOB at the pool company. Just like that. He stormed through the house tearing the embroidered name patch off his work shirt. The phone rang that night, one of his colleagues, Bill or Phil, I never could tell them apart. He wouldn't take the call.

He took a job counseling teens at a religious summer camp in Wisconsin. He said I'd written him a reference letter months before, but I didn't remember. As usual, I hadn't been paying attention.

Jane had largely ignored Maurice's vagaries, but this one caught her attention. She looked up the camp online. It was run by a small evangelical group that catered to wayward youth. The website spoke of light and recovery, dreams and journeys. There didn't seem to be anything fanatical about it. Emerson and Thoreau got equal billing with Jesus and Paul.

We agreed that it was probably the best thing he could have done for himself. What better way of getting him outside of himself than to focus on the problems of others? Most of life's woes are simply an error in context anyway. *Forget yourself*, pleaded the wife in Hawthorne's tale, and lo, the bosom serpent fled into the grass.

And maybe, we thought, that's all it was, the consuming paralysis of self-analysis, the serpent's fangs plunging deep into the boy's heart. You never really know your kids. You never really know anyone, but a kid is especially elusive. And they have a chameleon-like tendency to adapt to their environment. The Maurice we knew was not the Maurice those drug-addled campers would meet. He would tap into unknown reserves of strength to deal with their shit. He would be a better person.

He cleaned out the shed before he left. Stripped the walls bare of his beloved pinups. Every trace of his former self gone, the cigarettes, the bottles, the cloying gloom.

We wished him well. What else could we do?

I remember that time through the lens of Maurice, but I had my own concerns. Summer break for a high-school teacher is a time for taking stock. And I found I wasn't particularly happy. Jane wasn't all that happy either.

Our lives were creeping into middle age and we were starting to wonder what it was all for. What was this path we were on, and how had we gotten here? Most parents will say: it was for the children. We were proud parents, sure, but we needed more. We hadn't lost the itch that had once propelled us into our humanitarian careers. Despite time and experience we still felt that the life well spent was one that made a difference in the world.

When did it crystallize that we had to go back? Did we verbalize it one morning over coffee? I don't remember. But by the time Maurice was back from camp we'd decided that our future lay in Africa. And because this felt like a good change, the kind that brings renewal, we were both bouncy with anticipation.

Maurice came back from Wisconsin a bronze god, his hair chlorine-bleached, his blue eyes luminous, his spirits high. He saw the open maps and the new luggage, saw the new look in our eyes. And to our surprise, he was as excited about our plan as we were.

We got out the old Gabon photo albums. There was little Maurice holding a giant (probably poisonous) centipede by the tail. Maurice with a grinning gang of African children. Maurice hammering his first nail. He remembered none of it, of course, but he was fascinated as we always are with the dawning years of our existence.

We called our friend Pastor Kibula with the news. Yes, the old French farmhouse was still available. How soon could we come? What did we require? *I beg to be at your service.* Hearing his stilted English again we found ourselves lapsing easily into Fang, the local Bantu dialect. *There is much sorrow here, but you will bring us honor and joy,* said the voice in the crackling speakerphone.

It had never occurred to us that Maurice might actually want to come with us. He had just turned seventeen, was entering his senior year of high school. We assumed that no matter what path we chose, he'd point himself in the opposite direction.

— But you can't just go off and leave me here. I'm coming with you.

We wrapped him in our arms. It was music to our ears. And soon we couldn't have imagined it any other way. The three of us, back in Gabon. It almost seemed by design. Just as his childhood had begun in Africa, so it would end there, a final way station on the road to adulthood.

Little did we know.

Perhaps this time we would stay indefinitely. We were weary of western materialism. The house and everything we owned suddenly seemed an oppressive anchor. We renounced it all, disowning a dozen years of our lives. We couldn't wait to get the hell out.

Maurice didn't say much about his time at the camp in Wisconsin. He had no photos, nor did he betray any telling signs of love or loss, the awkward intimacies, the disarming silences. With the trip to Gabon growing ever closer, he seemed to rise above the emotional extremes that had been so characteristic a few months before, as though it had all been the nonsense of childhood. He practiced yoga, which he had learned at summer camp. He listened to classical music. He helped out around the house.

Jane and I were curious about the change, but we didn't want to pathologize it. We weren't the kind of parents to crawl around inside our kid's head and try to "understand" him. Our son was growing up. He wanted to help us save the world. He wanted to be *like us*. What better compliment did we need?

Blind with illusions, heady with our hard-won success as parents, we put our worries to rest, took our malaria pills and proceeded on to Africa.

I didn't think it would last. I was convinced that Maurice's enthusiasm would wane once we got there. The culture, the food, the unfamiliarity would wear on him. He'd start brooding again.

We could hardly believe our eyes.

See the boy a few months later, bumping along with us in a country-bound bus, plucking exotic flowers from the open windows, amusing the wide-eyed children with his guidebook Fang.

— *M'bolani*, kids!

— *Am'bolani!*

— *Ma wok ki Fang!*

See them press closer, curious, as though some celestial apparition had descended in their midst.

— *Wa dzon ah dzeh?*

— *Ma kobe ki Fang!*

They squealed with laughter at the crazy American teenager, absurdly thin in an Adidas T-shirt and stone-washed jeans. He wanted to be loved and admired. He pulled out every trick he knew, the disappearing thumb, the coin behind the ear, the ghoulishly inverted eyelids. They shrieked with excitement.

See the boy raising heartfelt hallelujahs during a sermon by Pastor Kibula, standing taller than everyone else by a chlorine-bleached head. And soon the congregants, warmed by the boy's enthusiasm, are raising the roof of the little mud-and-wattle church.

And during the last song, when the drums and tambourines come out for the rousing "Simama Imara," Maurice's clear tenor voice carries above all others. The congregation keeps singing as they proceed out into the red-clay churchyard. Jane glances back at me and her eyes shimmer with delight. *Simama imara jilinde* ... Maurice has been handed a drum. He walks up front, towering over the much-better-dressed pastor who gazes up at him with awestruck admiration.

There is a baptism down at the river. A very black woman in a blinding white robe is held underwater for a full three seconds by an associate pastor who seems to look upon her sins with a particular vehemence. The woman rises with a sputtering gasp to cries of *Amen! Hallelujah!* Maurice watches with tears in his eyes.

The pastor's eyes are wet. He can't take his eyes off the boy. No one can.

We were staying at the Okoumé Palace Hotel, a beachfront venue that was Libreville's nearest approximation of swank. The Formica counters were stippled with cigarette burns, and cockroaches would raise twitching antennae from the drains, but that's Africa. We were on the seventh floor with a patio that looked out on a turquoise sea. Jane and I would lean back in our wicker chairs and sip Gabonese palm wine out of coconut shells. We screwed like honeymooners.

We were so in love. Jane was returning to the shape and substance of the woman I'd married twenty years before. Not that there was anything wrong with Evansville Jane. But this was the Jane of my youth, the woman who wore crocheted caps and billowy skirts, liked to walk barefooted, hummed Pete Seeger while she knitted.

Almost imperceptibly, she relaxed her maternal hold on Maurice. She didn't track his movements or fret over his absence. I would find her on the balcony with a hamper of yarn and needles at her side, a new creation unfolding in her lap.

— Where's Maurice?

Her smile was serene, blissful, full of heady rapture. If I didn't know her so well I would have thought she was stoned.

— How on earth would I know? Probably down at the beach.

It was the same smile she'd had when she was pregnant. Except now she wasn't giving birth, she was being reborn. As she told me one evening, clicking coconut-shell glasses on the balcony, the salty wind tearing at our hair:

— I gave the best years of my life to being a mother. I enjoyed it, I have no regrets. But the rest are *all mine.*

She loved him as much as ever, perhaps more. We both did. And we might have been tempted to hold him close, to cling to the last vestige of his fading boyhood. But somehow this felt like the healthier course.

I had found a three-month consultancy on a USAID program.

It would give us time to find our bearings and decide what greater good was out there waiting for us. I was on the infrastructure team of the West African Health Initiative. I drew up plans for village water delivery systems that would both pump water and purify it. It wasn't a new concept, but because I'd done a bit of it on a Peace Corps deployment I was regarded as a hallowed expert. USAID was pouring millions into these water delivery systems. A lot was riding on what came off my desk.

I liked the team. I liked the young Chief of Party and the other visiting consultants. We lunched together, laughed at the same dumb jokes and did a little drinking downtown in the evenings. They were dedicated professionals committed to the cause. Not so common in the aid world, where dedication tends to be inversely related to salary, so that the more money you make the less you give a shit. Within two weeks the chief was talking about giving me a six-month extension. And I was sorely tempted to take it.

But Jane and I had other plans. We didn't yet know exactly how we wanted to be of use in Gabon, but we knew two things: (a) this was the place we wanted to be, and (b) we didn't want to draw a salary. We called it the Adirondack Principle.

Once upon a time, needing patio furniture, we bought some plans for Adirondack chairs and built a set over the course of a long weekend. Maurice cut the templates out of poster board, Jane did the sanding and I was on assembly. What began out of economic necessity turned into a memorable family experience. From the trip to the lumberyard on Friday evening to the sanded and varnished final product on Sunday afternoon, our entire focus and energy was on those damn chairs. And we'd never had so much fun.

A few weeks later some friends dropped by, loved the chairs, and paid us to build them a set. And because the initial experience had been so rewarding, we were happy to oblige.

And we hated every minute of it. Measurements were off, the jigsaw wouldn't cut right, everything came out wobbly. We argued and swore and blamed each other. The entire psychology was different. We ended up giving them their money back and chopping up the chairs for firewood.

Hence the Adirondack Principle. You'll love it more, and do a better job, when the work is its own reward. Provided your basic needs are met and mounting debt isn't dogging your heels, screw the paycheck. You can live without it. You'll live *better* without it.

And of course, where better to implement the Adirondack Principle than in Gabon, where the great humanitarian Albert Schweitzer focused his life's work. Without a paycheck.

Of course, it's easy to talk about saving the world from a breezy seventh-floor balcony with an ocean view, blitzed on palm wine. We weren't Peace Corps kids anymore. We were comfortably distanced from the realities of rectal worms and bilharzia. How long had it been since we'd had to boil drinking water or gather leaves for a visit to the latrine, praying they weren't poisonous? When had we last extracted bot fly larvae from our scalps or tugged an ascariasis worm out of someone's nose?

My USAID colleagues didn't understand. Why do good—for free—when you can do good and rake in some cash? No, Jane and I were navigating by a different light. And what a feeling that was, to resonate so totally with the passions of another human being, to follow a shared dream. We really did feel like soul mates.

It wouldn't last, of course. Tragedy was just around the corner, and we made our way toward it like a car hurtling through darkness toward a collapsed bridge.

30

Karimullah

Look in the sky to find the moon, not in the pond.
Persian proverb

THE MATTER OF NAZEEM FARAH and the fraudulent fertilizer delivery came at last to the attention of the Chief of Party, and in the worst way possible.

Karimullah could not prove that Leandro had altered the database, nor was that his objective. Nearly $600,000 had already been illicitly received by the so-called Nazeem Farah. Karimullah's primary concern was to warn the Finance Director to stop payment on the bank transfer for the remaining $900,000 scheduled to go out that very morning.

Of all the Americans on the project, Morgan Hayes, Director of Finance, was the one feared most by the Afghans. Karimullah would never understand how a man so lazy and vulgar could have been elevated to such an important position. His moods were unpredictable, his language always foul. On those mornings when he was hung over he was not a man to be approached for any reason. No one dared disturb him when the red sign was on his door, a warning in three languages not to knock for any reason.

At 9 a.m. Karimullah approached the dreaded door. Sure enough, the red sign was up. The Afghans who worked in the department glanced up from their workstations with grave forebodings.

Feeling his pulse racing, Karimullah took a deep breath and knocked.

Hayes was hunched over his laptop, his black face straining, as though he were holding his breath. Like most of the Americans on the program (except Hunter) he worked out a lot in the gym. Consequently he was a man of Herculean proportions, with massive arms and a powerful chest.

His eyes shot up at Karimullah.

— Can't you read the sign on the door?

— I have a matter that needs your immediate attention.

— What department are you from?

Karimullah had been to see him many times on contract matters, but Morgan Hayes seemed utterly unable to differentiate one Afghan from another.

— I am from procurement. I have information about the Nazeem Farah fertilizer contract.

Hayes stared down at his laptop, stabbing at the keys with his index fingers. Karimullah stood clutching a manila folder to his chest.

— Get on with it. What do you want?

In words that he had rehearsed through a long, sleepless night, he related the matter of the altered database and the discovery he'd made at the warehouse.

— The wrong fertilizer was delivered. Instead of 50 kg bags, only 2 kg bags were inventoried by the warehouse manager.

— Who authorized you to change the database?

— I do not have the password to make changes to the database. Only my supervisor, Leandro Palafox, can add or remove columns.

Hayes sighed, pushed back from his computer and tugged at his crotch. Leandro had once told Karimullah that black men had prodigious sexual parts. Leandro had once glimpsed Morgan's penis while the two were pissing in the guesthouse garden during a party. He thereafter referred to him as The Anaconda, thinking this detail might be of interest to Karimullah.

— Okay, Sherlock, so what made you go to the warehouse to investigate this thing anyway?

Unsure of the Sherlock he was referring to, Karimullah pushed ahead:

— If the contractor was delivering 50 kg bags of fertilizer, there was no way he could have done so in such a short period of time. It seemed . . . fishy.

— Fishy.

— Yes sir. Plus, I happen to know the contractor involved.

Hayes stared at him impassively. Karimullah went on:

— I know him to be a scoundrel and a thief. I have had dealings with him in the past.

— Professional dealings?

Karimullah looked down.

— No sir. Personal dealings. But my intention is not to slander the so-called Nazeem Farah. I only wish to warn you to stop payment until the issue can be investigated.

Hayes went through a pile of pink receipts on his desk.

— We've already sent the transfer request over to the bank. The payment is due to go out at 11 a.m.

Karimullah collected himself and said calmly:

— Sir, I *urge* you to call the bank and stop payment.

Hayes looked up from the invoice and stared at Karimullah through one eye.

— Why are you so interested in this particular contract?

— I am simply doing my job.

Hayes laughed falsely, the one narrowed eye pointing at Karimullah like an ineluctable judgment.

— It's not often that an Afghan cares so deeply about stopping corruption. What's your beef with this guy?

— My beef?

— Did he promise you a percentage, and then suddenly have a change of heart?

Puzzled, Karimullah said:

— I assure you that I would never—

Morgan Hayes slammed his fist on the desk.

— Don't raise your voice at me, *boy*.

And so at 11 a.m. a wire transfer went out from the account of ALAS to the account of Nazeem Farah, Inc. at the Afghanistan International Bank. The transfer of $905,320.52 was confirmed via e-mail to Leandro Palafox, Director of Operations and Procurement, with a cc to Karimullah and others.

Karimullah had taken the precaution of warning Quality Assurance and the various team leaders that they would have only 2 kg bags to distribute instead of the 50 kg bags the farmers were greedily anticipating. By now a myriad of e-mails and phone conversations was being exchanged between people who had no role in the swindle but who would have to account for it later.

Karimullah sat calmly at his desk, staring at the screen of his laptop where the ALAS logo was pinging from corner to corner as in a video game. He glanced at the clock over his supervisor's desk, waiting. He watched Leandro Palafox toil away at some task, glowering at his monitor, unaware that his life was about to change.

At 11:30 a.m. the secretary for the Chief of Party came to Leandro with a message. Belourine was as beautiful as her name, a quiet, conservative girl whose hair was pulled back in a bright red *hijab*. Karimullah could not hear what was being said, but he saw Leandro get up and follow her toward the chief's office, tucking in his shirt.

At 11:45 a.m. Morgan Hayes came into his office. His former irritation, so frightening at the time, had been replaced with an even more terrible calm. He placed both hands on Karimullah's desk and said in a low voice:

— There will be a meeting with the Chief of Party at 1 p.m. in the conference room. I believe you know what this is about. Bring all the relevant documentation.

— I have it right here.

— Nazeem Farah will be joining us.

Karimullah smiled and shook his head sadly.

— He will not come. By the time the meeting is underway his cell phone number will be switched off.

— In case you've forgotten, he's about to deliver a *substantial* order of wheat threshers. He knows he'll have to clear his name if he wants the payment to be processed.

— No doubt he has someone in this office providing him with information. He will be upset to find that his deception with the fertilizer was uncovered so quickly. And he may be stuck with a lot of wheat threshers. But in the end, it will be he who has the last laugh.

Karimullah skipped lunch and went to his room. He unrolled his prayer rug and offered an impassioned prayer. Following the prescribed recitation, he implored Allah to give him patience and wisdom in the upcoming meeting.

He took a shower and changed into his best clothes, choosing the *shalwar kamiz* he generally wore only at Eid, with its ceremonial design of gold thread against a black background. Then he took down his box of shoe-shining things and polished his best shoes until he could see his reflection in them. He had not forgotten Babur's long-ago advice about the importance of clean clothes and a good pair of shoes.

Karimullah was the first to arrive at the meeting, followed by Leandro Palafox and Morgan Hayes. A few minutes later the Chief of Party shuffled in with Belourine, who sat at a distance from them. Karimullah had hoped Hunter would be invited, though of course the matter had nothing to do with his department. He felt outnumbered.

The chief opened his briefcase and set a pocket tape recorder on the table while the other Americans chatted about unrelated matters. Nothing seemed to bother them, not even the prospect of losing nearly a million dollars. Their lives would go on the same regardless.

At 1:15 p.m. the chief looked at his watch and exhaled through his nose.

— I guess someone should call Nazeem Farah and remind him of our meeting.

Leandro quickly took out his cell phone and dialed the number, perhaps forgetting that the so-called Nazeem Farah spoke no English. It was so quiet in the room they could all hear the recorded voice squawking from his cell phone. As he didn't speak Pashto, Leandro put it on speaker and held it in Belourine's direction, though Karimullah could just as easily have told him what the recording said.

— This number is disconnected, Belourine said gravely.

— No worries, I have an alternate number, Leandro said brightly, tapping it into his smartphone.

In a moment he got the same recording. Karimullah glanced at Morgan Hayes who was regarding him coldly.

— Let's just begin without him, said the Chief of Party, like a kindly grandfather, and pressed the record button on the recorder.

Leandro led the discussion, describing in grandiose terms the goal of the fertilizer delivery program and the particulars of the procurement. Karimullah could see that the chief, who was scribbling out a chronology, had not been versed on the matter beforehand. With each of the old man's questions, Leandro had to shuffle through his papers to find the answer. No one asked Karimullah, though he could have answered every question by heart.

The chief again asked Leandro to dial the two numbers for Nazeem Farah. Hearing the same recorded messages, Karimullah felt it was time to speak up.

— Sir, Nazeem Farah will not attend this meeting. By now he has probably transferred the money to a bank in Dubai and gone into hiding. His real name is Obaidullah, and if you want to catch him you should call the police immediately and have him arrested. I can draw you a map to his orchard, though by now you will probably find him at the airport.

The elderly Chief of Party, who should have been enjoying his old age in a park somewhere instead of dealing with the corruption of Afghan vendors, removed his reading glasses and smiled sadly at Karimullah.

— Son, this is Afghan thinking. I have a western brain and a western way of doing things. We can't just go around arresting people without evidence.

— With all respects, you may have a western brain, but Obaidullah

264

thinks like an Afghan and has an Afghan way of doing things.

Morgan Hayes interrupted, leaning toward the old man and saying:

— This is what I was talking about. I think there's some kind of personal vendetta here.

Leandro Palafox said nothing, staring at the incriminating documents as though hoping his blazing eyes might burn holes in them and turn them to ash.

The chief held up his hands in a gesture that begged equanimity and respect. He turned his kindly gaze on Karimullah and said:

— Suppose you tell us how you were alerted to the mistaken delivery of those tiny bags of fertilizer in the first place. You deal with many contracts. Do you visit the warehouse and verify every delivery that comes through?

Karimullah sat straighter, counted to three and then looked the Chief of Party squarely in the eyes.

— The delivery was not a mistake, sir. It was an intentional violation of the contract. I knew there would be trouble when I met the so-called Nazeem Farah at a meeting to finalize the contract for the wheat threshers.

— Wheat threshers?

Leandro interrupted:

— He's providing the project with two hundred wheat threshers for agricultural cooperatives. Owing to his history of positive business dealings with the project, we—

The old man raised his hand, silencing Leandro. Karimullah felt his heart warm to the old man, finding in him the ally that he needed. The chief indicated for Karimullah to go on.

— I recognized him. I knew him to be a treacherous and deceitful man. When I learned about his previous contracts, I—

The English word briefly eluded him, but he pressed on.

— I . . . detectived the matter. I found that he had fulfilled a very large fertilizer contract that could not logically have been delivered in such a short period of time.

Leandro cleared his throat.

— I never authorized you to *detective* anything.

Karimullah ignored him, staring at the chief and saying:

— So many 50 kg bags of fertilizer could not have been distributed in the time frame indicated on the warehouse documents. And so I proceeded to visit the warehouse and found that the right number of bags had been delivered, only they were not bags of the correct size or value.

Leandro said:

— He says there was a modification to the warehouse database, but I made no such changes.

The three looked at Karimullah. The chief said calmly:

— Son, did you modify the database?

— Sir, you must know that Afghans do not have access to the database. Only the Director of Operations and Procurement has the password to make such changes.

At this he glanced at Leandro, who all but shouted:

— *Or someone who had my password!*

Karimullah was looking him in the eye for the first time since the meeting began. Who was this person seated before him? Long ago Leandro had helped him out of an awkward situation with a lecherous guard, then arranged for him to move into the training villa. Karimullah remembered the photos of Leandro's home in Oakland, California and the porch swing in which Leandro had inserted their images in a frame that said *Happy Together*. Karimullah had even trusted him with his story. Could this be the same person?

Again the chief raised his hands, as though stopping traffic.

— Please help us to understand the nature of your friendship with . . . what did you call him? Obaidullah?

— He raised me for a time when I was a boy. He abused me in ways that I cannot describe in the presence of a young lady.

Everyone looked at Belourine, who was placidly writing in her notebook, her face suddenly vivid red.

Leandro turned toward the Chief of Party and said in a voice waxy with insincerity:

— You raise a good point, sir. I think we need to know more about Karimullah's relationship with the contractor. I've never had cause to complain about his work before, but I'm seeing red flags here.

The chief nodded, not in agreement but simply to indicate that the point had been taken under advisement. He turned wearily toward Karimullah.

— So you are claiming that you had no . . . financial relationship with the contractor. He never promised you a percentage if you would, for instance, tip him off about the other fertilizer bids?

Leandro said:

— Nazeem Farah's bid was only one percent lower than the next highest bidder. That seems pretty strange to me.

Karimullah broke in:

— But you must know that the bids are sealed, Mr. Harbin. They are placed in a locked box until the day of tendering. I have no way of knowing the quotes of the other bidders. I cannot see into a locked box. Only my supervisor has access to that information.

Leandro pointed his finger at him:

— But you know who the other bidders are! *You* sent out the Request for Quotations. *You* could easily have contacted the vendors and asked them what they had bid.

They were all staring at him now. He knew he must say something, but what?

When he was a small boy someone once broke his mother's treasured porcelain vase. By process of elimination, Karimullah was believed to have been the culprit, receiving a terrible thrashing from his father. And though he knew he had been out playing when the vase was shattered, he could not shake the feeling that he must have been somehow to blame, else how could his father, whom he loved and respected above all people, be wrong?

No contractor would have ever told him the contents of a sealed bid. But because to the people seated around him it was theoretically possible, and because, being Afghan, he was the most likely suspect, he began to question his own recollection of events. How, after all, could these three Americans, who collectively made more than half a million dollars a year, be wrong, while he, the Afghan national who made barely thirteen thousand a year, was right?

The chief said:

— It seems there are two issues at stake here. We can deal with the matter of culpability by and by. Now, if it's true that Nazeem Farah knowingly committed fraud, what's our next step?

Morgan Hayes, flexing his muscular arms behind his head with apparent relief, said:

— He knew he'd be caught, but he didn't think we'd catch him so fast. He probably thought he could get his order of wheat threshers into the warehouse and receive payment before the fertilizer discrepancy was discovered. Or maybe he didn't count on being ratted out.

Karimullah addressed his next words directly to the Chief of Party.

— I would like to point out that Obaidullah is a powerful man with connections to the Taliban. He is dangerous.

— Well, I don't think we can legally pursue him on the matter of the fertilizer. He got away with it. Our control mechanisms failed. I want an investigation into how and why the database spreadsheet was changed, and why the warehouse manager didn't have the sense to raise the question when he saw those itty-bitty bags of fertilizer coming off the truck.

Morgan Hayes glanced at Leandro, his voice clipped and professional.

— We'll have to cancel the wheat thresher contract immediately.

Leandro produced a document. Though his voice was still shaky, he had the glow of one whose boat had reached safety after navigating stormy waters.

— This is the quote we received from the number two bidder. I'll call him immediately.

The chief frowned, not at Leandro but at the thought forming before his mind's eye.

— USAID will have to be notified. Morgan, we can talk about that off-line.

— Right.

Then the old man turned to Karimullah.

— You were good to bring this to our attention, son. But as you are a person of interest in the case, I'm going to have to put you on unpaid suspension while we investigate the matter further.

Karimullah wasn't sure he had heard correctly. As he tried to speak, he felt his tongue adhere to the roof of his mouth.

— You are . . . firing me?

The chief gave a hearty chuckle.

— Oh no, it's just for the duration of the investigation. I'm sure your name will be cleared by and by.

Karimullah nodded slowly, staring at the stack of documents

before him that no one had asked him to produce. He thought of the arguments that no one had asked him to present and the questions that had not been put to either Morgan or Leandro. Now the meeting was over and he was being put on suspension as the sole "person of interest." The others would simply go back to their desks and continue as if nothing had happened.

Leandro leaned back in his chair and folded his arms, staring at Karimullah with a level gaze. Anxiety gone, his cat-like face resumed its usual attitude of calculated innocence. Karimullah realized that it was this mask that allowed him to perpetrate his follies.

Karimullah stood up and gathered his documents to his chest. Setting off toward the door, he experienced a lurching sensation, as of the world dropping out from beneath his feet.

No sooner was he back at his desk than he became aware of a buzz of interest from his Afghan colleagues seated nearby. Gossip in the office moved like bees on a spring breeze. By now they all knew what had happened, and they looked at him as one looks at a man who had just lost his house in a fire—concerned, unsure what to say, and yet grateful that the tragedy had befallen someone else.

Karimullah spent an hour finishing up work on a contract. He felt weak with anger and shame, and several times fought back tears. But the work must be done; Leandro would only botch it up and then blame it on him later.

Everyone stopped working when they saw Hunter Ames fly into the office. His face was pale and distorted, his hair wild. He stared at Karimullah, eyes blazing.

— Is it true?

Karimullah nodded at his monitor, afraid that if he looked at his friend he would burst into tears. Hunter touched him on the shoulder and marched on toward the Chief of Party's office. He went inside without knocking, slamming the door so hard it sent a breeze into the room.

Karimullah finished his work, printed the documents, indicated the pages that needed to be signed, dropped them in Leandro's inbox and walked out of the office, realizing he would probably never be back.

Nothing had been said about his continued residence at the training villa. He assumed he would be asked to leave. He had not spoken to his former roommates Khan and Sadiq since their Eid feast, but perhaps they would take him in.

Then again, what did it matter? He recalled what Hunter had mumbled to him in Muhammad Ali's garden. Maybe he was right. Was death really such a tragedy? In moments like this Karimullah found little reason to go on.

Why try to do good? Why try to protect yourself and move forward in life when invariably someone was going to come along and throw you off the path? Why not let the circle of life carry you gently away?

As he lay on the bed he felt himself drawn into sleep as water is sucked down a drain. All the day's concerns disappeared and he found himself walking a sunlit path down into a green valley. It was as lovely a foretaste of death as he had ever experienced.

But he had forgotten to turn off his cell phone, and just as he entered the deepest and darkest part of the valley he was awakened by a beep indicating an incoming text message. He turned over woozily and looked at his phone. The number was unknown.

Hello my old friend. I am back. Can you guess who this is?

He puzzled over the message, then typed: *Who?*

A minute later came the reply, this time in Pashto:

Come dance with me.

His heart began to race. He typed: *Who is this?*

He waited. The phone beeped.

Voice so pure, spirit so sweet.

He typed: *WHO ARE YOU??*

And then the message came:

Have you forgotten your old friend? It is me . . . Babur!

31
When the Fat Lady Sings

Conversation has a kind of charm about it, an insidious something that elicits secrets just like love or liquor.
Seneca

HAVE I MENTIONED THAT my colleagues liked their booze?

Alcohol was banned under Afghan law, but they usually found a way. Some, like Jerry, received bottles through the APO mail. Others bought vodka off their staff, who found it on the black market, though at sixty dollars a liter, these sources were generally avoided. The vodka was often made from rubbing alcohol mixed with sugar and sleeping pills. There were rumors of expats who'd gone blind on the stuff.

Still others brought booze with them when they flew back from leave, hoping to avoid the random luggage inspections at Kandahar Airfield.

This is what happened to Hank Diebold. He had come back from R&R with a suitcase groaning with vodka, whisky and rum, only to see it confiscated by a very self-satisfied corporal who blandly reminded him of the prohibition on all forms of contraband on U.S. military bases.

The compound had been going through one of its periodic droughts. Hank had been the last great hope, and he had failed. And so followed a quiet, desultory week. The roof, scene of so many fire-lit saturnalias, was abandoned, and my colleagues moped around with the prickly combativeness that a week of sobriety can produce.

Then came salvation. Morgan Hayes announced that a friend who was working on an aid project in Helmand had managed to come by a shipping container laden with spirits. And this was not the dubious Pakistani stuff but black-label Johnnie Walker, Svedka vodka (in four flavors), Turkish *raki* as well as cognac, brandy and beer. Hundred-dollar bills flew like confetti as he went around the guesthouse taking orders and money.

But how would he get the booze from faraway Nahr-e-Saraj to Kandahar City, a 12-hour drive over treacherous roads frequently blocked by the Taliban? He met with the Afghans on his team, tempting them with money and promotions, but they were unmoved, knowing that any driver caught at a checkpoint with that much booze would be thrown into prison. He appealed to Dusty, head of the project's private security, who had no interest in risking confiscation of their armored Land Cruisers. Things looked bleak indeed.

But a few days later, word went round the office: *the booze is here!* Everyone stopped work and came out to witness a jubilant Morgan Hayes inventorying the contents of a dozen unmarked trunks piled in the garden. It was only that evening at dinner, when the merry-making had begun, that I found out how Morgan had pulled it off.

And really, it was the most obvious solution: Hayes had simply requested a helicopter mission to Nahr-e-Saraj and flown the load in on the project's tab. Thus the booze would be immune to bad roads and checkpoints, and safe from prying Muslim eyes.

Of course, the helicopter lease was expensive. I did the math. It was an hour's journey by air from Kandahar airport to Nahr-e-Saraj, then another hour back to Kandahar. At five thousand bucks per flight hour, the booze delivery had cost USAID and the American taxpayers just over ten thousand dollars.

It pissed me off, coming as it did on the heels of that Nazeem Farah business. A million dollars, and now this. Of course, it amounted to only a drop in the project's half-billion-dollar budget. To my colleagues these were just digits on a spreadsheet, never seen nor felt. But there was something so heedless and cavalier about it, as though booze was some kind of employee benefit, like health insurance.

I shut down my computer, went back to my room and fumed. I lay on my bunk with my hands under my head, thinking about the American factory workers and department-store clerks whose income tax had been commandeered to make this booze delivery possible.

I was nervously opening and closing my cell phone. Someone had to show moral courage. I brought up the number for the Chief of Party, but what did he care? Should I call someone at USAID?

I never made the call, and I found myself stewing in self-loathing as Karimullah and I sat on the balcony of the training villa watching the rooftop festivities from afar. The guesthouse was about two hundred yards away, beyond several intervening brick-and-mud walls topped with barbed wire. On the roof blazed an orange cone of light around which my colleagues could be seen as thin, Giacometti-like figures. With the shifting breeze I could make out tunes by Def Leppard and Journey cutting through the silent Kandahar night.

It had turned chilly; I'd forgotten how quickly the seasons change out here. Karimullah and I sat around a propane heater, rubbing our hands over the orange glow.

It had been a gloomy day for us both. Karimullah was on suspension and I'd probably receive a written reprimand after my confrontation with the Chief of Party. I had never dared use that sort of tone with a superior before. It hadn't swayed his decision, but at least he wasn't going to throw Karimullah out of the compound, much as Leandro had lobbied for it. At present this felt like a victory worth celebrating.

Karimullah leaned over the fire, his face lit from below. I was still experiencing flashbacks from his recent confession. I couldn't get the foul images out of my head, grunting, ill-smelling Afghans, trousers collapsed around hairy ankles.

I laid a hand on his shoulder and said:

— You know, we have a saying back home: this too shall pass.

He nodded, and when he spoke his voice was even and mechanical.

— I know it will. I am not worried.

— Sometimes the just suffer with the unjust.

— Except in this case there is no suffering for the unjust.

— Don't worry, Obaidullah's time will come. And Leandro's.

From the distant roof came a wave of laughter and screaming. Faith Woodson's shrill voice cut through the din like a plucked string.

— We need to get you out of here, Karimullah.

I had not known I was going to say it. The words seemed to change the flow of my blood, making my fingertips tingle. And then came:

— I want to take you home with me.

Staring at his hands, he offered no reaction; I wondered if he had heard me. I pushed ahead.

— This job has put your life in danger. There are visas available for people in your situation. My friend Bill Batson works at the

American embassy. I know he would help you.

I leaned back. As I put my feet up on the edge of the balcony, one slipped and crashed down into the propane heater, sending sparks and metal parts clattering everywhere. Karimullah grabbed the toppling device and laughed.

— Oh Hunter, how could I refuse? Someone must keep you from hurting yourself.

I frowned at him in disbelief.

— Really?

— I don't know how such things are done, but I would love nothing more than to join you in America.

For a moment we sat in silence, each absorbing the gravity of what was happening. And then I said, in as casual a tone as I could muster:

— We'd have a good life. You could be like, I don't know, a nephew or something.

He digested this.

— But do you think it could really happen?

— I know it could.

— I must fill out an application, go to an interview and that is all?

— Well, I'm sure it's more complicated than that. It ain't over till the fat lady sings. But I think we can do it.

— Then I can say without hesitation that this has been both the worst day *and* the best day of my life.

I had been working through this scenario ever since the night Karimullah unwound his tragic tale. In that moment I had a sudden image of our lives as two intersecting circles in a Venn diagram. And now this area where the two circles overlapped, this space that we shared, had abruptly expanded. I even drew it out for him.

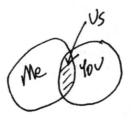

But what did it mean? Did Karimullah think I was helping him because I was just a nice guy? Surely he knew that all human behavior is driven by self-interest. Didn't that worry him?

What deep, unmet need had led me to share in the uncertain destiny of this kid? Was this just another impulse, like the monastery, that I would regret a few weeks down the road?

The wind picked up, sending us retreating back inside the training villa. We were out of wine, but Karimullah said he would put on some tea and stoke up the *shisha*. I went back to my room and changed into my *shalwar kamiz*.

The thought of another evening with Karimullah gave me a shiver of nervous anticipation. I realized that the joy I felt in his presence had become a physical sensation. I needed his hugs, to feel the solid curve of his shoulder. His vitality called out to me, awakened the primordial need for human contact. But was there more to it that I was still unwilling to admit to myself?

When I tapped at his door I could already hear the familiar sound of wind chimes. The lights were down and the room was washed in a rose-colored glow. Karimullah was sitting on the edge of the bed writing something in a notebook. It was the first time I'd noticed he was left-handed. The writing was all in Pashto. I caressed his shoulder with my fingertips. He muttered:

— Please, what was it you said about the fat lady, when she sings?

— You're writing down what I say?

He moved his arm, covering the page so I wouldn't read it. As if I could.

— Let me tell you something, Hunter. I was once a dancer. I once picked pomegranates. I once had wonderful friends like Marsha Kohn. Do you know what is left of those lives I once led?

He didn't wait for a response.

— Nothing. I have no photograph of Marsha Kohn or Babur or the foolish Sardar the Kalash. I have only the faintest memories of the things they said.

I sat beside him. My hand found the curve of his back and I stroked it comfortingly.

He continued:

— Yes, I write down the things you say. Not because they are especially wise or important, but because they will help me remember you when you are gone.

Astonished at his blunder, he interjected:

— But of course, you *are* wise, Hunter.

I began laughing hard, not so much from hilarity as pure joy. He handed me a tissue. I said:

— You know I'm full of shit, don't you? I really don't know my ass from apple butter.

I could almost see the strange idiom moving through the maze of his mental lexicon. I grabbed the notebook.

— You're not writing that down!

A friendly tussle ensued.

— I will write it down when you leave!

— You don't have to write anything anymore. I'm real. And I'm not going anywhere. I promise.

We stared at each other at close range. Then Karimullah leaned over and kissed me loudly on the cheek, hard enough to leave an imprint of warm saliva. Taking advantage of my surprise, he grabbed the notebook and spun away from me.

We smoked the *shisha* for a while and listened to music. There was so much to say, and yet wordless glances somehow befitted the moment. The emotion in the room seemed to crowd out language and render it irrelevant.

— Hunter?

— Mm.

— Did you know that Leandro also offered to bring me to America?

— He mentioned something about that.

— I never believed it would really happen. But I pretended to.

I felt a twinge of disgust being lumped together with fey Leandro and his misguided efforts to own this amazing creature.

— Listen to me, please.

— Yes, Hunter.

— Leandro was full of shit. You were just a fantasy, a kind of trophy.

— I do not know that word.

— It doesn't matter. Look, I don't make idle promises. If you want this to happen, I will make it happen. I will move mountains. I will throw a rope around the moon. I will call down the Furies.

I glanced over and saw Karimullah smiling. I continued:

— I'm going to call in a very big favor from my friend Bill at the embassy. This is going to happen so fast it'll make your head spin. You'll be home with me by the end of the year.

I suddenly had a vision of a Christmas tree and holiday cards with our picture on it—Karimullah and I by the fireplace wearing Santa hats. Jane and I had done that on our last Christmas with Maurice.

— I want to believe all of this.

— Then believe.

He shrugged.

— Maybe it will happen, he mumbled. Good things sometimes do. We may die for a while, but we'll live tomorrow.

— Huh?

— We'll live tomorrow. It's something my friend Babur used to say. *Mozhbaa sabaa zhowand wakroo.*

I tried to repeat it.

— *Mozhban sabraa* zum-zum something.

— You should learn Pashto, Hunter. When I am in America it can be our secret language.

And in that moment I wanted nothing more. To share secrets. To share a life.

The next morning was Friday, a day off. I woke up early, admiring my reverse-hourglass profile in the mirror on the back of the door. I had a fierce desire to visit the gym, now, while the other Americans were sleeping off the excesses of the night before.

I changed into my closest approximation of gym attire. I tied a bandana around my forehead, fished my MP3 player out of a drawer and put on a pair of sneakers.

As I left the room I was already pumping my arms in anticipation of the workout to come. Then something caught my eye, a half-sheet of blue paper taped to Karimullah's door. The writing was all in Pashto. It had the look of an official notice, stamped at the bottom corner in a way meant to suggest unimpeachable authority.

Peeling it off the door, I wondered if it was an eviction notice. I decided I'd leave it on Karimullah's desk so he'd see it when he woke up.

I opened the door slowly, hoping it wouldn't creak, then crossed the floor in three long, dainty steps.

Karimullah sat up, gasping in alarm:

— *Sok ye?*

I whispered:

— I found something taped to your door. I'll leave it here. Don't worry, go back to sleep.

Karimullah squinted toward the desk then threw back his bedding and stood up. I couldn't help noticing the curl of a morning erection hammocked in his sleeping pants. It was bigger than I would have imagined.

As he scanned the page his expression changed. He began shaking his head mechanically.

— What's wrong?

He looked up at me, his eyes imploring, his expression uncomprehending.

— Who was in the hall? Did you see anyone?

— I . . . don't think so. Why?

Something was definitely wrong. He shook the offending sheet of paper at me. When he spoke again his voice was almost a scream.

— *Do you not know what this is?*

32
Shabnama

Nothing endures but change.
Heraclitus

STILL IN MY WORKOUT clothes, though by now the gym was long forgotten, I sat at my workstation and stared out across the empty office. I had planned on spending today grinding out my first report on the inmate tailoring program, but there was no time for that now.

I had downloaded the instructions for the Special Immigrant Visa from the U.S. Embassy website, and now Karimullah was at his former desk working on his portion of the application. All we lacked was an employment verification letter from Human Resources. This would mean bringing Faith Woodson into the picture. Given Karimullah's recent suspension and Faith's weird bitterness toward me, I saw every possibility of sabotage.

I wasn't going to give her the satisfaction. Seeing that Bill Batson was on Skype, I rang him up.

— Hunter! How's it hanging, big boy? So did that kid submit his application?

— It's coming along. I'll send you a PDF by lunchtime.

— Great. I'll look it over and put it in the system this afternoon.

— You're amazing, Bill.

— It's a great opportunity.

—I know it is. This kid is worth it.

Bill laughed.

— No, I mean it's a great opportunity for me to have you in my debt for a *long* time.

— Listen, things took a bit of a turn this morning. There was a night letter taped to his door. It was from the Taliban.

Bill was silent. In a moment his voice surfaced from another part of the room. He was doing some kind of exercise, grunting a little.

— Shit, man. The dreaded *shabnama*. How did they get inside your compound?

— I have a hunch, but I can't prove anything. Someone on the inside.

— Make sure to include a copy with the application. Get him to translate it. It'll help his case.

— It might have come from one of our vendors. We just cancelled a machinery contract and now the guy is stuck with two hundred wheat threshers.

— Well, get me those docs and we'll have that kid in the land of milk and honey in no time.

— There's just one problem. Our HR director.

I ran through the range of lies at my disposal—*she's out on leave, she's in another province*—but decided to employ pure candor.

— She's a real bitch, Bill. I'd rather not get her involved. She's got it in for me right now.

— What about the kid's supervisor?

284

— That's . . . not a good idea either.

— Then get me a copy of his work contract. Sign it, stamp it and scan it. I'll make sure no flags come up.

— Thanks, Bill.

— You know you'll have this kid on your hands for a long time. Afghans don't assimilate quickly. He's going to depend on you.

I smiled. Funny that Bill would phrase it as a burden.

— He's pretty amazing, Bill. Wait till you read his personal narrative.

— I'll see that he gets his preliminary interview out of the way in the next few weeks. Has he ever been to Kabul?

— He used to work for the Kabul Children's Trust.

— No shit. I used to know the founder, what's her name. Marsha Something, killed in a rocket attack? Anyway, bring him up here, make a holiday out of it.

I was starting to imagine it when I saw Karimullah threading his way among the empty desks.

— I just e-mailed you the documents.

— How did it go?

He shrugged. His lips were set in the tight purse to which I was now becoming accustomed. He was so transparent. He had none of the cloaking devices that most people adopted to hide their most vulnerable moods. He simply was who he was.

He squatted beside my chair, resting an elbow on my great thigh as I clicked on his e-mail. The English would need some work. But no, I would leave it alone. The mistakes lent verisimilitude, an unvarnished truth.

Then I came to the translation of the Taliban night letter:

Islamic Emirate of Afghanistan
Kandahar Province
Memorandum No. 177

Karimullah, son of Abdul Bahram, your life is at its end. The time has come for you to lie in the bed of death. By your employment with the Unholy Invaders you have failed in your Islamic duty. We advise you to prepare for God's judgment and seek His mercy.

[seal]

Emir Ul Mominin
Mullah Mohammed Omar Mujahed

I read it through twice, recognizing the name of the famous Mullah Omar.

Someone had been paid by the Taliban to do this. And if they could tape a letter to a door, surely they could do more.

We went through the set of documents together: the application, the personal statement, the night letter, employment verification, my letter of support (succinct but tactfully emphatic) and the various proofs of identification.

Once everything was scanned and assembled into a single document there was nothing to do but attach it to an e-mail and stare at it until the 3mb file had left my outbox.

— Well, that's that, I said, tipping back in my chair.

I glanced at an open desk drawer and saw an unopened pack of cigarettes. I had pretty much stopped smoking except for the nights when Karimullah brought out the hookah. But now the thought of a cigarette put me in a dizzy state of lung-hunger. I slipped the pack in my pocket.

— Let's go up to the roof.

We leaned against the parapet facing the Red Mosque, a view of almost picture-postcard splendor. The sky was a deep cerulean blue. Against the mountain backdrop and the low rambling buildings, the old mosque was truly a thing of beauty, a note of harmony amid the dissonance.

The young inmates were noisily at play in the courtyard below. I peered down and saw them engaged in some sort of game with a piece of dirty red fabric tied to a stick, arguing over some infraction of the rules. Several of them, I noted proudly, were in my tailoring class.

Karimullah nudged me in the side.

— Why so quiet?

— Just thinking.

— I do not like it when you back into yourself, Hunter. You go into this dark place and close the door behind you.

I shook a cigarette out of the pack, ducked out of the wind and lit it.

— Hunter, I do not want to stay in my room any longer.

— Are you sure?

— I think it is dangerous. I have spoken to Muhammad Ali and he has agreed to let me sleep in his watchman's quarters.

I nodded, absorbing this new fact and wondering why it tasted vaguely of rejection.

— That's probably a good place to go.

— There is another thing I want to say. I want you to stop smoking.

I flicked ash, watching the grey lump tumble-weeding across the roof. Karimullah added:

— You are older than me, and our time together is already short.

I want you to live many years, Hunter Ames. Smoke the natural leaf of the *shisha* if you must, but not these poisonous things.

I began to tell him how little I'd been smoking lately, but he pressed on.

— You speak of the circle of life. You say that your life is not important. But it is very important to me, and I want you to live for a long time.

The prison kids had become alert to our presence, a fact signified by an empty plastic water bottle that now sailed overhead and clunked across the roof. They were looking up at us, hands on hips, wanting to play.

— Karimullah, if you tell me not to smoke, I will never smoke a cigarette again.

— Never say never. But try.

— No, I'm saying never.

I took the pack of cigarettes from my pocket and dandled it where the boys below could see. They froze at the trademark red and white package, like cats alert to a twitching string. I drew some cigarettes from the pack and tossed them into the air, not watching where they went. A second later came the slap of bare feet and an eruption of shouts.

— Never again, I repeated.

— Only the *shisha*.

—Yes, but only with you.

Karimullah sighed.

— I feel uneasy telling you what to do.

— I want you to always be open and honest with me about what you think.

— I will. And Hunter, do not worry that because I am living with you I will become a dependent. I can take care of myself.

— Think of it as a springboard to a new life. I know you won't be with me forever.

Karimullah pondered this.

— You are right. One day I will have to move on. But I will never be a burden to you. I will work in your garden and I will keep your house clean. You will be glad you have a Karimullah in your life.

— I want you to get an education. I want you to learn how to drive.

— Perhaps I could learn how to swim?

— I'll teach you myself. Most of all, I want you to relax and know that you're in a safe place where you will never have to worry about getting a Taliban night letter again.

Karimullah's old giddiness returned. He beamed and said:

— Do you think it will happen soon?

— Bill Batson will help us.

— *Inshallah*. Oh, and I must see my friend Babur before I go.

— Your dancing teacher?

— We have been texting. It is providential that he would return now, before my departure.

— He was a good friend to you, wasn't he?

— Most dear. He disappeared abruptly when I was a boy. We have much to talk about before I leave for America.

— You're going to miss your people, Karimullah. Do you think you'll ever come back?

He thought about this, clasping his hands pensively behind his back as he stared at the city outspread before him.

— I will come back in my dreams. There is nothing left for me here.

33
The Dance

He who laughs at himself never runs out of things to laugh at.
Epictetus

ALL THE NEXT DAY I was up to my neck in new projects. My team was on a roll, and whatever reservations I'd once had about them were being revised by the hour. They were energetic and startlingly full of new ideas. Even Nissar, the square-jawed boy who used to slouch in his chair like a bored model, was bringing me his designs and mock-ups with so much hope in his eyes that I wanted to tape them to my refrigerator.

Toward dinner time I rang Karimullah.

— Just wanted to see what you were doing.

— Hi Hunter! I was just having tea with Muhammad Ali.

Karimullah broke off and began speaking in muted Pashto. This linguistic shift brought a hard, masculine quality to his voice.

— Would you like to come over? He invites you.

— Actually I was thinking about dinner.

It was becoming harder and harder to make myself go to the dining hall. My unassimilated status among the other expats made mealtimes quiet and awkward. I felt like the private who'd wandered into the officers' mess by mistake.

I continued:

— Go back to your tea, I don't want to bother you.

— I have an idea. Let me cook for you tonight. If I am going to cook for you in Indiana, you have a right to see if I am any good or not. I will make you some mutton kebab and other things. Does that sound good?

— Sounds wonderful.

— Let me finish tea and then I will go to the market. But do you have something we can cook on?

I remembered an old hibachi grill somewhere on the guesthouse roof.

— That will be perfect, he said. I will buy some coal and see you in one hour.

I shouldn't have said anything about the hibachi. It meant a possible encounter with my colleagues. *What's up with the hibachi, dude? Party time at the training villa?* It gave me a sick feeling.

Slipping into the guesthouse, I was struck by how luxuriously it compared to my current address. I'd so thoroughly incorporated cockroaches and mildewy plaster into my sense of entitlement that the guesthouse now seemed sumptuous. How easily I'd taken it all for granted—the air conditioning, coffee service in the hall, the murmur of TVs in every room.

Reaching the top floor I passed my old room. I hadn't seen it since the renovations had been completed. Finding it unlocked, I stepped inside.

The transformation was striking. The walls were freshly painted and a new set of hardwood furniture now took the place of the cheap particleboard pieces from my day. What struck me most, though, was that the room was vacant, available. It left me feeling both liberated and left out, as though I'd been stricken from the guest list of a party I hadn't really wanted to attend.

Changwani. That was the consultant who'd died in this room months before. Somewhere in Pakistan a family was still reeling from the loss of its head of family, and who here even remembered him?

Out on the roof the relics of the previous night's festivities were on bold display. Empty vodka and whiskey bottles. Soda and tonic cans everywhere. And in one corner a telling splatter of hard brown vomit.

In the fire pit a thin finger of smoke was wreathing up from under grey ash. I looked up at the watchtowers on either end of the roof where Afghan guards sat silently in their sandbagged roosts. One raised the tip of his AK-47 in greeting. I tried to imagine last night's craziness through their eyes.

Hearing a scraping sound, I turned around. Hank Diebold was dragging a burlap sack of firewood toward the pit, preparing for the evening ahead. He stopped short.

— Huh. Didn't expect to see *you* up here.

I spotted the hibachi behind a satellite dish. I decided to wait until he went back inside. If I dragged it out now it would only offer further proof of my detachment from the herd. *He's cooking his own meals now. Can't get far enough away from us.*

Hank was having trouble getting the bag open so I handed him a miniature pocketknife that I carried on my key ring. He sawed away at the knot.

— Just need to find some kindling, he sighed.

— You've got some good coals down in the ash. Take a look.

I knelt and blew into the ash until I came to the hot embers buried within. I took some wood chips from the burlap sack, sprinkled them on the coals and blew on them until they started to smoke. Falling in with what I was doing, Hank began breaking down the sticks and twigs, setting them on the crackling tinder.

It had become a joint effort. As the small fire rose to life, Hank began to pile sticks over it willy-nilly. I rearranged them into a tee-pee, starting with the smallest and working up to the big stuff, leaving a chamber to allow good airflow. I thought: *When did rednecks lose the ability to make a simple campfire?* By the time I had dropped the last stick in place the fire was blazing.

Hank drew up a chair and indicated for me to feel free to do likewise.

— You joining us this evening?

— I can't stay.

He leaned toward the growing flame with his elbows on his knees.

— Nah, I didn't think so.

The quickness of the response implied a kind of churlishness that I found surprising. Was it possible that my presence was even *wanted* here?

At that moment Jerry Janace arrived with the evening's delights clanking in an open box. He wore a green camo shirt with the caption ONWARD CHRISTIAN SOLDIERS printed at an angle in military-esque stencil. His eyes widened in mock horror.

— Hunter Ames? To what do we owe this rare honor?

Hank said:

— This sumbitch knows how to make a pretty fair fire.

Together they arranged the cans and bottles on a nearby table. Again I recalled their method of delivery, the helicopter flight from

Nahr-e-Saraj that had cost the project so dearly.

— Think fast! Jerry shouted, whirling toward me.

I only just managed to catch a liter bottle of vodka tossed neatly in my direction. Hank handed me a glass and poured a generous amount of vodka, topping it off with Coke. I glanced in the direction of the hibachi, knowing now was the time to retreat, but felt anchored to the spot. We clinked glasses, leaned back and put the soles of our shoes on the rim of the fire pit. I felt a sharp clap on the back as Jerry said:

— Welcome back to civilization, man. We missed you.

Just one, I thought.

It was getting dark when Miso arrived, giving a little chirp in her high fluty voice when she saw me:

— Hunter, I can't believe it's *you!*

She seemed genuinely glad to see me.

They were soon off on some sort of office gossip that had nothing to do with me. I felt a clink on the edge of my glass and looked up to see Hank topping it off from the bottle of vodka.

Old Cleve Harbin shuffled in next, followed by Faith Woodson, light applause greeting their entrance. Faith could not suppress a look of surprise at seeing me, but then grabbed the unsuspecting chief around the arm, claiming him and her right to be there.

Dusty had strolled up to the group, a 9mm pistol holstered at his hip. Members of the private security detail weren't allowed to drink, as they were required to be on call twenty-four hours a day. I overheard him radio to the security desk the number of Americans currently on the roof. He smiled warmly at me and walked over.

— Haven't seen you up here in a while.

He squatted beside me and added under his breath:

— Maybe you could be the designated driver for the evening,

keep these people from going too crazy.

— I don't plan on staying.

— We're getting all kinds of security intel from the Afghan military. Insurgents have several VBIEDs circling the city today—Toyota Corollas stuffed to the gills with explosives.

I nodded, wishing that I hadn't started drinking. I knew how difficult it would be to stop now that I'd felt the click.

It wasn't the alcohol that kept me there as much as a kind of detached guilt, a sense that these people somehow needed me—which I knew to be bullshit. As a kid I would sit up with my father in front of the TV, watching the Scotch bottle move from the coffee table to his glass, back and forth all night. If I got up to leave he might whine for me to stay or throw the bottle at me, I never knew which it would be. It was always easier, then and now, just to stay put.

I thought about those vehicle-borne IEDs circling the streets of Kandahar looking for a target of opportunity—a slow-moving military convoy or perhaps a police checkpoint. Then again, most of the time such threats came to nothing. The boy had cried wolf one too many times.

By now Dusty had been spotted and the guys were teasing him with vodka that they knew he'd refuse. He took it all in stride. He was about thirty with a boy's face perched on a stocky well-built body. I envied his ability to fit in without sacrificing his scruples. Some people had that sort of strength of character. They knew what they were about.

A hoarse voice called out:

— Hunter's a religious man, aren't you Hunt? Hell, he's practically a monk, got his own monastery and everything.

It was little Jerry Janace, standing on the opposite side of the fire with Hank.

— The Israelites crossed the Red Sea, man. It's just been proved.

I nodded, thinking: *here we go again.*

— You can see it on the Internet. Undersea photos showing chariot wheels and all kinds of shit where Pharaoh's army drowned. Human bones! It's undeniable proof that the Bible is for real.

He was staring right at me, demanding a response.

— Forward the link. I'll look at it.

— I'm going to do more than that. I'm going to make copies for all the monkeys on my team.

I had never wrestled much with matters of faith. My parents were nominal Methodists who never made a big deal out of it. I had friends who would invite me to youth-group meetings where they talked about how their prayers were answered, and this was God's will, or their prayers went unanswered, and this too was God's will. I'd never understood the point.

I tried to imagine Jerry in church reading a Bible, holding a hymnal. I could not imagine what sort of prayer he would utter.

People were like computers, I thought now, the vodka making me oddly lucid. What was religion but a kind of operating system, like Windows or OSX? Jerry could no sooner have awakened one day as a Muslim than my Dell laptop would boot up as a Mac. It was just the way people were programmed, and you couldn't change them.

Trying to change the subject, I called out:

— Hey man, why don't you tell the story about the condom and the carrot?

Everyone went silent. I must have said it louder than I'd thought. Jerry seemed confused.

— I don't get it.

— Aw, man, you know. Your cousin?

It was actually Hank Diebold's story, told one day around the dinner table—redneck buffoonery of the most vicious kind. A distant cousin was in town and they had gone to a bar where the cousin proceeded to inveigh against gay marriage. When they got back home they sat around drinking with some of Hank's buddies, and the cousin continued to rave about how homos were destroying the moral fabric of America. At last the cousin passed out, good and truly smashed, and the others had an idea. They wriggled his pants off and stuck a condom partway up his ass with the end of a carrot. What the cousin thought when he woke up to find a condom dangling out of his hole, they never learned. He got out of there before anyone was up.

Jerry took out a can of Skoal. In the silence that accompanied the pinching and packing of the snuff I died a thousand deaths. Faith was on the opposite side of the fire. I didn't dare look up, knowing she would be smiling derisively.

Finally Jerry said:

— Yeah, man. That was quite a story.

And it seemed like a century of silence and throat-clearings before the conversation resumed. I had not stopped staring at the glass clenched in my hands.

Why am I here? I'm supposed to be having dinner with the kid. I'll finish this drink and then get the fucking . . . whatever it's called and get back to the training villa.

I felt my cell phone vibrating in my shirt pocket. I drew it out—KARMULLIAH. My finger hovered for a moment over the green button. Then, feeling someone elbow me in the side, holding forth the bottle, I slipped the phone back into my pocket.

Everyone was on the roof now. Damon and Eddie and Gene and the rest. They were playing eighties music. "Take On Me" came on, a bouncy little song that everyone but me seemed to know. As the lyrics soared into the upper register everyone sang along in an uninhibited falsetto that dissolved into laughter.

The chairs had been pushed aside. I was talking to Miso. I'd lost the thread of our conversation long ago, but I supplied affirmative grunts each time she looked up at me with her fiery little slits of eyes. She was a cutie all right. I wondered if this was going somewhere.

Leandro joined the party, but when he saw me he did a dramatic volte-face and went to stand by Faith on the other side of the fire. Here was just the person I wanted to see.

As I sidled up next to him he pretended to be in a state of rapture over Faith's elephant-hair bracelet, though it was the same damn bracelet she wore every day.

— Someone stuck a night letter on Karimullah's door. What do you know about it?

When he didn't respond, I gave him a shove. He swung around toward me, indignant. I repeated:

— What do you know about the night letter?

He turned to Faith.

— Faith, what are the rules about expats diddling with local staff? Her eyes widened.

— I don't think I want to know.

— Well, I want to file a complaint.

Clearly the drink in his hand wasn't his first, I realized, steeling myself for conflict.

If he had expected a show of solidarity from Faith, she surprised both of us by moving toward the drink table with a look that said we were both crazy. Jerry and Hank were just five feet away, yukking it up, drinks sloshing. I leaned close to Leandro.

— I'd better not find out you had anything to do with it, you son of a bitch.

Did I really believe he was involved? Sensing my uncertainty, Leandro wrapped himself in his own mysteriousness as if it were a mink stole.

— Well, wouldn't you like to know. Is your boyfriend nervous? Do you comfort him at night? Don't deny it, I *heard* you in there.

— He's just my neighbor.

His voice got louder.

— You were observed coming out of his room in a most *disheveled* state of undress.

Jerry and Hank turned around with their drinks. Leandro stepped back, like a showman presenting his finest exhibition.

— Ask him! Ask him about his *boyfriend*, one of our own staff!

They glanced between the two of us, eager to hear more. Faith was at my side. I felt the touch of the vodka bottle against my glass. I took a step toward him.

— You need to shut the hell up. You don't know what you're talking about.

He pointed at me.

— Lies! You're helping him get a visa so he'll come live with you. *Deny it!*

Somewhere beyond the firelight Dusty called out for us to keep it down. But Leandro wasn't done with me yet.

— And what about that little showdown in the chief's office, when you found out he'd been suspended? Playing the knight in shining armor?

I heard a shushing from someone near the fire. Leandro's eyes were wide, his face shiny with sweat. I couldn't think of anything to say except to deny all charges. And yet the more I denied it, the more I'd implicate myself. It was absurd.

— I just love that kid. I do. He's—

299

Leandro threw his arms out, appealing to the others as to a jury.

— You see? There it is, the truth will out!

I felt myself choking up. I looked down into my glass and through the jumble of ice and liquid I could almost see Karimullah's image, begging me to shut the hell up.

— He's got such a good heart. You don't know—

I felt Faith's hand on my arm. Leandro was laughing uproariously but she cut him short.

— Leandro, why don't you fuck off. You're drunk. Take your sad little drama back to your room and sleep it off.

He stared at her in voiceless outrage. This elicited a snicker from Jerry and Hank, who didn't know what to think of any of this. Then we heard Miso's little voice pipe up, trying to make everything all right:

— Let's have more music. Come on, let's dance.

It was over just as senselessly as it had started. Conversations resumed and Leandro slipped away. I had reached that stage of inebriation where I felt myself being carried from one episode to another as on an inflatable raft. Some time must have passed because now everyone was in a wide circle around the fire, dancing in place.

I heard someone yell out my name. It was Faith.

— Your turn, Hunter. Show us your move.

Morgan had made the observation that everyone had a default dance move that they always fell back on. His move was to raise his forearms like a black Santa as his body twisted right and left. Faith's was a conservative foot-to-foot shuffle accompanied by affirmative nods of the head.

— I don't really have a dance move.

— Yes you do, Hunter. Everyone does. Let's see it.

Miso was doing her move, tilting her head back and forth like one of those dashboard thingies on a spring. Everyone else was waiting to see what I would come up with. I took a long sip of my drink, set my glass down and pushed back my sleeves.

— You want my move?

— Damn right.

— You *really* want my move?

— Hell yeah! Morgan shouted.

All I could think of was John Travolta in *Saturday Night Fever*. Planting one hand on my hip, I pointed at Faith, then at each of them in turn, rotating across the group. I wasn't sure what to do next, so I threw my arms in the air and went into a crazy gyration that was part dervish, part Jane Fonda Workout.

They loved it. The volume of the music went up and every-one started dancing. Faith came up beside me and bumped her hip against mine.

— You're a terrible dancer, she said.

— Thanks for rescuing me back there with Leandro.

I was getting into the rhythm now, snapping my fingers and suck-ing in my lips. I felt a little dizzy. Sweat was accumulating in my underwear and streaming down from my pits, but I didn't care.

— I told you I could be a good friend to you, if you'd let me.

Our eyes connected for a long moment.

— You never told anyone, did you? About my son?

— Not on your life, Hunter. That's sacred ground.

34
Attack

Only the dead have seen the end of war.
Plato

I WENT DOWN THE steps two at a time, clutching the blackened hibachi to my chest as though it would somehow shield me from my self-loathing.

Stumbling out of the guesthouse and into the garden I tripped on the edge of the flower bed, falling headlong into the sudden materialization of a hydrangea bush. Losing the hibachi in the undergrowth, I gave up and lurched toward the steel door that opened onto Zone Two. The guard radioed something ahead, and like magic the various gates went up in perfect synchronicity as I jogged toward the training villa.

I couldn't believe it when I saw the time on my cell phone: 11 p.m. I had ignored four calls from Karimullah. I hoped he wasn't angry. Maybe we'd laugh about it later. It would be assimilated into our shared history as The Night Hunter Forgot to Come Down from the Roof.

The courtyard of the training villa was dark. The pervading silence seemed to shock me into sobriety. I took the stairs slowly, as though they led not to my room but to the throne of judgment. As I approached my door I took a deep breath, tapped softly and opened it. I switched on the light. No Karimullah—nor any sign of food.

I tapped on his door, then remembered that he'd moved in with Muhammad Ali.

I went back to my room, leaning in the doorway for support. I was very drunk. The room seemed to be tilting on an ever-rising wave. I fished my phone out of my pocket, puzzled by the greasy stripes left by the hibachi on the front of my shirt. I let it ring ten times. Then a recorded voice told me in Pashto to fuck off, or so it sounded.

Some time later I sat up in bed, feeling an odd sense of dread. The room was dark. Something had startled me awake, but what? I felt jittery without quite knowing why.

Maybe it was a protest from my bladder, which was presently tight as a drum. I bumped in darkness down the hall to the bathroom. I couldn't find the light switch, so I aimed a jet of piss in the general direction of the toilet.

I wasn't exactly sure what had happened to the evening. Something about the hibachi. And then all that vodka. On an empty stomach, too.

Then I thought of Karimullah. Chopping vegetables. Looking at the time. Wondering. The first call. Then the second, third and fourth. Then the transition from concern to weary disappointment. He had probably gone out on the balcony, seen the festivities on the roof of the guesthouse and drawn the obvious conclusion.

Hunter, you asshole, I thought.

I had trumpeted to the herd, and for what possible reason—approval? Why had it been so damn difficult to walk away? And that stupid John Travolta dance. I was going to pay for it tomorrow.

And then there was Faith. We'd walked away from the fire, and what was it I had said to her? Something, surely, for she set her drink down, stood on her toes and kissed me. And not in a merely friendly way. It was a kiss freighted with the promise of things to come. Now I could look forward to her prowling around the training villa again.

As I went back to my room, bumping along the dark hallway in a T-shirt and jogging shorts, I heard what sounded like fireworks popping outside. My colleagues were probably still up there, the party finding renewed momentum.

Was it fireworks? I thought I might as well stroll out to the balcony for a look.

As I was rooting my flip-flops out from under my bed I heard the unmistakable blast of a rocket-propelled grenade. I had heard my share of explosions, but this one came with such force that I could feel it in my organs. It was the kind of impact that seemed to suck the oxygen right out of the room.

I could feel myself transitioning into a terrifying new reality as I stumbled down the hall. I felt a sharp pain and realized I was walking on broken glass. The normally muted hallway was filled with the treble of outdoors, wind sighing through the stalactite edges of the shattered windows. Stepping onto the balcony, the door of which was standing wide open, I heard what sounded like war-whoops, as on a TV western.

I was unable to make myself believe what I was seeing. The guest-house roof was wreathed in flames rising to the height of the guard towers. My first thought was to wonder how they had managed enough wood for such a blaze. Its white heart seemed to be spinning cyclonically, sending a crazy Morse code of sparks so high into the darkness that I had to crane my head back.

I was overcome by a feeling of paralyzing lassitude. I knew I must form a thought, must perform some movement of my body. I looked at my hand gripping the splintered doorframe and saw my palm covered with blood.

My attention was drawn to the dark courtyard below where a silhouetted figure was approaching at breakneck speed, clutching a parcel of some kind under one arm. My first response was a desire to alert the person to what was happening behind him. I pointed mutely into the distance—*the guesthouse!*

But the figure drew closer, raising the parcel over his head like a basketball player lining up a shot. He screamed something in deranged Pashto, then hurled the unknown thing toward me.

The object fell loosely on the tiles of the balcony, rolling a little before coming to rest at my feet. Honoring the most primitive of fight-or-flight instincts, I fought my way over the broken glass to get back inside, realizing only then that the shouting voice down below belonged to none other than Karimullah.

35
Karimullah

Out beyond ideas of wrongdoing and rightdoing, there is a field.
I will meet you there.
Rumi

HE WAS SIPPING HIS THIRD glass of tea when Hunter called, inviting him to dinner. He and Muhammad Ali were reclining on plush red cushions in Ali's front parlor.

He had enjoyed his visit with Ali, who placed him in high regard because of his employment with the Americans. Today Ali had inquired into Karimullah's marital prospects, and hearing that he had none, became unusually curious about his family background. Was he considering Karimullah as a possible match for one of his three daughters?

In the foyer, as Karimullah was putting on his sandals, Ali laid a hand on his shoulder and said:

— I am concerned about the night letter. You must get away from here.

— Once I have my American visa I will be *very* far away.

— Are you sure this man will help you?

Karimullah felt a burst of warmth pass through him.

— Hunter is . . . a true friend.

He said this with such conviction that Ali glanced away, embarrassed for intruding on such depth of feeling.

Closing Ali's gate behind him, Karimullah began to think of the dinner he would prepare for Hunter. It was not often that he had the opportunity to return the American's kindness, and he wanted this meal to be special. The depth of their friendship still surprised him. As the Imam Ali wrote in *The Way of Eloquence*, they were like a single soul shared by different bodies.

And now Babur was back in town. They had been texting throughout the day. Never before had his heart felt so brimming with joy.

It was pleasant strolling through the produce market in the late afternoon, haggling with vendors, sampling their vegetables and spices. It was like the old days when he used to cook for Khan and Sadiq.

Karimullah bought fresh tobacco for the *shisha* and a kilo of coal for the grill. He bought some delicious yogurt that a vendor from Dand dipped out of a wooden barrel. He bought rice and onions and cilantro and lentils and four or five spices in little paper sachets. Then he visited a butcher's shop for lamb, glancing up at the second-floor room where he had lived when the Taliban had attacked him. It seemed like so long ago.

With this thought, he wrapped his scarf around his face so that only his eyes showed. He would take no chances. The Taliban, Obaidullah, he could feel their malevolent presence all around him. He had too much to live for now.

* * *

As he chopped vegetables in the dirty kitchen of the training villa he hummed a song that he had once danced to. The window was open and he could hear the late-afternoon chattering of birds in a nearby tree. All of God's creatures seemed to share in his joy.

As he was cutting the mutton into cubes he realized that he had no skewers on which to grill them. He borrowed some from Muhammad Ali—fine stainless-steel skewers with bone handles. As he was making the short walk back to the villa a sound caught his attention from the direction of the guesthouse—music, shouting, laughter. The Americans were at it again.

— One day they will be drinking around the clock, he said aloud, realizing that it was an unkind thing to say. He could stand in judgment of no man in the matter of drinking, given his own weakness for wine.

Back in the kitchen he impaled the cubed mutton on the skewers, inserting a tiny lump of fat between each for flavor. He was wondering what could be keeping Hunter when he saw a message on his cell phone. He smiled when he saw it was from Babur.

I need to see you, my prince

Babur was hiding out at Obaidullah's orchard. As Karimullah had predicted, Obaidullah had fled. He had been only days away from delivering the two hundred wheat threshers. Karimullah smiled when he imagined all those machines parked under the trees, ready for a delivery that would never happen.

He must warn Babur about these things, but it would have to wait until he could speak to him in person.

When he had cleaned the mutton blood off his hands, he tapped into his phone:

Soon, my friend. Find a place where we can meet.

He sent this, and then added as an afterthought:

O. has new reasons for hating me. Much to tell. Not safe for me to come see u now.

Soon came the reply:

Do not fear, O. is far away. Come!

He resumed cooking, switching on the light for it had grown dark in the room. He wondered again what could have delayed Hunter.

With everything now prepared, his hands sore from all the chopping, he lay down in Hunter's room. Again and again he rang, but there was no answer.

As time wore on his curiosity got the best of him. This wasn't like Hunter at all. Ignoring the awkward fact that he might encounter Leandro, he went to the guesthouse in Zone One. As he entered the garden he could hear, issuing from the roof, the sounds of laughter, music and cheering. A cry went up: *Hun-ter . . . Hun-ter . . .*

So that's where he was. He stood for a moment, stunned, fighting an instinct to go upstairs and confront him. Instead he walked back to the training villa and gathered up the prepared dishes and the uncooked kebabs. He considered leaving a note for Hunter, but his mood was uncharitable and he knew he would regret whatever he might say.

When he arrived at Muhammad Ali's gate, the watchman remarked on the armload of covered dishes. Karimullah said to the gentle old man:

— Have you eaten yet, Amanullah?

— I have had a delicious dinner of fresh bread and tea, thanks be to God.

— Old friend, you shall be my dinner guest tonight.

In the low room that he had lately begun sharing with the aged watchman, Karimullah swept the rug, laid out the oilcloth and arranged each of the dishes. Amanullah made a small fire and they transferred the coals into a pan, using it as a brazier. They sat together on their haunches as Karimullah turned the skewers and the room filled with the aroma of roasted lamb.

— It is quite an occasion, the old man said, the fire bringing the deep wrinkles of his face into sharp relief.

— Courtesy is owed to you, uncle, for taking me under your roof.

— But why are you sad?

Karimullah shook his head and did not answer.

After they had eaten, the old man returned to his watch. Karimullah cleaned up, set the room in order, and lay on his pallet.

He sifted through the events of the day, looking for some overlooked bit of evidence that would exonerate his friend. He could not understand how even an American could so brazenly forsake the conventions of hospitality. But then, you never really knew a person. Hunter often talked about intersecting circles and how they converged in friendship: *this is me, this is you, this is us.* But was it the overlapping parts that mattered? People always kept something to themselves, and perhaps that was as it should be. But in Karimullah's experience, those unexplored regions were the places where lurked the darker shadows of human nature.

He found himself wanting to purge his heart of friendship forever. What had it gotten him? Every friend who had ever mattered to him—Babur, Penny Jones, Marsha Kohn—had left him for one reason or another. He'd once thought Sardar the Kalash was a true friend, only to be shown his moral depravity. What surprises and betrayals could he expect from Hunter Ames?

He had come to this compound looking for safety, and now the Taliban had found him. He had tried to stop corruption, and instead of being praised for his initiative he had been put on suspension. Had he not tried to live a virtuous life? Would he continue to be punished while the wicked were rewarded?

An explosion shook the room, followed by a shower of plaster and mud raining down from the ceiling. He dressed quickly, numb to the terror he knew he should feel. When he got to the gate old Amanullah was trying to drive in place the heavy security bar that was seldom used. Karimullah saw fear in the old man's eyes.

— It is another attack, much worse this time, the watchman said in a trembling voice.

By now they could hear the sound of automatic rifles and the ricochet of bullets. Behind this was a low human murmur, like crazed spectators at a sporting match. The shouts of warriors. Karimullah ran back inside the room he shared with the watchman. From a high shelf he took down a bulging plastic bag.

— Where are you going? What is in that bag?

— Lock the gate behind me, uncle.

The old watchman laid a hand on his shoulder but Karimullah broke free, wrested open the gate and slipped outside. All the noise and violence in the universe seemed to be concentrated on the roof of the guesthouse.

His steps faltered as he saw it in the distance, like a blazing beacon in the night. Then he saw a flash of light through one of the windows followed by shattering glass. The Taliban. They were kicking in the doors and tossing grenades into the rooms. He prayed that Hunter had gone back to the training villa.

He ran in that direction, and as he rounded the corner his heart leapt with joy when he saw Hunter on the balcony. Karimullah had only one thought now: he must save his friend.

He screamed:

— Come down, we must get out of here. Take this!

He said this in Pashto, finding in his anxiety that he could not speak English. He tilted the bag over his shoulder and threw the awkwardly light bundle onto the balcony.

But Hunter, seeming not to recognize him, backed fearfully away over the broken glass.

When Karimullah found him, Hunter was standing in the center of his room in a T-shirt and shorts. His face was pale and he stared at Karimullah with wide, fearful eyes. He seemed dazed, holding his laptop over his head as a weapon.

Karimullah drew from the bag a jumbled piece of blue fabric.

— Put this on. Quickly.

As he shook the folds free, it took on the dimensions of a crudely made burka, custom made by the child felons for this day that he had so grimly anticipated.

— The compound is under attack. We must leave immediately.

Confused, the American did what was asked of him, raising his arms in the air.

— No, Hunter, there are no sleeves. Here—

Karimullah threw the burka over Hunter's head and wrestled it down his body. It fit just right. The boys' first attempt had been far too tight; they had made it with a typical Afghan woman in mind. He'd made them do it again, certain that this day would come, and that everything must be perfect.

Karimullah centered the oval mesh over Hunter's face. Wide glassy eyes regarded him somberly.

— Listen to me. You must do exactly as I say.

— We're leaving the compound?

— Yes, Hunter.

— But it's against the rules. I can't leave . . . I'll be fired.

Karimullah caught the sour stench of alcohol on his friend's breath. He impulsively hugged Hunter, wondering if this might be the last time.

—There are no more rules, he whispered into the fabric of the burka.

Then he added quietly, his voice catching:

— There is no more project. ALAS is finished.

Hunter's feet tripped on the bottom of the burka as Karimullah led him out through the dark courtyard. The guards had fled their post at the main gate. It stood open and unguarded, but so far no one seemed to be coming in. This could only mean that the insurgents had succeeded in breaching Zone One. The guards had either joined them or were presently fleeing for their lives.

Hunter held Karimullah's hand as the latter drew him quickly toward the home of Muhammad Ali. Karimullah felt him hesitate, staring at the inferno now sweeping through the distant guesthouse, tongues of flame lapping from every window. The fire shone in Hunter's eyes staring blankly behind the mesh of the burka.

— *Oh my God.*

— Don't look, Hunter.

Karimullah was reminded of Lot, the nephew of Abraham, trying to drag his reluctant wife away from the immoral cities as God's fire rained down from the sky. He gripped Hunter's hand tighter and pulled him forcibly along.

He pounded at the gate of Muhammad Ali, fearing that old Amanullah had retreated to the main house. But in a moment there was a skirling and clanking from within and the gate creaked open.

The watchman stared at the huge burka-clad figure with alarm.

— Who is this woman?

— Do not be afraid, old friend. This is one of the Americans.

— But why—

— We will leave by the market gate. Please bolt the door behind us.

Karimullah swatted dust off the seat of his motorbike; he had not ridden it in some time. He jumped on the starter four times before it reluctantly belched to life.

Hunter was disoriented. Karimullah had to shout to persuade him onto the back of the bike. As Hunter straddled the seat, Karimullah saw the fabric climb up his legs, revealing pale, hairy shins.

— Hold onto my waist, Karimullah shouted, revving the motor and proceeding toward the back gate.

Passing alongside the house he saw the figure of Muhammad Ali standing in a lighted second-floor window holding a cell phone to his ear. At that moment Karimullah heard his own phone begin to ring. He waved up to Ali; there was no time to talk.

In a moment they were out in the dusty silence of the market. The shops were shuttered, the loud commerce of buyers and sellers still hours away. Stray dogs slept in the dust, oblivious to the mayhem happening nearby.

Karimullah sped past the Red Mosque and turned onto the main road. Hunter's hands tightened on his waist. The wind quickened, whipping the burka wildly about like an untethered sail. Karimullah drove the little motorbike as fast as it could carry them.

Hunter was regaining his coherence by degrees, shifting his weight on the motorbike and causing it to swerve about.

Karimullah shouted into the wind:

— You need to be still, Hunter.

— Where are we going?

— To the apartment of my former roommates, Khan and Sadiq. We'll be safe there.

— And then what?

Karimullah didn't answer.

Minutes later, coasting into the courtyard of the building, Karimullah raised a finger to his lips, indicating for Hunter to be silent. He led Hunter up the dark stairwell with its familiar domestic smells of cooking oil and laundry.

He tapped on the door. When no one answered, Karimullah turned the knob. It was locked, but thankfully Karimullah had his key. He switched on the light and saw that the room was in its usual state of youthful disorder. He called out, but no one was home.

They sat together on the sofa. Through the burka's facepiece Karimullah could see Hunter's face gleaming with perspiration, his eyes darting nervously like a caged animal.

Karimullah wondered what to do. He knew he had to take Hunter somewhere safe before sunrise, but where? There was no American Embassy in Kandahar. Would the Pakistan Embassy take him? No, that would be foolish; everyone knew the Pakistanis were not to be trusted.

He chewed his lower lip in restless anxiety, tasting blood. He had not thought to grab Hunter's passport or any personal items. With a passport they might have been able to get him on a flight to Kabul, though even that would be dangerous.

Hunter said softly but hoarsely, his voice muffled behind the burka:

— I'm sorry about dinner. I know it must have hurt your feelings, going to all that trouble.

— It's okay, Hunter.

This was so like Hunter, to worry about a breach of etiquette when the world was crumbling all around them.

— I do not know what to do with you, Hunter.

— I'm a shit, I know.

— No, I mean, what to do with you now, where to take you.

— Where are those famous roommates of yours?

— Probably out with their whores.

It was an unkind thing to say, but it made Hunter laugh. He squeezed Karimullah's hand.

— It's funny, but I feel safe with you, right here.

— Soon the roads will be blocked with barbed wire and police checkpoints. The Afghan Army will be out in force. Tanks will be everywhere.

— Then I'll flag a tank.

Karimullah laughed heartily.

— You cannot just walk up to a tank and ask for a ride. They will think you have a bomb and shoot you.

Hunter rose, pulled the burka impatiently over his head and tossed it aside, surveying the room like a prospective buyer.

— Maybe I could stay here until things quiet down.

— That is impossible. Obaidullah will be looking for me.

Hunter seemed oblivious to what he was saying. Perhaps he was still in shock. Then he brightened on a thought, snapping his fingers.

— Where's the nearest military base?

— In Arghandab, twenty minutes by road.

— That's probably our safest bet, little buddy.

— You are right, it is our only hope.

Hunter stood still, his expression rigid, and Karimullah saw his mood undergo a change. He turned away and his shoulders began to quake. He mashed a pillow over his face, emitting a high wail. It seemed that something had snapped inside him. Karimullah sat close beside him and gently lifted the pillow.

— I killed him. I did, it was my fault!

— What are you saying?

— I wasn't listening . . . I wasn't paying attention.

— You did not kill anyone, Hunter.

— My son. My dear Maurice. My beautiful boy.

— We will have much time for talking, please—

But Hunter was adamant.

— I have to tell you!

Karimullah held Hunter tightly, and soon the shaking stopped. His face had come to rest against the scruff of Hunter's cheek. He could feel the warm tears.

Despite all the shameful abuse he had suffered, the myriad ways in which his body had been demeaned, one thing had never been asked by his tormentors, nor would he have given it willingly: a kiss. It had happened with only one person, the American woman who had been his teacher in the art of love.

Between his hands he took the big face, bloated with so much unknown sadness, and pressed the lined forehead against his own. He stared into Hunter's unfocused eyes, then gave Hunter a kiss, tasting the salty tears. It was not a long kiss; he did not want to add more complications to an already dramatic day. But he needed Hunter to know how much he was loved.

When he drew away and saw Hunter's wide-eyed gaze, he knew it had been a rash and foolhardy thing to do. He waited for Hunter to push him away. But after only the briefest hesitation he felt Hunter's arms tighten around him and again their lips came together.

36
Eucalyptus

Time is a game played beautifully by children.
Heraclitus

A CHILD IS A SELF IN the making. A work in progress, like an artist's studio with newspapers over the windows. Stay out, no peeking.

Sometimes they'll offer you a glimpse onto their inner lives. But it's up to them. You can speculate, but at the end of the day all you really know about your kids is what they want you to know.

Maurice still had his demons, his bouts of darkness, but Gabon seemed good for him. He volunteered as a counselor for the Sea Brigade, teaching kids about sailing and tying knots. They'd sail down to Port-Gentil, anchor out in Lopez Bay and catch fish. He'd stay gone for whole weekends and return sunbaked and glowing.

He got a job tending bar at one of the waterfront cantinas down by the casino. It was hardly bartending, he said; mostly he just listened to drunk tourists pour out their stories. The owner thought having a white boy behind the counter might reel in a more sophisticated clientele.

This would explain his sudden interest in clothes. Suddenly he was going around in bone-white Egyptian cotton shirts unbuttoned halfway down his chest, setting off his dark tan. He wore linen suits and Italian leather deck shoes, a bracelet with his initials: MHA. A small silver stud appeared in one earlobe, then the other.

He was becoming his own man. They say the apple doesn't fall far from the tree? This one had landed in another orchard. And that was fine. I never wanted to create another being in my image. One Hunter Ames was enough.

He must have been making lots of new friends. We could hear the phone in his room ringing constantly. Often we'd hear him come home in the early morning while we were making coffee, and sometimes he wasn't alone. He'd turn up the music to drown out whatever it was he didn't want us to hear. Sometimes a moan or a cry would reach us, sometimes male, sometimes female.

I'm ashamed to say, the revelation that our son might like women was a relief. We were inheritors of the old notion that homosexuality equaled suffering. And we didn't want our boy to suffer. AIDS was never far from our thoughts; this *was* Africa, after all. But we'd raised a smart kid.

Libreville is located just inside the Gabon Estuary, a wide inlet that protects it from the rough waters of the Atlantic. It provides a sanctuary for fisherman and other seafarers, not to mention the occasional yacht and pleasure craft.

One morning Jane called me to the balcony to witness the arrival of one such ship on the horizon. It was huge and white, its decks stacked like Legos high over the water. At night its port lights shone like neat strands of pearls arranged one on top of another.

Jane said:

— When did the Love Boat start putting in calls at Libreville?

We learned from the desk clerk that it was the yacht of a certain Rémy Champlon, an elderly Frenchman whose family had made a fat fortune on Gabon's timber reserves back in the colonial days. The ship's name: *Le Mistral*.

Apparently the Frenchman still had some sort of business interests out at the Port à Bois. A few times a year he anchored off Libreville, came ashore in a landing craft that was a veritable ship in itself, loaded in provisions and left. He was feted like visiting royalty.

Jane and I were strolling the beach one evening when we saw him with his entourage. He was a lean, twitchy figure with overstated elegance, rather like some self-assured fashion designer, looking all the more vivid in a bright white suit. He must have been in his late seventies, though his face was smooth from years of suntans and Botox. He was surrounded by guys in dark suits wearing no-see-um sunglasses and stony expressions. As they strolled along, Champlon would toss coins over his shoulder to a crowd of children who followed like screaming seagulls in his wake, a gesture that seemed more a boast of conspicuous wealth (*Look at me, so rich I can just throw it away!*) than an act of true compassion.

The guys at the office had mixed opinions about him. Some thought him a benign humanitarian who had contributed greatly to Libreville's youth through scholarships and training. Others said he was an unrepentant old pederast who only came ashore to troll for new additions to his harem of boys, especially the ones who could dance. He reputedly dressed them in belly-dancing costumes and feathers. An entire deck of *Le Mistral* was dedicated to housing these catamites. Or so the rumor went.

He was a mystery, that's for sure, one of those eccentric personalities who can set tongues wagging in a backward town like Libreville. Jane had heard the same stories in the Red Cross clinic where she volunteered. In her version, the Frenchman would come ashore in the afternoon, drink heavily and then prowl the muddy back streets of shantytown in search of boys. Local mothers called him the five o'clock menace.

I saw his entourage one afternoon while I was wandering the back streets of shantytown in search of a locally produced herbal laxative. There he was, the white suit, the tan, the inscrutable smile. You could smell his cologne at fifty feet. Shopkeepers were standing at attention in front of their doors, hoping to be dignified with a visit. I saw him pat the cheeks of a few boys, but I saw him just as attentive to the girls, with a coin for one and all. Some menace.

— You can't be as rich as Champlon and avoid being vilified, Jane said.

— Still, at the heart of most gossip is a kernel of truth.

— Not always, Hunt. Keep an open mind.

I didn't think much more about it. Champlon would be gone soon enough anyway.

One evening I went down to the lobby to see if the English-language newspapers had arrived. I bought a copy and took it to the bar. Champlon and his henchmen were sitting at the round VIP booth in back. That wasn't so unusual; the Okoumé Palace had practically the only luxury bar in town.

I had a vodka cranberry at the bar, rather hoping Champlon might see me and invite me over for a drink. I wasn't immune to the charms of the rich and famous. Now and then I could hear his raucous cigarette laugh penetrating the din. Soon I forgot about him, absorbed as

I was in the news from back home.

We had just started bombing the shit out of Iraq, and commentators were remarking on what this might mean for Afghanistan. I hadn't thought much about Afghanistan before. I certainly had no clue that my vocation might one day lead me there. I had mixed feelings about that damaged decade. I understood the *zeitgeist* that had brought us to war—the thirst for action, for vengeance—but my aversion to herd thinking made me wary.

I had to walk past Champlon's table to get to the restroom. Two of his bodyguards were standing by the table as a kind of screen. I tried to get a look at Champlon at close range, but all I caught was a sleeve and a manicured hand on a glass.

Coming out of the restroom I heard the high, raucous laugh again. The guy sure liked to have a good time. The bodyguards were still at parade rest, exuding seriousness and self-importance. Behind them I saw a variety of well-dressed guests, all young and most of them black, with the exception of one young man sitting close to old moneybags. I felt a change in my body temperature, a quick hot flush, when I realized it was my son.

Our eyes connected for perhaps a second, and then he looked back at his host. He sat up straighter, proud of his triumph, holding forth his glass for more. Champlon's hand was under the table, stroking his leg.

Heart racing, I returned to the bar and ordered another drink, wondering what to do. I thought maybe Maurice would call me over, if only to rub my nose in it. I debated walking right up to the table and introducing myself. But after half an hour, tired of all the damned laughter (which now seemed directed at me), I folded my newspaper and went back up to the room.

Jane asked what took so long.

— Champlon was in the bar with his cronies, raising hell as always.

— Did you meet him?

I considered.

— Nah, why would he want to meet someone like me?

I didn't tell her.

A few days later we were on a train to Ivindo Province, in the Gabonese interior. The Red Cross needed Jane's help with a startup clinic near the wildlife refuge and we'd decided to make a family outing of it. The plan was to drop Jane off at Ivindo, then Maurice and I would travel back alone. One of my colleagues had loaned us the use of a cabin near Makokou. It would be a nice break from the noise and pollution of Libreville.

Jane and I had always dreamed of traveling on the Trans-Gabon Railway. The route follows the mighty Ogooué River, offering glimpses of some of the darkest, densest rainforests in all of Africa. The service was spectacular, the dining car all brass and paneled wood; examining the menus we salivated over pictures of filet mignon and lobster and *crème brûlée*. A liveried waiter in white gloves brought us gin and tonics, then turned down our beds for the night. All to the grinding, mechanical rhythm of rail points, a purple sky and the distant wail of the locomotive. It put Jane in the mood. But I was too busy brooding about Maurice in the next compartment, and his secret.

I was sick with morbid curiosity. He knew me well enough to know I wouldn't breathe a word about it to Jane, that I would try to protect her. Through fey glances and ambiguous smiles he communicated as much. *Oh Dad, there's so much you don't know. And you're not going to like any of it.* And he couldn't wait to tell me.

We got off the train at Booué and rode on to Makokou on a local bus. It was a foolish time to be traveling. Heavy rains had made the roads treacherous, and that old bus threw us around like dice in a cup.

We hired a driver to take us to the cabin we'd borrowed on the river, stopping along the way for provisions at the only grocery around. How clearly I remember that grocery and the sound of rain battering its rusted tin roof. Jane had to make an emergency visit to the outhouse, not an easy feat during an equatorial monsoon, and Maurice and I were waiting under the store's eaves, inches away from the falling rain. It seemed like I'd only seen him in profile the entire trip, staring off into the distance. But now he turned to me, his face gleaming with mist.

— Rémy offered me a job on his ship. Will you let me go?

Not Mr. Champlon. *Rémy.* I felt a knife turn inside me. The question was a formality; he knew he didn't need my permission anymore.

We stared out into the grey rain, listening to the grinding *scrunch* of windshield wipers on the Land Cruiser where the driver was waiting.

— Have you told your mother?

— I don't want to ruin the trip. I'll write her a letter when I get back to Libreville.

I felt myself settling into my usual attitude of compliant resignation. I knew better than to fight him. The appearance of an adversary would only cause him to tighten his grip. He was like a wolverine. If you didn't fight back, eventually he might let go.

— How long will you be gone?

Pointless question. I knew he wasn't coming back. But it seemed to rouse his spirits.

— We'll put in first at the Canary Islands, then on to Antibes. It's a really first-rate ship, Dad. Two diesel engines, satellite phones . . .

I wanted to ask about the harem of dancing boys, but decided against it.

Maurice sighed:

— The South of France. I've always wanted to go there.

— Yeah, I'm sure it's nice. Then after a while it's just like everywhere else.

As he stared ahead, I glanced at his handsome profile and saw something I'd never seen before: shame.

— What's it like to be such a cynic, Dad?

— What's it like to be a Frenchman's whore?

I didn't know I was going to say it, and I was sorry I did. I saw his fist tighten, his knuckles turn white. Jane arrived just in time, sloshing up from the outhouse, offering a pleasant shriek in the rising torrent of rain.

Maurice looked at me as though he might be sick. He wasn't disgusted at me, I told myself, but with the whole situation. He'll never join Champlon. It was just one of those deviations meant to test his limits, find his boundaries.

The driver got us to the cabin. Mostly we sat around playing cards and dominoes. We read. We took naps. Jane found a guitar and taught herself a few chords. The constant downpour was a comfort, filling the silence.

We made only one trip on the river, during a brief respite from the rain. But no sooner were we out in the boat than the clouds rolled in and the rain returned with a grim vengeance. We turned back, bailing for dear life.

Jane kept trying to cheer us up, wanting everything to be okay, clueless as to the cause of our gloomy looks, our terse replies. Maurice listened to music on his headphones, a talisman to ward off unnecessary conversation. We decided to cut our sojourn on the river short.

We delivered Jane to the clinic where she would be working for the next month. Maurice, plugged into his iPod, embraced his mother almost as an afterthought.

With Jane safely conducted to her Red Cross clinic, Maurice and I took the bus back to Booué, an old trading village whose fortunes had fallen in recent years. We took a room in the only hotel still open. The Libreville train, we were told, would arrive in the morning.

We had hardly spoken since the scene in front of the grocery. I was fine with sweeping the whole thing under the rug. It's what we did best. But a voice told me: *if you want to know this boy, it's now or never.*

I apologized for my rough remark, though it was probably a mistake exhuming it for further scrutiny. Maurice was sitting by the window with his bare feet on the ledge, watching the treetops clash in the driving wind. I was lying on the bed watching him. I cleared my throat and offered in an upbeat voice:

— So how is that going?

— How is what going?

— Whatever you've got going with Champlon.

He smiled at the rain-drenched window.

— You're asking me about my *love* life?

The bold confirmation was the last thing I wanted to hear. But I blundered ahead.

— I thought he was your boss. I'm just curious about your . . . life. Or is that off limits?

— This is kind of weird, Dad.

— I'll drop the subject.

His feet came down from the window and he stood up, poised for a showdown.

— No, I'll tell you. What do you want to know?

— How did you meet him? At the cantina?

He stood over my bed, arms folded.

— Let's just say I pour a mean gimlet.

— So it's true.

— What's true?

— He's more than just your boss.

— It's always been true, Dad. Remember that time you saw me and Corby in the shed?

— So what do you guys . . . You know.

He had paced back to the window, but I could see him watching me through the reflection.

— Jesus, Dad, are you really asking me sex questions on a Sunday morning? That's so awkwardly like you.

— I didn't mean—

He spun around, his expression oddly animated, as though this was exactly what he'd been hoping for.

— Corby wasn't my first lover. If you *really* want to know.

Not really. Not at all. But I sat up, scrunching the pillow under my arm as though this were any other father-and-son conversation.

— It started when I was fifteen.

I closed my eyes, fearing the worst. And it was worse than I could have imagined.

— You remember the old Domino Café out on Albertson Drive?

— That honky-tonk place?

— I picked up a trucker. I wanted to blow him. I'd seen it in a movie and I wanted to try it. So we went out to his truck and did it. I guess I was pretty good, because every time he rolled through town he'd come looking for me.

— He came to our *home*?

— No, he'd wait outside school.

— Jesus Christ. You were, what, a high school freshman?

— And pretty soon we were doing it all, Dad. The whole nine yards. You know what I'm saying?

I was rewinding back to Maurice at fifteen. He had gone in for a seventies look, as most kids had that year. His beguiling purity had only just begun to be encroached upon by the dark inwardness that would soon become characteristic. I tried to imagine it, this complex and beautiful being going down on some trucker in the cab of a Freightliner.

Tapping his finger on his lip, his expression became contemplative.

— I don't remember the guy's name. He had this friend named Bill who worked on pools. Bill was hot, he kind of looked like Patrick Swayze. He got me a job.

I stared at him as the horror grew. The kind of horror that makes the hair on your arms stand up like quills.

— Is this ringing any bells?

I closed my eyes, telling myself not to go on the attack, not to fight him. I was here to learn about my son, not to moralize.

— I'm not going to say the obvious, that you were taking real risks in this … line of inquiry.

— What would you have done if you'd found out?

I leapt from the bed.

— Done? I would have killed them!

— But I asked for it. I wanted it.

The forced hilarity on his face grew stiff. He edged away from me.

— You were just a *kid*.

— You think kids don't know what they want? There were some

women too, if that makes you feel better. Cougars mostly. I met them online. Housewives looking to spice things up.

I paced around stupidly then sat back down on the bed.

— What does that mean, you're bi?

There was no heat in his voice, just a bullheaded resolve to bring everything out in the open, whether I liked it or not. And to be honest, this new level of candor was refreshing.

— Why do I have to be one thing or another? That's so ... binary. So black and white. There are other colors on the spectrum, you know.

I repeated impatiently:

— Which means bisexuality.

He was affecting an annoying new mannerism, pursing his lips and sucking in his cheeks condescendingly, something that struck me as vaguely French. God knows what else he was learning from *Rémy*.

— That's just another label.

— Well, if you're not gay and you're not straight, then you must be bi.

He shook his head.

— You know, Dad, it must suck to be from your generation.

My voice was as tired and croaky as if I'd run a marathon.

— Believe me, the day will come when your own offspring will lob the same grenade in your lap. But I hear what you're saying. To hell with labels. Do what you want. Screw who you want. Have I got the gist of it?

He laughed and glanced over at me, the skin crinkling around his eyes. He was so damned handsome.

— Not really, but keep working on it, Dad. Explore the whole spectrum of sexual experience and leave your binary world behind.

— I'll take that under advisement.

Later, after a shower, he came out of the bathroom in a towel and sorted through the clothes in his suitcase. He made no attempt to hide the tattoo on his shoulder, the amulet of two blue triangles one inside the other. Seeing me staring at it, he smiled strangely. It was on the tip of my tongue to ask him about it, but then he grabbed some underwear and toiletries and went back to the bathroom, closing the door as solidly as a vault.

No trains would be running out of Booué, we were told by an unfriendly stationmaster the following morning. Passenger service was delayed for two days owing to a large ore shipment that was currently making its slow, trundling way from the Mounana mines.

— Uranium! the stationmaster proclaimed, waving away the relative unimportance of passenger service.

Maurice and I contemplated the bleak prospect of two days together in this drab town. I gathered that he was urgently needed on board *Le Mistral*. We both wanted this holiday to be over.

As we were leaving, the stationmaster called out to us:

— There is a charter flight this afternoon. Perhaps they can make room for you.

The airport was near the river. Once a hub for daily flights into the interior, it was now used by only the occasional charter flight. Sad with neglect, the roof of the small terminal was covered with grass and small saplings.

We found a small, gleaming twin-engine plane whose owner, a Frenchman, told us that there was indeed a flight. Some South African businessmen would be leaving that afternoon. The plane was full but he thought he could squeeze us in, quoting a rather hefty fee.

The rain had stopped and the plane's white paint seemed oddly bright against the grey sky. I leaned into the cockpit, admiring the maze of buttons, switches and dials. The small cargo area was stuffed with suitcases labeled in Afrikaans.

I asked:

— How old is this plane anyway?

The Frenchman wore an old safari hat with two greasy spots on the brim that corresponded to thumb and index finger. I wasn't in a mood for elderly French colonials. He didn't seem in much of a mood for me either.

— The plane is old but well maintained. You can take it or leave it, *mon ami*.

Maurice stepped up.

— We'll take it.

When the Frenchman was gone, I said:

— We could always wait around for the train. What's the rush?

— You can poke around this gloomy town all you want, but I'm flying. I don't need your money. I don't need *you*.

On cue, thunder rumbled across the sky. Maurice popped in his earphones and strolled angrily away, the wind tousling his hair.

See the boy: bitter, wounded, proud and vain.

It's one of my last memories of him.

The plane seated eight. There were four rows with a narrow aisle running down the middle, one seat on either side. Maurice and I were crammed in back. There was no room for our bags so we were told to carry them on our laps. We sat there for the half hour it took the pilot and copilot to go through their pre-flight checklist. They wore matching orange jumpsuits and spoke a tribal dialect I didn't understand.

The old Frenchman came over to check on things. The pilot led him away from the plane. Together they looked over something on the pilot's clipboard. The pilot's arms were folded, as though perplexed by some problem that he doubted his boss would be able to solve.

They inspected the cargo compartment, shuffling the large parcels this way and that. The plane, I began to realize, was too heavy. I glanced at the open door. There was still time. In less than a minute Maurice and I could be strolling down the tarmac—snickered at by the South Africans, an enigma to the pilots, but free. *Let's go back to the hotel. Let's get dinner, have a few beers, find something to laugh about.*

Maurice nudged me with a stick of chewing gum, a conciliating gesture I chose to ignore. His mood had relaxed. Clearly he was thinking ahead to Libreville and his new job. Visions of the Côte d'Azur, lounging on the foredeck of *Le Mistral* while the old Frenchman coated his shoulders in coconut oil.

I love you. I don't want to fight with you.

They never leave us. We wear them like scars, all the things we should have said.

At last we were ready to go. The pilot climbed inside the cockpit and the Frenchman saluted the South Africans, giving the plane a light slap. Pilot and copilot put on headsets and began flipping toggle switches, bringing the plane humming to life.

Certain details stand out with stark clarity: tufts of weeds poking through the clay runway, the dilapidated airport, the ragged child vendors with their baskets of fruits and nuts. But I don't remember the faces of the other passengers. They're a blur, like the faces on TV reality shows digitally masked to hide the identities.

I went through my mantra: bad things happened in the world, sometimes catastrophically bad things, but they happened to other people, didn't they?

Most airplane disasters happen during takeoff and landing. If you're on one of the world's top twenty-five airlines the odds are negligible, around one in ten million. If you're on any of the bottom twenty-five carriers, your odds are ten times worse. But still, one in a million isn't worth worrying about.

The two engines came alive. The burly South Africans let up hoots and applause. Maurice was bouncing around in his seat, trying to line up a photo in the dirty window. I sat there with my bag in my lap and stared at the hairy neck of the guy in front of me, noting the odor of whiskey wafting from his sweaty pores.

The airport was situated in a bend in the river, which snaked around both ends of the runway. A mindful pilot would want to squeeze out every available inch, which is just what ours presently did. I could see the landscape halt and pivot as the plane taxied to the end and turned about, positioning for takeoff.

To my alarm, I saw Maurice standing in the aisle, dragging his bag to the front of the plane.

— Where are you—?

— I'm moving up front. I want to get some pictures.

I saw him bending over one of the South Africans, a man with flaming red hair. After a brief conference the man shrugged, surrendered his seat and joined me in the back of the plane. We had begun some sort of banter when the engines rose in pitch, the propellers became a blur, and the plane lunged forward. The other passengers grew silent, either because of the shrill noise or in deference to the miracle of flight. On a small plane it really does seem like a miracle.

The pilot was leaning hard on the throttle. I was with him, straining in my imagination. The bumpy runway became smooth as the plane gently left the ground, but in a moment it dropped again with a hard thud, swerving a little.

The plane was going more than 80 mph now, too fast to brake for the ever-shrinking length of runway: the point of no return.

Again the plane began to achieve lift. We could all feel the angry struggle between gravity and human engineering. I glanced up the aisle at Maurice fussing with his camera, though there didn't seem much worth capturing but dense green forest and a smoky veil of mist.

We were airborne.

Then: a loud thump, a sickening metallic screech and the plane heaved violently to one side. I glanced out the window just in time to see the wing tip strip the leafy top of a eucalyptus tree. Someone else saw it and had about half a second to find it funny before we felt the almighty plunge.

I remember nothing of the impact itself. When I came to, I was still strapped to my seat, thrown like a crash test dummy from the cracked fuselage, face down in the undergrowth.

It was oddly quiet. I remember hearing the reproving squawks of crows returning to their roost atop the eucalyptus tree. I remember the smell of scorched plastic. The air was greasy with fumes.

There was none of the screaming human drama you would imagine in such a scene, not even a moan from my red-headed neighbor, now sitting up a few feet away from me. Our faces were as bloody as newborns. One of my arms was sticking out at an unlikely angle. I was too stunned to feel any of the pain that would soon be screaming through half a dozen cracked ribs.

I took in the scene: torn metal, a trail of luggage, bits of foam. But where the hell was the plane?

Behind me I heard the pat of bare feet slapping on wet clay. I turned with difficulty, expecting for some reason to see Maurice. But it was a group of kids, the ones who had been harassing us to buy their fruits and nuts.

I was so happy to see them, I don't know why. I stumbled forward on my knees, holding out my one good arm, wanting to embrace them. I was laughing as though this were the funniest thing in the world, exhilarated by the precious gift of life transposed onto the sweet faces of those children.

They stared at me as at some malignant forest spirit, then edged past and made their way toward the smoking disaster that awaited us down by the river.

37

Karimullah

Your task is not to seek love, but merely to seek and find all the barriers within yourself that you have built against it.
Rumi

IT WAS NEARING three a.m. when they finally left the apartment. The motorbike moved sluggishly under their combined weight but soon picked up speed. Karimullah felt weak with emotion. Hunter, on the other hand, seemed light, unburdened.

There was no awkwardness between them. They were the same people, and yet not. Everything was new. The last veil had been lifted. And Karimullah was certain, after the sad story he had just heard, that their lives would be forever entwined.

They passed several green pickups of the Afghan National Police, sirens blazing, racing toward the compound and their own likely destruction. The ensuing gun battle would rage on until late the following morning. Americans would die, innocent Afghan civilians would die, the police would die. And in the end the Taliban would die, but by then, with the attack appearing on every network in the world, their primary objective would have been achieved. They would have succeeded in bringing down one of the largest aid projects in Afghanistan, and everyone in the world would know about it.

Leaving the city, the small motorbike began to groan as they began the climb into the Arghandab hills. Kandahar lay spread out across the valley floor behind them, its streets and rambling mud buildings mostly dark save for a single pillar of fire near the Red Mosque.

The bike swerved as Hunter turned for a last glimpse of the atrocity. His head came to rest against Karimullah's back, his hands tightening around his waist. He muttered:

— Mother of God.

Soon the road crested and the motorbike came alive as it began the downhill course toward Arghandab.

FOB Arghandab was not used to receiving guests at 3 a.m. As Karimullah turned the motorbike up the gravel incline toward the main gate, a bright light snapped on and Afghan voices shouted for him to stop. He could see the silhouettes of AK-47s turning in their direction as fear swept among the soldiers. He stopped the bike and raised his hands in the air. He said to Hunter:

— Remember, this base is now controlled by the Afghan Army. The American force is very small.

The Afghans were shielding themselves behind Hesco barriers, weapons raised, shouting at them to get off the bike. He knew that he had only a few seconds to explain his errand. In Pashto he called out:

— My brothers, this is an emergency. We need to speak to someone in the U.S. military.

As he spoke, Hunter climbed off the bike, righting the burka, which had climbed up his legs. The bright searchlight panned between Karimullah and the odd figure next to him.

A megaphone clicked on.

— Stay where you are. Do not come closer!

No one wanted to take the blame either for killing them or letting them in. Hunter, not understanding what was being said, was now sauntering toward the entrance as though expecting only the warmest of welcomes. Karimullah tried to stop him.

Two soldiers stepped out, jittery and confused, aiming 9 mm pistols. Hunter, now realizing what was happening, began flailing his arms beneath the fabric in an attempt to raise them in the air. But this skirmishing only further upset the wide-eyed guards, who saw his pale, hairy legs and cried out:

— It is not a woman!

Tangled up in the burka, Hunter froze and shouted desperately:

— Please, listen to me. I am an American citizen and I am in need of the services of my military!

It was some time before an American officer could be brought to the scene. By now Hunter had removed the burka and was wearing it across his chest like a Greek toga. The Afghan duty sergeant, who spoke some English, had allowed them to approach the gate but no further. He and Hunter were now chatting about the disaster that had befallen the compound. Hunter recited the facts in a quiet, matter-of-fact way, as though it were something he'd only just heard on the news. And then, unexpectedly, he brought his hands over his face and began to weep piteously. Karimullah tried to rouse him, fearing another scene like the one he had witnessed back in the apartment. He prayed Hunter would not try to confess his sins to these men.

This was the scene that greeted the colonel and his retinue upon their arrival. Col. Paul Donovan commanded the small American support unit at FOB Arghandab. He put a few questions to Hunter, but each time Hunter tried to answer, his words dissolved into loud wails. The dazed Afghan soldiers standing around him began brushing back sympathetic tears. Exasperated, the colonel barked an order to the duty sergeant to let the poor man in.

— Raise the fucking gate, Anwar. This man is no suicide bomber.

The colonel clapped Hunter on the back as he led him inside.

— Let me make you some coffee. You look like you've just been to hell and back.

Hunter turned and pointed at Karimullah standing on the opposite side of the gate.

— Wait, he's with me.

The colonel looked at Karimullah and wasn't so sure.

Karimullah called out:

— It is okay, I must go, Hunter. The streets will soon be full of police checkpoints, and I did not bring any identification.

— But it isn't safe out there.

Karimullah looked at his friend—the gleaming, sweat-stained face, the burka slanting down across his chest like some warrior of old. He thought of the kiss, and how natural it had seemed. Here was the ally he had sought for so long, his protector. *My friend*, he thought. *My best friend.*

— I will return tomorrow, my dear Hunter.

He got on the motorbike and began to ease it down the gravel drive. Then he heard a shout.

— Karimullah!

The searchlight was now aimed at Karimullah's face. He raised his hand to shield his eyes. He sensed that Hunter wanted to say something for him alone.

— What is it, Hunter?

Hunter looked down at the ground, trying to find the words. Then he raised a clenched fist in the air and cried:

— *Mozhbaa sabaa zhowand wakroo!*

Karimullah smiled, recalling the one Pashto phrase Hunter had managed to learn.

He eased the motorbike down to the main road and saw the dark expanse of Arghandab orchards descending toward the river. He thought of Babur. They had only exchanged a few text messages since Babur's arrival, but now he felt a terrible urgency to see his long-vanished friend, even at this hour.

Karimullah knew that his life was about to change in profound and dangerous ways. By morning his escape would be noted, both by the police and by Obaidullah, wherever he was. Owing to Karimullah's recent suspension he might even be implicated in the attack. There was no place on earth that he dreaded more than Obaidullah's orchard, but if he hoped to see Babur again, it must be now.

He took out his phone and sent a text, hoping it would wake him. He told himself he would wait just five minutes for a reply. If none came, he would return to the city.

He sat on his motorbike in silence, listening to the night sounds of insects and baying dogs. He could hear police sirens whining faintly in the distance.

The five minutes had passed. And just then, as if in answer to a prayer, his cell phone lit up.

Yes, come! I will meet you in your old room.

Karimullah wrote back:

I must stay with you. I am in danger.

In a moment came the reply:

Do not worry, Prince. O. is far away. Come quickly.

His heart beat wildly as he started the motorbike, turning it in the direction of Obaidullah's orchard.

In a while he was pushing the motorbike quietly along a dirt road flanked by majestic poplars. He could hear the trickle of water in the irrigation canal. The moon was bright, casting a chalky, ethereal light through the branches above.

The orchard was fragrant with the odors of harvest, a combination of fruity lightness and putrid decay. It had been a record-setting year for pomegranates in Arghandab, largely a result of USAID programs in the valley, he thought proudly. Harvests were up by thirty percent, and though the mullahs praised the beneficence of Allah, Karimullah knew the Americans could be given some of the credit as well.

He was surprised to find that he had retained some good memories of this place. He could remember flying through these trees like a trapeze artist. He could remember the songs of the workers, with their refrains that spoke equally of happiness and suffering. Beneath a certain tree he remembered a picnic that he and Babur had once shared.

And of course he remembered the dancing.

He would never dance again. He knew that now. He would go to college in America, study engineering, learn how to build bridges and buildings. But he would never again feel that electric joy tingling through his senses. Just as it had begun here, it had been corrupted here, and here it had died.

In a break between the trees he saw the moon's reflection repeated many times over something metallic, like staring eyes repeating far into the distance. He grinned as he drew closer and realized what he was seeing. In the pale light he discerned the word SUPERIOR stamped on the smooth metallic surfaces. Here were the two hundred wheat threshers specially ordered from China and ready for delivery to ALAS. No doubt Obaidullah would get rid of them somehow, but Karimullah took pride in having put that particular pebble in his shoe.

As the road curved, the dark outline of the main house came into view. He felt the old apprehension, the old terror. The last time he was here he had been but a boy, running with pockets full of jewels stolen from Obaidullah's wife. It was as though he could see the shadow of that fearful boy now running past him, bound for a Kuchi camp and the promise of freedom.

None of this Babur knew yet. They could talk for days and Karimullah would not have time enough to recount all the events of recent years. He felt as though he had lived many lives already, and the best was yet to come.

He soon came to the low outbuilding where he had once lived. His heart began to race with the exhilaration of seeing his friend. They would only have a few hours before sunrise, but those hours would be sweet.

He tapped on the old door.

He wondered why Babur had returned to this place, with all its painful memories. He could still remember Babur's furtive, downcast eyes when Karimullah was in training. Had he known what was to befall the child? Had the same thing happened to him?

He tapped again, whispering Babur's name.

Karimullah had been through many traumatic events in his life, none so terrifying as what had happened tonight. But he had been ready for it—the motorbike, the burka, the friendship with Muhammad Ali to gain access to his market gate. It was like one of those elaborate domino courses, vast in design, which could only be deployed once, either to succeed or fail. And it had succeeded.

Pressing against the old wooden door, he felt it give with an abrupt creak. As his eyes adjusted to the faint light, he realized that the room was very much as he had left it—the rough-hewn table where he had once studied, the pallet on the floor, a calendar from many years ago.

The door slammed behind him. Turning, he felt hands of incredible strength seizing him. He giggled, thinking it was one of Babur's games. But then he felt his arm wrenched painfully behind his back and Obaidullah's voice grunted into his ear:

— Welcome home, Prince.

38

The Head Sometimes Remains Intact

Skillful pilots gain their reputation from storms and tempests.
Epictetus

I SLEPT THROUGH breakfast and lunch. I had a vague memory of someone knocking at the door of my tent, or had it been a dream?

When I finally awoke I found at the foot of the bed a pile of what looked to be bits and pieces of many men's wardrobes—briefs, a T-shirt, sandals, some fatigues and so on. Pulling on a pair of track shorts and a shirt, I flung a towel over my shoulder and went in search of the showers.

I felt fine, if a little dazed. The sky could not have been a more cheerful shade of blue. I must have slept a long time. The sun was already past the meridian and sinking toward the tall hill, drawing long shadows from the tents and conexes that I passed.

I stopped a female soldier and asked directions to the showers. She pointed the way, but then, realizing that I was the civilian who had turned up at their gate that morning, led me there herself. She was a plain, long-faced woman with hair gathered up in a bun, but in that moment she was one of the most beautiful creatures I had ever seen.

— Any idea what time it is? I don't think I've eaten a thing in twenty-four hours.

She glanced in the direction of the sun, as though taking a bearing.

— Must be nearin' four. This your first time here?

The accent: South Carolina? Georgia?

— I've never been to this base before. Spent some time at the FOBs in Zhari and Maiwand, though.

I kept on talking. I needed badly to connect with another human being. She smiled and nodded, like a therapist letting me ramble on.

Having arrived at the steamy entrance of the shower conex, she clapped me on the shoulder.

— There you go, sir. Enjoy your stay.

She walked off, smiling back at me.

There would be no three-minute combat shower today, I thought, undressing. I stepped under the blast of hot water and closed my eyes. I held the showerhead as though it were a microphone. I felt like singing.

And then a flashback: flames exploding from the guesthouse windows, the staccato sound of gunfire, the faint but discernible wail of human screams.

I leaned against the shower's plastic shell, trembling. Where were they, my colleagues? Who had survived and who had perished?

This was going to be more difficult than I had thought.

After an uninspired dinner of franks and beans I met with Col. Donovan at the command center. The colonel went out to find his major, who would be taking notes, as the embassy had requested a full debriefing on the attack. In a while the colonel returned with a red-haired young man fiddling with a tape recorder.

We were introduced, and for a moment I was amused; the man clearly had no memory of me. I was in no doubt—the freckles, the smug expression, the hair like coarse sandpaper. It was Maj. Frost from Zhari, the one who had sent me into the wrath of the angry *shura*.

We took our seats at the head of a small conference table and a staff sergeant brought in a tray of coffee. I stared at Frost, who was now awaiting the colonel's command to start the recorder. He glanced indifferently at me, still carrying on the pretence that we were strangers.

At last, stirring his coffee, the colonel said in his homey, southern manner:

— Before we begin, Ames, I'd like to know a little more about what it is that you do.

— I'm a civilian aid worker.

— I know that, but parse it for me. What does that mean?

— I work for a company called Global Relief Solutions. We're funded by USAID to provide agricultural—

— Right, the ALAS project. Unfortunate acronym, isn't it?

— I worked in infrastructure. We—

Hearing it in the past tense, I felt my throat tighten. Trying to compose myself, I stared down at my hands, lips clenched and trembling.

— Excuse me, sir.

Abruptly the colonel leaned over the table and laid a gnarled hand on my wrist.

— Son, I can only imagine what you've just been through. If you're not ready to do this, fuck the embassy, we'll try again tomorrow.

— I think it's just starting to sink in.

The colonel thought for a moment, then said to Maj. Frost:

— Major, you can turn off your device and go.

— Sir?

— I want to talk to this man alone.

Frost took up his things and rose, familiar with the colonel's shifting moods. I tried to reach him telepathically—*come on, remember me.* At the door he paused to gather up the recorder's electrical cord that had slipped through his fingers. *Remember me, dickhead.* But then he was gone, without a wink or smile.

I glanced around the room, storing it all away in memory: the military-issue desk, the obsolete dot matrix printer, a jar of ancient Jolly Ranchers hardened to a dusty clump. Already I was feeling Afghanistan beginning to recede, like an exotic port viewed from the deck of a homebound vessel. Yes, I was going home. What little I knew about this bewildering country was all I would ever know. I wouldn't be back. The last bit of film was threading through the projector. Time now for the closing credits.

— I'm supposed to be debriefing you, Ames, but I believe you're the one who deserves to be briefed. Is there anything you would like to ask me?

When I didn't respond, he went on:

— Four of your colleagues lost their lives in the attack.

I glanced up at him pleadingly.

— Don't tell me their names.

— Fair enough.

— I'm not ready for that.

— What we know is that two suicide bombers climbed over a wall and entered by way of your main office building. You may know that there is a children's prison attached to your compound. The suicide

347

bombers were inmates of that facility. They had improvised a rope out of strips of fabric. We don't know how the Taliban smuggled in the explosives, but I suppose it's easily done. We estimate around a dozen insurgents then entered through a breach in the wall. It was well orchestrated.

I leaned down with my face in my hands, moaning:

— How do you know the suicide bombers were children? Someone else could have done it, maybe a prison guard.

— When a body vest explodes, the head sometimes remains intact after detonation, depending on the placement of the charge.

I looked at him in disbelief, tears streaming unchecked down the side of my face. My lips curled in disgust.

— You mean you know which boys they were?

The faces flashed in my mind like playing cards. Boys with pimples and weirdly shorn hair, eyes bright with intelligence or dull with apathy. There was Hamid, the thief who might yet be redeemed. And the sad smile of Alaamzeb—the beauty of the world.

— We do. One was a—

I stopped him:

— No, don't tell me. I don't want to know what they looked like. I knew those boys. Please.

The colonel slid a box of tissues across the table.

— I'm sorry about this, Ames. Is there anything we can do for you?

— I want something from the compound, from my room.

The colonel was silent, marshaling his thoughts.

— The recovery is in progress, but there isn't much left of the guesthouse.

I grabbed a tissue and impatiently smudged the tears streaking my face. My nose was running copiously now and for some reason this infuriated me. I nearly shouted:

— I wasn't living in the guesthouse. They had me stuck in a building in Zone Two.

— Zone Two?

— The training villa. It's near the main gate. I'll draw you a map. If you've got men over there, ask them to drop by my room. Ask them to find my cell phone.

— We'll see what we can do.

— Please. It's important. I need my phone.

Karimullah, I thought.

39
Karimullah

And still, after all this time, the Sun has never said to the Earth,
'You owe me.' Look what happens with love like that.
It lights up the sky.
Hafez

THE VALLEY WAS GREEN and narrow, chilly from recent rains. As
he made his way down a rocky trail, birds called out gaily from one
to another as though telegraphing the news of his arrival. *He is home,
home, home* . . .

He was nearing a river. He hadn't known it would be there. He
smiled as he heard its gentle susurration ahead through the trees, like
a chorus of voices whispering: *You are home, home, home* . . .

He awoke with a start, feeling a damp washcloth moving stickily
up his arm.

His eyes ticked wildly from side to side. As they adjusted to the
darkness he could make out blurry points of light in a mesh pat-
tern. He wriggled his nose, feeling a scratchy burlap sack covering

his head.

Sensation returned to him like lights switching on in a darkened house. He became aware of the string that fastened the sack around his throat, the ropes binding his wrists behind his back and biting into his ankles, the dank must of the burlap.

And then the pain in his back and ribs, a dull numbness on one side of his face. He opened and closed his mouth and tasted caked blood. One of his front teeth moved under his tongue like a toggle switch.

He could hear the washcloth being rinsed in a bowl. He was aware of a smell, distantly familiar. A woman's smell.

He took a shallow, trembling breath, gasping against the shock of broken ribs. Again he heard the cloth being dipped into water.

— Who is there? he whispered, finding his voice.

— Be still.

How long had it been since he had heard that voice? Even in those few syllables he recognized Afsana, Obaidullah's unhappy wife.

Taking his hand she lightly raised his arm and brought the wash-cloth along the inside of his bicep. He felt a sting as the cloth daubed at a cut. Her touch was tender, motherly, yet at the same time fueled by haste.

— Please take this off my head. It is difficult to breathe.

— Be still! she hissed

He tried to turn over and realized that he could not. His ankles were tied to the bedpost.

— What has happened? he whispered.

The woman paused in her ministrations. Her voice was as stern as sacred text.

— You have been punished for your crimes.

— What crimes?

351

Her laugh was joyless, bitter with long-festering resentment.

— Have you already forgotten about the jewelry you stole from me?

— Afsana, I will repay you for my past offences. But please remove this sack. I cannot breathe.

She snorted.

— You? Pay me? You are just a poor dancing boy.

— I am not the indigent slave who once lived here. I have a job and money—

— Be silent!

He moved a little on his side, trying to feel the lump of his cell phone in the deep pocket of his *kamiz*. But it was not there.

Despite the harshness of her voice, he remembered Afsana to be a compassionate woman, the kind who rescued wounded cats and set eggs back in nests but could do nothing to protect herself from the moods of her violent husband.

She was still for a moment. He felt her hands exploring the rope that bound his neck. It tightened as she worked with the knot. As she slipped off the burlap sack he felt his face drenched in cool air.

She pursed her lips as she went about her work, careful not to look into his eyes. She was probably fifty, with thin, arched eyebrows and the merest hint of powder on her cheeks. She had aged in the intervening years, her unhappiness recorded in deep grooves bracketing her mouth.

He had no idea how long he had been here. It might have been hours or days. There was scarcely a spot on his body that wasn't numb or throbbing with pain.

It was as though she had read his thoughts, for now she reached into a drawer and drew out a bottle of pills.

— You must take this for the pain.

She laid one on his tongue and offered him a drink of water from a chipped cup. He sought out her eyes, trying to read her intentions. Through the open window he heard the call to prayer.

— You are too good to me.

— It is no more than I would do for a wounded animal.

— You were always kind.

— Ha. Do not attempt to flatter me.

— I must ask a favor.

— I owe you nothing, she said, as though insisting on her right to resent him.

— Untie me, old mother, so that I might offer a pleasing prayer to the Almighty. I feel it may be my last.

She looked at him uncertainly, glancing out the open window.

— How can I trust you not to escape?

— I offer you my word. It is the only thing of value I still possess.

Hesitantly she began unfastening his bindings, first the rope around his ankles, then the one around his wrists. He rose to his feet, wobbling.

He saw a prayer rug rolled up in a corner. She indicated the *qibla* to which it should be pointed. Karimullah knew that he was filthy and should perform his ablutions, but he would have to depend on Allah's mercy.

Kneeling with some difficulty, he prayed. His mind was muddled, and each time he prostrated himself on the rug and rose again he fell over. At one point he lost his way in the prayer and had to start over.

When he was finished he rolled up the rug and returned to Obaidullah's wife still sitting on the edge of the bed. He squatted, matched his wrists and extended them.

— You may tie me up again.

Her eyes grew wide. She glanced around and hissed:

— Leave this place.

— I gave you my word.

The hand holding the rope was trembling. He could see that she was close to tears.

— Do not be a fool. I release you from your promise.

— Auntie, I could not escape if I wanted to. I am too weak. And you would be severely punished. But do me one favor. Find my cell phone.

He reclined in his previous position and she tied one rope about his wrists.

— Bring my cell phone, he repeated.

She sank back on her haunches, her face pitiable, like a scolded child.

— What will you do?

— There is one who can help me. He is nearby, at the military base.

He saw that she now held his cell phone in her hand. Her expression hardened, and where before he had seen kindness he now saw an emotion that he could not name.

— Twice you stole from me. Do you even remember?

— Auntie, I was but a child. Please—

Her eyes were blazing with indignation.

— First you stole my father's watch, three strands of pearls, a gold brooch and three rings that had been passed down to me from my grandmother.

Never had it occurred to him to consider her loss. He had acted recklessly, focused on only his freedom.

— My brothers pooled their money together and bought me a set of emeralds and rubies. Green and red were always my favorite colors. But next thing I knew you had stolen them too!

354

Her face was twisted with grief over the ancient loss, a woeful refrain she must have come back to many times over the years. Karimullah felt impotent against the charges. What could he say?

He glanced at the phone clutched in her trembling fist. As she turned it this way and that he knew this simple woman had never operated a touch screen before.

A sound entered the periphery of his hearing. At first it had no more significance than the droning of a fly. Seeing Afsana's sudden alarm, he knew it was an approaching truck. As it drew nearer to the house he saw her face become frantic with indecision.

— Please, the phone. Give it to me. Quickly!

The truck stopped outside the window with a squeal of brakes. Two doors slammed followed by men's laughter.

He seized at the ropes binding his wrists, managing inadvertently to tighten them. She was staring at him, unsure what to do.

— Call Hunter Ames.

— What is the number? Hurry!

— It is in my list of contacts. Call him. Tell him I am here.

— I do not know how, she hissed, stabbing at the inexplicable device.

— Hunter Ames, he repeated urgently.

Booming voices entered the house, enlivening the silence with overtones of doom. Afsana dropped the phone and threw the sack once more over Karimullah's head, affixing the rope awkwardly about his neck. Her voice was quick and unsteady, pitched not for his hearing but for the Almighty's.

— Forgive me.

There was no need. He felt himself entering into a strange detachment. He was tired of fighting. Maybe Hunter was right. *What does my life matter? What's so important about me?*

His soul was empty, but the emptiness didn't frighten him. He had fought hard to preserve a place in the world for Karimullah, son of Abdul Bahram. It was time to stop fighting. He recalled the green valley of his dream. *He is home, home, home* . . . He longed to be in that place again.

His muffled voice said, quietly and simply:

— I do not blame you, Auntie.

He felt her hand linger a moment. He was sure she wanted to tell him something more.

But with a sudden rush of footsteps she was gone.

40
Here at the Frontier

A ship should not ride on a single anchor, nor life on a single hope.
Epictetus

IT WAS REALLY TOO cold for an outdoor barbecue, but my friend Ron felt my return merited nothing less than a soirée. He promised to bring over a few teachers he thought I should get to know. My future colleagues. Ron was now assistant principal at Evansville High School, where I would soon be back in the faculty ranks. Brush up on your schmooze, he said.

— You're a celebrity. Take advantage of your fifteen minutes of fame.

Ron brought Eddie, his new boyfriend. Others followed: Mary, who taught French, a biology teacher named Scott and some others, I forget their names. It wasn't a great party, but the food was good and we had some laughs. Music played on crackly outdoor speakers that hadn't been fired up in years. We stood around in the firelight holding drinks. Later we moved inside and played board games.

I braced myself for the inevitable questions about the attack. By then it was all over the national news, and the Taliban had posted photos on their Voice of Jihad website. As before, there were pictures of body parts scattered all over the compound, but this time some of them were American.

My guests only seemed to care that I was okay, that I'd made it out alive. That was nice. But it's amazing how thoughtless the questions could be. *Did you know anyone who died?* Sheez, I knew them all, you morons.

But we had a good time. I was networking, learning what I needed to know about my new colleagues. I'd only been home a week when I landed the job. Ron had urged me to drop off my resume; they had a science vacancy for the spring term. The teacher I'd be replacing had just been sacked for screwing one of her students.

We talked about that, of course. Endlessly. Ron said the kid was a hunk, who could blame her, which offended Mary. They were all pretty drunk. I was sticking to cranberry juice and soda. While Ron was setting up a game of charades, I went to the kitchen to throw some more drummies in the oven.

Hunter, what are these things called drummies?

I had been imagining you a lot lately, remembering little things that I hadn't been conscious of when we were in Kandahar—the teardrop-shaped mole on your wrist, the way you always draw a deep breath before laughing. Now you were at my side, squatting to peer into the oven window. My hand came to rest on the crown of your head.

— They're tiny chicken legs. I don't know if you'll like them, they're kind of spicy.

You'd probably be wearing some garish shirt from the mall, one that you'd later discard as your taste in American fashion evolved. It's hard to imagine you in jeans and tennis shoes. Try as I might, I can only see you in that pale blue *shalwar kamiz.*

You have nice friends, Hunter.

I looked at my reflection in the window and turned in profile. How badly I wanted to deflate that fucking beach ball.

— Yeah, they're okay, but I'm getting tired. Might be time to shut things down. What do you think?

A throat cleared behind me. I turned and saw Mary, the French teacher, leaning in the doorway. I felt my face turn scarlet. How long had she been standing there?

— Anything I can do in here?

If she had heard me, she was too polite to say. She was an energetic, matter-of-fact woman who liked to be of use. She found the garbage can and dumped out an ashtray. We'd had a nice chat earlier about France, where she'd once lived. Never heard of Meuze, of course, but the monastery intrigued her. She wrote her e-mail address on a napkin and asked me to send her some photos.

I wasn't entirely sure I wanted to sell it. I was starting to sense that the monastery of Meuze might be the next stop on our journey. Not right away, of course, but someday. Yvette was amazed when she received the wire transfer with payment in full; she thought I'd given up.

You said you once dreamed of castles in the sky. Is the Hautes-Pyrénées high enough?

Mary leaned over the sink, admiring the garden in the fading firelight. Then she turned to me, smiling sadly.

— I thought your name sounded familiar. Now I remember.

I knew that tone of voice. She meant Maurice.

Your reflection appeared in the window between us.

Stop running, Hunter. Talk to her. She's beautiful.

You were right. The woman was making an overture, reaching out to me. And she *was* beautiful.

— I'm so sorry. I'm sure what happened in Africa must have been devastating. And now this.

I was rinsing dishes. I stopped and stared abstractedly at my hands.

Talk to her, Hunter.

She tried again:

— I taught seventh grade at La Salle Middle School. He wasn't in my class, but I remember seeing him in the halls, such a lovely boy. He had a kind, sweet disposition. An old soul.

In the other room a glass shattered and Ron's boyfriend squealed. I felt Mary's hand clasp my arm before she turned and rejoined the party.

Go, Hunter. They're waiting for you.

— You're all I need.

Ron blundered into the kitchen in search of a towel. He saw my phone and asked for the fourth or fifth time to see your photo. It was one I'd taken at the children's prison. You were standing next to Tulai, the instructor, deep in earnest conversation. The sun caught in your eyes, making them glow like searchlights.

While I was calling up the photo he put his chin on my shoulder. His breath was so pungent, I wondered what would happen if I put a match to it.

— So you haven't even heard his voice since you got back?

— Just some text messages.

You've been sending a lot of those messages lately, always asking for money. Something has happened to our old intimacy, the endearments that once fell as naturally as raindrops. But I know you have other things on your mind. And I'm sure Babur keeps you busy.

— I hope it's not some kind of scam. I mean, what do you really *know* about this kid? You're really going out on a limb.

I thought about the night of the attack and what happened in that apartment. I wanted to tell him, just to see his expression. But it would only have aroused an evangelistic frenzy, a desire to win me over to his team. And I knew I didn't belong there. Maurice was right. I had wandered into that middle zone he used to talk about, and there I found you. It didn't change anything about who I am. Forgive my bluntness, but I am, at the end of the day, a man who likes the body of a woman. But I like you too. And somehow those two contradictory facts have found sanctuary in my brain. *Travel the spectrum*, my son once told me.

I found the photo at last, turning the phone toward Ron. He sank back helplessly, holding an invisible arrow over his heart.

— Those eyes.

It was so tempting. But no, you can ruin something once you put it into words. Like opening a rare bottle of wine, exposing it to all that oxygen. I just wanted to keep the cork in a while longer. I know it will still be as fresh and sweet as that last night in Kandahar. My memory of you, my love for you.

I try to stay busy, stay in motion. It keeps the questions at bay.

The furniture for your room arrived the other day. The Sears guys asked me how I wanted them to arrange it, and I said, which way is Mecca? Ha, you can imagine their expressions. Later I got a compass and moved everything around so there would be space for you to pray. Turns out Mecca is directly out the window overlooking the garden. I couldn't have planned it better.

Today, despite the cold, I sat on the back porch and read poems, something I haven't done in decades. Sonnets by Shakespeare and

Elizabeth Browning and Edna St. Vincent Millay. I had a weird desire to write a poem of my own. Touched by love (Plato tells us) everyone becomes a poet, even though he had no music in him before.

I got out pen and paper, but the inspiration fled as my thoughts of you got tangled up in the other ones. I felt the peculiar remorse of losing colleagues I never really liked—their grisly end. The volume of that grief came up full blast, forgotten details now frighteningly vivid, like Leandro's sassy walk or old Harbin's peculiar way of blowing his nose, a descending two-note honk. Both gone now.

Easier to just sit there with my cell phone, hoping it would ring, memorizing every nick and scratch. And what venom I felt for Ron and Mary and a local landscaper for not being you.

Then it happened, a beep and a twitch. You needed money again.

I texted: *Take it all, but CALL ME! My kingdom for the sound of your voice!!!*

I got a note from Bill Batson. He says he has been e-mailing you and getting no answer. The visa is ready to be processed, pending an interview. Bill assures me it's just a formality. With any luck you should be on a plane in a few weeks.

Don't let that kid get away, Bill wrote. *He's your lucky rabbit's foot.*

I forwarded this to you, adding: *Get your ass up to Kabul!* Still no reply.

I also got an e-mail from Faith Woodson, still in the hospital. Burns and lacerations. She wants to lead a class-action lawsuit against Global Relief Solutions. *For the world's most vulnerable people, in the world's most hostile environments.* You can say that again.

I'm not getting involved in any lawsuits. We all signed the same waiver when we hired on; there's a reason they call it danger pay. I went through five years of litigation after the crash in Gabon and never collected a penny. I won't go through that again.

Let it go, people. You're alive, for God's sake. Don't waste a minute of it.

There once was a war, a long and nasty war. But it's not my war anymore. Still, I'm glad I was there.

People ask: Was it worth it? Did you do any good over there? Maybe it wasn't worth half a billion dollars, but yes, we did some good. My canal retaining walls were solid, my reservoirs sturdy. They should be serving Kandahar farmers for some time to come. Or until the next war carries it all away.

And perhaps Kandahar is a few tailors richer because of that course we started. You never really know what you'll leave behind. All you can do is the best you can do. Isn't that what you told me?

People talk about outgrowing their home, but I think this 1950s ranch-style has outgrown me. I've lived too long in compounds. My needs are simpler now; a bed, a hotplate, a laptop and maybe some porn, what else does a man really need?

The neighbor lady, Mrs. Haskell ("No relation to Eddie"), came over the other day with a big bail of my mail under her chin. Mrs. H. is a brain cancer survivor and a widow. Her cancer left her with a bad case of vertigo, but she refuses to use a cane or a walker. The police sometimes stop her when she's out for a walk, thinking the stumbling woman in a muumuu must be drunk.

I've had problems with wistful widows in the past, but this one leaves me alone. No casseroles or invitations to join canasta parties. She's not an unattractive woman. She's certainly as much woman as a guy like me deserves. Despite her limitations, she likes living alone—a trait that does give her a certain sex appeal.

Anyway, I was going through the mail and circulars, tossing most of it into the garbage (I pay everything online—why do I still get this shit?) when a letter caught my attention. It was addressed to The Ames Family, meaning the sender was being polite or else hadn't kept up with time's cruel whittling-down of the Ameses. We are one aimless Ames these days.

The letter, dated a month earlier, was written on one sheet of unlined paper in a neat, slanting hand. It's not often that I'm so entirely caught off guard.

> ... didn't find you home, and looked into the windows to see if you'd moved away. Seeing those African masks on the wall brought back a lot of memories. I'm sorry I lost touch with you and Mrs. Ames. I heard about Maurice, but I still can't believe it's true. I wanted to hear the story from you.

The return address was a dormitory at the University of Evansville.

I read it through twice, put it back in the envelope, then read it a third time. I went out to the porch with a pad of paper and tried penning a response. But it was no good. My heart was racing; I had too many questions.

I grabbed my coat and drove out to the University of Evansville to find Corby.

Jane and I had many questions to ponder in the bleak weeks after Maurice's death, each secretly blaming the other. I told her about the strange bruises I'd seen on his chest when he was working on pools. I told her what I knew about his connection to Rémy Champlon. I even told her about the Domino Café and the trucker. Each revelation was a new agony for her, a nudge toward that precipice called Divorce. It was absurd how little that poor woman knew.

It was weeks before we could get Maurice's body released from Gabon. I asked the funeral director if the tattoo on Maurice's shoulder was still visible. With some misgivings he e-mailed me a close-up photograph. The skin had the color and texture of bacon, but you could still make out the two triangles, one inside the other.

I took it to the police station. They recognized it right away, a symbol by which pederasts and willing boys identify one another. A detective pulled up a website where pedophiles chatted. There at the top of the page, as my heart exploded, were the interlaced blue triangles. I had to run to a trash can to be sick.

I brought up the website for Jane and showed her the photo of the tattoo. At first she wept. Then she slapped me, looked back at the screen, and slapped me again.

She stuck around long enough for the funeral, then got her stuff and cleared out. I didn't blame her. I even helped load up her car.

I told Corby most of this, but not everything. There would be time. Mostly I had questions. Who was Maurice? What can you tell me about the men he was with?

He hadn't changed much. He had filled out, of course, the gangling teen replaced by a lean man in his twenties, but I would have known that shy smile and that funny Southern drawl anywhere. He was in his final year of law school. He drank white wine and smoked an electronic cigarette. From his mannerisms I figured he was gay, but I was learning not to assume anything anymore.

His father had recently died and he was pretty much on his own. He had come back to study in Evansville because it was the only place where he'd ever felt at home. By that, he meant at home with the Ameses.

— Maury liked older dudes. He went in for the truck-driver type.

— Yeah, the Domino Café.

Corby seemed surprised that I knew this arcane little tidbit. I added:

— It was one of the last things we talked about. Freightliners and pool guys and God knows what else.

Our hands were clasped over the same table where the teenaged Corby had instructed us in the nuances of Yahtzee. Hearing my voice catch, he tightened his grip.

— I thought he was over that phase.

Was it my imagination or did I detect a note of jealousy, hearing that the Domino Café was more than a one-time vagary? Nothing is sadder than revelations of deceit in the dead.

— I must have been blind not to have seen it. What the hell was I thinking?

— There was nothing you could've done, sir.

— There was plenty I could've done. I saw the bruises. I just couldn't make myself believe it was true. I was weak. I knew the plane would crash, but I let it happen—

The box of Kleenex sat untouched by either of us; better to let the tears roll down our faces unchecked. Corby stared down at our joined hands, shaking his head, his voice soft.

— I loved y'all so damn much.

— We loved you too. I can still remember the day your father came and took you away.

— It all sucked after that.

— What happened? Where did you go?

He shook his head, didn't want to go into it. I didn't really want him to either. Another fucked-up childhood. Aren't they all pretty much the same?

— Well, I'm glad you're here. I don't want to lose you again, you understand?

— Do you mind letting me look around?

— Anything in particular you want to see?

But I knew: the shed.

It was dark now, but Corby tapped his smartphone and a bright light came on. He led us to the back corner of the garden, remembering the way. I warned him there wasn't much to see. When Jane left me I started doing my drinking out there. I'd lie on Maurice's mattress, trying to think his thoughts. I'd play his Beatles and Barry Manilow records. Then one drunken night I fell asleep with a lit cigarette and set the damn thing ablaze.

It was still there, what was left of it—the charred joists perched over ash now dusted with snow. Corby sat down on the icy grass and I sat close to him, our knees touching. He panned his light across the wreckage, then turned it off and we sat in darkness.

There was so much left to be said, but I didn't want to reminisce anymore about Maurice. Those conversations can end up slipping uncomfortably into phony idealization. *He was too good for this world.* No, he died in a plane crash. His time was up. Through some design fluke the tail section broke off with me in it, leaving him to proceed with the plane into the Ogooué River. If he hadn't changed seats at the last minute . . .

We didn't say anything more. We just sat there, staring into the darkness, letting it speak for us.

Corby spends the night. It's not that he's too drunk to drive, but we both sense that it's too early for this to end. I bed him down in Maurice's old room—your room now—and offer him a pair of pajamas. But he's not of the pajama generation. He strips down to his underwear and slips under the blanket, holding out his arms like a child entitled to be hugged. I squat beside the bed and hold him, rocking a little.

— Breakfast in the morning, Corby?

— Mm-hm. Do you still know how to make them potato pancakes?

— There's not a damn thing in the fridge, but I'll run out to the store first thing.

Corby stares up at the ceiling, smiling.

— I used to love coming to the Ames house. It felt like a real home, you know?

— The other place doesn't even have a kitchen, not yet anyway.

I didn't even know I was going to say it. I was already thinking of Meuze as a second home.

— Other place?

— I bought some property in France when I was on leave.

— France, that's cool.

— Just an old fixer-upper on forty acres. I'll show you some pictures tomorrow.

He wants another hug, so I oblige. It's a long one, with a moan from us both. I turn off the light, glancing back from the doorway at his long legs skating contentedly under the blanket.

I know I won't be getting to sleep anytime soon. I carry a glass of wine and a blanket out to the back porch. I plunk myself down in the big round papasan chair, setting candles all around like votives for a Buddha. A little Chopin on the outdoor speakers. Could anything be more exquisite? The ringer on my cell phone is turned as loud as it will go. I'd kill for a cigarette, but I gave you my word.

The snow has stopped and now the garden is muted and still. I hung some wind chimes out there, the big tubular kind pitched to produce musical chords. Tonight, though, there's not a breath of wind; all is silent and still.

Inside I hear footsteps on the second floor, then the flush of a toilet. One day those will be your footsteps, Karimullah. I want you to be part of this.

I pick up a book of ancient Chinese poetry and hold it up to a candle to read. It's pretty good. Poems about blue mountains and lotus leaves and flowing rivers. Poems about friends who are soldiers, friends who are children, friends on long journeys.

And then I read:

> Here at the frontier, there are falling leaves.
> And though my neighbors are all barbarians,
> And you are a thousand miles away,
> There are always two cups on my table.

I smile and dog-ear the page. Sometimes you find just what you need when you need it most. How does that happen?

A toast to you, unknown writer from the Tang Dynasty.

And to you, my elusive friend.

I take the phone from the table and clutch it to my heart, willing it to ring. My eyes close and open. Then close. I start to nod off.

And in that moment between consciousness and sleep you come to me.

We're seated on that bright Kuchi carpet in your room. You're dressed in pale blue, your hair combed and shiny, your heart-shaped face holding all the joy in the world. Your brow curls on a thought. You look at me and open your mouth to speak . . .

But then the vision switches off, everything goes black. My eyes snap open and I feel a twinge of panic.

— What were you going to tell me, dear friend?

At that moment I hear a faint rustling in the garden, a gathering of energy. A breeze picks up. And then I hear them, the wind chimes, soft but distinct, as though grazed by a hundred tiny fingers.

Rising . . . falling. Like a coded message. Like spoken words.

Then gone.

EPILOGUE

Thirty Years Later

IT WAS A SIMPLE teahouse of the kind you didn't see very often anymore. Just that. No cakes or sweetbreads, although they could certainly be sent for, the proprietor assured the stranger, knowing a promising patron when he saw one.

Half a dozen old men sat around smoking cigarettes and sharing local gossip. It was dark and startlingly cool after the blazing noon-day heat. A boy brought him tea with a saucer of nuts and raisins. Nothing cooled the body on a day like this than a pot of scorching hot tea. He took a sip and closed his eyes, feeling sweat trickling coolly into the folds of his *shalwar kamiz*.

A soiled, tattered cloth served as the main door. It opened with a flash of blinding light as a woman shuffled inside, though she was of such an age that she could hardly be said to possess any gender at all. She was like the sexless embodiment of Time itself, hunched over a walking stick that seemed an extension of her twisted, knobby hand. She wore a ragged blue burka from which the grille had been cut away. It was odd to see a woman's face so unapologetically exposed.

But then, the stranger laughed to himself, not even the cruelest of *talibs* would find moral cause to cover such a face.

So crooked and bent was the woman, so crippled with arthritis and the weight of the years, that she had to stop and raise her head to find the person she was seeking. Spotting the stranger, she shuffled purposefully toward where he was sitting. He stiffened, thinking she was a beggar.

Her voice was surprisingly loud.

— *Salaam aleikhum.*

— *Aleikhum salaam.*

— You are the *kabaar wala*?

— Yes, old mother.

— I saw your scrap truck parked in the road.

— Then you have found me. Have a glass of tea and rest yourself.

— I have only a moment. My pomegranates are unattended.

So she was one of the old women who sold fruit beside the main road. Not a beggar but not far removed.

— But as you know, mother, I am a *kabaar wala*. I buy scrap metal, not fruit.

— Finish your tea and follow me. I have something that may interest you.

These days there were more donkeys than cars in the Arghandab market. As he rumbled behind her in his huge truck, finding it almost impossible to drive so slowly, he met the eyes of vendors laughing in their stalls, enjoying the absurdity of the great truck idling behind the old harridan with the creaking cart.

The sad little pyramids of fruits and vegetables—the diminutive cucumbers, the limp greens, the oranges that looked as though they were deflating—were reminders of how mightily fortunes had fallen in recent years. He had come here as a boy during the years of the American occupation. He remembered swimming in canals and picnicking with his family near the Arghandab River as it ran high with the spring opening of the Dahla Dam. Was it some trick of memory, or were the markets not exploding with rich colors and smells in those days?

It all came down to water, of course. Who could forget how the Taliban celebrated their return to power by blowing up the Dahla Dam, proudly obliterating one of the most conspicuous legacies of American interference. It was an event bigger than the destruction of the Buddha statues in Bamiyan. He had come out with his family from Kandahar City to witness the churning rapids. The new leadership had certainly timed it right. It was the first year of the Great Drought and the farms and orchards needed just such a drenching.

The following spring there was no water, of course—no dam to trap the runoff from the snow-covered mountains, most of which was captured by the farmers upstream. This left Arghandab and the farms to the south at the mercy of the seasonal rains. A few farmers dug wells, but as the aquifers lay deep underground, such wells were within the means of only the wealthiest of farmers, and even those didn't last.

Glancing down at the woman's slow-moving rump, he felt a sudden impatience to get back on the road. He wanted to reach Spin Boldak by nightfall with his load of scrap and join the queue of trucks crossing into Pakistan. What could this woman have that would interest him?

Reaching a turnoff, the old woman stopped and pointed a crooked, bony finger down a weed-choked lane, intending for him to proceed ahead of her.

It seemed to be the entrance to a farm of fallen glory. The way was almost too narrow for the enormous truck, which lurched and pitched on the deep potholes. Branches scraped the sides of the cab with a sinister screech, as of many tormented souls begging him to turn back. Through his mirror he saw the woman advancing minutely behind him.

He was in a pomegranate orchard, the ground littered with brown and broken shells that crunched under his wheels like gourds. In the distance he saw a house, or the ruins of one. Its roof beams rose straight up from the wreckage as though shattered by the fist of Allah. Its old walls seemed to be dissolving back into the soil, reclaimed, as all things must be, by the immutable will of time.

He stopped the truck and idled, rolling down the window and smelling the composting fruit and dust. No one was buying these old farms anymore. With diminishing underground aquifers and the inexorable approach of the surrounding desert, Arghandab's days as the breadbasket of Kandahar Province, capital of the Islamic Emirate of Pashtunistan, were long behind her.

He turned off his motor, not wanting to waste precious compressed natural gas, as the nearest CNG station was in Kandahar City. He was beginning to resent the old woman and her intrusion. Why had he agreed to this? Pity had always been his undoing. He would offer the woman a few *rupees* and be on his way.

But where was she? He turned this way and that. And then he saw her huddled blue form crouching in the weeds with her back to him, relieving herself. Funny how social niceties become irrelevant with age. Who had this woman been in her youth? Her round face and the rosebud set of her wrinkled mouth hinted at long-ago beauty. Half a century ago she would not have been seen by any man outside of the home, her identity guarded as a great family treasure. And here he was watching her urinate.

What had happened to the men of this family, leaving an old woman to toil through her last years alone? Victims of the partition, no doubt, that great social experiment that turned Afghan against Afghan, north against south, Pashtuns against all others, and led to the formation of Pashtunistan.

He had spent the whole of the Pashtunistan War in Iran. There he turned his energies toward tailoring, a skill he had first learned in a Kandahar prison as a boy. He opened a small shop that catered to Afghan émigrés, for where is the Afghan who doesn't need a new *shalwar kamiz*? He was nearly forty before he returned to Kandahar, setting up a prosperous tailoring shop. Later, entrusting the shop to his three brothers, he bought a truck and started a business shipping scrap metal to the greedy recycling centers in Quetta and Lahore.

Who would have thought that scrap iron and steel would become the second greatest export of the Islamic Emirate of Pashtunistan after opium? Who could have foreseen that a new economy would emerge from the looting and decommissioning of old factories and infrastructure? The line of trucks at the Pakistan border sometimes stretched for more than a kilometer, each laden with the beams and girders of Afghan industry. Old bridge members and grain silos. Crushed cars and corrugated tin roofs. Little by little, Pashtunistan was being sold off to the highest bidder.

The new leadership didn't care. So long as the poppy farmers paid their taxes, so long as foreign meddlers stayed away and Afghanistan respected the Treaty of Partition, so long as sharia remained the law of the land and women were confined to the home, the experiment could be viewed as a success, if an imperfect one.

It had become something of a national motto: *God never promised freedom from suffering.*

* * *

The old woman now led him down a path in the undergrowth. She probably had nothing better to show him than the rusted carcass of some old work truck that would scarcely be worth the effort of extracting. But by now he had formed an attachment to this woman and her mysterious errand.

— How long have you lived here, old mother?

She paused, tilting her face in his direction.

— If I have ever lived anywhere else, I no longer remember.

She would not have known how old she was. Women of her generation never did.

— You seem to live a hard life.

— We are all at Allah's mercy.

— He takes good care of you.

— When he is finished with me, he will find me ready. What we seek is just there.

Just ahead he saw a dark shape in the undergrowth. It was quite large, though too low to be a building. Covered by years of falling debris, it stretched on into the gloom like a burial mound from some lost civilization.

He picked up his pace, striding ahead of her. Parting the brambles he felt his heartbeat quicken, sensing that his journey might be rewarded.

He lifted away a layer of dead leaves that years of compaction and moisture had bound like a mat. Beneath this he found a plastic tarp that dissolved into flakes as he tried to lift it back. At his feet he saw part of a wheel and a flat tire.

The woman had now come up wheezing behind him. She leaned forward, trying to help him find the end of the tarp, now lost in the confusion of leaves and wild growth. With a polite gesture he indicated for her to step back.

It was a machine of some sort. The paint had mostly flaked away, but as he swept away the leaves he distinguished the word SUPERIOR. From the object's general shape he took it to be some sort of farm implement. He had done plenty of business with farmers, hauling away their old plows and disk tillers and the occasional tractor too far gone to be resuscitated, but this was something unusual.

— What do you call these machines?

— I do not know.

He gestured across the sprawling mass.

— How do you happen to have them?

— My husband acquired them long ago for some purpose that was never explained to me.

Having excavated the first of the machines, the one beside it came forth more easily. He brushed the dirt from a small metal plate. Its stamped letters provided the name of a Chinese manufacturer and identified the unit as a wheat thresher.

The mystery suddenly took on a new complexity. There had never been much wheat in Arghandab, even in the days of plenty. Why so many wheat threshers?

He stood up on the wheel and began digging around in the cobwebby darkness. Leaves plugged the opening of the hopper like a cork. After a moment of digging he was surprised to draw out a plastic sandal. He turned it curiously in his hand, as though it were an artifact from the tomb of a pharaoh.

A warm breath of mold and decay rose out of the machine's dark maw. Among the leaves and twigs he drew out what seemed like the remains of some large rodent. But as he turned it in his hand he saw that it was a section of human skull with some hair still attached. A pair of blank eye sockets regarded him coldly.

Reaching deeper still, he felt something sharp clinging to the teeth of the machine. As he wrenched it out he saw that it was a grey femur connected to what was unmistakably a length of pale blue fabric.

He stepped away from the machine, cold with horror, brushing his hands on his trousers. He offered a quick prayer, realizing he had trespassed upon a grave.

It was dark when he reached Spin Boldak, and the queue of trucks was as bad as he had feared, stretching from the border checkpoint as far as the eye could see. The crossing was now closed to cargo traffic and most of the trucks stood empty, their drivers having gone in search of dinner and conversation.

Needing human contact, he locked his truck and began walking toward the border station. Along the side of the road he saw drivers sitting together around small fires and drinking tea from metal thermoses. Some of the trailers were bulging with straw, others carried sand or produce. But for the most part they were all hauling jagged, twisted, towering piles of scrap metal.

He waved to a friend, another scrap dealer from Kandahar City, sitting up in the cab of his truck with his legs propped in the window of his open door. The friend jumped down from the truck and shook his hand, holding his forearm affectionately.

— Alaamzeb! *Salaam aleikhum.* Come join me. I have more food than I can eat.

Alaamzeb looked up at the dark cab of the truck, which didn't seem particularly inviting. In his present desultory mood he wanted voices and laughter.

— Let's find a tearoom instead, my friend. Let's celebrate.

The friend went back to the truck for his ragged scarf and wrapped it around his neck, his eagerness showing in a broad, suggestive grin.

— What are we celebrating?

With an inward shudder Alaamzeb remembered what he had brought up from the hopper of the antique wheat thresher. He would never forget those bones, hinting at some dark and terrible tale. Who could it have been? What passions and dreams had been so savagely snuffed out, and by what corrupt, hateful hand?

But no, it was in the past, leave it there. The nation was one sprawling graveyard. What difference was one more body? Some people go on forever, like that old crone back in Arghandab. Others struggle and are defeated. In the end, we are all born to die.

But he shook the dark thoughts from his mind, clapping his friend on the back.

— Life is all too short, my friend. Each breath we take is cause for celebration, wouldn't you agree?

The friend looked at him slyly.

— You are in a rare mood, Alaamzeb.

— I don't know. But come, let's find what makes us happy. Tonight the world seems beautiful, and I suddenly feel alive.

AUTHOR'S NOTE

It's always enjoyable to read, in an author's note, of the many friends and loved ones, the spouses and children and helpful readers, who witnessed a book's creation. Like so many doctors and nurses gathering around a difficult labor.

For some writers, writing is a way of looking at themselves. For others it's a purgative. The mirror or the toilet. I wrote this novel to help me make sense of the often baffling realities of aid work in time of war. I wrote what I knew, the rest I made up. And while a few kind readers helped me avoid humbling errors of culture, religion and lazy writing, any mistakes herein are all mine.

Those readers include Robert Calderisi, Joel LaMar Cruz, Rhea Fitzgerald, Howard Freeman, Gracie Holloway, Barbara Miles, Tessa Nordin, Eduardo Peris-Deprez, Shannon Rednour, Jan Seale, Ray Stewart, Serena Stewart, Elizabeth Sweeten, Fru Teston, Valerie Vanneste and Cliff Williamson.

In Afghanistan, special thanks to Abdul Hamid Ansary, Fazelrabani Qazizai, Mujtaba Hashimi and H.Q. Special thanks to Amanullah Nadeem for his image on the cover.

For music, life lessons and courage: Chuck Wild.

This book is dedicated to the hundreds of humanitarian aid workers who have perished trying to rebuild this lovely, shattered country.

After fourteen years of conflict, and despite a widespread drawdown in troops, Afghanistan continues to lead the world in attacks on aid workers, twice that of the next highest country.

Of this number, eight times more Afghan aid workers are killed—most at the hands of their fellow countrymen—than their expatriate counterparts.

Kabul, April 2015

ABOUT THE AUTHOR

Will Everett is a native of Texas. As a journalist he has reported from the Middle East, South Asia and West Africa for National Public Radio, the BBC, *Newsweek* and other outlets.

With Walter Cronkite he wrote and produced the 2006 documentary *World War One Living History Project*, honoring the last surviving veterans of World War I. His work has been recognized by the Society for Professional Journalists, the New York Festivals and the National Headliner Awards. He holds a master's degree from the University of Southern California Annenberg School for Communication and Journalism.

In 2015, his choral collaboration with composer Joseph Martin, "The Message," was published by Hal Leonard.

He currently lives and works in Afghanistan.

willeverett.net